ak

děbrady

Chlumec
nad Cidlinou

Hradec
Králové

BOHUMIL HRABAL
WHY I WRITE?

MODERN CZECH CLASSICS

Bohumil Hrabal

Why I Write?

And Other Early Prose Pieces

Translated from the Czech by David Short

Karolinum Press

KAROLINUM PRESS, Ovocný trh 560/5, 116 36 Prague 1, Czech Republic
Karolinum Press is a publishing department of Charles University in Prague
www.karolinum.cz

Cover and graphic design by Zdeněk Ziegler
Typeset by DTP Karolinum
Printed in the Czech Republic by PBtisk, Příbram
First English edition

ISBN 978-80-246-4268-0 (hb)
ISBN 978-80-246-4324-3 (ebk)

CONTENTS

Until the age of twenty I had no idea what writing was, what literature was. At high school I consistently fell at every hurdle in Czech language and had to repeat years one and four, so extending my adolescence by two years… After twenty, that first solid plank of my ignorance snapped and I then fell headlong for literature and art, so much so that reading and looking and studying became my hobby. And to this day I am kept in a state of permanent euphoria by the writers I came to cherish in my youth, and I know by heart François Rabelais' *Gargantua and Pantagruel*,[1] and even Louis Céline's *Death on Credit*[2] and the verse of Rimbaud and Baudelaire, and I'm still reading Schopenhauer and my latest teacher, Roland Barthes… But at the age of twenty my real inspiration was Giuseppe Ungaretti, who so impressed me that I started writing poetry… Thus did I set foot on the thin ice of writing and the force that drove my writing was the sheer delight at the sentences that dripped from my soul onto the pages in my Underwood typewriter, and I was bowled over by the chain being strung together from that first sentence on, so I began keeping an intimate diary, my self-addressed *billets doux*, my self-addressed monologue combined with interior monologue… And I had a constant sense that what I was writing was mine and mine alone and that I'd succeeded in setting down on those blank sheets something that was quite an honour, but simultaneously startling. Back then, whenever my mother's friends and neighbours asked how I was getting on with my legal studies, she would just brush it aside saying that "his mind's forever on other things"... And that's how it was, back then I was obsessed with writing, a young man in gestation: the only thing I looked forward to was the weekend, when I would return from Prague to Nymburk,[3] and the main thing was that, back then, it was so quiet in the office of the brewery and I could spend a whole two days at my Underwood, and having written the first sentence I'd brought with me from Prague, I could sit at the typewriter and wait, fingers held aloft, until that first sentence gave birth to the next... Sometimes I might wait an hour or more, but at other times I wrote so fast that the typewriter jammed and stuttered, so mighty was the stream of sentences... and that flow, that rate of flow of the sentences kept assuring me that "this is it"... And so I wrote for the sheer pleasure of writing, for that kind of euphoria in which, though sober, I showed signs of intoxication... And so I wrote according to the law of reflection, the reflection of my crazy existence... I was actually still only learning to write and my writing amounted to exercises, variations on Apollinaire and Baudelaire, later on I had a go, under the guidance of Céline, at the stream of city talk and then it was the turn of Izaak Babel and in time Chekhov and they all taught me to reflect in my writing not only my own self, but the world about me, to approach myself from inside others... and to know what destiny is. And then came the war and the universities were closed[4] and I ended up spending the war as a train dispatcher and new encroachers on my writing were Breton's *Nadja* and the *Surrealist Manifestos*... and every Saturday and Sunday, in the deserted office of the Nymburk brewery, I carried on writing my marginal notes on things I'd seen and things that had befallen others, I was frightened, but also honoured to have become, by writing, an eye witness, a poetic chronicler of the hardships of wartime, and at the same time, having spent so many years writing on that Underwood of the bleakness and brutality of reality, to have been forced gradually to let go of my adolescent versifying and replace it with a woeful game played with sentences that tended towards the transcendent... and so I went on setting down my self-addressed, interior monologue, but without commentary, and so, being my own first reader, I could have a sense, gazing at those pages of text, that they'd been written by someone else... and I have continued to feel it an honour that I was able to write at all, that I could testify to that huge event in my life, that I was at last able to start thinking thanks to my typewriter... And so I carried on writing as if I were hearing the confession not only of me myself, but of the entire world... And I continued to see the driving force of my writing in that fact of being an eye witness and in the duty to note and set down all the things that excited me, pleasant and disturbing, and the duty to offer, by way of my typewriter, testimony not on every single event, but on certain nodes of reality, as if I were squirting cold water on an aching tooth... But I saw that, too, as a divine game, as taught to me by Ladislav Klíma...[5] And then the war came to an end and I completed my studies to become a Doctor of Laws, but I yielded so far to the law of reflection in writing that I took on a string of crazy jobs with

the sole object of getting smeared not just by the environments themselves, but by my eavesdropping on the things people say... And I never ceased to be amazed at how, every weekend, in the deserted office of the brewery where on weekdays my father and his accountant would work, I could carry on jotting down the things that had befallen me in the course of a defamiliarising week and that I had dreamed up in the arcing of my mind... And I went on playing like this, with a sense of having my chest rubbed with goose fat by a beautiful girl, so strongly did I feel honoured and anointed by the act of writing... And then it dawned that my years of apprenticeship were over and that I must snip myself off from the brewery and abandon those four rooms and the little town where my time had begun standing still... and I moved to Libeň,[6] to a single room in what had once been a smithy, and so embarked not only on a new life, but also on a different way of writing... And then I spent four years commuting to Kladno and the open-hearth furnaces of the Poldi iron and steel works and that gradually made a difference to the way I played with sentences... Lyricism became slowly regurgitated as total realism, which I barely even noticed because, working as I was next to fires and the milieu of the steelworks and the rugged steelworkers and the way they spoke, it all struck me as super-beautiful, as if I were working and living at the very heart of pictures by Hieronymus Bosch... And so, having snipped myself off from my past, the scissors actually stayed in my fingers after all and, back then, I began taking the scissors to what I'd written, applying the 'cutter' technique to the text as to a film. Eman Frynta referred to my style as 'Leica style', saying that I captured reality at peak moments of people talking and then composed a text out of it all... And I recognised this as an expression of respect because, back then, I already had my readers and listeners because I, as they put it, I had the knack of reading without pathos... And so, back then, I went on writing with my scissors close at hand, and I would even write solely with a mind to reaching the moment when I could slice up the written text and piece it together into something that left me stunned, as a film might... And then I went to work as a packer of recycled paper and then as a stagehand and I invariably looked forward to my free time and the chance to write for myself and for my friends, and I would make *samizdats* of them so as actually to be a writer, a top sheet and four carbon copies. Then I became a proper writer; from the age of forty-eight on I published book after book, almost falling sick with each successive book, because I'd tell myself: now they're publishing things that I've thought were only for me and my friends... But my readers ran into the hundreds of thousands and they read my things as they would the sports pages... And I wrote on and on, even training myself to think only through the typewriter, and my game now proceeded with a hint of melancholy; for weeks I would wait for the images to accumulate and then for the command to sit down at the typewriter and rattle off onto the pages all the things that by now were just scrambling to get out... and I wrote and kept receiving honours for my writing, although after each ceremony I felt like a nanny goat that's just given birth to a litter of kids... Now I can afford the luxury of writing *alla prima*, resorting to the scissors as little as possible, with my long text actually becoming an image of my inner self, rattled wholesale into the typewriter by my fingertips... Now that I'm old, I find I can genuinely afford the luxury of writing only what I feel like writing, and I observe *ex post* that I write and have been writing my long *premier mouvement* texts in time with my breathing, as if the moment I wave my green flag I start inhaling the images that are impelling me to write and then, through the typewriter, I exhale them at great length... and again I inhale my pop-up picture book and again exhale it by writing... So it's almost to the rhythm of my lungs and a blacksmith's bellows that I galvanise myself and calm myself rhythmically so the act of my writing works with the motion of a grand drama, like the workings of the four seasons... Only now am I becoming aware that writing has brought me to the realisation that only now have I pinpointed the essence of ludibrionism, which is the essence of the philosophy of Ladislav Klíma... I believe that it's been only through the act of writing that, several times in my life to date, I have reached the point where I and a melancholy transcendence constitute a single entity, much as the two halves of Koh-i-Noor Waldes press studs click together, and I rejoice that, as there is less of me the more I write, so there is more of me, that I am then a permanent amateur whose prop is the one little word: *Amo*... and so love... I blithely consider even the suffering and those particular strokes of fate to be just a game, because the most beautiful thing about literature is that actually no one *has* to write. So what suffering? It's all just one great masculine game, that eternal flaw in the diamond that Gabriel Marcel writes about... When I began to write it was just to teach myself how to write... But only now do I know, body and soul, what Lao Tse taught me: that the greatest thing is To Know How Not to Know.[7] And what Nicholas of Cusa whispered to me about *docta ignorantia*...[8] Now that through the act of writing I have achieved the acme of emptiness, I hope I shall be treated to some means by which finally to learn in my mother tongue, through the act of writing, things about myself, and about the world, that I don't yet know.

THOSE RAPTUROUS RIFLEMEN

A short story

Searching some old wardrobes for something,
I came across my first attempt at prose,
possibly a novel that I've since given up
for lost. So just for interest's sake, here
it is for my friends...

I/

Jan came out. The glazed door opened, the handle having
been depressed. Twice did the laws of reflection and re-
fraction meet the Stargazer half-way. Once at the opening,
once at the closing of the glass surface. "What a gorgeous
morning. Good day to ye, Morning! *Küss die Hand*, Sun-
shine! *Küss die* bare arse, more like!" As Jan strode along
the pavement he tipped his hat back to the very top of his
head, his hand dribbling the ticking of his watch into his
right ear as it passed. He was also careful not to tread on
the cracks between the kerb stones and repeated to himself:
"What a gorgeous morning! Have you had breakfast? You
haven't. Is the city breakfasting? It is. On what?... Wagons, cars, motorcycles and wicker baskets laden with fruit
and veg..." And Jan Stargazer lost touch with himself. He
walked past the wagons, cars and motorcycles and time
and again waved his gaudy handkerchief, convinced that
he was sailing through a lake-town paved in swirling H_2O,
where the cars and wagons were boats bound hither and
yon, their bellies filled with wares and sightseers. But Jan

wanted more than this; he wanted everyone who met him to recognise at once that Jan wasn't Jan, but a craft that had broken its moorings. He asked the first passer-by to moor him next to a sodium vapour lamp in the harbour. He leaned against a railing and asked an old man to wait by his clothes while he took a dip. And he dabbled his foot in imaginary water. The old man wiped his spectacles, then a second time, and still he could see neither clothes, nor waterway. When the waters of insanity had risen almost to his mouth, he bowed, withdrew out of range and, from desperation, bought himself a hat. This is why Jan Stargazer enjoyed transferring the coordinates of smile and confusion onto passers-by, knowing they would ask: 'Is the man mad, or what?' They'd smile, then forget. But one time they'd come along entirely alone, with only their footsteps for company. Along a paved road or a footpath. And suddenly, Where am I? In the third projection plane of dreaming. Lips move, a hand addresses the blue and is accountable not only for third persons, but for entire assemblies. And then, beneath the waters, a foldaway field altar opens out, and who's this leaning out of its gold frame? Jan Stargazer. And what's he doing? Waving to the car-boats and testing the temperature of non-existent water. Now the former fun-poker doffs his hat and bows: "Yet it's wonderful to dream aloud!"... But that's not what Jan wants. He's unhappy with dreaming. That's precisely why he's kissed imagination's hand farewell, so as to be rid of it. That's why he's bouncing up and down on an enormously long plank and can't touch the ground because what about the tens, hundreds, thousands at whose floors the lift of intellect only pauses and why not let the regions we pass by come gushing out? But snap a gear lever at full speed, bounce on a plank without being able to touch the ground! It's wonderful, daredevil, but how such things can end… These were Jan Stargazer's thoughts as he passed from one shopfront to the next. He stopped, stepped up close to the glass and breathed on himself, sniffed at himself. He screwed up his eyes and checked to see how fetching it was. Then at once he started thinking up metaphors for eyes. A pair of minus signs; twin knife slashes in a fur coat. In line, not one above the other. But how about some accessories? A white stick and a metal sign with the legend: *Blind from birth*. Touch, hearing and nothing else. This was the very moment when Jan became like the young man who stands outside the fairground booth within whose depths lies a naked mermaid, and wonders whether he should or shouldn't. Though he knows in advance that he should enter. All it needs is to think quickly how to go blind. First, close the eyes. And in we go. The peelings that are his eyelids admit a pink light, and touch is also a useful device and the walls are warm. The voices to be heard, how different the sound they make, and the sense! And the images to be seen! Six hummingbirds, no two the same, embroidering an inscription on a curtain: *Just what do the blind see in heaven?* That would be a good heading for a cook book too, look you. Nothing better than to contrive a new world for oneself out of nothing but noise. But then along came something that had nothing to do with the game. "Permit me, sir, let me lead you…" "It's all right, thanks, I only live round the corner,

I'll make it..." "Sure it's all right, so I'll take you round the corner..." So what now? Jan was the old passive Jan again, weighing ninety-five kilos. Somewhere from a desk at the back of his conscience a little voice piped up: "What did I say, sir?" There was nothing for it but to hold out an arm and go. Ah, another's arm, and warm. I wonder who it is. He half-opened one eye and out of the corner saw a skull with thick, black hair. Not wearing a tie. The stargazer opened his eyes wide, turned and said: "Fritz!" But he immediately lowered his gaze before Fritz's, he wanted to say something, apologise, but those eyes. The earth, apples, elderberry, granite. He was embarrassed, and with his little eyes half-closed he watched the receding Fritz Milkin, his schoolmate, who was reciting as he went: "At the age of twenty-six...," shook his head, "who'd have thought, at twenty-six..," and putting a forefinger to his temple, Fritz Milkin repeated to himself: "Twenty-six and a constant repeater of stupidity..."

II/

Every day, the Milkins get up, have a quick wash and prepare all the day's meals. They pee out in the garden. Oh, how wonderful it is to empty one's bladder in the morning, that rapturous whistling sound. Then they kick-start their tandem and off they'd go. On a bicycle for two, Ferdinand by the bell, Josef at the back. They lean into bends, step on it on the level, brake going downhill, and ring the bell at pedestrian crossings. A twice-a-day journey. Once there, once back. Josef sits there and pedals, seeing neither wires nor handlebars, seeing nothing at all. He just pedals, using the smells from shops, bends in the road and the stones on the roadway in town to determine his location here, in Europe, in the world. At the third turn of the pedals after the first bend you have to duck. It's the first low branches of some linden trees. Then comes the war memorial. An alphabetically arranged seating plan of the fallen and missing soldiers of the First World War. And whenever, meaning twice a day, the brothers ride past on their bicycle, they always get a whiff of simple graves. They ride into a cloud of reminiscences and their hearts join hands and dance off hippity-hop deep into the past only to pop back into the bodies of pedalling automata a moment later. They invariably catch the unkind salutation of passing shrapnel and tell themselves: 'Back then it would have taken just one little step and the plaque, the black marble plaque with space for just two more names, would have been filled.' But they don't complain. And they don't even say it to each other. They just think it. And not even that. They're like the bell that they ring as per the highway code, they laugh and are glad that the war memorial's safely behind them, that they're breathing blue air, that they're selling mineral water. That they are Ferdinand and Josef Milkin, deserters from the war memorial... By the booth with a cottage attached, where Ferdinand's son Fritz lives, they hop off by command like in the circus. They'd trot on a few metres and stop. Then Josef sits next to the nickel-plated pipe and takes maids', ladies' and pensioners' bottles from them and listens to the liquid steadily rising until the fizzing at the neck shrieks *done!* And then other flasks, company casks, flagons, whatever people bring with them. First come, first served. Josef loves listening to the pensioners who so relish every burp as they jubilate in their infantile way: "My, that's some water! So good for the health!" And Josef nods, understanding why they cling to every litre of air that could prolong their life by one tenth of a second. Ferdinand, he tears off the receipts, and as the one in charge of the money box, alternates between 'Good bye', 'Cheerio', 'See you again', ''By-ee' and savours the women's backsides, slurping on his saliva, because he's still only sixty and a widower. Whenever there's a pause, Ferdinand leaves his booth, takes a look round and says: "Yes, it's going to be a lovely day." And behind him the trickle of mineral water tinkles away and Josef cools his hand in it. "D'you remember, Ferdi, that time we were taking the post up on the funicular and had to chuck that St Bernard off 'cos it freaked out?..." Ferdinand is staring out over the hills somewhere in the direction of Tyrol... "And how I had to bop its owner one? I thought he were done for. What a crack it was! Thought I'd killed him. But then I still had both thumbs...." And he looks sadly at the fin that used to be his right hand, where there'd once been a thumb. Josef, his chin raised, says: "I should have knocked the fathead out at the bottom. But what's done is done. Like with that kitten..." And now comes the moment that Ferdinand's been anticipating for the entire last quarter of a century... when Josef will start cursing the kitten that cost him his sight and Ferdinand his thumb. For a long time he's had his speech ready, ready to say that if they hadn't gone to get the kitten, the shrapnel would have made the same mincemeat of them as of their comrades, while they were only hit by fragments. He's had his speech ready to say that if they'd smoked even one extra cigarette, or even if they'd denied themselves that pleasure, everything would have been different. He'd tell him that that scrap of fur, or rather his love of all living creatures, had prevented the black plaque that they rode past twice a day from being engraved in its entirety in letters of gold and with a photo of Josef and Ferdinand Milkin... Now he's looking into the blind, cross-slashed face of his brother and sees that any exercise in oratory is pointless. Josef is stroking the flow of water with his fingers and smiling. "You know what, Ferdi? Let's go and buy ourselves a kitten, just like the one back then, you know, a tabby with a white bib, white socks and a little pink muzzle..." Ferdinand doesn't reply, blowing his nose instead. He can see a bunch of navvies coming from the railway. He glances at the calendar and thinks: "Aha, Friday! Hello!..." But no. Workers. On a Friday. Nothing to smoke. Proletarians from Thursday to Saturday. 'To hell with it!' 'Life's a pig!' 'Bugger it all!' 'We'll be beggars till the day we die, the bosses do what they like with us.' They'll have been raining abuse on the New European Order since first thing, banging their tools viciously. Now some sit on the table, others astride the bench in revolt, while from Monday to Thursday, when they still have something or other to smoke, they sit properly. Ferdinand taps his forehead: two missing, ah yes, they'll have gone into town to pick up dog-ends... and he sets glasses of mineral water down in front of the navvies. Suddenly the whole gang jumps up and stares hard towards the corner of the square. "Got some?"... "Got some!" the two tatterdemalions exult, raising their cupped palms high. And the rest dash towards them. They share out the dog-ends and in silent concentration re-roll them. And they start puffing away. They inhale the smoke and something nice shines out of their eyes, and they aren't even listening to their comrade as he sketches, in the sand, on his knees, a map of his little field on which he's marking an avenue of cherry trees as a line of dots. Through the billowing smoke the navvies draw inspiration from any woman who passed by. "What a roly-poly!..." "Hell, they must be feeling the heat... sweating..." "Between their legs!" And one old boy with a face full of jolly wrinkles exhales through the smoke: "The Tartar women used to shave it. We'd spy on them through a chink in the bathroom, single or married, wow..." And he half-closes his eyes and the others, Ferdinand as well, follow suit. "They give 'em a good soaping then shave 'em with a sharp knife." And they can all envisage, at arm's length, the Tartar women bathing, stropping their knife, propping their legs up on a bench and shaving themselves between the legs, or one another... "When we was in Algiers we 'ad a hell of a time with 'em, filthy bitches...," a gaunt fellow takes over, "...filthy, I tell you, we always 'ad to give 'em a bath first, an' if you'd seen the diseases, scary..." And again they all grimace at the image and reach for their flies. "Best know where you're putting it..." "Let it loose on some Turkish bint..." "You could end up wi' it drippin' slivovitz, a whole Danube..." "Christ, we 'ave to go, or the supervisor'll do his nut..." And one by one they pay their twenty hellers, for

Ferdinand lets them have it cheap, he really appreciates this bunch, who've taught him so much about Africa and Asia, whither two of them once wandered. Every day he asks them things, or they start of their own accord. And that's why they get a discount, likewise the retired pastry-cook Marvánek. Every time he turns up, he unbuttons his waistcoat and takes out a silver tube that looks like a chalice taken from a shrine. Then out comes a little funnel that he fits into the tube and then dribbles the mineral water into it. Kids and grown-ups alike come to sit and stare at Marvánek's silver tube. But now Ferdinand is staring after the departing navvies, mentally filling in the details of the tale he's been told and plucking hairs from his nose. Hell no! That man's back on his knees and drawing his little field again, this time in the gutter, marking with a cross the line of cherry trees planted for his daughter, and Ferdinand guesses that at that moment he's adding his neighbour's field to the diagram, and wingeing about the neighbour's unwillingness to sell him the strip that will make his cherry orchard whole and enable him to plant another row of trees. Ferdinand has heard it all a hundred times before and knows the sorry tale of woe by heart, and he understands. He sees the dreamer rub the pretty geometry out with his foot and his mates thumping the poor guy in the back. When Ferdinand turns round, he sees that his brother, his head on his chest, has fallen asleep.

III/

At that moment Jan Stargazer turns up, as is his wont. Head held high and hatless. Now and again he runs a comb

through his hair and watches, against the morning sunlight, his dead hair being borne away on the wind. "Good
morning, Mr Milkin," he says, saluting with one finger,
"Is Fritz in?" "Not sure, he could be still in bed...," says
Ferdinand, offering Jan his hand. "What's up?" "Nothing
in particular, I want to see Fritz," says Jan and he opens the
little gate. He crosses the yard and knocks on the cottage
door. Not a sign. Just some wasps hissing about under the
overhang. He takes the door handle and stares gormlessly
at his wrist watch. Quarter past ten. And in he goes. Once
he gets used to the change of light, he looks about him. The
pictures they'd been talking about were lying on the floor.
Jan treads on the work, the face of a portrait of a girl, as it
happens. He quickly steps back and finds himself standing
in a bowl of apples. And under the flowers on the window
ledge there's a little mat cut out of sunflowers. Jan Stargazer
mutters to himself: "What *is* the man up to, turning himself
into carpets and mats to go under plant pots?" Instead of
a cloth, the table has a moonscape covering it, held in place
with shingle nails. The moon itself is covered by a promotional ash-tray from the Olla company. Jan is most sorry for
the girl nailed to the floor through her eyes and ankles. And
for having trodden on her face. He wishes he could strip off
and lie down next to her. Warm her with his own body and
bring her to life. Instead, his eyes are drawn to the wall,
where some pictures are hanging of which it is impossible
to say that they are pictures. He looks at one face made up
of bits of newspaper and fabric and finished off by hand to
wear the expression of doleful workmen, sentimental whores

or kids waiting for a bit of coal to fall from a passing truck. There are workmen stepping out of a frame made of welded pipes, whores surfacing out of cleverly wired-up corks. And suddenly they're all gazing out at what Jan is wearing, the tie with which he expresses his own taste... And a beggar sitting at the foot of a wall under a bridge looks at Jan as if Jan is wearing nothing at all. A fist with galvanised veins leaps from one picture to bop Jan Stargazer on the nose. Goodness knows what might have happened if the door hadn't opened to admit the egg-shaped, curl-coated cranium of Fritz. He places a little packet on the table and unwraps a rectangular glass sign of the League Against Tuberculosis bearing the legend *Thank you for not smoking*. "Fritz!" Jan cries. But Fritz starts hammering a nail in above the mirror, whistling as he checks he's got it dead centre. And he hangs up the sign with its *Thank you for not smoking* inscription. Then he gleefully dances a few steps back, rolls a cigarette and strikes a match on the sandpaper belly of a worn-out old biddy. "So, what do you think?" Jan Stargazer claps a hand to his forehead: "Wow, Fritz!... That's brilliant! Something I've been dreaming of for ages. Nicking that sign from the patisserie. To give us a conscience. We know what we're supposed to do and we don't do it. But I do know..." And Fritz breaks into a dance. "So do I. We crap on all values from a great height. Thank you for not smoking. Thank you for not smoking. D'you fancy a roll-up? Thank you for not fornicating. For not stealing. Thank you for understanding man's basic needs. Eh?" And Fritz grins a toothy grin with all his gleaming-white teeth and strolls across the girl from her fingers to her head. Suddenly he holds his gaze. "Well I never. Her lord and master has washed her face. Was he trying to bring her round?" And Jan has no idea what to say; he drops his own gaze. "Am I trampling on beauty? Eh? There was a time when I wanted to stir people's emotions with Beauty, but people still live like beasts and still work till they drop and get bludgeoned for their trouble. And those places I've supplied pictures to? Where did my soul in inverted commas go? Big houses, the cars of subtropical beauties and gorgeous idle whores in bed. Yes, thank you for not smoking. The League Against Tuberculosis. The whole world can go blundering into war, but something as simple as a sitting room, kitchen and bathroom, no way. I'm done with it! Causing a stir, raising the alarm with a bop on the nose..." Fritz is shouting now and pointing to his latest pictures, while in desperation Jan Stargazer reaches under his armpit and sniffs his fingers. Then he mumbles: "But Fritz, I want to be rid of *my* self, too, I want to turn myself into a carpet, just like you, but there's so much beauty that just escapes, escapes." And Jan Stargazer kneels down and wipes the face of the portrait. Fritz hops across to him and yanks him away by the shoulder: "Life and art is reality, not a daydream, not going about the street like a blind man, but with the eyes open, idiot! And now beat it! And give me a whistle tonight." Jan Stargazer struggles to his feet, calm restored, and offers Fritz his hand. "Thanks, Fritz, I needed that, I've been born..."

Then at that time in the evening when lovers come out and regret having only two hands and one mouth, Fritz and Jan Stargazer are sitting together. Like gravediggers out of *Hamlet*. Sitting in a graveyard and making jokes with the gravedigger and boiling a skull in a skillet. In wartime a gravedigger will, in exchange for ten cigarettes, steal a corpse, gravestone and all, so what's one skull from a ten-year-old grave. And a Czech table calls for a Czech skull, one that will raise in the beholder a full-toothy grin to match its own… "Every household should have bones on the table," Fritz cries. "To act as an exclamation mark!" And Jan is happy for that to be so, though he keeps turning his head away. It makes him feel sick each time he registers the water bubbling as it makes its way between the skull's teeth and around its cavities. The gravedigger is smoking and a bit on edge. "If anyone asks, then you just found it…" But Fritz waves that aside and says he's got nothing to worry about. He goes on talking. "Come and join us sometime, Stargazer, and listen to the navvies. They'll have cycled twenty kilometres to work. To do track-laying. For 450 crowns a month. If you touch their hands, it's like touching a three-dimensional map of some hills. And when they get back home, they have to go out to get grass. In the night. Not their own grass, but to steal some. And if there's a moon, then after midnight. And then up again at four. Can you be at all affected by a Rubens when there's this in the world? Pass me a cloth." Jan hands him a small rag and Fritz drains the steaming soup, then, using his handkerchief so as not to

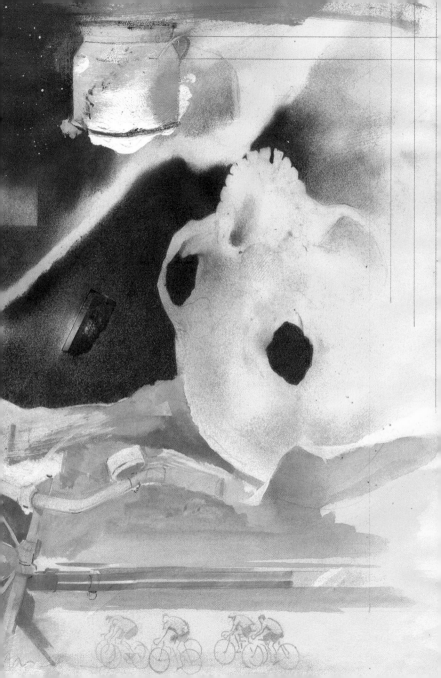

burn his fingers, he takes the skull out. He sets it down on a greasy newspaper. Jan looks at the table and whispers to himself: "It's a skull, a skull, nothing but a skull, bone..." But in vain: like woodworm the spiral of a question mark comes winding out of the skull, climbing up and up, and the dot at the foot is a human skull. What Jan keeps trying to suppress just won't vanish from sight. He sees a house bombed out and laid bare, bath taps dripping on every floor, one floor up a picture, a wardrobe, a carpet ripped away. The boiled skull keeps grabbing at different things, things that are receding in seven-league court shoes, things that are not beautiful, but true. Inside the skull he can see the world all abuzz, a huge trug full of painted Easter eggs, revolving round the pins of his mother's hat. Somewhere at the back the skull's owner rises, sadly swinging both arms, nothing else, just sadly swinging his arms. But Jan Stargazer wants to see nothing of this. He wants what is. Or what's there is, and what's here isn't? He feels awkward again, and when he looks up he sees Fritz finishing a drawing. He rises and is blinded. Fritz wraps the skull in the newspaper, shakes hands with the gravedigger and they depart into the star-filled night. Beyond the cemetery wall they stop. Fritz hands Jan the parcel. "Mind you put the skull on your table. It might help you, good bye..." Fritz makes to leave, constantly trampling on his shadow. Jan calls after him: "'Bye. See you. Look, Fritz, isn't this a beautiful wall?" Into the silence of the night Fritz replies: "Yeah, just the place to whip your cock out and pee all over it..."

Next morning Jan Stargazer woke up knackered. If they'd put a virgin to bed with him, she'd have woken up still a virgin. He hopped out of bed and, as he dressed, gazed on the skull gleaming white on his bedside table. That day he had to do *something* of benefit to human society. He went out to the back and chopped some wood, brought some coal in and had meant to dig over the entire garden. Now he was digging and listening to his mother's ethico-medical tags coming out through the window, the tags she'd stickered all over her son, the low wall and the old pear tree stumps. "Mind you don't catch cold..." "Jan, oh Jan, what are your bronchial tubes going to say to that..." "Oh, woe is me, would that I'd never conceived you..." And Jan thought brutishly: "Well, you shouldn't have held tight then." He also thought how wonderful it would be to bash his mother over the head with the spade and be left alone in the world. "Jan, oh Jan, by your father's memory, stop what you're doing and sit down, you're all hot and sweaty...," comes at him from this window or that. But Jan wanted to shout back something rude, but hadn't got the nerve for it yet. "She *is* my mother," he mused. He tossed the spade down and washed his face and hands in the water barrel. "Oh, my own dear, dear child," his own mother went on badgering her own flesh and blood as she came running out into the garden. At that point the gate opened and in walked Fritz. His curly hair glinted like steel swarf. He weighed the situation up in a trice and said: "Howdy, Stargazer! Get your clobber on, Bobby's waiting... Ah, a very good day to you,

Madame…" "And who's waiting, Mr Milkin?" she enquired over her spectacles as if inspecting a beetle in a box. "Bobby, Ma'am, a sweet little strumpet with a beautiful behind!" And Jan Stargazer got the message: "That's right, Mum, a little strumpet with a beautiful bottom. And what's wrong with that?" And Fritz, chewing his nails repeated: "Yes, Ma'am, what's wrong with that?" At which point, Mrs Stargazer, a justice's widow, staggered as if, there in the garden, she were playing blind man's buff. Jan was about to run across to her, but Fritz held him back. "Come, the umbilical cord that ties us to our parents has to be cut…" But she didn't hear. She mounted the steps, whispering under her breath: "Bob-by bot-tom…," until, as she closed the glazed garden door, she trapped the heady word *strumpet* half-way so all her maid heard was the condescending, barely appropriate little word *pet*.

VI/

It's a wonderful day in a lifetime that brings the discovery of something new, something stupendous looming on the horizon, something with which we communicate solely by means of signs, but which we know is coming our way and solely for our benefit. Jan Stargazer had ceased to be a letter box for the receipt of sealed envelopes. He'd been promoted. Now he was a post office that stamped all the percepts to be sorted and delivered to the correct addresses. An express parcel is an express parcel, a letter a letter and a packet a packet. That afternoon he was sitting by the window and staring into the glass at himself. Unawed. By a half-open window at that. A wasp flew up, clad in its striped jersey, and was crawling up his nose in the glass. Crawling about his hair. Another time he'd be sure he had a beetle on his brain, dashing about on its hot feet and vanishing amid the junk of his mind. And he would suffer from the notion all day long. This time he knew it was a wasp crawling over the glass and from his imagination he supplied the extra tiny footsteps of a golden spiderling. In short: he was beginning to split into two worlds like a strangled amoeba. His old longing to spew up his dreaming and clear-fell some space for his imagination had been cast out. He amazed himself with the observation that it sufficed to place a sheet of paper between himself and the wasp so as to create two worlds sufficient unto themselves, two worlds of equal beauty. One this side of the curtain, the other behind it. And through the window he watched the cyclists, the old women with packs of mown grass on their backs, the cars, in short reality running on the drive-belt of the road. He manoeuvred the wasp onto the paper, opened the window wide and – fly, fly away, you wingèd, stripy skittle, freedom is the most beautiful thing man can have, fly away, fly, you girl of the 1800s, tight-corseted at the waist, fly, wasp, I am free to decide whether to free you into the air or kill you without a pang of conscience. In the air you'll crash into nothing, in the mind you'll crash into nothing, Jan Stargazer, but life is full of sharp-cornered objects that can bring you down. At that point, without knocking, his mother entered, her white scarf sopping wet. For several hours, Jan had known that he'd have to hear out his blood-related flagellant: "Oh, son, my son, what have you done to me…" Jan relented. "But, Mum, stop being silly, go back to the kitchen, I know…" But instead his mother started shrieking: "You know, but I don't. This needs looking into! My son shall not consort with whores! Shame on you! Did your daddy go with whores? I ask you, did your daddy go with whores?" At which point Jan started to titter, suddenly he couldn't care less what he said to this play-acting woman. He knew it was entirely up to him whether to go and see Bobby or not, just as, whatever happened to be on offer, if he wasn't interested, he wasn't interested. He wanted to leave her one last opening. Stepping up close to his mother, he said: "But Mum, silly old Mum, what are you thinking of?" But his mother carried on shrieking in her high-pitched voice: "I ask you, did your daddy go with whores? Who'd have thought it! When I was going out with your daddy…" "…we would visit your gran's grave in the cemetery and prick our thumbs on a rose thorn and suck each other's blood to seal our deep love," Jan Stargazer picked up the thread, because he knew it by heart. And he severed his kinship forever. At that moment he detached himself from his mother, from that moment he would only see a woman, this woman who'd turned her isolation into theatre and so too into his prison. He saw his own isolation and the fact that henceforth he'd be surrounded in his house by objects, and he smiled and watched the screaming woman dispassionately. Even before that day he'd have gladly become a policeman, taken out his non-existent notebook and issued her with a fine for disturbing the peace. That might have made her laugh, and all would have been well. Now, though, he'd entered a world of objects and saw in his mother only his landlady, concierge, cleaner... raising her eyes to false heavens. And as she ripped invisible rags to shreds, beside herself with rage, she shouted: "My son's not going to go with whores, he will not. No, he will not! Which brothel does that whore live at? I demand an answer!" And Jan, bowing courteously, said: "The Tunnel..."

VII/

"Ever since then, every time I see roofers, I get spots before my eyes and have to get off my chair..." The company all nodded, but their minds were on why they'd come. For the racking of the redcurrant wine, that beautiful, red, redcurrant wine that had been bubbling away for four weeks through the fermentation tube and feeding the imagination. That day it would all be drunk, bar two bottles to be set aside for Christmas. Meanwhile they were skinning a rabbit that the bandmaster, Vaňátko, had been rewarded with at a funeral, and keeping the fire going in the iron stove, and it was stifling hot. Josef and Ferdinand Milkin and the retired confectioner Marvánek with his silver tube were gazing at the top of the cupboard from which a ten-litre vessel would soon be taken down. "So let's get started..." Ferdinand climbed onto a chair. "God, my head's starting to spin just looking at it, and my fin's probably not up to this; I might break it... Fritz, Fritz," Ferdinand shouted into the green tendrils of the Virginia creeper. Fritz parted the green curtain, stood on a chair and got the ten-litre vessel down. "Here you are, and after you've drunk yourselves stupid, give my son a call, he'll come and paint you and... Thank you for not smoking!" And Fritz patted his father on the shoulder, winked at him and nodded to give his father, uncle and the assembled company to know he didn't mind if they did. And he left. "Quick, out with the cork! A spoon!" Ferdinand sampled it and "Aaaaaaah..." And the whole company, even blind Josef, beamed. "Josef, shut up shop, we're not selling mineral water today. Put a notice up: *To-day's allocation exhausted.*" "To hell with mineral water! Turns my stomach just thinking about it," Marvánek bellowed and, unbuttoning his waistcoat, took his silver tube out as if wanting to fraternise with every available drop. "Glasses!" And that first swig, delicious, the knack of taking in sun and sugar and fermented juice with the tongue, the wine, the *fine drop o' wine* as the old 'uns grace it, the way they do with anything fit to drink. A rum isn't a rum but *a fine drop o' rum*, a kirsch *a fine drop o' kirsch*, and this wine was *a fine drop o' wine* and they gulped it greedily from their glasses or straight from the nozzle with their eager snouts. "Those were the days, eh, Josef, when we brewed us a fine drop o' grog and it caught fire on the hob, eh?..." "And then you went and puked in the tomatoes, eh, Ferdinand?..." "And you, me old pastry cook, you puked in the toilet and we had to pull the chain for you and you came back covered in droplets..." "And you, Beethoven, do you remember on the way back from Ostrava and you puked all over your crime disclosure certificate, and then knelt on it?" "Oh, happy days, such happy days, my friends," said Ferdinand, raising his glass against the sunlight. "And you, bandmaster, play us a tune, but with your fiddle behind your back, like the time you played on top of that ceramic stove!" "And when the cops then carted you off like a roll of lino." "Play, Beethoven, or I'll pour this down your neck!" The bandmaster played and the company stamped their feet and shouted: "Bravo! Hosanna! But back then?" Ferdinand began protesting: "No, lads, it wasn't my fault. It was that greengrocer's bookkeeper, kept on about some fabulous recipe, he did, so I copied it out and then brewed it up. Well, folks! All I know is that we went outside and slap, bang, wallop! Like when you knock down a pensioner, and I was just lying there!" Marvánek transferred some wine to his stomach via his little funnel and cried: "I know, it was called the Royal and Imperial Regulator!" "Bollocks, Marvánek, you poured a nice drop o' Nuncius[1] into your silver tube and you were more than happy with it: 'That Wantoch, he might be a Jew, but he makes a good brew!' you said. Then having puked all over your waistcoat, you started shouting: 'What's that Jewish sod brewed us now?'" And so the company chatted away, they ate the rabbit and even drank the bottles set aside for Christmas. As dusk fell, they loaded the almost sleeping confectioner Marvánek, along with his little tube that he was still holding his thumb over, into a wooden washtub, decorated it with strands of Virginia creeper, made garlands of it to go round their own soggy foreheads and carried Mr Marvánek home. They got his key out of his pocket, unlocked the door, found a cork in the spoon drawer and stoppered his silver tube with it. The bandmaster stayed on guard; he'd left his fiddle at the Milkins', and the company staggered off into the dark of evening. At the crossroads next to the mineral spring they shook hands and said their good-byes. The Milkins linked arms for support. At the gate they undid the lock and, Ferdinand having wheeled the tandem out, Josef said: "I say, Ferdi, d'you know what I've just remembered?" Ferdinand knew at once. "That kitten!" "Right, the kitten. We shouldn't have gone there. You know, it's really terrible when I can't see a thing." Then Ferdinand shouted in his brother's ear: "Closing time! Closing!" and he jangled the keys to drown everything out because that really was Everything. "We're closing up and then we're off," said Ferdinand, stumbling next to the second handle bars. And blind Josef swung himself up and they rode off. As they reached the lindens and the war memorial there was a glimmer of light amid the gloom and both Milkins looked up and saw a tabby kitten with a white bib and little white socks and a little pink muzzle, sitting by the war memorial and miaowing pitifully, just like that time a quarter of a century past outside their trench. And the closer they rode, the more pitifully the kitten miaowed until it suddenly dawned on Ferdinand that he was riding on the back saddle and blind Josef was in front, steering, with the expression of a bird that knows where it's going. He wanted to shout out, keep shouting, but some little gnome had taken a hooked pole to his lips and pulled the shutter down with a clatter. He'd barely ducked ahead of the linden branches and suddenly a massive wardrobe opened its mouth and clamped its jaws... A crunching of iron and bones. And silence. Alone the kitten hopped off the memorial and ran silently across to the bus and the brothers crushed beneath it, licked their faces and curled up in a ball next to Josef, like that time five seconds before the explosion of shrapnel. Then two airy shades, clear in outline, crawled out from under the bus, dusted their clothes down and, holding hands, ran with an unbelievably velvety tread towards the war memorial and engraved on the blank, black marble two names to make up the numbers: Josef and Ferdinand Milkin.

VIII/

Huge tears rolled down Fritz's cheeks, and they were more like tears of helpless laughter. He was glad it was all over for his father and his uncle and he kept laughing and playing the dead men's favourite marches on the gramophone, so greeting death with jubilation and birth with tears. A few hours previously he and the neighbours had dressed the deceased in bright clothes and laid them in coffins. He had crossed his father's hands behind his head, the way he used to take his nap in the garden after a good lunch, and he laid his Uncle Josef with his palms clamped to his temples to conceal the deep gash from the mudguard. His relatives, who'd been there since first thing, found it offensive and prophesied bad things, and each time they knelt by the coffins to pray, they couldn't get a single prayer out. If the wound hadn't been oozing blood through his coat, you might have thought he was asleep… It's all that heathen's fault! And they shook their fists at Fritz through the glazed door. But the time of the funeral was approaching, so they got down on their knees and started wailing. "Oh, poor dear uncle of ours, what have you done to us?" "Uncle, oh Uncle!" "Oh, Jesus of mine, holy Virgin Mary…" "Dear old Ferdi, my only true friend…" Thus did they wail, wailing across one another and, above all, across the blaring of the gramophone. But Fritz was smiling, pouring himself one glass of rum after another and munching open sandwiches, and whenever one of the relatives stood up from the coffin to take one, Fritz raised a finger and declared: "When the soul doth grieve, the stomach shall sleep…," and put the sandwiches on top of the cupboard. Through the open garden door two male relatives could be seen trying on the dead men's shoes. "I'll have those, if you don't mind, Ferdinand promised them to me." "Oh, no, no, no, no, no, not true! Those are mine, they're Uncle Josef's and he promised I could have them!" And they were actually Fritz's! He leapt up and snatched them back, hitting the relatives over the head. "Don't play games with me!" And he was smiling again, knowing it was going to end badly. He knew things would hit a slippery slope and everything would come crashing down. That's why he put one record after another on the gramophone, each one louder than the last in order to drown out the ever crazier things his relatives were saying. "And I'll have these trousers, Josef liked me best." "And I'll take this duvet for my daughter, she's getting married. What good is it here?" "No, that one's mine." "All right, but never darken our door again!" "Let go of those wellingtons, I saw them first!" "Oh, what a lovely vase! Mother *will* be pleased!" Now Fritz leapt to his feet and his eyes focussed on the white stick that he'd placed in Josef's coffin. With a few leaps he flew into the room and yelled: "Out! The lot of you, out!" And he grabbed the white stick from the coffin and lashed out left and right, aunt or not, uncle or not, he went furiously for his relatives, who fled, tripping over the wreaths of wax flowers. There could be no understanding reached with this world, just a sound, a very sound thrashing. Then in their flight someone tripped over the stand and Ferdinand fell out of his coffin, face down and with wood shavings showering over his back. But Fritz kept battering his relatives, even jumping over his dead father. And the relatives gathered outside the window, next to the pump, wiping the perspiration from their brows and exhibiting their bruises. The white stick broke in two. Fritz, his whole body trembling, held the two pieces together, then apart, like the vacillating pointers on a balance scale. An unknown hand slipped some blotting paper between his next thought and his acting on it, and he hesitated. He glanced in surprise at his father, seeing his father for the first time, seeing that he'd been his father and would never be his father again. He was about to drop to his knees when the undertakers arrived; they placed the coffin on the ground and rolled Ferdinand Milkin into it, but Ferdinand's arms had become so springy that they had to bend them into the coffin by force. And then Jan Stargazer showed up, dressed in black and wearing an agonized smile. "Some funeral, eh?" Fritz came back to his senses. And the undertakers started nailing the coffin down. "Aren't you even going to see your dad off?" Jan asked. "No…, let the dead bury the dead, come through to the kitchen…," said Fritz, pale as a sheet. And the minute they were in the kitchen he put the gramophone on. Jan Stargazer stared at the rucks in the carpet and his throat went dry.

IX/

Evening again, and probably after the funeral was over. Jan Stargazer and Fritz Milkin, somewhat the worse for wear, had left the house of mourning, gone across the square to the booth and through the yard to Fritz's den and studio, and now they were drinking again, in silence, one glass after another, each immersed in his own space. Fritz, with his head thrown back, was reliving his moment of weakness beside his father's coffin. He sensed that everything had been a forced lie, that for all his intellect, that useless adjunct, he'd made everything a lie, he sensed that he'd actually been quite fond of his father, loved him even, though without once talking about it, that he'd played the titan and deluded himself and his father and everyone else. Never again would the stream of mineral water gurgle at his side, and never again would his father's voice be heard thundering through the cottage. In a sweat he rose to his feet and for the first time he felt sad. He looked at Jan Stargazer and saw that, quite the opposite, Jan was all aglow, somehow revitalised, even though in that drunken state he could hardly sit. Fritz saw that Jan had been saved at the expense of his own loss, that Fritz's own world that had just collapsed had been accepted in full by Jan Stargazer. While he, Fritz, would be going on rudderless. Fritz sat down, laying his head on the table, and Jan stood up, wobbled, opened a cupboard instead of the door, but then did get out into the yard, overgrown with

Virginia creeper, finally to grasp the door handle of the little mineral water booth. He was thirsty. He turned the tap on, successfully aimed the neck of a bottle under it at the very first go and started gulping the water down. As he went to switch off the light he spotted a half-open drawer. He opened it and took out an old photo, all grimy and dog-eared. It was a photo of a boy with a dog on a lead. At the top it had written on it in pencil: *This is my little son and Bubík the dog when they were seven.* "But that's Fritz!" Jan muttered to himself and put the light out, then he parted the jumble of Virginia creeper and staggered back into Fritz's den. He collapsed into an easy chair and fell asleep. When he woke there was already a glimmer of light. Through the window he could see, across the yard, a light on in the little mineral water booth. Fritz wasn't in the room. Jan slowly rose to his feet, fell, got back on his feet and lumbered outside, then, holding onto the wall for support, he made his way to the half-open door. By the light of the lamp this is what he saw: Fritz was lying sprawled across the pewter countertop, his left hand touching the running mineral water and his right hand clutching the childhood photo of him and the dog, and he was weeping silently. Jan Stargazer closed the door, opened the gate and went out into the square. Staggering as he went, he reached the lindens and the war memorial, where there was a large black patch on the tarmac. He stared dully ahead of him and then, as if having just come to his senses, he walked away at a brisk, military pace.

CAIN

An existentialist short story

I/

I went up to the ticket window and said to the girl: "One ticket." The cashier replied through the window: "Where to, sir?" She knew me as the station dispatcher, so she was mildly surprised. I thought for a moment and said: "I'll go to wherever the ticket your eye first lands on says." And the young lady, thinking this had the makings of a conversation, smiled: "What do you mean, first? I look at the tickets all day and every day." And she laughed and you could see her gold canine. "Right, miss, look me in the eye and like a fairground parrot, pull me out a ticket," and I rubbed my hands and thought I'd got the better of her. But she was cleverer than that. Without hesitating, she replied: "I can issue tickets in the dark. I'd end up giving you only the ticket I wanted you to have." She laughed again and swung impertinently on her chair. "Right then, seventh column, seventh row down going from right to left, like the Jews," I whispered with a quiver in my voice. Then I heard the ticket being punched in the date-stamping machine. The window had a light on and some ginger locks now leaned through it: "Bystřice by Benešov. That'll be six crowns fifty. You're looking a bit sad today, sir." I said: "Something like that," and turned away from those obliging eyes.

Then I was standing on that borderline when it might be said that it isn't night yet and it's still daytime, or when it might also be asserted that the day is over and evening has come. On the platform, the station odd-job man was getting the luggage ready to go in the brake van. I mused: "So Bystřice by Benešov it is. A little town I've never been to, a hotel I've never slept in." And I found it odd. The station odd-job man lit a lamp and I, having no lamp to light, sat on a bench and scuffed the decomposing leaves with the tip of my shoe. I scraped a layer to one side and spotted a scrap of paper. I bent down and by the light of a match read a snatch of the piano score to the hit 'The springtime of my love is here'. When the match went out I repeated to myself: "How right, the springtime of my love is here."

The train entered the station. I entered a compartment, unlit as the Protectorate[1] required, and without fuss set off on my journey. As I passed the dispatcher standing there on the platform, he waved his green lamp up and down three times, like a priest sprinkling a coffin. On this trip there was no one playing cards, and I was leaving on a quest for simple human happiness, to harmonise my life to my thoughts. I was sitting in my coat and because I had a degree in the history of law,[2] I was thinking about the Austrian law under which suicides had to be interred out of the way, with no fuss, or be passed to their relatives for quiet burial. And the order shall go out to whole companies of maggots to gnaw at my eyes, divisions will be sent to my intestines and lungs, and several armies will be charged with taking my bones by storm come what may. And all that quietly, out of the way. That's what I was thinking about and I listened as the click-clack of the wheels slowed because the train was stopping. It stopped. A dark-haired woman and some big boxes squeezed into the compartment. I wondered: "What on earth has the woman got there," but I said: "Where are you travelling to, ma'am?" And she said: "Home, sir. I'm going home and taking empty fruit boxes with me. I have some orchards, you see. I pick the fruit in summer and deliver it in winter." Woe or exhilaration in the voice, hard to tell in the dark. "And are you happy, ma'am?" I asked. "How could I not be. It's what I enjoy. Up a ladder all day, picking the lovely fruit, and when it comes to putting them one at a time in a basket, that's the best moment of all. I've been doing it for twenty years." Her voice careworn, but exhilarated. "And have you ever fallen off?" "Goodness! Not so far. And I climb higher than even my husband dares. I set the ladder on branches and twigs and rummage about in the very tops of the trees. I've probably got a guardian angel," she said with a chuckle. "And where are you going?" she asked in turn. "Me? I'm going for razors," I clicked my tongue. "Two razors, one to go in my hand and one into a limewood plank." "Razors? And going where to get them?" The woman's voice betrayed regret that she'd broached the subject. I gripped the razors inside my pocket and said: "Bystřice by Benešov, dear lady." "And why?" For no obvious reason I started to rant: "Ah, dear lady, I shall climb a tall ladder and for a full hour I shall stand there and wait. The branches and twigs shall make my body move. Then someone will shout and not shout, shoot and not shoot, but I shall fly, not downwards, but up." That's what I shouted, or what was actually shouting inside me, and I leapt to my feet. The woman's voice, though you couldn't tell if it was a woman's, a human voice, and you couldn't tell if it was human, said something unintelligible in reply. The dark-haired woman who so enjoyed fruit-picking, had fainted.

11/

Over the prostrate body I told myself I shouldn't have done that. I summoned the ticket inspector with a little light hanging at her breast and together we brought the orchard lady back from the dark. I rubbed her hands and the ticket lady poured a little coffee into her mouth. Finally she raised a hand to her eyebrows and breathed out. And I still had hold of her free, motionless hand, breathing into her fingers and begging her forgiveness. Then the ticket lady shone her lamp in my face and said: "Well, well, sir, what are you doing here?" And with her voice a little posy flew into the darkness of the compartment. A familiar voice, pleasing to the ear and capable of bringing back events both snowed-over and fresh. I was still holding the orchard lady's hand, but the sickness of the past had begun to gnaw at my brain, my heart. I reached my fingers towards the lamp and shaded it with the palm of my hand. The orchard lady was quietly groaning: "Good lord above, oh, good lord." And she tried to stand up. I helped her. She took her seat and straightened her scarf and the light of the lamp watched us. The train drove onto a deafening bridge and slowed. To a halt. I turned, crossed to the window and slid it down. I was swathed in fresh air as I gawped at the signal indicating Halt. The train whistled dolefully. Behind my ear the ticket lady said: "Nothing to cry over. It's probably because of the milk train." I turned and took the lamp from the voice's chest, shone the light and it was her. I said: "We've already met the milk train, Máša, at Kostomlaty." And I hung the little lamp back round her neck. I leaned out of the window and looked at the red signal light. She touched my back and said: "Well that's something, you recognising me. Do you remember, you horrid man, that fence? Do you remember all the rest of it?" And her lamp pressed into my back and I could feel the warmth of its lens. I said: "How could I not!" I swept a dismissive hand into the darkness, because there was no point to anything. This ticket girl had messed up my jigsaw and I knew I'd have to re-do it all. As usual, she'd shown up at the wrong moment. Not that I didn't like her, on the contrary, I liked everything about her, it turned me on, but even back then, that time by the fence, I'd had another plan, another construct had excited my brain. Now, just as I was in a hurry to give it life, she'd appeared and her existence placed me in peril. I could feel her breath on my shoulder, hear the beating of her heart and the hiss of her lamp. Then there was a noise in the signal post and the red light was replaced by a cold green one. Máša whispered "Yippee" in my ear and broke into a laugh. I sat down and the train moved off. I said: "Do you remember how we pinched photos from each other's pockets?" Máša said nothing, from her coat pocket she withdrew a timetable held together with a rubber ring from a bottling jar, extracted from it a stiff roll of paper and handed it to me. She ran out into the corridor. I lit a cigarette and scrutinised the paper by the strip of light from the station lamps. It was a photo of me. The orchard lady strapped her boxes to her back and, as she went to get off, made her farewell: "Goodbye, sir." I said: "Goodbye, ma'am, goodbye," and I looked at the photo of a child with a fringe and eyes that had been crying. The photo was stained with coffee and soaked in grease. I switched my gaze from the photo to the platform. Below the window Máša was walking up and down and calling out: "Čelákovice, Čelákovice." Her voice receded and came back again. Such an assured and steady voice. It twinkled and flickered in space as sure as the flame in her lamp and I felt awful. The death I was longing for was receding and laughing. I was coffee-stained and grease-soaked, my hair trimmed into a fringe and my eyes like I'd been crying. That was me. And that's what I was going to be like. Then the strip of light in which I was caught slowly started to spin. When I looked back at the photo, I saw a little girl's head with a ribbon. I turned it over and on the other side was me. Even as children we'd leaned on each other. That did for me. The past, which half an hour earlier had been a single point, had now carved itself an opening through which a grown man could pass. And an ever mightier tingling stream flowed from me and the longing for death shone white. It was stronger than anything. There was nothing to be done about it and I wasn't one to resist. I had always yielded, because that was safer, because I believed in some destiny which, whenever it fancied, might well stiffen my resolve, but only to break my back in the next instant. It was a cosy philosophy, but it had served me well, which is why I stuck to it. When she reappeared in the compartment doorway, her clippers were dangling and the sudden rush of light was irksome. I screwed up my eyes and handed her the photo. She reached out to take it. I stood up, held her firmly by the wrist and shaded the lamplight with my body. I even gave her a kiss. It was dark and whenever I moved, light spurted out along the length of her coat. My hand felt her firm breasts. Everything was fine and I acknowledged right there and then the truth of the Cubists' claim that objects exist even in the dark. As I had seen it three years before through the wire fence, so it was now, too. Then I asked her to douse her little lamp. I didn't do anything to her because she was wearing long trousers. I just stroked her hand and she squeezed my fingers as if she meant to pump her whole life into me. I told her: "Go and call out the stations. Someone might break a leg in the dark." She brushed that aside and said: "So they'll have to take more care." And she kissed me for a full three minutes. On the approach to Prague she told me, relighting her lamp: "Wait for me by the main entrance." The train was stopping and her voice could be heard: "Prague, Vltava Station.[3] All alight here." She was moving further away and the desire inside me grew stronger. I alighted into the Prague blackout. The trams were running in a blue obscurity and pedestrians were magical. I went and stood opposite the exit and watched its openings and closings, the stream of refracted lights, and the passengers who were fabulously beautiful in appearance. The swing doors seemed to be opened by a draught. As if I was in a sunken ship, where the current was opening and closing doors, giving admittance to the drowned and fish. When she appeared, it was a prettier and more engaging sight than I could have imagined. She opened the door just as a tram was passing, flooding her in a suppressed blue and amber. I noticed she had a new latex collar and that she was looking about her. I waved my whole body to her and the nickel buttons came trotting down the steps and you could tell she would have loved to give me a kiss. But I was seeing how well her coat fitted and how pure she was. She was carrying a tiny case, the kind engine drivers have, and a blue coffee flask. As she walked she had a huge backside, as if she had some physical deformity. She stood in front of me, swinging the flask, and I laughed at her. I took her little case and she asked me to hold the mirror of her compact so that she could recast her lips and make them more beautiful. I liked that and she turned her eyes towards me and looked at her quivering lip. She looked and could probably see her kisses there. I thought: "Hell, she doesn't care whether I love her or not." And then I told myself: "Idiot, she's further gone than you. She's happy with the knowledge that *she* loves *you*." And I felt embarrassed. I took her arm in mine. She walked along beside me and with every step she brushed her thigh against me. I started to enjoy it and without warning I said: "Máša, I love you." And I meant it in all sincerity, just as sincerely as – if I hadn't bumped into her – I would have slit my wrists with the razor. Máša replied: "Well I never, and I've loved you for ages." And she laughed. I compressed her radiant lips and said, with as much tenderness as I could muster: "My little muzzlet." Her dimples refused to subside and she dragged me off somewhere to the top of Letná. There, in the pitch dark, she told me, pointing into the darkness: "That darkness over there, sir, that's the National Theatre, that lighter bit, that's the monument to the resistance, and that over there, well I've no idea what that might be." And she prattled on and on while I was in contact with her hips and enjoying being on the move. I nodded at everything she said and was genuinely happy because not once did she ask if I would love her always, nor did she put the wind up me with talk of her relatives. She took me all the way home with her and all she wanted from me was my presence. Then at some point or other she lay a finger on my lips, though I hadn't said a word for half an hour, and hissed: "Shhh." I thought: "Jesus, how idiotic," but said nothing. I let myself be hauled up the stairs, and again I had to wait a moment while she found the key. With a flick of a switch eyes slowly got used to the sewing machine, a cupboard full of stuffed orioles, and a picture of the Heart of Jesus. I sat down on a rocking chair and closed my eyes. In my coat pocket I could feel the razors – lying ever so close to my genitals. When I half-raised my eyelids, Máša was taking her blouse off. She'd also made the bed and set the picture dancing with a corner of the duvet. I closed my eyes. I heard the light switch. The rustle of blouse and underwear, the tap of one shoe against the other. The Heart of Jesus was still swinging. Through a chink in the blackout curtain a dim blue light was forcing its way in. I lifted the curtain a little and down below was a pure, lovely blue night. The city was exhaling its carefully dimmed lights. I let go of the strip of wood in which the curtain ended. Darkness. Even the picture had stopped swinging. I undressed in silence and devoted all my powers and juices to Máša, as if using love to wash away suicide. I've always done with sincerity whatever has happened to come my way.

III/

Towards morning I found myself alone and the start of the day was being provocative. I was in a sorry state. Máša was sleeping like the dead and a great bubble by her nose testified to her being alive. Her right leg was hanging out of the bed and a vein was transporting oxygenated blood to her tentacles, which provided me with more evidence. Her right breast wasn't hanging, but billowing and seemed about to drag her body to the ground. The bubble by her nose kept billowing and shrinking and I couldn't lie there anymore. I got up and without a word or any other noise got dressed. The Heart of Jesus shone helplessly from the colour print and the thorns and blood were new and fresh. The confusion was presided over by the Son of God and he couldn't prevent any one kiss or any one cry. He hung like a guard who had nothing to do with the man condemned. Only a little garden, crowned by a blazing wisp of straw, was capable of receiving anything that sprang from pain. And as I was tightening my belt, he was coming ever closer, and as I knotted my tie in the glass of his picture, I made him my brother and he raised no objection. I understood that he had taken his fate into his own hands, that he knew exactly what the end would be, and yet he didn't avoid it because he needed the evidence of his sacrifice. As if he'd lain down on a railway line and waited for a train to come. He knew what awaited him, but he hadn't flinched. He committed suicide as proof of the integrity of his thoughts. I became aware of my own self in the mirror and made up my mind. Máša, even through the solid wall of sleep, sensed it. She whispered something and the bubble at her nose burst. I quickly left the room. The street door was still locked. I opened a window into the yard, climbed over the wall and ran to meet myself. Nothing stood in my way. I alone was holding the tiller and steering. I could feel my willpower being transported to the remotest parts of my body. That day for the first time did I know myself, and how to express myself mathematically. I was neither sad, nor happy. Only my senses had sharpened. When I reached the station at a trot I realised that I'd left my ticket at Máša's. I bought a new one and the first train bore me off towards Benešov. I clutched the two razors in my pocket and quite near them were my genitals. I sat there and found the arrival times in my timetable and, watch in hand, checked the train's progress. I'd have preferred to be beside the engine driver, as fireman, and ignore all the signals, and only stop when we got to Bystřice. Only one thought bugged me. Would there be a bathroom? After that I thought of nothing else.

And there was a bathroom. At the hotel, I had them make a fire up for me and signed the register. Under 'Reason for stay' I wrote: *Visiting brothers.* I paid in advance and told the fat licensee I was going to bed because I'd been travelling all night. I unlocked room No. 7, undressed and lay down on the bed. Outside it was raining and from the bathroom came the ever rising sound of water. I lay facing away from the window and in the mirror I could see the window panes, blurred by the trickling rain. In the same mirror I could see a headless hat, a hollow coat, trousers and bits of the stand. It was such a sorry sight that I rose and went into the bathroom. I turned the taps off and took the razors out of my pocket. Suddenly I began whistling the waltz from Lehár's *Der Graf von Luxemburg*. I stuck the blade of one razor to the bath step with putty and lay the other one next to it. And hesitated. I'd already felt uneasy from having started whistling. Though it was more as if the whistling was inside me. I fell silent and picked up the other razor. I could feel my fingers shaking. Then it happened. I plucked a hair from my head and tested the razor's sharpness on it. The fingers holding the hair were quivering. I wiped the misted-up mirror with my shirt sleeve and looked at myself. Yes, there was fear ensconced there. All the whistling and testing had been invented by a frightened body. In the mirror I was that little boy in Máša's photo again, with a fringe and eyes that had been crying. For the first time I had an exact view of myself and not a single fold escaped through the eye without my doing an autopsy on it. It was terrible. I placed the razor back on the step and went out into the corridor. I leaned against the doorframe and closed my eyes. The humbling I'd put myself through, the fear that I'd caused myself had tied my guts in knots. I could feel the pallor in my face and the irregularity in my arteries. So I stood and waited until I began to subside. A rhythmical rustling gradually brought me back. I opened my eyes and down below an old man was standing at a bend in the stairs, plugging a hooked nail into the wall with his gnarled hands. I watched his deft handiwork. And in the corner stood a Minimax fire extinguisher. I rallied somewhat and the old man hadn't spotted me. I slipped back into my room and lay my face against the cool door. Silently, I edged it open and through the tiny chink I meant to watch the old man and his hands. Then he who all the time I was there hadn't once looked at me was now staring my way. His gaze was fixed on the chink that was only a few millimetres wide so that his eye seemed to be set dead opposite mine and to know everything. I banged the door to and ran into the bathroom. I was exasperated. I slipped off my dressing gown and went and stood in the hot water. Without thinking twice I picked the razor up and with one swipe commenced the concert of death. At the initial pain I came over faint, but as soon as I put my hand in the water it eased. It was more like fatigue than pain, more like sleep than a keen wakefulness. I had neither the strength to press my good wrist onto the blade held in putty, nor any reason to beat a speedy retreat. It was too beautiful. I raised my arm to check that it was true. The blood was streaming and I willed it to escape by the centilitre. Slowly and silently. I willed my transfiguration to be as slow as possible. Reproach couldn't have been further from my mind, no distant memory of things read came to me. I began to see myself as the very substance of poetry, music and painting. Not even Máša's heart came to wish me well, or hold me to blame for something. I now belonged to other things, and fear and dejection were things of the past. I had no such wish as *Father, if thou be willing, remove this cup from me*. On the contrary, I prayed: "Father, if thou be willing, let me drink of this cup." I was prayer personified, and I was begetting myself in the beautiful. Not my father, not my mother, not even the station master came to hinder my transformation. Nothing tainted the moment, just as no one had ever tainted my happy life in the past. I absolved everyone and hoped they would all absolve me. Once Máša told me through that wire fence: "Bogánek,[4] do you know that actually man only lives for the benefit of a few hours?" And she was quite weepy. Back then I'd thought her a bit stupid. Now, as my life was coming to an end, I had remembered and granted that she'd been right. Man does live just for the benefit of a few hours. As I approached the finishing line, I wished for nothing more than to be prepared for the sight of the dying seconds, when present, past and future rotate in a single flash. But I had passed that moment, or it hadn't arrived yet. The bloody water was becoming oppressive and I had an idea that any vision of that one clear second might be a delusion. I was only thinking of what had just been. As if I were returning to my mother's womb, as if I had re-grown an umbilical cord. I was being sucked into something. I was holding on to the edge and the force was gaining force. Finally I had to let go. As if the hands with which I was clinging to the shore had been snatched away. I had missed myself, and the final seconds that had seemed to matter so much were disgusting and desolate. My eyes were open and I saw not, I heard voices and could not call out to them. I was gulping bloody water and threw up, because my head had begun to topple. All I could see above me was laughing faces. I also wanted to laugh, but the mask was now static. The light bulb had gone out.

IV/

Dr Gall had pumped the blood of three donors into me, at the top rate. So I hadn't died. The novelty I'd longed for had become a reality and I was now someone else. The name on the black board above my head might have been mine, but the blood was stacking up different kinds of thoughts in me, washing off the soot and wallpapering my brain with other kinds of ideas. If it hadn't been for the wound on my wrist, I'd never have remembered. To my new blood the razors appeared non-existent. I couldn't fathom how I could have done it, how I could have zapped my wrist with a blade without it hurting. I must have been given the blood of none but the most prudent of citizens, so I broke into a sweat at the recollection of what had happened in Bystřice. Dr Gall looked after me and whenever I began to wake, there would be his steady, bespectacled gaze as if he were trying to knock a hole into my head and find out how it had all happened. One afternoon he told me that the lady ticket inspector who had saved my life was coming in to see me. I kept my eyes firmly on the door, like that time at Vltava Station. This time the door was white, at peace and artless. When she came in, she was afraid and out of uniform. Her eyes travelled from one bed to another and she held her right hand to her heart. She smiled at me and came slowly over. I could tell she wanted to kiss me, but was feeling coy.

I said to her: "Sit down, Máša." And she was so confused by so many eyes that she sat on my sore arm. I yelped and the tears that sprang up reminded me of Máša's love and I was utterly dismayed. I couldn't imagine where her unbounded love sprang from. It was as if she'd taken it into her head to authenticate Christianity. She wiped my tears with a corner of her headscarf. At such close quarters I noted that she was wearing a brown dress with a purple belt and brown high-heeled shoes and that her hair was combed up high like in a locket. When she sat down, she crossed her legs, her calves flashed, and you could see that her knickers were the colour of mallow. Fourteen pairs of eyes were watching her swinging leg. When she realised, she stopped and blushed. Then she told me about trains, the station master and the dress she'd made. I was staring out of the window and wanted Máša so badly that I place my bandaged hand in her lap. It lay there like a helpless kitten. I had a clear sense of her warm flesh and pure contours. I also registered how small her ankles were. I wanted to say something nice to her. I leaned towards her and whispered: "Oh, Mum." And she got the message and, smiling, lowered her gaze and nodded to show she understood what I meant. At the far end of the ward a motorcyclist was coming round from his anaesthesia, following the amputation of both legs. He was waking up and shouting: "Let go, Max, let go of the handlebars, Max!" He was held to the bed with straps that his chest was stretching to snapping point. Máša looked on anxiously and took hold of my good hand. The motorcyclist was trying to stand. Shrieking with pain. Suddenly he disengaged his right hand, reached under the bed, grabbed the glass urine bottle and flung it with phenomenal force. The urine-filled vessel flew over fourteen beds and smashed against the wall above me. Splinters of glass landed on my white duvet cover and glinted in the sunlight. Máša went quite pale and droplets of urine shone in her hair like tiny bits of amber. She suddenly burst out laughing and pressed the bell to call for help. The motorcyclist was yelling and trying to lever himself up, but the straps held. Máša leaned towards me, gave me a kiss and took a book from her bag and said: "Goodbye." At the door she turned and blew me a kiss. I raised my bandaged hand, then let it drop back. I told myself: "If she'll have me, I'll marry her."

V/

Dr Gall saw me every day and constantly asked me questions. Then he listened closely. I thought he wasn't much into reading, or that he wanted to write a scholarly article, so I didn't omit a single twist or turn. Good old Máša had brought me Karolina Světlá's *The Cross by the Brook*,[5] so I read that bucolic narrative in bed and it felt like leafing through Máša's soul. One evening I was summoned to the doctor. By now, the three donors' blood was obeying the commands of my brain, so I could relocate my body wherever I wished without a hitch. Dr Gall poured me a glass of plum brandy and I sat there on the couch, dangling my slipper. He removed my bandage to reveal a purple scar and said: "Listen, I can't get my head round the fact that you did it for no reason. For example: Life gives me no joy, so I have a reason for suicide because of being tired of living. But you're happy with everything, you know how to laugh, you know how to joke, you've got a girlfriend you can't keep your eyes off, you insist the world can be perfect only in its totality, meaning that good and evil are both necessary, otherwise it would come crashing down. Fine. I've nothing against any of that, but you can, or could, run five kilometres without getting tired. Mentally you're entirely normal. But now, how can I make any sense of a suicide arising from plenty, the fact that you merely wanted to triumph over yourself, I just can't get my head round it." And the doctor wound the bandage into a ball and looked at me questioningly. Suddenly I was scarily keen-witted. I saw everything before me and calmly explained it all to him. "Right now I can see before me man's entire happy future. A mankind sound in mind and body, but obsessed with a longing for death. I tell you, suicide will become the ethical and aesthetic realisation not only of the individual, but of families, dynasties and nations. It will be the climax of cultures and will become a conceit of artists and aesthetes. One day, God will start praying to man triumphant, because He will have become superfluous. Just look at the history of suicides, doc. Before this war came along, and before I was redeployed by the regime, as I recall, I was a law student, with a special interest in the criminal law. Look at the avant-garde, look at all those gems scattered throughout the history of mankind. I remember that when I was just a kid, a friend, during a game of hide-and-seek, hanged himself in a chimney on a triple wire, completely overwhelmed by the idea of how surprised we'd be when we eventually found him. I used to know a very religious man who so craved holiness that one night he raised the cover of a crypt and having got himself tangled up in vestments and fossilised entrails and limbs put a bullet through his head. But really, isn't it wonderful, departing with all your powers unimpaired? Freely and totally aware. And while I'm at it, I can tell you the manner of my own grandfather's departure, in 1919. He was a station master. He stripped naked in his office and covered his body in rubber stamps – I've no idea where he got so many different ones from. For his back he rigged a clever contraption to ensure that even there no spot was left unblemished. He checked in a mirror. He also used all shades of ink, so he ended up looking like a leopard. Then singing a song, he got his revolver out of his drawer and shot himself in the temple. He'd been so thorough and thought of everything down to the smallest detail that as the district medical officer drew his foreskin back one letter appeared after another until they made up the name-board of the station where he'd served as a lad. The doctor, a notorious card player, cried out: 'Cripes, it's like successive hitting at blackjack.' And he laughed at the rubber-stamped corpse and slapped it jovially on the back. Well, wasn't my grandad a giant? Is he not the *magnus parens* of the future?" I asked, but Dr Gall was lost in thought with his fingers clasped to his head. I went on, chasing the pace of my thoughts with hand gestures. "And so instead of pointless wars there'll be collective suicides of whole nations. Like in pictures of the cinquecento. Hauliers' trucks laden with ingenious configurations of corpses will be dispatched as samples.

The discipline will be taught at universities. People will be nothing but happy. The idea of heaven will disappear. We'll humiliate God and give him a taste of what he did to our forebears. We shall drive him from our hearts." Thus did I let myself get carried away, and I let everything that had grown within me long before and had been swept aside by my act get borne away as well. Only now could I talk about it because the deed was done, because I had accomplished what it had been mine to accomplish. Which is why I now saw my case as unrepeatable, unique and remote. Nothing worried me anymore. The top-price blood they'd pumped into me had made me into something else, something cautious, timorous, literary. I'd been telling the doctor about someone who had died, or was alive, but whose address I didn't know. I had become the real me there in Bystřice by Benešov and had been brought back against my will. There was nothing more I could do and now I was forced to accept life under these conditions. Because I was sincere and had never known despair and never sought the impossible, I began to manufacture life. The little factory had commenced production and I longed for nothing but Máša, a job to do and a little house.

VI/

It was as if I had just left a cabinet of curiosities and was seeing the natural world again. I was not beset by a single memory of either the past or Dr Gall. Under my arm I had a little bundle of underwear, and the blood of three donors infused me with an eager warmth. Everything was a source of amazement and I happily stood with legs apart beneath the lance of St Wenceslas[6] observing unknown faces as they approached and receded. My sole uncertainty was whether I was the whole me. When I clamped my hand inside my pocket, I had to run a quick check that it wasn't someone else clenching their fingers into a fist. I felt as if I'd been stretched out over an area of several square kilometres. It was only my own eyes that gave me the assurance that it really was me, that it was my hand, and it wasn't half an hour's journey away from me. And so people looked surprised to see this passerby shoving his hand in his pocket, then opening it in front of his eyes. But as soon as I hid my hand in my pocket again, it again felt as if I'd left it somewhere and that it was lying abandoned somewhere like a stick or umbrella. And so I walked down Wenceslas Square and felt the first wrinkle etch itself into my brow. In shop windows I saw myself slithering among bottles, flowers, fabrics and furniture. If I passed a mirror, I stopped and had a fit of the shivers. The impression was of not yet having reached the point, or of having passed it long before. I went back, and the one I'd seen had been me. I hadn't recognised myself. I stared at the apparition, stock-still. I still hoped it was someone else and that he would suddenly move and vanish from the amalgam. But the other was still standing there, as motionless as a headstone. I found the courage to raise one hand. The other raised his. I unclenched my fist and so did the other. It *was* me and tears of disillusion dripped onto my bundle of underwear. Back at the hospital among all the pale faces and corpses I hadn't noticed it.

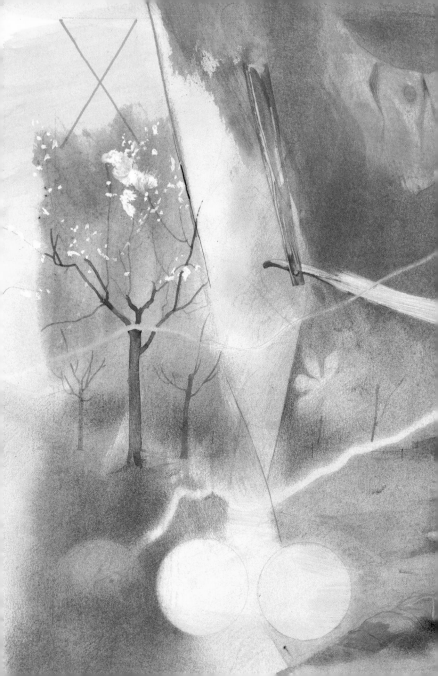

I'd assumed everything was all right, and now I was being gawped at by this man with his loose tie and baggy coat. This was the me who had so loved his seventy-five-kilo body, who liked to sniff his armpits and sponge them down. The me who had blood, and so a life that he hadn't sought, the me they'd given blood to without me being permitted to choose which. I had brought my life to its own free destruction, and now I was to be responsible for the blood injected into me. My so-called honour might be supplanted by a criminal act, and I wouldn't be taken to court because I'd died. And so, putting my blood on trial, they'd be trying the me who wasn't. I'd been made part of a game that not even death would end. I'd been abandoned and cheated. I needed just one tiny finger of Máša's for something to be made of me. I needed someone to whom I might be needful. So I stood at the bottom end of Wenceslas Square and stared into a shop window and saw Máša's neck bent over a sewing machine, I saw myself touching her, fearful that she might dissolve, vanish. However, life has to be lived; that much I felt clearly. In the mirror I tried to guess how much I'd lost. Eight to ten kilos. Easy enough to make up again. I strode on with a firmness in my stride. My brow was bedewed from the horror of seeing myself, but I went on because I was sincere and always did what dangled before me. I had to live because I was afraid of death. And since I had to live, I had to live as agreeably as possible. And with Máša things would be quite easy. I'd be as heavy as I used to be and in space I would occupy a shape the image of which was reassuring. Yes, I had to so as to give Máša my weight and with that everything. I walked with an easy tread. Towards me came a fireman in his shining helmet and I saw my face approaching. As we passed each other, my distorted face saw that on his shoulder he was carrying a Minimax fire extinguisher. Bystřice by Benešov. The old man. My eye to that chink. I groaned. I should never be rid of that past. It would keep exploding like a land mine. It would be with me to the end. All the firemen of the world, all the helmets and all the fire extinguishers would take me back, whether from the wildest part or even from my wedding. But then, my own wrist would remind me of that day several times a day. The past, instead of diminishing, would gather strength, blossom, grow in intensity, because the superfluous details would disappear, leaving only the myth behind. It was going to be enough just to brush against the remotest of realities and at the opposite end a neon hand would light up. My compliments! I closed my eyes and passersby kept bumping into me.

VII/

At the end of April I set off back to work on my bike. I weighed seventy-one kilograms and I pedalled so furiously along the main road that I ran out of breath. I no longer thought that I would cross from one present to another. The perfume of the past was fresh and nothing could be done about it. I'd annealed the friendship that I'd embarked on with the Heart of Jesus. Passing a metal wayside shrine, I said to myself: "Look, there's my mate." I hopped off the bike and went to say hello to the man nailed to the cross.

But he didn't budge. He hung there and rust trickled from his nails. Across his loins some kind master decorator had painted something like swimming trunks in red, white and blue, and he, good bloke that he was, had let it happen. There beneath the linden trees I wanted to say something nice to him, but I was quite tickled by the trunks and laughed, and Christ couldn't aim a kick at me or give me a clip round the ear because he was well and truly nailed up, and then he never clipped anyone anyway. From a good way further on I looked back and the only thing shining out of the grey of the morning were those swimming trunks in the national colours. As I rode into the station it was ten to seven. The station odd-job man went to stick a number on the bike. I blocked his way and said: "Good morning." I offered him my hand and he his. But I could see that the only bit of me that he was seeing was that wrist. He bowed to the scar and said: "Good morning, dispatcher, well are we, well?" – and he blushed. I'm sure the idiot could just see me, slashing my wrist with that razor. But then he was quite entitled to see me like that, so I didn't turn nasty. I told him: "We'll be doing the day shift together," and entered my office. The telephones and telegraphs were clicking and ringing away and I kept turning round and round in circles. I took my cap off, opened my locker, and my red uniform cap was covered in a layer of dust. The tiny tracks of the tiny feet of mice had created a decent relief design. I got a brush and brushed the dust off. Then the duty dispatcher grabbed me by the elbow and looked over my shoulder at my wrist. I could tell. And he, to explain his look, said:

"Hi, what's the time?" – then pulled my sleeve up beyond the wrist. Sternly I said: "I slashed my wrist," and held the scar right up to his eyes. "Don't worry, I'll take over right away." And I set my cap on my head, signed in and took charge, and phoned through to the signalmen that I'd come on duty. And to say Good morning. They, invisible men, wished me Good morning in return, but I could tell that they'd like to see my wrist. I felt as if I'd just been run over by a train, or like a murder victim, and as if people were gathering round to take a look. I could tell that they'd like it if I'd cut my hand off and could show it to them preserved in alcohol, and I knew that if I had a prosthetic device they'd have no qualms about asking me to unscrew it and let them hold it. And the same when I summoned linesmen to the phones in their huts to report delayed trains to them or the intercalation of military transports. As one hut after another responded: "Understood!" I knew that what they'd like to have understood was my wrist. And I was in a state in which I had no inkling whether they saw me as a hero or a coward. I glanced at the purple scar and had to tell myself that that was the end, that I'd never be able to do it again. It began to seem as if someone else had done it. But for the whole station it had only just happened, only now were they taking possession of me, only now were they being disconcerted by me. For me, only now had it become an object, an animal, a life. While I was back on a firmer footing and trying to focus my attention on the transition from Monday to Tuesday, Tuesday to Wednesday and so on, they were turning me back, hurling me into a bleeding bath and pressing a razor in my hand. They were rewinding my film, back to breakfast, lunch, dinner, and I had to grant that it was their right. When I went out to a train, the public got on and off. People I knew looked at me and I could see that I was seen as the man with the spurting wrist. I felt like screaming: "Go fuck yourselves!" but I remembered the garden of thorns around the Heart of Jesus, remembered the swimming trunks in the national colours, and had to concede that things were all right as they were. I had to whistle the signal *Train guards: to your posts* with my fingers because I couldn't find my whistle. I waved my green command staff. The faces at the windows stirred and the train began to move off. Suddenly I heard her voice: "Dispatcher, sir!" and on the running board I saw Máša. With her right hand she was holding onto an iron handrail and in her left was an apple she was offering me. She was wearing her white neck warmer again and the dimples in her cheeks were radiant. As if she'd looked out the prettiest smile she thought she had in store. I was struck dumb. I'd been deprived of speech and watched as the vision slowly vanished. I was holding a yellow apple and she was being borne away by the train. I slowly went in to confirm the departure. In the doorway I was stopped by the station master who said: "Listen, don't whistle using your fingers. Take my advice, it's well-meant. That way we'll both stay out of trouble." And he wagged a finger at me. I looked down and said: "I won't do it again." But the station master's fleshy lips went on with their reproof: "I hope so. The other day I was coming back from HQ, sharing a compartment with a lady and her infant. As we approached Kostomlaty, the mother told the little girl: 'Watch closely, Georgie, this is the station where the dispatcher whistles through his fingers.' You should be ashamed. Suppose our controller or an inspector had been on the train." And the station master brandished his little fat fingers as if warding off doom. I went into the office, reported the departure and was full of Máša's smile, which couldn't be smothered even by the station master's severity. On each passing train I hung a smile, and onto the backs of all the passengers I projected the face that was so dear to me. And passing through my station were the last trains carrying fugitives, hospital trains, military transports. The Russkies were approaching relentlessly. I saw trainloads of sad-looking Hungarian oxen, I saw Silesian sheep, so hungry that they were grazing each other's coats. I leached the image of Máša onto them all and forgot about my wrist. The three telegraph lines, eight telephones and ticket sales left me exhausted and I coalesced with time, above which floated the image of a woman and a sense of duty. Transports of well-fed Germans were calmly hastening towards safe zones. I and the rest of the Protectorate's train dispatchers were seeing them safely on their way. From wire to wire I passed reports of their safe passage. I was guilty and by midday I wanted to puke. Only the image of Máša remained pure. Everything else was doomed to devastation.

VIII/

I saw open trucks with legs leaking from them. I saw hands raising a morsel of pork to lips, I saw shiny one-kilo tins of food and had to look down. I was ashamed. Someone could have gone *Bang, bang!* for a joke, and I wouldn't have batted an eyelid. They'd told me to come and work at Kostomlaty, near Nymburk, and so I was standing by the track, and because I had eyes, I watched the carriages laden with blonde hair, tanned faces and automatic pistols. I marvelled at the Silesian regiment, of which some soldiers had their hair in pigtails and rings in their ear lobes. They had their sleeves rolled up, were sunbathing and laughing in my direction, because they were young and knew they weren't going to fall in battle, but live. I ensured their safe passage although in the office hung the death notice of my colleague from Rovensko pod Troskami into whom pals of this lot who were fleeing past us to war-free zones had emptied entire magazines. And I was doing my job just as properly and nobody came up to me to say: "Quit it and come with us." Perhaps I mightn't have gone because I was afraid, but there would have been the chance to go and I would have known that things were happening in my area. And so my life was constantly made unpleasant by the notion that the Germans saw in me a vassal who, though hating them, served them to the last wagon. However, that day two men dressed as road menders arrived and told me: "We've had notification of an SS special coming through, so we're going to dismantle the rails." I said: "I've been waiting for this for ages. But do it about half-way between Nymburk and Kostomlaty." They replied: "OK, you stay put, we'll make ourselves scarce." And they left. *Right, I'm to stay put and you'll make yourselves scarce.* Because I was used to obeying orders, I stayed put and followed the special's progress by asking questions. The linesmen reported in: "They've just passed here and at the back there's a truck carrying tools and two corpses." I thought to myself: "Oh dear." And I went out onto the platform and looked into the distance, towards the bend by the home signal. They entered the bend slowly and came to a stop. That's great, partisans. *We'll make ourselves scarce and you stay put, they'll leave you alone.* I also wanted to make myself scarce when I saw them jumping from the locomotive, but there had to be someone here to set the signal to 'clear'. Every five minutes I ran out and stared at the signal post, where the Germans were putting the track back in place. I went back into the office and my blood was up in arms. If it had been up to my blood to decide, I'd have been hidden in the hay in a hayloft long before this. I re-read the death notice from Rovensko pod Troskami. Nymburk kept badgering me for a notification, and I sent the station odd-job man home. Eventually the train began to move and entered the station with caution. I came out to the trackside, green staff in hand. The signalman was hiding and apart from me there wasn't a living soul in sight. The sun and a handful of chickens intensified the desolation. The engine, hung about with SS men, was creeping forward like a leopard. They were all wearing leather trousers and they had their sleeves rolled up and their fingers on their triggers. They were sunburnt as if on the way back from the seaside. Their paws were vibrant with muscles. They were anatomical men and some of them were slowly eating pork from 1-kilo tins. They were getting closer and the details of their faces were coming alive. I could tell they meant business. I was becoming a mere cipher. The train stopped and on the farm opposite someone slid back a metal cover on the roof and the German immediately aimed a machine gun that way. Some little guy climbed out onto the metal roof. The captain roared: "*Halt!*" And the little guy, having stared at the station, got lockjaw. He raised his arms and turned to stone. He stood there like a weather cock on a windless day, like a metal chimney stack. I wanted to look up, but the gleam from the weapons and the locomotive left me blinded. Two of the men in leather trousers jumped down from the running board and looked at me as if I'd been the one who'd removed the rail. Explanation was pointless. Then the captain jumped down and indicated with his chin that they were to take me onto the engine. Now I was beyond all help. I was pale, my eyelids had a tremor and the whole world went out of shape. I'd become a hero against my will. I'd done them no harm, and they were prodding me upwards with their pistols. The train jerked and the guy on the hot tin roof was still standing there. The station was receding into the distance and the only thing I'd registered was the door bearing the legend *Ladies*. I laid a hand on the hot engine workings and looked about me. Beside me stood a lookout, whose hairy hands raised his binoculars. I took to the man because we were in the same boat. He too had been told: "You're to stay put and keep an eye on the track." Having set down his binoculars, he looked at me and his eyes took me for a lost cause. *You shouldn't have been standing there, you should have run off*, those grey eyes were saying and they didn't pity me because he was inured. Only the captain looked at me in a different way. He knew that I'd stayed put out of stupidity. I knew he was the only one who saw me the way I'd been. He could just see me, saluting the German engines and ensuring their safe passage to the Reich. For him it was suddenly unpleasant, so to defile the war's happy ending. I didn't fit into his conception. I watched him half-close his eyes as he slotted my fate into the unfolding picture. I hung onto the air vents and waited for his first look. And I wasn't even thinking about Máša or about how I'd be dying a hero's death. I was scared for my life and fighting in silence for it. And I didn't even suffer from being found guilty though blameless. I'd rather have been found innocent though guilty. And I wasn't even bothered that the captain meant to appease his God by my non-sacrifice. I wanted to live, and that was all. The captain opened his eyes and bellowed: *"Halt!"* I looked into that wrinkled, rapier-slashed face and thought to myself: *I'm grateful to you, you devil, for giving me my life back. I pronounce you an angel.* And I began climbing down the steps without asking a thing. The engine stopped. I jumped down onto the gravel track bed. Above me, the captain was leaning out, smiling. It was the cockcrow of the angels. The others also smiled at me and one of them handed me a packet of cigarettes. I smiled back and the train moved off. Blood was coursing through my veins. I waved to the men as they moved off into the distance. They were moving off into the distance and now they were reduced to ovals and grey blotches. Other, properly defined faces went past me. Female camp followers sat in their striped dresses with their hands folded in their laps and probably thinking of home. I stood next to a telegraph pole and stared at the SS special and it was all clear to me. There was in me something of those tradesmen of old, of those loyal retainers of old. That dawned on me after the last carriage had passed by me. I knew how to serve. Next to the brakeman's lookout lay two naked, yellow corpses, clinging together at rib height. One hand came lose as the train jolted and described a hesitant arc. I remembered that the station lacked my presence, that I hadn't given the all-clear and that the telephones and telegraphs were calling. I quickened my step. By the signal post I turned and it had all been true. By now the train seemed like a tiny box and the two corpses shone out like a tight-closed pair of bloodless lips. I unbuttoned my work jacket and ran non-stop all the way back to the station.

IX/

I was a cipher that indeed mattered, but was only there for someone to look good and inspired. Unfortunately, I was no such prime mover and so I couldn't care less. Whether I'd been serving to suit the Protectorate, the Reich or with reservations, it was all the same. The fact was that the Germans had taken me for an idiot in service to them. And whether that was willingly or with reservations or with venom in my eyes, they didn't care. On the contrary. Venom made them feel good. They were still conscious of their might and I was proof of it. I did their signalling, I operated their telephones, while my brain churned out question marks. That day my mind also went back to the partisans removing the rail and to how I might have ended up deceased, because I'd stayed put. I saw before me the smiling face of my colleague from Rovensko pod Troskami, I saw him raise an arm against the automatic and he wasn't even given time to say: *But I haven't done anything, there must be some mistake. I don't want this.* And they still emptied an entire magazine into him. I could see his crumpled face and its questioning of the injustice. All morning the question mark floated about in the shapes of smoke, settling on passengers' backs, their necks, their hats. My fingers, too, were obsessed with a longing to figure as a WHY. I stood alone with my mundane duties as a train dispatcher and utterly alone in the face of all eventualities, chances and mistakes. That trip to Bystřice by Benešov struck me as a miracle, like total freedom, like an act arising out of me and me alone. For the first and only time I'd been my own accused and judge. I alone could have borne the responsibility. I had been king in a kingdom inhabited by the king alone. I began to see both the Christ in Máša's room and the one at the crossroads in a different light. It wasn't the burning bundle of straw, or the garden of thorns, but the hands. As I worked on the railway and against that mass of random events that could have placed my life in jeopardy, his hands would appear to me whether I would or not. The right forefinger pointed to the heavens. The left forefinger to the garden of thorns. Yes, capitulate while there's still time. And Christ could do nothing but mitigate for me that which was relentless in its inevitability. Without me, but about me. Just like on that German railway engine. Praying means preparing for one's execution. Not as my will, but as thy will be it done. Yet I bore Christ no malice. There was nothing for which I could reproach him or of which I could remind him. On the contrary, I found I liked him the more. He'd been afraid, just as I was on that locomotive, he had sweated because anxiety was choking him. And if he pricked himself on a nail, it hurt. The blood of those three donors had made a sissy of me. I was a puppet, just like Christ our Lord, over whom a higher being had a lucky win at cards. In fear and the relentless tide of events we were all equal and no one on earth, apart from the suicide, could fail to change places with Christ. That day, Christianity was me. I with my top-price blood. That was clear to me. When I was in the water-filled bath, there were plenty of things I could do, except not be in the water, and when I'm dead, there'll be plenty of things I can do, except not be dead. That afternoon, Máša left her train. I'd hardly seen it off and away and stood before her when Christ disappeared and the question marks straightened up into crosses. At once I was free of thoughts and affliction. She had a latex collar and her hair combed high. Her buttons gleamed and continued up into the two dimples in her cheeks. I wanted to say it suited her, but she was the wiser one: "Hi, Bogánek, Hello. Pop and give the all-clear and pop and drop the departure signal." And she pointed at the departing train as it tucked itself in behind a knoll. She was right. I pulled the lever, went into the office and rang through to say the block was clear. And then looked at her through the window. She was standing next to a bench. She had one knee on the seat and one arm on her hip. She was looking about as if the station belonged to her. I stepped outside the office and said: "Come and sit in the office." With a smile she replied: "Oh no, that would make your job so nice that you could cause a crash. I'll just wait here for you. Then I'll tell you something that'll knock you flat. You're going to be very, very surprised." The telegraph started calling my station. The station master came in and asked me over his shoulder: "Is that the ticket girl who found you?" "Yes, it is, sir." And I ran out to meet a goods train. The station master was looking out of the window at my back and I could sense him seeing me in that bath. And seeing Máša bent over me. I knew that right then he was feeling sorry for Máša, as well as for all my friends and relatives. I think he also shuddered and ran a hand across his sleeve as if the spurting blood had reached that far. I was a prick to his conscience because by now I had no conscience of my own. I was tramping the earth to no good end and the mark on my wrist would follow me for the rest of my life. To all the initiated my face would conjure up my crime. And not just me: the very existence of razors would remind them of me. My station master and everyone else except me had set a mark upon my pure brow for all time.[7] I had my security. As far as they were concerned I was all done. On the flickering sides of high closed carriages, as on a cinema screen, I saw parading before me all the faces that I had made to blanch with the knowledge of my act. I looked into their eyes and saw everywhere a fear of me. A dread blanketed by an anaemic smile. Even my parents seemed to be being sorry for themselves. Of all those mugs only Máša saw me without a distorting prism. And only she knew me and knew that there was something in me that had to be protected. As she'd looked at me through the fence at Nymburk, so she looked at me still. Something unchanging, something everlasting permitted her to see my life as a whole. I dedicated the last three carriage sides to three ovals, the three donors of my blood. Though they couldn't care less. If the blood for which they'd been paid at the going rate had been guzzled by dogs, they wouldn't care. The train departed without a trace of being defaced by my vision. I re-set the signal to Stop and saw Máša from inside my box. She was sitting on the bench and staring into the distance. As if she were talking to someone at that distance. Her lips were moving. I went up to her and jingled my key behind her ear. She didn't hear it. I slowly headed back to the office. It was her right to be distant, her right to enter a dialogue with invisibility. Her body, which she had forgotten on the bench, was idling. It was the body of my bride-to-be. I went inside, relayed the train's departure and sat at my desk. I wrote out the handover note. Train No. 811 brought my colleague. I handed over to him. I took my red cap off and washed my hands. The station odd-job man brought my bike round. I went out. Máša took hold of the bike, stepped on one pedal and kicked off with her free leg. The sun was dipping and the open country rolled away into the far distance. I kept to the path, my eyes on Máša's shoe heel. I was pure, and at that moment I wanted nothing more than to walk on like that, worming deeper and deeper into the warm air. At the level crossing Máša stopped and read aloud: "The grazing and driving of animals alongside the track is strictly forbidden." She glanced at me and narrowed her eyes: "Here, hold your bike while I pretend to be an animal." And she ran off down the path. I only just caught the bike by the handlebars. I hung my briefcase round the bell and walked on, perhaps in her footsteps. I watched her flashing heels. Sometimes she turned and blew a strand of hair away from her forehead. Before reaching Zboží[8] she stopped and waited for me to catch up. She looked into me and wanted to tell me something. I could see her trying to form sentences. With one hand I held the bike, putting my other arm round her waist. She wriggled away and said: "Come here," and sat down next to a telegraph pole. I propped the bike against it and sat down next to her. She undid her coat and said: "Look." I looked and since I thought she wanted me to give her a hug, I put my arms round her. She pushed me away and said again: "Look, Bogánek." I made to kiss her, but she shook her head. "There's a train coming," she squealed. I ran down the embankment and Máša flung herself in my arms. The clatter of wheels and buffers bombarded us, sparks and steam likewise. Amid all that thunder and din Máša cried: "I'm going to have a baby." I held her close. The sentence floated about amid the noise and droplets of steam. I was a father and I was neither elated nor downcast. The last carriage took the noise away with it and the steam and sparks bedded down in the clover. I looked at Máša and she was in tears, and she kept nodding as if repeating over and over again that she was a mother. She said: "Lend me your hankie," and she blew her nose. To my right stood a willow tree and a little way ahead of me wound the narrow lane along which I used to ride to work. I was a father and I couldn't find the sentence with which to express the fact. Because Máša had sat down I sat down next to her, leaned towards her ear and whispered: "My bride." She kissed me and with that kiss became a mother. It was a kiss that lacked passion, deferential, polite. By now I was afraid even to touch her belly. I was surprised not to have noticed it, quite an innocent little hillock. Máša placed her head on my knee as on an executioner's block. I pushed back her hair and stroked her velvety skin with my forefinger. Then she turned and laid her head in my lap. She looked up into the blue sky, held up the fingers of her right hand and let them drift back like the water of a fountain. I watched the hand and wanted to say: *Come on, Máša, get up and let's go. You'll catch cold*. But it was such a stupid sentence that it really would have been better to get nephritis than disrupt the song rising in her arm. An icy peace came over me and I saw my future next to this woman, I saw a little house and garden and the baby who would inherit my longing for death. I suddenly saw that nothing was over, that death solved nothing, deferred nothing. Even if I had killed myself four months before at Bystřice, life would have gone on. So it was good that they'd saved me, because the baby to be born to me would need protecting. It would not and could not be in any way different from how I was, how my ancestors had been. So it would need someone to explain to it who it took after, it would need to be apologised to for having been brought into the world. I knew that the child would be born with an invisible scar on its wrist because the wound's source would be in its soul. Neither I nor Christ could change that, because the sphere had been launched down an inclined plane long before. The sun was setting and Máša's hand had fallen silent on her breast. A stopping train came rumbling along. It was too late to run down into the ditch. I covered Máša with my coat. The draught caught my cap. Sparks and droplets of condensed steam rained down on us. I was still thinking about the baby and Máša cried out happily: "I'm going to have a baby, a sweet little baby." After the train had trundled past I spoke into my lap, to the girl huddled there: "Did you say something?"

X/

One particular evening Máša was supposed to come to our place and I wanted to show her to my parents. She was to help me pack some things, because I was moving in with her. As I returned by the main road, I passed Christ, still girt with those coloured swimming trunks, and was thinking about the wedding and leaving home. Yes, severing the umbilical cord. At a crossroads I passed an armed patrol, because there was a scattering of Germans roaming the area. But it was peacetime now and they were just frightened individuals who willingly put their hands up. I was riding along, thinking of Máša. Then I noticed that the road was littered with letters, postcards, rags, sticks, bandages and helmets as if a tornado had come coursing that way. Among the green corn lay two German soldiers. They were dead and lay there wearing looks of surprise. Although it was early evening, the countryside had taken on the silence of noon, a dangerous silence. I hopped off my bike and wasn't even surprised to hear groaning coming from the ditch. I approached the edge. In the bottom of the ditch lay a German private, lying, though his legs were still marching as if having a message to carry. I stepped down and the air closed in over me. The road carried on at eye level and was a mess of rags, bandages and letters. The shaven-headed soldier boy was still walking his legs and he looked like a toy. I walked round the injured man and bent down towards his eyes, over which death was visibly drooling. He'd been shot in the stomach, his hand clasped to his abdomen. I undid his flies, rolled his shirt up and saw three bullet holes. Faeces were mingling with blood and the lad continued marching on the spot, killing time. And on the way he cried: "Mutti, Mutti, Mutti." I didn't know if he was calling to his mother, or the mother of his children, so the best I could do was pat his hands. Looking down on those bulging eyes, I understood that there was no other justice now. He was in the same predicament as I'd been on the locomotive, or as Christ on the cross. Though actually not like Christ, because he'd been much better off, having wished for death, death being the crown of his teaching. But the squaddy wanted to live, he'd been bearing his life somewhere westwards, to his family, and a week after the peace he'd been shot by stray bullets. And all because he'd been in a marching column of prisoners of war and he and a few comrades had attempted to escape. Which was why he was still marching, why he was trying to escape justice, escape the death that he was having to accept as an insult, as a ghastly hallucination. I squatted over him, unable to leave. I couldn't leave him there like a scrap of a tin can. I stood upright, whistled to a passing patrol and beckoned them down. Then I said: "Shoot the poor guy. He's fatally wounded." And I pointed to the marching boots. "Never, I'd never kill even a chicken. Shoot him yourself," the farmer replied and slung his rifle off his back. "Here you are," he said, handing it down to me in the ditch. I took it. Because I loved life, I couldn't stand slow, sadistic perversion. I gripped the army rifle and my fingers didn't even quiver. I aimed at where I thought the heart was. I pressed the trigger. The squaddy marched stubbornly on, staring ahead of him with his bulging eyes, and yelling himself on his way: "Mutti, Mutti." I took aim again, this time between his eyes. I pressed the trigger again and the eyes narrowed as if they'd been bullwhipped. The legs, those creepy legs, slowly stopped. The mill of his life was grinding its last and the world he carried in his head was spilling out through the hole between his eyes. He was lying on his side and I said: "Here, catch it, mind out." And I tossed the rifle up to the patrol. I bent down and I felt like the centurion who had speared Christ's suffering heart. I attempted to straighten the cooling fingers and clasp them together. I could tell that the dead man was holding a chain. I forced his palm open and out fell a silver chain with a medallion inscribed *Bringe Glück*. I said to myself: "If it didn't bring you any luck, maybe it'll bring me some." And I clipped the medallion round my neck and made the dead man my brother. I was thinking of the brotherhood that I'd concluded with the Heart of Jesus in Máša's room. It was the same again, give or take. Then a vision of things to come swept over me. As if someone were weaving wickerwork before my eyes. I had long been planned to be a particular patch in someone's carpet. Now my turn had come and I couldn't leave this road strewn with postcards and misery. Máša's face was so far away. I was standing over a dead man. My head was the dot under a question mark. I picked up my bike and my flask, looked around, and the patrol was walking up and down the road again. The sun had started to dip. I hopped onto my bike and my shadow did likewise, while the soldier boy's shadow lay beneath him. In the distance another column of prisoners was approaching and I drew near. My shadow, riding ahead of me, quietly suggested I turn back, but I rode on. I passed the first few rows and saw their skinny faces and to me they seemed to be singing. It was ghastly. I knew precisely what role these chaps, herded together from all corners of Germany, would play in my life. I rode on. On one side there were blossoming plum trees, on the other side of the narrow gangway was the kilometre-long straggle of prisoners. I tried to stay on my bike, but I knew for sure that there was no point. Something was closing behind me, pincers of a sort or a thousand-fold gate. Through the gaps I could see the accompanying guards, automatic weapons at the ready. I kept pedalling, but it was as pointless as the German squaddy's marching. A few metres ahead of me a soldier had fallen. A few others had stopped and a huddle had formed. Two or three made a run for it into the thickening evening gloom. Shouts, the crack of pistol shots and I felt a pain in my neck. I tumbled over the handle bars and rolled over into a ditch. Blood was gushing from an artery. I pressed a hand tight over the wound. Desperate prisoners were running up above me and the guards were shouting *vorwärts, vorwärts*. They were running and casting aside anything that was holding them up. After the last boot to land set the dust whirling over my head I remained alone. No one could do me the kind service of finishing me off. And anyway the rush of blood from my neck had abated somewhat. I knew this was the end of me and that I had to abide in an agony that I hadn't wished for and for which I wasn't to blame. I lay in the ditch with a scarf of blood, and with every puff of the breeze a shower of plum petals descended on me. I dug my fingers into the soil and tore up tangled masses of young grass. I could think neither of Máša, nor of the wedding. There was nothing left of me but an acrid dryness in my throat, through which someone was drawing a thick twist of barbed wires. With the pain I began marching on the spot like the shaven-headed squaddy a few hundred yards away. I kept walking so as somehow to fill the void that separated me from the abyss. No beautiful thoughts, no faces. I just kept gulping and beneath the palm of my hand my life was draining away. In just a flash, or rather in the chink of an almost closed door, all that appeared to me was my suicide, and it was so adorable and sweet. All other deaths were brutal and unjust. Even Christ appeared to me only in the guise of a traffic policeman, like a postman in a sorting office. If I had ten thousand arms and gardens around my heart, he still couldn't have helped me. He would merely have pointed a finger upwards. *Not me, it's the boss that wants it this way*. And yet I did tell myself: "I believe in you, Christ, because you're a beggar exactly like me, because I'm a beggar exactly like you. I speak to you unheard, and with the same unhearing you go to your unhearing Father. It was as if there were a traffic policeman directing, with a right-angled sweep, a car from one street into another. I believe in you, poor chap, because the blood gushed from you exactly like this and no one could rid you of the notion that you were suffering though innocent. Not as Thy will, but... I didn't do any harm to anyone either. All I wanted was to have fun in this world with the bride with whom I've made a baby. I wanted it to be not a vale of tears, but the paradise from which you drove us so cruelly. And for that, Christ, Your Father has repaid me and the smoke from my burnt offering is sinking back to earth without me knowing what for, without me knowing why." Then I was visited by spirals and circles. I yanked the medallion from under my shirt and hurled it into a field of clover. Alone this earth, green and fresh, promised me nothing, only ever prepared to comfort me with birdsong and the charm of shapes and colours. With an effort I hauled myself up to the edge of the road and gazed, close to death, at the evening landscape. A train was just leaving my station and its tender was lit up because the fireman was just shovelling coal. It was the train that would bring Máša to our house. Her eyes used to be bright and indulgent and she wore a neat neck warmer that was like a rising crescent moon. I rolled back down into the ditch. With every puff of the breeze a shower of flower petals descended on my face. I kicked my legs like a child and the world vanished.

Your childhood was a by no means happy time. People born in this period have to cope with lots of grief. That's the thing! And the gloomy streets in Habeš and The Colony[1] haven't helped matters. Especially of an evening, when they're hung about with those mop head maples and streetlamps as dim as inflated pig's bladders! It really is no joke to be walking about beneath clean-shaven trees. That never bodes well! The hours wasted walking need to have something to show for themselves! And you can no longer tell people you know from people you don't. Nocturnal passersby get so disfigured by the shadows. But you're a nice fellow and well-disposed. You heed the interests of others and that's why everything gets the better of you and gives your heart a hard time! And that's also why from now on you'll never be able to wipe that little face from your memory!

And so up and down the pavement you go, counting the miserably lit street lamps. And you jump when odd figures say hello as you pass. Hands rise so mournfully to hats as if the people concerned are surrendering, or cursing someone. As if they're cursing their lot or can't stand the thought of someone.

And here am I, a fortune-teller with a green parrot, telling you that you've set yourself on the threshold of eternal life. Which is why, when the going gets tough, there's uncertainty with regard to those you love and wouldn't want to hurt. And it's why you look up at a window and wait for proof that you've been dealt with! That you've been done for, given the old heave-ho! That you've had your chance! You yourself know in advance that it would be better to leave and let that first floor be. Leave and let it go its own way. Ah, but no. You're too much the hotshot for that. It's that all too forgiving nature of yours, which relishes doom and destruction! But that's the great and good thing about your heart! And you're canny enough never to blame yourself for not having done everything that could have been done.

But that little face couldn't care less. The only snag is that it leaves you being swept off to the great hearts of the stars, where tears are just tiny droplets of light and sorrow nothing but an airless space! Which is why it's also better for you to play the buffoon to the end and take a look at love's little corpse, so base and corrupt. Your tearless weeping and sorrow give you that right.

So you're padding along beneath the tingling maples again, you turn, hesitate, but you're on a tight leash. If there'd been a snowfall, you'd be startled at the number of footprints you've been making just on account of her having said: "Come!" Just because you've taken it into your head to show her your crumpled face and to ask How are you and What have you been up to. Isn't that right?

And just as you raised your hand to ring the bell, you saw a woman in black with a dog on a lead turn towards the house. And after you hid in the cypress right next to the door, the lady actually had one foot on the scraper and was carefully cleaning her shoes. And having switched her handbag from left hand to right, she rang the bell. And then things started going like clockwork. Just as I'm seeing it now in this crystal ball. A light's gone on upstairs. Then briefly nothing. And now there's the glinting fold of a dressing gown and a patent leather carpet slipper. Isn't that right? And a hand leads a rhythmical, well-kept body down by the banister. And a beautiful and imperious head comes rolling down towards the door. A head beautiful and perfect, truly suited to kissing, or to bashing with an axe for the sake of peace, so there'll be peace and quiet for evermore. The not unexpected opening of the door, and hands go up as in a psychic trance and impeccably reach out to the lady. Those hands! Then some chitchat that matters not in the slightest and the bang of the door closing. And the dog runs up the stairs first. Then the well-bred hostess and finally the lady in black. The stairs abandoned and innocent, then nothing but darkness and silence.

I, an old horoscopist with a green parrot, am prophesying that your marriage will be happy, because you have learned how to appreciate each other and because you'll have put this cruel life behind you. But there will be unpleasantnesses, chiefly owing to relatives.

Now you have to go back onto the pavement and remain in the dark, the better to watch the window. Again you must while away the moments of sadness by watching how the shadows of passersby pass from the tips of their shoes to their heels and vice versa. Again, some will recognise you and reach for their hats as if meaning to tear their hair out over lord knows what crimes! But this is a moment of repose, this watching the street in the dark, and so time isn't such a total blank.

Of course your married state isn't and won't be enhanced by a large number of children! In that area there'll be much worry and concern. But you'll live to see their brilliant future and advancement. One will be very clever and gifted and in due course hang himself, but the other child will be a major responsibility, because it will wish to remain innocent.

And so you go on to-ing and fro-ing below that first floor window and keeping your eye firmly on it. Eventually a light goes on again and the ladies and the dog come down the stairs and I can see that you're now so distressed that you can't even move. As if you've come to an end thanks to the waiting and submissiveness. Neither the departure of the lady with the dog, nor the dressing gown's return upstairs, neither the dark, nor the silence of the night... Only Satan has kept commanding you to wait awhile and wait some more and get a grip and look into the jaws of fate.

I, a fortune-teller with a green parrot, prophesy that this way you won't live to a ripe old age. Your love, though dead, will outlive you by far! It will no more enter the married state and will only live for memories of you, because it will have lived to twenty years after its menopause.

But what obsession has possessed you, man, to ring the bell and have the head come down and then to tell it: "Here I am and here I stand!", when you know that her unwavering, clear and unerring voice will reply: "Oh, what a shame! I've got Mrs Schulz with me right now."

What great and horrid hankering after the truth makes you, young man, ask again: "Is that the lady who keeps coming here with a dog?", when you know that her unwavering, clear and unerring voice will reply: "Yes, that's her. She's got it with her now, upstairs."

Why have you gone on, young man, to whisper: "But that's not true. I've just seen her leave with these very eyes! With these eyes I saw her!", when her unwavering, clear and unerring voice is going say: "She's with me upstairs! Upstairs with me on the first floor!"

And she gives you such a look in the eye, with such a power of truth, that you sink to your knees and beg for forgiveness for not believing, for doubting. You made a mistake. Deceived by your senses. Now you know for sure that the lady with the dog is upstairs, even though you've seen her leave. You hurriedly beg for another day when you might come, and you quietly take off like a reptile through the trapdoor of darkness and disgrace, while she majestically bears aloft her victorious, true profile, so suited to bullwhipping and kissing.

I, a fortune-teller with a green parrot, am offering you the hope that fortune has begun to smile on you. Above all, that no sickness is on the way, but that a joyful old age is getting closer. Just don't be too cocksure and think that the worst is over. The change that you so long for will not let you down. Thank you and I wish you every success. I don't take private clients. But be assured, I promise that every day I'll be reading the 'Tragedies and Disasters' column in the papers.

At half past eleven in the morning, a light bulb observed the following sequence of events: a station master was seized with love for his wife as she leaned out of a first-floor window! A passenger strolling along the platform mentally noted: "Oh, there's the station master's wife waving good-bye to her mother." Three minutes later he redoubled his attention because the lady on the first floor was still waving, though the train was long gone. But he told himself: "I expect she loved very dearly the face that's just vanished into the distance!" And for him, that was that. He went on walking up and down with an occasional glance at his wrist watch.

But the light bulb on the first floor was further witness to how the rhythm of love merged with the rhythm of an arm waving. And it was only then, my dear lady, that you realised the situation you were in. Only then did it dawn that regard for your husband's social status had obliged you to remain in an unusual position that was, incidentally, defamiliarising because your husband would, as a matter of principle, only ever take you in the dark and only ever in one and the same way! Which is why you froze. You were unsure whether lover and husband were one and the same! But the sight of your husband's hands gripping you at the waist set your mind at rest. You were troubled, however, by the fact that suddenly you didn't want it to end. You even wanted things to revert to the previous state and start all over again. You wanted the train carrying your mother to reverse into the station and set off again. You, a Catholic! And just as you felt your uterus being bombarded with seed and sensed that you were fated to conceive in the window there, you glanced at the clock tower and saw, and heard, that it was quarter to twelve. At that moment something inside you snapped. You buried your face in your scarf and the hands of shame imprinted themselves on your neck. But he who seeks out causes and contrives them into effects will say it was *Difficult Death*[1] that, tied up with string and supplied with a shelf number, was broadcasting its forceful views.

Although, dear lady, you have, since that occasion, frequently tried to lean out of the window in anticipation of your husband's again attempting to add some colour to your life, I have to tell you that such anticipation is in vain. It's all down to *Difficult Death*, which some passenger left on a train and a snippet of which showed up in an innocent house. So you needn't have been surprised that thereafter your sole pastime has been to watch, from your window, trains, faces and luggage departing. For you rightly suspected that he'd never show up with amorous intent again. *Difficult Death* also knows why you became a specialist in toilet windows being kept slightly open! Why you, a Catholic, have caught yourself pleasurably catching men with their yellow wands of urination, why, mesmerised, you watch women sitting down on that revolting seat! And your eyes have even attested instant love-making! The pleasure of it! Your life fulfilled! Over those few years the whole of mankind has projected itself onto second and third class toilets! And whenever someone's been introduced to you, you've squinted as you tried to imagine how that person behaves in the toilet! And there and then you have judged accordingly whether he was a good or bad person! You've erected your entire Catholic ethics on the toilet! Poor wretch!

But he who seeks out causes and contrives them into effects will say that you're innocent. It's all down to *Difficult Death* that, tied up with string and supplied with a shelf number, tormented you, once such an exemplary woman. It has so distorted the upbringing bestowed by parents and conscientious teachers! You, a woman who, every Sunday, gazed up with unfeigned emotion as the monstrance rose aloft, today, with the same pressure on your brain, lie in wait for men to drop their trousers or unbutton their flies.

Let it not be thought that *Difficult Death* confined itself to the wife. Far from it! It was on you, station master, that it wanted to test the sharpness of its teeth! Just remember how it began. How suddenly and out of the blue you heard the call of that long-drawn-out yen for light years! It was the same day that the station odd-job man brought in *Difficult Death*, which you put in a safe place as the regulations require. It was the same day that you made your wife pregnant! Don't you recall that window? Just remember the painful sensation in your temples that time. You still don't remember? It was the evening when out of the blue you made contact with the trajectory of the stars with your left leg, while with your right leg you were standing firmly by the North-Western Railway! But that didn't satisfy Difficult Death! In the fifty-second year of your life and the thirtieth year of your service to the railway it forced you to lift your other leg as well and break contact with the earth! Ever

since, you've been up there with the stars. Try and remember, station master! Station master, do remember! Have you remembered now? And you'll never forget it again? Never ever?

After all, it was after that that you began seeing your duties the way a poet sees reality. You would calculate the travelling time of trains down to five decimal places, having duly corrected it with regard to the sixth. You decked the waiting room and traffic office with photos of the constellations and those beautiful milky ways of the Swan constellation, and the little cluster of extragalactic nebulae in Andromeda. Do you remember that, station master? For God's sake remember! Don't you even remember the day you replaced the locomotive entering Wilson Station with a picture of the sun's neighbourhood up to a distance of thirty light years? So you don't remember! All right! It was the day you went out into the August night and found vanity of vanities, all was vanity, apart from the desire for transformation!

But he who seeks out causes and contrives them into effects will tell you that it was down to Difficult Death, which had crushed you underfoot beyond recognition!

But that still didn't satisfy Difficult Death! There was still the window daughter! That most precious flesh and blood! Tabula rasa! Virgo intacta! The girl who it would bring downstairs to the office, where on a waxed-cotton sofa she would listen to talk of the expansion of the Universe. And of canals on Mars, and she was led at once to beg her father to milk the most beautiful stars into the bowl of her brain! And if you've got a handbook of astronomy to hand, just read some of the fairy tales the station master read aloud to his little daughter! Perhaps the one about Neptune: Major axis 36.154, sidereal orbit period 217 years, eccentricity 0.10751, length of perihelion 284° 45′, mean length on 1st January 318° 47′, mass 1/9300, true heliocentric length on 1st January 326° 32′, distance from the Sun 33.06 astronomical units. And after a few minutes, before the girl's amazement and rapture began to wane, a craziness gave her innocent lips a boost: "That's beautiful! Oh, it's so beautiful, Daddy! And now tell me about how the moons of Saturn were born!" So it was no surprise when for her birthday she got a subscription to an astronomy journal, while other girls of her age were leafing through books about princesses and fairies! No surprise when for Christmas she received a globe, while at her age other girls were pushing doll's prams and playing hopscotch.

But he who seeks out causes and contrives them into effects will tell you that it was all down to Difficult Death, which had eaten out the family brain and left behind nothing but divine cinders! And a thirst for the cosmos. But that didn't satisfy Difficult Death! It was after bigger and better results! The seed that Difficult Death had spurted under the cranium had proliferated hypertrophically! It had thrived! Rutted! Because the situation was now hurtling downhill!

And so with both feet hooked firmly to the stars, he dangled head down towards the earth like a pendulum. Like a skinned rabbit! Like a slaughtered pig! And from the pockets of the station master's brain the world went rolling all over the place, and now all he desired was to be dwelling, any moment now, in the stars! To disperse the atoms of his soul and rock away to his heart's content!

"I'm sure you'll remember *that* afternoon, station master! That glorious afternoon that everyone for miles around remembers. Your memory's failing you again? You're too far away from us, but maybe it'll come back to you, how you peeled the shelf number off *Difficult Death*, as if you guessed where it all came from. You'd reached the very gullet of your doom (or salvation?)! And you'd sucked the curse into your last tiny blood vessel! Or, to put it a better way: you'd matched an imprint to the matrix! You'd become the equal of your tutor, your master! You'd found your God! Your everything! And having locked yourself in your office, you stripped naked and covered your entire body in all the rubber stamps you used. In every colour, so after half an hour's meticulous endeavour you looked like a giant parrot! For your back you'd made a contraption out of the poker, some string and a pair of sugar tongs so even your spine got its fair share! So you left out not one single spot! And then you put a bullet through your temple from a tiny pearl-handled revolver.

The district medical officer, examining your calm, cold body, realised that you'd composed your suicide exactly following the rules of aesthetics. As he drew back your foreskin, lo and behold!, one letter appeared after another until they formed the name of the station where you'd so enjoyed working in your younger days. Can you at least remember, station master, that station out near the frontier? And the district medical officer, a notorious card player, couldn't help himself and he slapped you on your ice-cold back and laughed: "Cripes, it's like successive hitting at blackjack." And he gave a little laugh and failed to recall that from now on you were going to remember nothing, because NOTHING was what you'd just become![2]

And yet he who seeks out causes and contrives them into effects will confirm that this was the neat handiwork of Difficult Death. That same Difficult Death that indulges a certain lady in a mental institution and lets her lean out of a first-floor window twice a day, even if it happens to be on the ground floor, from which she waves good-bye to her departing mother, despite the fact that she's been dead for two years. It's that Difficult Death that has indulged the lady and let her fall pregnant twice a day, although she's long past the menopause. It's simply that kindly death that allows the lady to have a baby girl once a day, although all anyone can get from her are jumbles of words and deaf-mute intimations! That, my friends, is all down to Difficult Death, which came easy to a lass (so long ago it is now) as she leaned out of a first-floor window to see the whole of Orion. But enough! Enough, for God's sake!

And yet even you, my gleaming rhombus on the hypotenuse of ordinariness, you too will pass along Wenceslas Square and your unsuspecting arm will be taken lovingly by HER. And you too will go on like a magic billiard ball and not feel the bouncy ricochet in your brain, nor a measure of sterilisation in your genitals! You too will joke and laugh and be unaware of being preordained to go on, predetermined to hurtle towards the unknown, which will suddenly be known so well! Your whole world will collapse, apart from the longing for transubstantiation, which, like a neon snake, will writhe above the red-hot integument of your body! My good and beautiful one, lose not sight of the terrible hole in Doctor Faust's ceiling! Then your salvation will be ever so close. Lovely young lady of mine, cast *Difficult Death*, by a man whose name should have been Clever, away, over here to me.

MORNING: you were listening at the door and really there was nothing to hear but your own heart and a quiet sound of water falling or laughter. In the end you decided you should enter and say: "Here's that four hundred from Marie! And I'd like a receipt, miss! And good-bye! Farewell!" But for now your heart was beating so loud that it might have been audible from inside! And you thought you heard someone answer your knock in a stifled voice: "Enter!" So you depressed the door handle and the fierce sunlight almost knocked you out! It was beating down into the little room with a determined density! When you'd got used to it, lo and behold! There was a naked statue sitting in the wash basin holding a red flannel in its upraised hand! Not in your wildest dreams did you think it could be alive! And yet it was she, rigid with surprise at your presence! "You!" Then the image of her brought the little room back to life with the movement of the hand wetting the flannel again and applying it to her neck and under her chin and between her breasts. She said: "I say, sir, how very nice of you to come! And a good morning to you! Do sit down next to me here!" And she went on washing her legs, which were outside of the wash basin! Blimey! And she wasn't the least bit abashed, the bitch! Added to that, she now rose up from the basin and started going at her vagina with the red flannel as if she meant to rub it out! As if it was a spelling mistake! But when she bent back down to the tap, she went PEEP-O at you between her legs! So you got a view of her lifeline! Christ! It was looking out at you like a gnome or a musketeer. And she even had the gall to remind you: "Take your hat off, will you? I'll be ready in a mo! And pass me that terry towel from the oven! And do take that hat off!" And she stamped her foot, fit to knock a hole in the wash basin! So you went slowly over to the oven, totally befuddled, stupefied. And, sir, you did take your hat off and you placed it on top of a cupboard. But now you were in a predicament of sorts! You could scarcely imagine stepping up to this bare-bottomed, topless wonder and telling it something about the four hundred crowns you had in your trembling hands! And when she saw them, she stole a march on you and said: "Let's not bother with the money for now. Put it on the coffee table over there and come and dry my back, my back, my little piggyback!" And indeed you did place the four hundred on the coffee table, the four hundred for which you were to collect a receipt, and you began drying that wet, pretty, female frame, like a verger giving St John a once-over before the patronal festival! And you completely forgot about the circular regarding bicycles and tyres! And you even forgot about the cash on the coffee table! Your attention was totally fixed on the deep furrow that ran down her back from her sopping wet hair to her bottom. And when you checked yourself and hesitated, she urged you on: "Don't worry, sir! Dry me everywhere, and spare nothing!" And again she splashed her fingers in the basin, sending water everywhere. And she kept calling: "You sweetie, sweetie, sweetie-pie!" And she shook herself as a mark of how good it was making her feel (the sight of the four hundred crowns)! And when she turned to you with a smile, you felt such freedom as never before! Her breasts gleamed and her whole body shone with a dull lustre, the credit for which was down to the towel in your hand. She looked at you and said repetitively: "And call me pussycat baby, pussycat, pussycat, pussycat baby! Come on!" And tentatively at first, then more intimately, you repeated it after her, as if you'd learned it by heart! So far had you been borne away from bicycles and tyres! You'd been fired high up over the co-op and still hadn't landed back on all fours! Nor did you want to land! "Have you never had the urge to go back to that brothel next to the station, sir?" You'd been turned into a total imbecile by the sunlight streaming in through the window like sea water into a sinking ship. You thought it was coming from the sofa and the cupboards, the dirty water and her body! So much sunlight in one place. And yet you did remember about the four hundred and reached out your hands. But the young woman saw through you and said quickly: "And now come and sit on the sofa in the sunlight! Come and lie down! Come and plant kisses all over me like chickenpox. Come on, now, surely you're not afraid, you naughty boy!" You merely protested that the blind might be pulled down. But she said no, on the contrary she had to see love. Like during an operation she had to see each intended move, each position! And: "If you wanted, sir, I'd make love with you on the square, on the statue of St Wenceslas!" And that knocked you for six. The image of you on the statue of St Wenceslas cast you, sir, into such an agreeable light that you fixed your eyes on the girl's lips with real gratitude, and by now you were done for! You stroked her quivering body

and started to shake. And you told her that, anyway, the fire brigade would come and take you down their ladders, but by then you were already on the sofa resolved to let God's will be done. And from that moment you weren't sitting on the sofa, but on the statue of St Wenceslas in Prague II, and you could hear the distinct hum of the crowds and agitated calls of "Police, police!". And she was still whispering to you like crazy: "Come, my little imbecile, come my little staglet with doe's eyes, come!" But you weren't taking it in, because you were trying hard not to fall off the rear end of the saint's horse! You stripped like a tightrope walker, casting into the depths, into the cries of the people, your coat and waistcoat and shirt and vest and the rabbit fur you wore for your sciatica. My! And she kept on and on: "Come here, come on, for heaven's sake get a move on," and with glazed eyes she reached her arms out to you! And she begged you: "And put that cushion under me! No, not that one, the one with the red tulips!", but you demanded that she lean back properly on the holy horseman and not wriggle too much in case you both fell off into the depths! "And quick, quick, before the fire brigade gets here. Hurrah! hurrah!" you cried from the sofa down to the floor! "Hurrah, victory is ours!" you cried into her face, while from the abyss rose the voices of the outraged thousands, who were jumping up and down and grabbing for your hands to drag you down to them, sir, and rip you into a thousand pieces.

AFTERNOON: We have a considerable number of bicycles on order and so, as soon as we receive them from the factory, we'll send them to you. And will your sister require a receipt? And the four hundred are down the pan! In her little room! Added to which, quadrangles and rectangles are abandoning sheets of every kind of paper and symmetrical furniture and doors and windows! They're being a real nuisance! They're trying to break you down, do for you. We will notify you by circular letter and inform you whether subject to our allocation of bicycles we will be able to supply you with the same! And to think you rose to the bait! These circulars really call for a lawyer. Wherever you look, these symmetrical figures are moving about! And new ones abandon their objects and wander about the office of their own accord. And when your eyes are closed, it's concentric circles that start spinning, and they go on forever and ever! Because they can't get a hold on anything. When you chuck them out of the window, again there's all those symmetrical flowerbeds and windows and roofs and dormers! And no peace for the wicked! How good it would be to escape it all for twenty-four hours and cover oneself in darkness. Exactly the way it is with bicycles, exactly the way it is with tyres. Of which we are pleased to inform you. That stupid girl Mary should have delivered the four hundred herself! Four hundred, holy Moses, four hundred! Given that the shortfall at tyre factories is an established fact, we are accordingly unable to allocate bicycles as we might wish and desire, of which we are hereby also giving you notice! And those business managers will make a pig's ear of it anyway! This really does call for a lawyer! And if only the cupboards and shelves would stop spinning! If only their shapes would come crawling back! Even those four hundred were shaped like rectangles, and the stairs, and the tiles! Given that as of today we cannot give you a guarantee that even the tyres will reach us from the factories, and squares, squares, squares and that you will have the tyres delivered, delivered, delivered, delivered, delivered, delivered... Christ, Mr Slavíček, stop me, I'm going mad like a gramophone record. A rectangle, no, they're squares, a trapezium! Enough now! Enough of this! Finish writing this for me, would you please, Mr Slavíček, I have to get away. Far from here, wherever my eyes carry me. I can't cope anymore, all this geometry! Whole textbooks have ganged up inside my brain! And don't ask! Wherever my feet and chance take me. Any old where, just to get away, to forget, or it'll be the death of me, all these symmetries. Look, there's one, smirking and waving at me, signalling its intention to put me in the loony bin. And that girl didn't help either, unless by helping herself to the four bloody hundred! If the chairman asks, then I've gone to the regional division to pick up a bulk allocation note! Or who cares, just tell him I've had a breakdown, I've flaked out! That I've had it up to here! The main thing to say in the circular is that we'll supply the tyres and bicycles as soon as they reach us from the factories! Put it intelligibly and legalistically, the way I always write these things! Before that they can't have them! Right, I'm off now, I'm off, I'm going to get blind drunk, if I know me! No one can stop me now. We've taken civilisation too far! A spot of culture, a few flowers and nice smells and getting away from myself, that'll do me just right! Better than ten psychiatrists! Listen, Mr Slavíček, I've got an entire production line running inside my noddle! There's Taylorism[1] for you! The peak of socialisation in a nutshell! There's all this superstructure being erected inside my noddle out of stuff in the office! Listen, Mr Slavíček, hand me my coat! Wuff-wuff, grr, grr, grr, wuff! May my hallucinations return to their objects! Pray for me, mercy!

And you, sir, our manager, you tottered off out and down the stairs. Then you stopped by the gents, unzipping yourself and zipping yourself up again, because you hadn't had the call. And the tiles carried you back out, ran outside with you, and the whole world was made of squared paper! As if? No, really! And then you were ingested by a rectangle into a passageway, a rectangle presented itself for opening, just right for sitting down behind. Only the pewter countertop like an altar retained its shape, and you drank and drank and drank. And half an hour later you were on your way back, and objects were settling down and all a-gleam in an identity of form and matter. You looked about you diffidently and the cupboards and chairs were once more offering you their winning friendship. You were able to smile and remember and analyse the obsession that would overcome you four times a year. A revolt against symmetry. Yes, it had begun, as you recalled, eighteen years before. At the time you kept a plank of lime wood in your office at the Track Maintenance Department. When objects began to push you towards the gates of the madhouse, you would eventually grab the plank and say, for all to hear: "I'm off to the archive. If anyone asks for me, that's where they'll find me." Having reached the basement archive, you'd open a cupboard that was quite unsuitable for the plank and tell the bearded underling: "I have to go and see the in-house carpenter and get this plank trimmed down. If anyone asks for me, that's where they'll find me!" And you headed off to find the carpenter, but on the way you concealed the plank behind a small cupboard out in the corridor. You would offer the carpenter a cigarette and say, out of the blue: "Oh bother, I need some nails to fix a plank. I must pop and get some. If anyone asks for me, would you mind telling them that's where I've gone?" Then either you'd go for swim, or take a walk along the bank of the Elbe to let nature defer the devastation, to let all things green soothe your soul, to let the running water wash away the production line that kept imprinting itself on your brain. "Four more brandies, waiter!" One down! Two down! Three down! Four! So much for *them*! Now they could get on and warm your cockles! And suddenly, sir, you'd get to thinking that as matters stood with tyres, so they also stood with bicycles! And you weren't leaving the place until you spent the very last of your small change!

I wonder, how many steps does this subterranean concrete passage have, so skilfully constructed? And where are you taking us down these cold steps? You go first, sir, and we'll follow, lest we stumble on the spirals! But how can you actually be alone like this? We don't like it one bit! The utter isolation! Say, what would you do, who would you call for help, if you were to fall with cramp on the concrete and couldn't budge? And even if you did manage to call for help, what can anyone do for you if you won't even be able to get back on your feet? It's no laughing matter, because the times are bad, and so are people! So forgive the inept remark and lead on, let's have some light from somewhere. To us, your place is like being permanently got the better of by something. It's bitter cold, and just that glimmer coming down from the light well. It must be grim, living so far from people and your pension. We seem to be walking waist-deep in the earth. So do get on and open the door with the Hebrew inscription, let's not be a light burning under a bushel.[2] Oh, my, this isn't bad. Who'd have thought there could be such a nice flat in a cellar! And there were we, thinking that any such dwelling was degrading! And quite the reverse! The windows might be up there by the ceiling, on the other hand you do get to see the trees' ankles. Ha, ha! And you've got gas! Look at this – a little flame flowing from a little metal pipe, such a delicate, tiny little flame, such a wise little flame, gothic, abstract. There's really nothing in this world so faithful as an eternal lamp indoors, shining daily for two crowns fifty! You're saying nothing, sir, and we understand! We do understand! One word and you'd breach the integrity of the companionship between you and the gas flame.

But we too haven't come here to talk about merging and escape. We too are on a mission! We've come about something quite specific and urgent. We've come to make this little flame safe! We've come to give you a guarantee that this flame will accompany you right up until your death, or the start of your new life, as the case may be. We're here so that you'll be able to pay the charge joyfully even in your old age. But, sir, forgive the digression, what is the meaning of that tree trunk, so horribly eaten away by bees or ants?[3] It looks like a decaying corpse! What? Well, well, that's wonderful! You say it's your nephew who has such peculiar interests. A bust of Robert Desnos.[4] A poet, you say? Indeed so! Poets? Goodness no! And he died in a concentration camp of starvation and beatings? Not a bit of it – no regime can silence people like that. In the arms of doctors? They're everywhere, but haven't we come to just the right place! It really is a fine cautionary object, and created by nature! And where its face is supposed to be your felicitous nephew has plastered it with moths! And he's placed an inscription on its chest! Don't explain a thing! We've got the message! The inscription might well mean: *Do not lean out of the window!* or: *No spitting*, or whatever, because who on earth understands Aramaic, though to your nephew it means something really nice, a prophesy or something of the kind. But anyway, you must permit us to take a photo of this bust of Robert Desnos! We can make it into a promotional leaflet: *Secure your old age.* When all's said and done, it carries a clear warning. And now to business! The matter of your future happiness, sir! Look at these tables. For a trifling sum, you can, and we believe you will, enjoy a very nice pension. You won't be looking out on the world from a basement, but from street level or the first floor. You'll be able to buy a nice picture to go on the wall or an alabaster statuette, and not have a horrid artificial limb hanging on the wall like this here, all fiddly levers and nickel clips.[5] What? How d'you mean? What altar? It really is priceless, this home of yours! You're such interesting folk hereabouts. But then what you say is quite true. One may not even be aware of walking about and breathing. Of being fit and well! It's no bad thing, actually, that the prosthesis serves you as a reminder of your obligation to the Creator! When all's said and done, it's God's mercy that He attached it to someone other than me. After we've gone, say a prayer for us, ask for the prosthesis to give us a wide berth! It's not a thing anyone would want much. Though it's still a fitting symbol of something terribly important. Your only option is to join the Tradespeople's Fund. We've half a mind to force any tradesman who's still unprovided for to visit your home and let these objects get to work on him! Hand on heart, sir! But really, what inexcusable negligence is it that makes you roam the earth without provision for your old age? That is irresponsible both to your family and to the entire nation! Look at us! Although we have no direct interest, we shudder at the very idea! Having an artificial leg

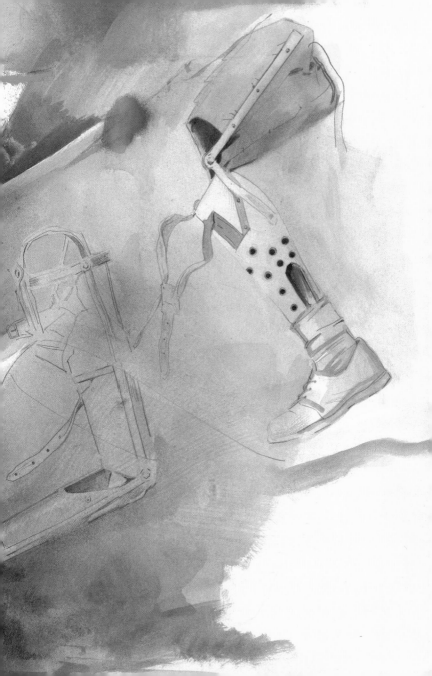

where you carry on your trade, that already sends a shiver down our spines! How it would sadden and disturb anyone with a kind heart. How, you unfortunate man, how could you kick-start a bike with a false leg? No, no, no, no-o, this is no time for joking. It's quite obvious now. If you fail to join the Fund, that makes us co-responsible for your future life. We'd have you on our conscience from now to eternity for having failed in our efforts. Right now! We already have your name and surname. So, if you just show us your certificate of apprenticeship so we can take down the number. You'll be thanking us with tears in your eyes! What, you never did an apprenticeship? What sort of oversight is that? Do you realise, sir, that you're guilty of deceiving public officials? So why the hell didn't you say at the outset it was your brother? Behind the curtain? So move it. So we can draw it up with him! He's dying? Ah well, if he's dying, there's nothing for it. Though you and he are sharing a household, and after his death you'd get half his pension, as a widow would. We'll add that to the application form, and it will all be settled to the satisfaction of both sides. So the artificial leg is your brother's? We'll add a note on that, too. But it's quite simple. If he can't get to the table, we can bring him in. And he can sign it here! We can hold his hand. Right, take the blanket away. Now, sir, put one arm round each of our necks and let us take your weight. After all, the Fund is your support in old age. It hurts, does it? Ah, but everything in the world hurts these days. Even our very existence! Have a drop of water, that'll refresh you most likely. Come on, move! And I'll guide your hand. Go-o-od.

And again, slowly does it. Now the dot on that *i*. Done, and now you can pop back behind the curtain. Quick-quick, the water! It'll pass, it's just a moment. We get this all the time. It's terminal frailty. Careful dammit, mind you don't smudge the signature! And rub a bit of vinegar into his temples. He might come round. He hasn't worked for ten years? This is the best sign that we've arrived at the twelfth hour, though it's only half past two in the afternoon! Ha-ha! And now, we are duly authorised to receive your first three months' payment in cash. Scour the flat, we can wait. It would be very odd if you couldn't come up with such a trifling sum! See if there isn't some lurking in those mugs. Think about it, your brother will only be paying for ten years, then he can start drawing his pension at once! In a mere ten years! Though it looks as if you might be needing a doctor. He doesn't seem to be coming round. Try the neighbours, they might lend you it. It doesn't matter, just as long as we see the money because if, at some later stage, you came to the Fund on bended knees, we wouldn't take you on. Your nephew? Why? To what purpose? It's now or never. It's the law of minimal pain. It's not of our doing. Because he's dying? He might be. Man is mortal. But my colleague here saw he was fully self-aware and composed as he put his signature to it, didn't you? There, where there's a will, there's a way. We'll send confirmation of the payment. Rest assured, yes, and as we're passing the vicarage, we'll leave a message for the priest to stop by. God bless you and goodbye!

You were seen, sir, hurrying across the footbridge linking the bridge to the island. You were clearly in that state where it's hard to tell the difference between quarter to twelve and three o'clock. The simple fact is that you were in a hurry, and counting up and counting down the hours was irrelevant, especially now that sap was heading down towards the roots and the sky was turning grey.

But resistance is futile! All you may wish for is that the leaves fall thicker and faster today, and tomorrow perhaps snow! Ever thicker and faster, one leaf after another, one after another! After all, you too entrusted the frills of your soul to the questionnaire and now you are nothing more than a ragged puppet, nothing less than a corpse with no domain! My friend, what's left of you is your sex without love, a snail without a shell, beauty without form! You now have nowhere to return to, to huddle down in. You need to dream yourself up again, reinvent yourself.

So you've no grounds for doing a Cossack dance on the way home. Likewise, you've no grounds for fighting back against the falling leaves and holding something against them! Your sole option is to walk on for now down the avenue of plane trees, even though your avulsed rectum makes walking difficult. You also need to keep your head held high, even though gobbets of spit from the mouths of others haven't dried up yet and are trickling down your cheeks. Fain would you say something, but that knocked-out tooth inhibits verbal precision. My friend, yearn you may, but there's no heart left.

Ever more insistent blood pressure is exhausting your liver. Only an untied lace of the shoes you bought last year at Vetera is forcing you down on one knee to do something. So you're kneeling on your right knee and the leaves are shifting about beside you in soft footprints. Over there, a stone statue is rooted firmly in the air and leaves are streaming past all around, so it doesn't take much imagination to come up with the idea that it could easily be the leaves fixed firmly in the air and the statue dropping silently through the trapdoor of oblivion. But one persistent leaf has hidden your mouth and one cold leaf has covered your eyes. You tear away the red dressing and donate the leaf to the wind. However, you're still down on one knee, and the leaf buds being turned on nature's lathe bring you the consolation of the new foliage fermenting away inside. The delicacy of the future leaves is already assured, but your entrails are too scattered about faculty corridors. You're also found wanting on the grounds that the colour of your heart has lost some of its lustre!

And as you kneel with both ends of the shoe lace in your hand, you're still being bombarded with insults! You can't fail to hear your young lady being ordered to place her womb on a plate! Loud voices recommend that your wife cut out your baby's tongue as proof of her compliancy! And even at this stage they pin to your lapel the number you are to wear! And even thank them for it! Other matters will be left out of account!

But the avenue of plane trees in which you're still kneeling – it has also left you out of account! As you look back, it's as if you've never been this way! Not a single shoe-print have you left! Perhaps if you were wearing muddy boots, it's just possible you could have formed the ground plan of the tunnel your person has hollowed out! You've arrived at the realisation that all things come to an end and merely start over and over again. That whatever has been done to you, whether or not the avenue has taken you into account, you have to walk on notwithstanding and not keep looking back. It's blooming pointless. You've also come to the realisation that in this posture of a kneeling bowman the only things of worth are scandal and a headstone. That that's the end of it though. You've had your lot!

Leaves of every kind keep coming down and you've just done up your shoelace. The warming ticking of your wristwatch is marching onward in order to stay fixed on one spot. Throughout the region there isn't a single metaphor to warm the cockles of the heart. But it's time to rise to your feet and with no going back to go back home, with your jaws clamped and pale, guided now by no more than lights in windows that, cut in four to form crosses like Norwegian flags, warn of the risk of becoming shipwrecked. As if elsewhere is all shipwrecks and melancholy. You're returning towards buildings whither, in their folly, birds and dead leaves fly to spend the night, as if in other places death might reside. And some horse, disturbed in the darkness, having whinnied with a pain that was human, you've raised your arm in that direction as if two kindred pains were easier to bear. And suddenly a clock has begun striking like mad! Without cause, reproachfully, it has begun to weave onto your shoulders a crushing iron grill as heavy as a manhole cover!

The time is not far off when life will be one long hooting to get you to work on time, hooting you to table, hooting you to go to bed! Chains of complex hootings so that you know that you've grown old!

Only now do I know why you weren't expecting me in the abandoned garden and why you didn't look me up at work. I now also know why you stick swallows' nests in the mouths of beautiful young women! I now also know why you didn't break down when she refused to carry your shadow. I know now why you were in two minds whether to hang yourself on a silver cross or ruin your life in its name! Only now, my friend, do I know why you were looking for a small, round pocket mirror and in that mirror a table and on that table a book and in that book the kiss that you last refused to give in the Garden of Eden!

Don't go to bed yet. It's not worth it. Go to the cemetery instead and wake a few corpses just for the hell of it.

Since there's nothing else in the world but larking about anyway.

So you tapped on the first sarcophagus and said: "Get up, dead-o, and tell us: what use were you in the world. We'd like to know."

And wouldn't you know it, the deceased, being well used to the dictatorship of heaven, saluted like a doorman and reported: "Yessir! My reason for being in the world was to come to know that I don't know anything."

And you, my friends, gawped at him like your granddad at a goose fair. You hadn't a clue what he meant, but then you twigged and laughed like bloody drains.

The kindly old corpse had cheered you up so much that you kept stamping on his chest for luck till his heart came oozing out of his mouth. As if he'd just hanged himself, or had been gorging himself on the misfortunes of others.

And then you toddled off to another burial pit and settled its occupant's hash with a stick of dynamite. And right away you told it: "Out you come, zither, play us a tune to show us what you got up to in your lifetime." But that yellow harp of bones stayed lying at the bottom and crapped itself in terror. What a treat! All over the shavings inside the coffin. And it said: "Have mercy, sirs, all my life I was shit-scared of doing anything wrong. So I thought it best to do nothing. That's how frightened I was of sinning."

And you, my brave lads, hollered down at it: "Come off it, you silly ass! You're a right one! And so you can't complain, we'll piss you a bathful. Faradic current therapy,[1] hydrotherapy and electric shock therapy to keep you warm...

"... Do you fancy Poděbrady, Sliač, Velichovky?"[2] But you were already craning over the third grave, above which you declared: "Third time lucky!" And so it was.

One dig of the spade, then a couple more and suddenly a howl came from out of the earth: "What the blazes, right between my legs, just like when I was alive, you swines." And a skeleton scrabbled its way out of the sacred ground like a mole, and it sat on the surround and shook out its rotted hair.

"Come on, you buggers, give us a drink. I'm a girl that unrequited love made slash her wrists in God's honour. How stupid was that!"

And she made no bones, so to speak, about making up to you, flinging her actual bones this way and that. And so, me hearties, you had a bit of a warm-up and turned yourselves on with several slugs of Old Tom Gin.[3]

You poured the spirits non-stop into the corpse's cracked skull to cries of "Hosanna, hosanna, we baptise thee in the name of the Lord, for thou art the corpse that hath taken our fancy."

And now nothing could hold you back, you rustic crew, and in the twinkling of an eye you'd performed a caesarean and yanked her old bones out of the earth and loaded them onto your shoulders.

And you took the bones out into the street to perform their confirmation.

But only after you'd ripped all the dry skin off its head – by contact with the cemetery gateway, so it flapped about like an Indian scalp.

It was her own stupid fault; she should have ducked.

And so, my children, you broke into song and, glowing with glee, you made to drive knives into one another's backs and snap each other's hands and ribs in a token ritual.

And you were still plying the cankered lips with liquor, which leaked onto the ribs and vertebrae and down them onto the pelvis and from the pelvis onto the raw earth.

The lucky ones who were closest sucked on the gin-soaked fingers. And the ribs. And the pubic bone.

The ones at the back, the socially disadvantaged, they at least sucked at dear mother earth wherever any drips dropped.

Though they then missed out on the fun caused by her skeleton-ness: as she was being borne along, she flung her arms all over the place like at a Sokol jamboree. Twisting her hands this way and that, she kept slapping the lads round the face. Then she put on a charade of rinsing the weekly wash or playing the piano. One nice move was when she appeared to be delousing someone.

On the square, by which time the procession had swelled to fifty persons, you adorable lads jammed an empty bottle between the rattletrap's ribs. But then you tripped and the bottle got smashed to smithereens. But that only made your progress more fun as the bits of glass clinked in step and your spirits rose even higher as at the Elevation of the Host. You were a sight to behold, boys, as you swept forward in closed formation.

But the main thing was that you were fearless in your frolics with the dear departed.

You who were closest, that was a great trick you did with her tendons. You stretched her arms out like elastic then paused briefly while the rest of her body carried on forwards, and then you let go.

Golly, what a jangling racket and how the splinters flew!

And then another one took over the closest position and as he marched along he waggled the corpse's lower jaw so that from a distance it seemed to be laughing horribly at something, or yawning. Morning, warning, mourning.

And just outside the Bohemian Brethren church the first disaster struck. One of the brethren thought the dead old bird was making fun of his inflamed trigeminal nerve, and, ever ready with his fists, he landed one so hard that her head went spinning round on its vertebral column.

And the shocked swillpot who'd been working the jaw forgot to remove his fingers and it bit two of them off. Well! They lay on the ground after the procession had passed like two little mice waiting for a dog to gobble them up.

But the high point was still to come. Suddenly there's this crowd of cops and the order to hand over the corpse at once for quiet burial. Without fuss and right now.

But you lot, true to your glorious traditions, weren't having that. What must be must be, but only with plenty of fuss. Let the plods know the meaning of history.

And so you went at each other, but before long you had to leave the police in charge of the head and arms, while you hung on to the rest. The police were almost on their last legs and about to send for reinforcements, but the inspector in charge had his fingers so firmly jammed in the corpse's maw that he couldn't get them out.

And as you tussled over the bag of bones, the teeth just sank in deeper. And deeper.

And you, lads, you might have done a runner by then as well, but you couldn't either, because some of you had fingers jammed between the ribs.

And so you kept on wigwagging the ghastly thing and the broken Old Tom Gin bottle kept clinking like it was the Resurrection. You this way, the cops that. And the corpse kept cracking and popping and clacking and grinding. And then it gave.

So now it was the cops this way and you that.

The spinal column split from the bony remainder along with the head and the inspector's fingers. That's how firmly the gum ridge had closed on them.

And now you were haring down a side street, each brandishing his particular bit of booty above his head.

One had a rib, another one three, someone had a thigh-bone and the rest had glee in their eyes.

You only paused when you reached a pub, and, looking at one another, you couldn't help laughing, laughing like mad at what idiots you were. At how you'd played the game to the end in all earnestness, like kids, like people in love.

You gathered up the leftovers, wrapped them in newspaper and tied them up with string.

When you entered, the publican's missus thought you'd brought some nice bits of veal to go in the soup.

But by now your minds were elsewhere. In triple, nay, quadruple ecstasy. You now had other plans. Something really great was brewing inside your bonces.

But before you settled in, you refreshed yourselves with a few swigs of Old Tom Gin. To get a clearer view of things.

And you broke into song. Specifically: "Oh, Lord, stay Thee not the windless shaking and the trouble that our glands are making."

Then you leapt to your feet and decked yourselves with garlands from last year's village shindigs and stuck paint brushes and pokers in your hair.

And in time with the song you burped and snorted and puffed and shouted: "One, two, three, one, two, three, yo, ho, ho."

And again you were all on heat, on the dance floor and on a hiding to nothing. And again believing that this was the best thing ever in this vale of tears.

That is, until your knackered guardian angels asked you to slow down. To start thinking about going back. Offering re-emigration to paradise.

But you, great guys that you are, you'd been here before and retorted with a jingle. To wit:

"Fill not the blanks inside our heads, Lord,

far rather set dynamite to our hair

than send us back to paradise. Oh gawd."

And those shits who'd claimed to have driven you out of Paradise boasted of the flames that had engulfed them.

But you argued back: "You, you chased us out of Paradise? Ha, ha. Back then we were just lying with our hands behind our heads, taking the piss out of Adam. It wasn't you that booted us out of Paradise, but us who drove God out of the Paradise of our brainboxes. And pretty smartly at that. And we whacked Him with a rod of juniper to give him something to think about, to give him a taste of what it's like to be different. After all, back then we already knew that life's only worth living when it's you in charge."

And you went on: "Beat it, you young whippersnappers, and take your halberds and your wings with you before something bad happens, before we whip your hides, before we turn your arses into fiery furnaces. Not one ounce of common sense has come from you. Nothing but aggravation."

We, asses that we are, the worst thing we did to ourselves was to have longed to convert our forelegs into hands and arms. Christ! Since then, the only good use we've had for our hands has been to get a grip on the mucous gobbets of sentences that come straggling in and mess about inside us like a bogey in our nose. And never again can anyone be of no account. And so just out of spite, however far removed we are from one another, oh, oh, oh. Hence, too, that passion for scandal.

At which point, some man wielding a cow's tail came bounding in on this self-abuse, bellowing into your conscience. "Here's a fine thing. A fine howdy-do. No wonder you're all over the place, and you'll never patch yourself up again, dimbo. By turns, you'll be, to judge from things you say, a wardrobe, a cow and a streetwalker. God almighty!"

And after each word he slapped the tail across the table.

"Great heavens above. Don't forget, citizens, that you are citizens. That the state needs you. That your morale matters to it. Dammit, You've been edging away from the grass roots. A few seconds more and the transformation will be complete. Make peace with your guardian angels. Kiss their swords and wings, you bastards."

And another slap and bang with the tail across the table.

And you, drinkers of Old Tom Gin, you preserved decorum. You stood your ground and stuck to your guns. Stuck to your point as the very thing. As the thing you hanker after. And what makes you say screw citizenship. And maintain that your kingdom is not of this world and vice versa.

And also that one of the brethren became a kitten and another some moss, a third a teat, a fourth a tinkling pendant, a fifth an umbrella and so ad infinitum.

And I can also testify that you lot haven't been much fun. Least of all when you go all rueful and your little ravaged frames start talking to your rime-coated soul that isn't. It's better to steer clear and avert the gaze.

And when a startled liver imprints itself on letters and they're not there, even God gets the blame for it.

I saw you that time when you all jumped onto the running board of his Ford and made such a mess. When you shouted in the ear of the ordinand: "You are the architect of our slow disappearance. You, the intellectual begetter of our contemptible existence. We're gonna show you what's what. You bastard. Take note."

And I'll testify that, when you were in that holy ecstasy, you snapped his halo off bit by bit, then munched on it like donkeys munching at wreaths.

And he didn't say a word. The slyboots. Just hunkered down inside his car with nary a peep.

You were getting on his wick and he didn't even flicker.

But as soon as you started getting at his heart with knives, he yelped for the first time in his life.

And as you elevated that steaming goulash of heart towards heaven, the heart began to wail: "Forgive me my transgressions, dear friends of mine. I did go too far. I've coughed up so many terms of abuse because of people. I went wild, letting loose at them, and then by contrast let them get too close."

And again I'll testify how you chucked the leftovers from mass back in the car, that you tightened your belts and besought God with your fist: "Lord give us the strength to continue despising you."

"Lord, give us the will to treat Thee so for evermore."

"Lord, swear that Thou art not and shalt not be homosexual."

And he, putting the pieces together, says: "At last, lads, you've got the hang of it. I'm not one for hearing otherwise than by insult. It's a shame I can't join you and go against myself. That really would be fun."

But you, my lads, weren't thinking about that. You were already infatuated with other madcap stuff.

You'd pee into tar-coated urinals and sing: "As I left the little grove along a forest track", as if you'd just been born, or had at that very instant forgotten everything. Adieu.

I says: When the time's right, but the old biddy just wouldn't put a sock in it: You're a nice clean lad, as if that mattered, an' Mum said afterwards: Don't worry about it, before long Uncle'll be pushing me along in a wheelchair, an' everyone keeps asking me if I go to visit the girl an' if I'm going to marry her, I'm going to the barber's to get my neck shaved, so we've started rehearsing this play together an' she can't make any headway with even the difference of opinion, You're beautiful, Miss, you're divine, it's good training, an' Dáša, she also likes it an' the lady from the chemist's stuck with us an' her old man came flying in, Good God, what are you up to? he's the nervy type, It's nothing, just an ordinary row as we imagine it, she said, Never mind, sir, my dad doesn't understand, an' that's how I got into dramatics, or tragedy or the sick business, Korbelář meets Štěpánek an' Štěpánek plays the doctor an' Korbelář[1] the patient, they're both huge guys an' the one being the patient is moaning an' holding his hand, it's quite an art, holding your hand like that, an' he says Doctor, my hand's really sore, aaaaaargh, it hurts, an' he says, Let's have a look, it's only a sprain an' we'll get you to hospital, Thank you, doctor, an' another doctor examined it at the hospital, Hmmmm, come, come, it's nothing, you're fussing like a girl, you have to remember all your lines an' you have to know how to do it, the way it's set out in the notes, it has to be played right, he could play it different like, but then the directions would also have to be different, an' one young lady an' an older one laughed so hard they had to leave the room when I told them about it, the lady herself said He's a good actor, do you know what part you're playing? You the prince an' me the princess, I wear a very low-cut dress, I couldn't care less, even if you were stark naked I wouldn't be bothered, but then with that face, never mind, not all princesses were pretty, so while we were at rehearsal I had this idea of running it myself from the side, though they said Don't worry, man, it'll all come right, but Dáša said she'd put the radio on for us to dance to, An' I'll tell you what we're supposed to say to each other, all that stuff, just so's you know, Miss, what's passion an' what's just extravagance, so passion's when someone's real keen on something, he mightn't achieve it, an' it gets a bit like being half-crazy, whereas extravagance, or profligacy, that's like when you've got to have a thing even if it costs you your life, like love or smoking an' it goes together the same way as passion, except that extravagance is harmful, as Batista[2] writes, he's got things there you can't make sense of because he's so learned, an' she's a pharmacist an' she can't fathom why he keeps asking questions like some kid, so extravagance has unpleasant consequences, it's a sickness an' even the fittest among us can have nasty things happen, spread over three generations, though kids mightn't get it straight off, but the kids of the first ones, but the main thing people forget is it depends on the semen at intercourse, that they had their gobs wide open, it's no fault of mine that there's some people, some as don't get it, why they don't have kids, it's either because their semen's gone off, or it doesn't take, you might discover what's behind some freak of nature, or about roaring fertility, there's one woman in the book's had twenty-five sons an' another, even if they went at it hammer an' tongs, nothing would come of it, but even a man can be, as we say, a freak, not having his member the way it should be, needs two nice testicles an' one epididymis, but some only have one testicle an' there's some as die early, an' you too, if you study medicine, you'll also know what goes, but what Batista knew came from bitter experience, I'd love to see a photo of the man, he must have been a genius, no professor has ever gone one better than him, in his research an' writings, what's good for one an' harmful to another, one might take a ride on a filly with no ill effects, while another might get himself an ulcer on some beautiful mare, an' that's the point, knowing what's what, like in the army, when there were syphilis, no one were allowed out in public, like if a bloke went blind or deaf, they lopped it off, if the troops could control themselves an' not go after any old cow, they wouldn't get ulcers on their pricks, if it's not treated it's bad, an' even if it's treated it comes back again, an' a bird advertising for a husband, she'll put she's of pure character, but it's no good a bloke saying he's a virgin, anyone can say that, it's just not enough, so if a girl wants a husband, she'll have him examined by a specialist to make sure there's nothing wrong with him, but if he has it off with every woman in sight an' drinks a lot an' has had kids with four different women, then it does get a bit suspicious, there aren't that many ideal ones at all, it's like your Strauss or young Mozart an' some others, after something that hasn't been done before, an' they get so worked up about it till it gives them a headache, then there's folk that are far from dim, but the daftest of women can get one over on the cleverest of men, it weren't something she'd heard, she says, she just thought he were some stupid old geezer from the brewery, an' when I started to say something, they both shut up, but you'll be able to act out that difference of opinion, without any kind of rehearsal, don't get to thinking, young lady, that we'd have fine clothes to wear, anyone can, they're just for show, but being able to speak an' leave the stage refreshed an' undefeated, without rehearsals, if with a prompter, she gets the message, but when her feelings want to put it into words, not everyone can do it, we've still a way to go, the practice itself is an art an' an actor's gestures an' what he has to learn, the pretending, how to move, crying, laughing an' getting angry, Vlasta said it once, You're useless at gesture, she said, you're just a bloke from the brewery so you don't know anything, stupid cow, but knowing how to smile, move or weep with polish, knowing the right way to stand, an' do this or that with your hands, or just let them lie in your lap, an' there's some excitement, or tension you might say, then there's knowing how to express things with your hands, how and when to cross the stage or sit down, that's how an actor has to do things, an' not go about picking his nose, least of all when there's a bunch o' critics around, it takes a professional to get things right, like Jára Pospíšil,[3] Holzinger[4] or Voborský,[5] folk who do it all the time, ordinary folk don't have the knack, an' when some ordinary bod in costume opens his gob, it ain't the real thing, an' such throat experts don't get sent to war, an' when there's money you can get away with a lot, but if you're on your beam ends, girls are forever asking An' does he gamble? An' does he drink? An' is he a whoremonger? because won't that just lead to divorce an' fighting? it's all well an' good for you lot, you get to ask questions like that from a safe distance, but when other women start showing an interest, then you reach for axes an' knives, like that Šoupal guy at our place, she liked 'er tipple so he beat 'er up, that's when you get marital discord, he called 'er a whore an' a slag, an' so she wouldn't forget he dragged 'er down the corridor by 'er h'air, but if you bumped into them in the street, he were quite posh like, he'd come from nothing an' grown rich, but his wife drank like a fish so he were forever knocking the living daylights out of her, you bitch, you been at the bottle again, you reek o' booze, let me smell your breath, then bang an' wallop till her teeth flew out of her gob an' other such, then there's those who hang themselves, one or other of 'em, like that guy as lived behind the station an' used to steal from people's fields in the night an' he kept a cow an' did a bit of cobbling an' she were German, an' because she were useless in bed, he got so pissed off he went an' hanged himself from a cross-beam in the loft, then opposite there were this Chytil, his wife hawked fabrics an' sold shirts, but suddenly goodness knows what got into 'er, she started stealing an' the cops caught her an' all he could do was hang himself, an' that good-looking fellow Korec, worked for a health insurance company, he had a son studying in Olomouc an' he had his fingers in the till an' Doctor Karafiát, he was the auditor, an' people had been complaining about not getting their money, an' he had a goatee an' he comes into the insurance office an' says What's been going on here? an' that there'd been complaints about him not paying out, an' he said he had a son studying in Olomouc an' that he'd taken the money, Don't be daft, man, you can do what you like but you're going to court, an' he downed a litre of rum an' got hold of a scythe an' slashed his throat, an' there were a guy called Karásek, another waste of space, he were a foreman in a woollen weaving mill, fifty women they had working there an' the stuff used to get sent to Vienna, to a bloke called Goldschmied, horses' hair, from their tails, gets added to the worsted an' makes the loom go ratata-ritata, so he wet his finger an' caught one hair an' drew it across the shuttle, an' he put his foot down like in a car, jerked it an' broke the horse hair an' the thread, but he were a cheat an' ripped off the workers an' he charged a lot for his wares an' the Jewish fellow in Vienna asked where's however many metres it were of this or that gone?, clever fellow he were, college educated so his company didn't cheat people an' weren't going to collapse, an' the guy tells him I were destitute an' sold it off, so what did he do when he were tried an' found guilty, he went into the forest with a rope an' hanged himself, there's more to justice than what's said an' written down, no boss misses a thing, take Baťa,[6] the poor guy had plenty to worry about, thirty-six thousand employees he had an' knew every one of them, an' like when there were that tornado an' we needed to get some salami from Tóneček, so we went breaking rock an' while we were out rock-breaking by a wayside cross, the light started to fade an' suddenly there's this great black cloud, everything went dark an' there were a thundering wind fit to perish in, so we lay down in a ditch an' when we got home later, Mum says What have you been up to?, an' the forest where we were breaking rock, that were the one where Karásek hanged himself, an' that's a fact, an' as for stories of unhappy marriages, there were this Mařena at our place, a real cow, belly like a two-pint beer glass an' tits like pint pots an' they wanted me to marry her, I were seventeen an' hadn't a clue, but her brother said you're spending the night here today an' you can give Mařena a hand, ah, but there's nowhere for you to kip, so we lay down next to the stove up where the brewery workers' quarters were an' I made a sudden move in the night an' dished my nose against the leg, an' I did what I could but the bleeding wouldn't stop, so I went to soak it in the tub an' Are you crazy, man? In the night? What you been up to? We just turned over an' I banged my nose, So how about marrying my sister? I've no idea what I'll end up doing, she bought me a tie an' a gilt nickel ring, cost her twenty florins, but I didn't really fancy 'er so a guy called Jetrudka wooed an' won her, I'd never be able to keep her, he said, so I says to myself: You can keep her, mate, his mother chucked him out, an' the girl were called Jetruda, Gertrude, an' so she were his an' he were forever getting drunk an' they were destitute an' six kids they had, an' when the parents died of consumption, the parish shoved the kids onto various people an' half of them hanged themselves an' the other half were crazies, like he'd been, used to show off something rotten at dances, caused quite a stir, an' then she died of starvation anyway, the mayor can do that, loads o' kids, but he? kids crying from hunger, but to send them out begging, that's beneath his dignity, as for me, I were never short of a pretty girl or two, the Jewish girls, the postmaster's daughter at the post office, an' I went out with the sister of an embezzler an' she said we ought to think of him, so I started going out with the mayor's daughter an' Sloupský shot himself because she went wi' others, gorgeous she were, like Kamila, an' she often said: Come on, let's go for a walk round the cemetery, one evening when it were all silent, but I were agitated an' she were in a pretty white dress an' she kept calling, but I were busy right then, as soon as I get back, so she stood out there by the churchyard an' I dashed off to find her anyway in my best bib an' tucker an' she were like a queen an' she said, tenderly: Let's go up Birch Top, it's up in the hills, an' she sat down on a rock, An' what are you up to all the time, you're never around? an' I says how much work I've got on an' it's making me ill an' they run me ragged, an' she lays this sunshade thing down on a patch of grass an' lies down next to it an' I'm sitting there propped up on my elbow an' she bends her knickers an' hasn't got any legs on, no I mean the other way around, an' it drove me crazy, an' do you know my mum's very fond of you? she said, an' would you come round for dinner? but I said I were too busy, an' it were a sunny day, a sunny afternoon, glorious weather, an' we were lying there on the grass, Have you got a girlfriend? suppose we make a go of it? an' my balls were tingling an' I felt awful, an' her brother contracted syphilis, must have had it off with some gypsy girl, but he didn't give a damn, an' her other brother were in the dragoons, an' how did it happen? He'd spotted something, he were a miller an' he grabbed a revolver an' bang! there in the garden, he were a happy soul an' we used to go hunting together, an' he'd say: what d'you reckon, not a bad day today, but then he'd turn his thoughts to his wifie sitting at home, an' there were other girls, more, I'll show you the memorial, she were tired all the time an' used to say: I'm having trouble breathing, I can't wait to be here, as we passed by the cemetery, an' her dad would also have a go: Won't you come an' work for us? but I didn't know if I'd be any good at it, an' he weren't one to be messed about, an' she had two more brothers, hand-some guys like Soukup an' Novák, idiots the pair of 'em, but one embezzled an insurance company then shot himself, that's friendship for you, an' this other girl, she drowned herself, used to go around dressed all in velvet an' her hus-band, he were a drip, but she were as beautiful as the Dou-dová girl, a giant of a woman, though wi' more style, but given as 'ow she drank, they got their water from a well an' as she went to draw some, pissed as she were, she had a gid-dy turn an' fell in an' he didn't find her till next day, all swollen she were, an' there were this other crazy, Kalvoda, he used to kiss the ground, mad he were an' very religious, an' he hanged himself anyway, a big bloke, like Verner the baker, his wife an' daughter took his money an' squandered it whoring around, so he went to his mother's grave to shoot himself, but right now his name escapes me an' the priest had to re-consecrate the graveyard an' people used to crap there, an' if he'd shat himself there it still wouldn't have done

him any good, an' the company doctor at that law firm? –
a jewel of a wife, like our Líba, for seventeen years, while
still single, she came to us for milk, all the way from the
manor to our humble abode, an' she, Helena, said: Won't
you come round to our place for a while? an' I said: To do
what? an' it were true an' her mum came from the chateau
the other side of Přemyslovice, or whatever the dump's
called, belonged to a Bochner, it did, thirteen kids they had,
oh, I know, it were called Hlochov an' she were vast, like
Maria Theresa, a mammoth beast, weighed over a hundred-
weight an' a half an' she were filthy an' her husband the
lawyer, he were huge like Vaníček an' he were called Svatoň
an' he were German, an' he owned White Horse House,
where he had cows an' stables an' six black-an'-white dogs
an' he did his ploughing with four big greys an' the brutes
would follow him, an' so they got married an' had seven kids
an' my mum did for them when she were young, an' they all
became officers an' the oldest were an army RMO covered
in stars, velvet epaulettes with silk batting an' a sky-blue
coat, black trousers wi' red stripes, what's the world coming
to, dressed like convicts they are nowadays, my dad's coat
were pale blue, his trousers blood-red an' he had a helmet
on his head, a gold helmet an' a sabre, tall boots with spurs,
you can well imagine an army like that, the finest guards in
the world, when he came home on leave, the whole village
came out an' the girls were pissin' oil, that RMO, when he
were alive, he had two rows of gold buttons an' loads of gold
all round his collar on red silk batting, we're having it for
the play an' Verner's going to see to it, the gold stars are here

an' the stripes above an' below an' the wavy stripes of a medico, the whole collar tricked out in gold, the prettiest girl's going to crap herself when she sees it, an' the full rig an' discipline that must have made weakling soldiers desperate, an' they'd end up shooting one another the way they got bullied, an' they'd be flogged an' locked up an' made to get up at three, concentration camp's a doddle by comparison, an' he were so proud he didn't know what to say, an' he went to war like going for a walk with a girlfriend, educated, a doctor an' a soldier an' he got murdered, but he also had him beaten an' kicked an' he kicked him himself, down there, by Maribor, an' the dragoons were there an' the soldier were on leave, an' when he got back from seeing his mum, he'd got money with him an' his mate killed him an' poured spirits into his mouth, so the doc thought he'd been drunk on duty, an' he didn't see the dead man's mate, an' the man confessed an' got locked up an' hanged himself with his towel, an' they buried him at home with his mum an' his sister Helena put her arms round me when I came to pay my respects to the coffin, beautiful girl, an' his mother fainted an' she'd have gladly demolished the church an' paid in gold for him not to be buried discreetly, in the evening, in a remote spot an' without a priest, but money! – an' so all that velvet an' all that silver, because she paid fifty thousand crowns an' tore her hair out before all those people in the church an' lay against the coffin an' cried out Moric, Moric, what did you do? an' the priest sent for the cops an' they put her inside the vicarage an' locked her in 'cos even at the time people knew they were burying a suicide for money in a consecrated plot, an' that were a bit naughty, an' so the people might have killed her an' he, God's representative, shouldn't have allowed it, at the front they bury you like a hanky an' here they'll allow it for money, just like today, those millions again, an' people don't give a shit when there's no money around

It's okay, he can come, I said, I'd like to see him, an' right now, as if I hadn't been doing it, ha-ha-ha, since the age of ten, I were doing it again, sorting potatoes, chucking out the bad ones, picking the sprouts off, an' he says, quit that, man, an' come work at the brewery, an' right off they assigned me to some boilers an' filthy I were an' with a candle, an' it stank an' then the malting started an' the Director said Come, let me show you, but I said no, I know how to toss barley, an' I took it on an' got a pat on the back, an' girls started coming after me, do let us help you sweep up the grains at least, then along comes him, reeking of Cologne, a cigar an' all dolled up, an' What are you doing here? that broom has to be shaken out properly an' do you know how to unload coal? an' we go across to the coal truck an' he doesn't even know how to open it so I ups an' gives it a tap, an' there's all that coal at his feet, Christ, you could have killed me, an' by evening the ten-tonner were done an' in the past it had taken three blokes to offload, an' once it happened to be pay time an' I came into the office a total wreck an' they said: You done? you were snappy, an' all by yourself? but I were thirty-three an' scared o' no one, I'd taken the Římský course an' went to town on him, made mincemeat of his Adam's apple an' for good measure landed a knuckle sandwich between his eyes with keys, an' this lass said You couldn't get it up now, you're knackered, so I took her in my arms an' she giggled like a little kid an' begged, gosh, you're so strong, a pretty lass from Humpolec, a tall blonde, all silk an' silvery shoes, came to find me at the brewery because Karel Procházka an' me, we were drinking an' he owed me some, the director came up to our loft an' said There's some young lady looking for you! me? so I goes down an' sees this red sweater an' silk skirt an' the shoes, an' the guys gathered round an' gawped as she followed me to the men's quarters an' there she told me about it, in tears, but nothing to do wi' me, miss, all I had to drink were lemonade an' he's not here, but when he comes, I'll tell him, then she put a blanket across the window an' locked the door, an' the guys climbed a ladder to see what were going on, an' I handed her a quart glass of beer, an' then the blanket came down an' she sauntered off an' the Director came to me with Blimey, I like your taste, an' they congratulated me, but I didn't know her, except that she were from Humpolec, an' after I started seeing her, she had a name, Marie Klapková, an' the Director began keeping bees an' he put gloves an' a hood on an' set about fixing those little window things with the honey in an' they kept flying about but not a one did anything to him, because he had the back of his neck covered as well, an' anyway it's a shitty business with all the bother an' the cost, an' when they swarm, they fly up onto trees an' they form these big clumps an' little clumps an' the branches have to be sawn off an' set next to the hive, but the guy who owns the trees, he doesn't want it done, so they start scrapping an' the bees sting them, an' if they're out of reach they have to be hosed with water to bring 'em to their senses an' make 'em come back, an' that's dangerous, an' you must never be sweaty, an' Šišler now, he's a right sight, crazy he is, forever going on about bees not stinging their gaffer, but then he'll turn up again, eyes puffed so he can't even see an' he's totally depressed 'cos books tell him they're not supposed to attack him, he's got a little green hut there, with a little red window, it's like a dog kennel facing east, an' they fly about there, grazing on the trees, Anka turned up there, the one the guys had rogered in the lumber rooms, an' she thought I'd want to have her, but I didn't fancy her, when she took her stub-toed shoes off her legs were covered in lumps an' thick as bulging sacks, that must be something, then Kamila an' Líba have got lovely slim legs an' beautiful bodies that would make Batista himself rejoice, because that's a guarantee of marital bliss, as he wrote, an' when you get back from the bees, the manager said: So you're done now an' can go chasing skirts? but I said I didn't have any money, an' he said, well, my maltster lad, I'll lend you some, an' when I declined he said, all right, you can learn a bit more about beekeeping, we can help Mr Haňka move his hive, an' we carried the hive with great care, me being mindful of my childhood, an' the manager had his protective veil on an' gloves an' his neck covered as well, an' then I tripped over a brick an' from no higher than a quarter of a metre I dropped the hive an' we flew, fled, but to no avail, the bees havin' spotted us, an' they went for us, eyes or no eyes, an' they even got under the manager's coat an' Haňka were kneelin' there wringin' his hands at the bees an' beggin' 'em because 'e'd got a family, an' after it we were bein' treated in the shed, an' next day the Director gave us a bollockin', he'd rather give us our cards an' a kick up the arse instead of our pay, 'cos two of them had stung his prick, which were the size of a waterin' can, an' then I were knockin' about with Štěpánek an' Milota, goin' to bars, an' one barmaid asked where I'd been so long, an' how come I'd put on so much weight, but I didn't tell 'er that much 'cos I were forewarned havin' read that thing of Batista's, they're all ragtails, all these girls bein' treated for venereal disease, an' I were gonna rain on my own parade, were I? I wouldn't be able to get down to it, wouldn't have the right temperament, it's so debilitatin' for a man, he starts avoidin' women 'cos they're obnoxious, but a man who's fit? – he's cracklin' wi' electricity an' rarin' to go, an' Bobinka the barmaid at that sleazy joint said What are we having then, milord, an' I said, what are you offerin', I haven't got any money anyway, an' I asked 'er if she'd 'ad a wash, got a pitcher of water an' she 'ad to wash an' she put a silk dress on an' we chatted about dancin' an' singin', she had 'em play summat for me an' I 'ad to dance wi' her an' she lay down on a sofa, drew the curtain round it an' said, is this gonna work or not? I'd like to get married an' right now, an' here, an' let's do our weddin' night, lad, you've nothin' to fear wi' me, I'm clean, an' this other one came at us an' said Scram, bitch, this one's mine, an' she were raven-haired an' chased Bobinka away, said I'm Edita an' they tell me you've never been with a woman, right? an' I told 'er if I'd gone with all the ones who wanted me, I'd be dead long ago, an' the other side of the curtain the publican were arguin' with the blacksmith, they'd over-charged 'im for the room, an' the pretty girls refused to go wi' him so 'e'd taken the old bit of rough that never stopped powdering 'erself an' sent her back from the stairs to put more powder on, that Slovak girl from Hradiště, she'd stripped off an' it were cold upstairs, so she said let's go down an' be near the stove instead, an' there were a girl there called Jana, an' when I showed up, all the guys there were put out, old Švec 'ad got nowhere with her an' she voiced the opinion that there were a huge difference: you so full of beans, an' he just the booze an' cards, an' she all for singin' an' dancin' an' pure art, to this day the girls remember her an' they're scattered all over the republic, an' back then I'd get flowers even from people's daughters an' some real beauties an' they'd say, tell me, good sir, where did you learn that? an' Vít 'ad been a sailor an' played the drums an' cym-bals an' little Novák played the fiddle, he'd say let's play *Violeta* an' the girls would climb onto chairs an' clap me like the president, at the time it cost a crown to get in an' the bloke on the door said to forget it an' just go in, an' for half an hour they'd play for me an' wanted me to do *The Sultan's Wedding* until they were sweating buckets, I still think about those girls, there's that lady who were still single back then an' she's beautiful to this day whenever I bump into 'er, she danced wi' me so much that she still says 'ow beautiful it were, as if it were only yesterday, an' there are others, an' more, the wife o' the counsellor at Dočekals', an' her husband counselled her well, you'll tire yourself out an' be done in wi' that man, 'e's done for better ones than you, an' while we was dancing she asked, How d'you keep it up, I can hardly breathe, my peritoneum's getting clogged, an' I were utterly exhausted an' the hotelier, when he saw it, said come into the kitchen an' lay her down an' he offered me his hand an' his wife chimed in with What'll you 'ave to eat an' drink an' it were me who 'ad that solo played for you, an' Futurista[7] were also there an' 'e came into the kitchen an' gave me 'is hand an' the first thing 'e said were Autumn's here an' you're not in Prague yet? an' so I became famous an' then I sang wi' some lad playin' the accordion an' at the National House Járinek asked who it were that sang so well, an' no one wanted to compete with this guy of world renown an' the women screamed I should 'ave a go, an' they shook my 'and an' he helped me up on the stage an' said quietly Sit 'ere an' I said I couldn't an' he, still in a low voice, said why? – well I've only got a ticket to stand, anyway I did sing an' then it were all 'im, an' the women said That explains it, he's divorced, but what matters more is his art, the perfection of it, just being that good at it, That's the honest truth, said Dáša, we should make notes, it won't come to you just like that, then several times you could see 'er red as a calf with the effort, 'specially when Sprémo the director turned the heat up, though he were more of a poet, he were better at writing an' Miss Krušina kept looking round an' were keen to rehearse her own bit, get a move on will you, keep straight, an' she had to come in again through what would be the door an' we sang the waltz *Parting is oh so sweet*, last year she were sitting wi' us on the pump surround an' she asked When's the performance going to be? but she's moved to Hradec since, an' they had a cat from us, she'd said I want a tom an' she took that brindled teddy-bear of a specimen, an' then I went out with 'em, but old man Řepa didn't like that, 'e wanted me on the spot, All you do is go around gawpin' at women's legs! I says put that knife down before summat bad happens, 'cos if I jump you, you old buffer, I'll rip your insides out, an' he went on, wanted me to take 'is turn on night watch, an' I damn near did go for 'im an' they'd never 'ave scraped him up off the ground, there were that time when some blokes 'ad their knives out an' the girls wanted to run away an' tables got knocked over, an' I stood there with the girls an' someone shouted from the bar, you're a brave 'un, no wonder they all fancy you! an' I grabbed a chair an' there'd 'ave been four more dead if they'd come anywhere near, none too bright they were, half o' them would 'ave met their maker, all it'd 'ave taken were one knuckle sandwich between the eyes, an' if that didn't 'elp, then a Browning would, this standard bearer guy come up an' I floored him, on the parade ground they teach you to treat 'em like the enemy, an' 'e were expectin' arms right! arms left! an' only then a clean thrust, but I just bopped 'im a one-two on the chin, good thing the flagstaffs were un- furled, anyway the Bosnians brought 'im round an' I weren't gonna hang about in the face of the enemy, but right in there, straight into the flesh, an' the Bosnians were pretty good at that, they bayoneted one after another, an' if a hand grenade landed, they'd chuck it right back, an' there were one old boy, seventy 'e must've been, sittin' up in an oak tree an' firin' at us through the leaves, an' that old soak of a maltster Mertl did the same trick as old Řepa, got an advance from the office, then queued up for 'is full wages, holdin' 'is 'ead in 'is 'and, now then, Frank, if you want your full wages, you can't go askin' for advances, which is why people prefer to wait a week, 'e were always knocking back the hard stuff an' I used to fetch 'im some beer, an' 'e raped 'is own daughter, that's why the blokes didn't like him, wrecked 'er an' she died, partly of grief, then 'e drank twice as much an' went mad, 'eld his 'ead in 'is 'and an' kept jigglin' it till he died, an' Vykydal the tailor, brilliant tailor, 'e raped 'is daughter an' got five years in Mírov, 'e were a widower an' she did for 'im, an' 'e were drunk most of the time an' because 'e didn't 'ave a wife 'e did that to 'er an' she screamed, it being 'er first time, then she'd most likely have kept 'er trap shut an' bled till it stopped, but you know them interferin' women, they asked who an' she said my dad, it's a tale like from those days o' plague an' starvation in India, they murdered Ghandi at 'is prayers, they did, the idiots, all 'e wanted were for people to be a bit more pious an' love one another, an' 'e were carin' about India's independence, but then this anarchist shot 'im, 'e were the type that can't stand discipline an' 'e went on hunger strike for a fortnight, in short, in 'is cups a bloke turns to crime, not me though, if a girl won't give I can't be bothered wi' 'er, there's a skill to winnin' over a virgin, but a scrubber, she'll spread it for any old bloke, but a girl who's been brought up nice like, there's an art to that, those guys are all dead now, or they 'anged themselves from shame, then there were that one who came home drunk an' knocked Káča Rypová's daughter, 'is wife, down on the floor an' gave 'er a rogerin' wi' the kids lookin' on, an' us too, through the window, 'cos the buildin' contractor 'ad sent us to fetch 'im, so the man of promise may die an' the villain lives, she were only with 'im a year, an' we were out in Remanence[8] once an' she were there, she 'ad several marriage offers, but rather than chance it, she didn't respond, but she did like bein' held tight while dancin', an' when she were out an' about there were few people she liked, the guys at the brewery thought 'er weird, given she 'ad a fabulous figure, an' she did let me take 'er to the pictures, though she paid for 'er own ticket, an' it were a film with Štěpánek in it an' we were in the gods, we'd met on the bridge, she lived nearby wi' some other girl an' they're secretaries an' the other one's from Tábor, got the same talent as Božena Němcová,[9] a brilliant sense for such things an' never says much, she'd been to the dentist's an' the pair of them called across, come an' join us, an' we wound up at Měšťan's, you, young lady, are forever thinkin' about your trousseau, bein' ready in case you get married, but 'ow does it end? some even in divorce, but once you've married 'im it's your affair an' you can stop complaining, my old mum used to say, that's 'ow it goes, you love 'er, but you didn't really mean it when you told 'er so, an' I told 'er, if you didn't keep going on about doctors an' officers, so I didn't dare, but she did come to the woods with me, she 'ad 'er swimming things on, took 'er skirt off an' started askin' me about Jews murdering people, true, but only a few cases, only when they're after circumcisin' some girl, an' the scallywags draw the precious blood from 'er veins, that's them worshippin' Moses an' in the Moses way, 'ow 'e prayed for the liberation of 'is nation, there's that cord an' 'e puts a little black thing on 'is 'ead an' prays, it don't make sense, then a woman has to be worth her salt, I took that pledge when I was young, but she might say, what good would you be! and I have to protect myself, I couldn't fancy you, girl, but I could have it away with you, except I'm about to take up a short-time job so I have to go easy on myself, one just set the murder up an' the other beat her to death, slit her throat right across an' took her to that spot an' covered her over with mournful conifer branches, it were a real mess there an' the baby had spilled its potty an' he couldn't find a job, slept in a cubby hole where there weren't room to swing a cat, an' the Jew turned up sharpening his knife at the head of the bed, a machete, an' Adolf pops up an' what's up? – nothing, sleep on, and what were you sharpening that knife for? what did you have in mind? and he raised a hand to the Jew and he stopped sharpening the knife, my dad told me there was a Jew in Boskovice, Zeisen, who was going to employ a girl and he waited in the cellar with a rope and his missus found a pretext to get the girl down the cellar steps, but she punched the coachman in the mouth an' broke away from them, an' so naked, in nothing but her snow-white skin, she ran for the police, and they, having given her a good look-over, put some clothes on her and locked the Jews up and kicked their arses till they lost consciousness, or in Olomouc, Waterworks Lane, where the distillery and bleachery are, some girls went for a swim there and there was a Jew living nearby, a Nidrle or Vekrle or something like that, and one girl had been waiting there, waiting loyally for her friend, and when nothing happened, she raised hell and the cops came flying and found her in the cellar, and another lot were koshering poultry and a headless cockerel was spurting blood all over the ceiling and a grotesque shadow was dancing on the wall and the Jew waited knife in hand till it stopped dancing, it might strike someone that it's the fairy tale about Little Red Stocking, but that's how it is, and anyone eating bacon with a knife, well they'd rather throw it away, just like the Turks, who believe something similar and can't bring themselves to eat pork, but they dress in finery and have lots of perfume, all silk and velvet, and because our emperor was pals with the Turkish sultan 'cos of women, we had a Turkish doctor in the army an' he wore a black kaftan and a round cap on his head and helped the wounded out of Christian charity, the Poles, bastards, kept shouting *God's wounds*, *heart of Jesus*, how sick is that? – and my lady doctor put me down as a four and the staff doctor said, right, you son of the fatherland and nation, you're going back to civvy street, though there were patients with degrees there an' none o' them went home, couldn't, least of all in wartime, so they let 'em die instead, and who let you out, the cops asked me at home, the general himself! an' my dad also had a lot o' bother before they let him out, so much bother the whole time like with the five-year plan, you run out of some stuff or other after five years and people are penniless again, like under old Austria, when there was plenty of everything, but in those days people were backward and believed silly things, the Revivalists[10] chivvied things on a bit, but then it went back to sleep, an' it's not grown-up even today, even nowadays there's compulsion an' Catholics sing the praises of their earthly authorities an' the Pope in all his glory, like back when Bechyně the black-hatted Social Democrat[11] walked the earth teaching people that God's a mere spirit that can't be shut away in a box, but is inside the hearts of all good men, Havlíček[12] had started that, a natural scholar through an' through, he was, but they locked him up an' he got consumption because he cared about people an' could have been an archbishop, only his wife Julinka, Juliánka, understood him an' that all he wanted was the truth, but they brought him to grief an' madness, an' it were only after he died that they appreciated his stuff an' picked up on it, an' now his writings pass from generation unto generation, an' he didn't have enough to eat an' she hungered after truth an' they had a daughter an' she were called Naděžda,[13] my dad liked his stuff an' he got hold of the supplements with his picture in them, things like that don't come from a muttonhead! – he had charisma, black hair an' a black coat, but where does it all come from? – his brain's got an estimated value of several million an' it's in a museum, an' that comes from the folds in his grey matter, an' when a head's small an' doesn't have that many convolutions, it's a nutcase, Edison's another one, it's a gift from God, like my teacher Mr Vaníček used to say, an' who's to say if the Five Year Plan will do the trick, Nejedlý[14] himself said it'll take us twenty years to get over the catastrophe, an' all those millions an' nothing in the shops, an' if a farmer does raise something, they nick it off him or he eats it himself, an' loads of people are communist only in writing an' ranting, while a true one's supposed to work an' share things wi' others an' not just shoot his mouth off an' do nothin', if I did nothin' an' shot my mouth off, they'd tell me to get stuffed, in the old days folk drank more an' there were a brewery in every village, an' people also had enough to eat, if you buy a coffee an' add a bit more sugar, it's a treat, but if you add less, it's nothing, an' I wonder how much saccharine goes into beer these days? – an' if a guy gets totally pissed, he can't give his wife anything

There were no other like Římský, I didn't know him, but Adolf, he were a baker an' they got to know each other at the hostel where bakers gathered when they were out of a job, a northern Moravian from the 54th, green epaulettes, they're the ones that fought at Bakhmach,[15] an' no one dared say a word to him or even look his way, even soldiers an' cops had to make themselves scarce, they were no use anyway, you 'ad fifty people in a pub an' someone started something, an' he joined in, an' when it got sticky he used his revolver, smashed a table in two, knocked out the ceiling light an' reduced the furniture to matchwood an' four died in hospital an' the rest jumped out of the windows, the cops were just idlin' about along wi' some Prussian soldiers wi' their pointy helmets on, an' he still hadn't had enough, so he grabbed two blokes an' smashed their heads together, that's how strong the bugger were, an' in the cooler he

bashed the door in an' carved up the prison warders an' warrant officers, an' he filed through a hefty chain, an' before they knew where they were they'd been heaved outside along with the door, how could he do it? – an' one trollop that got in the way, the cops tryin' to make 'emselves scarce knocked her over, an' as Římský were kickin' at 'em 'e kicked her false leg, smashin' it in two, an' it were only when they sent for some troops an' the fire brigade an' they aimed their 'oses at 'is eyes that they got 'im an' the spirit went out of 'im, an' there were this other waste of space, a bloke called Benda, Wallachian, another baker, Adolf did his apprenticeship wi' 'im, an' once 'e said What? to 'im an' got what for an' blacked out, an' when they brought 'im round, the guy says Where I come from we say Pardon? an' in the end 'e drank too much an' almost froze to death, then 'e got 'is mother's dowry an' did all right out of it an' stayed on in the district, then that crowd from Přemyslovice, they were an even worse bunch, poachers the lot of 'em, an' when recruitin' started, they beat up all the Germans, including the mayor, an' hounded them into the brewery, an' one of them stuck a knife in the mayor's back as a reminder, a really edgy lot they were, give 'em one black look an' you 'ad your teeth come flyin' out of your arse, but fine figures o' men they were, 'ad their own bands, an' when the day they was to enlist came, it were all ribbons an' roses, all 'ung about wi' garlands they were, their boots gleaming an' wi' filthy great knives stuck down them, best to give 'em a wide berth so as not to wind up takin' your innards home in a bucket, I used to go there to see this girl, but she went an' married someone else, he had epilepsy an' he died, he'd fall down without warning, frothing at the mouth an' shaking all over, he hadn't told her at the outset that he had it, an' later she told me it was her fate an' that she'd rather have married me instead, she owned a thatched cottage an' a patch of garden, an' he, when he wasn't falling about, he used to make slippers, an' I were making thirty-six florins at the brewery an' he wouldn't make that much in six months, but he did go out boozing with his mate, there were a folk custom thereabouts that either blokes died on the way from the pub or they hanged themselves, an' several girls drowned 'emselves on our account, her dad, he went boozing with some guy called Trávníček, anything they earned they immediately drank away or lost at cards, good thing they played together, an' another that they weren't the suicidal type, then at the church annual fair young Karlíček, the priest an' a great-looking guy, used to pass his fags round an' he stopped by for a glass of water at my place on his way home from a meeting, an' here's a groat for you, laddie, handsome he was, very tall, an' he wore a gold pince-nez, an' Archbishop Khon[16] took 'im on because 'e were also a six-foot bastard wi' Jewish roots an' hair as white as flax an' a gold pince-nez an' that ring on is finger worth millions an' 'e reeked right royally of musk an' when 'e were out in 'is right royal carriage, the smell billowed out behind like behind a steam engine an' the old womenfolk wanted to kiss 'is 'and, but the canon pushed 'em away in case they left snot on 'is sleeve, though as for the young ladies from the manor an' the notary's pretty daughters, 'e kissed their hands 'imself, an' 'is footmen, every day they had different stockings, red trousers, red tailcoats wi' gold buttons an' braids, an' there were six of 'em, with two on hand each day, an' as they accompanied 'im to church they carried guns, an' he had lots of red silk an' a shirt an' a gold cross that were worth even more than the ring, an' a little cap on his head an' pretty shoes with gold buckles like some barmaid, a get-up fit for the theatre, an' next day he'd be all in white for a change, wi' plenty o' gold braid, an' at church time of a Sunday Trávníček would call out to my dad, Greetings, František, ain't seen you in ages, an' 'e looked like a gypsy, stripey jacket above the waist an' a cap, an' what'll you have to drink, me ol' mate? – whatever you fancy, an' they both fancied rye, an' it were flavoured with aniseed, so off they went to Fidler's bar for a litre, a tumbler the size of a tub, an' they poured it off into quarter glasses, looked like lamp chimneys, they did, an' 'e gave my dad the first one, an' when they were well-oiled, they'd both sing, beautifully, an' or-dered a liquorade to take away,[17] an' they'd go an' sit on the cemetery wall an' sing that song – *an' there I spied a huntsman wi' such a pretty lass* – an' the priest come out wi' a hanky the size of a napkin, an' 'e starts up, dammit man, Trávníček, what d'you think you're about, making that racket while there's a service on, off to the woods with you, or I'll have you locked up, by which time the local constable 'ad shown up in 'is Sunday best, the girls turned their noses up at 'im an' refused to talk to 'im, that's bad, it's bad enough when one of 'em says If you were married I wouldn't even be talk-in' to you, I'd never sit in a corner wi' a married man, not for a million, a chap 'as to be rock-solid an' not let things

176

get 'im down, one dame said, Lord knows what'll become of you, an' a girl can be from a poor family an' wear coarse linen dresses an' 'e become a director, the mayor were surprised an' didn't believe it anyway, it's the same everywhere even within the church, without a doctorate an' hard work there'd be no archbishop or Pope, but Trávníček had forgotten all that an' bought 'imself a stick of rock an' my dad, covered in filth an' pissed, came home an' my mum slapped 'im across the face, 'cos if you're fond of a drink you need something set by, otherwise it's madness, it gets into your brain an' there's no point, take Lojza Továrek, 'e went mad, that time we were on the square because of the re-paving, 'is son were up to no good, made babies wi' several girls an' then gave one of 'em a beating, an' then the kids of those kids were up to no good so 'e'd keep banging 'is 'ead, an' at first 'e used to hum *for god's sake Joseph! for God's sake Joseph!* then when 'is madness really took off 'e'd sing *all devils liberated, all devils exorcised*, an' having observed it over a period they stuck 'im in an institution, an' 'e'd been a clever bloke, sat with Bechyně on the town council, ran the local Sokol, an' it were such a waste, an' my uncle's daughter shot 'erself, never said much, she gave in to 'im at some point, 'e'd knock off anything in sight, an' she shot 'erself with the revolver they had hangin' there, an' my dad got locked up, 'cos it weren't allowed, an' we used to get meat an' bacon from the butcher's wife an' she 'ad a pretty sister, could 'ave been as pretty as the Glanc woman, she asked me over once to do some flailing, over beyond the square somewhere, an' we lay on our fronts together in the barn, an' before they married their surname was Klíč, daughters of that photographer an' conductor, an' she tickled my nose with an ear of grain, young, she was, eighteen or so, an' she asked Are you mates with Lojza? an' I said I was an' what of it? – well, the bitch would come to me through the window, an' then she'd receive the locksmith's son, an' her husband went into town to buy grain, but he knew that bonny lad came visitin', so he pretended to go an' sent his apprentice to spy, then he nipped back on a certainty an' gave the guy such a beltin' that he lay out in the street unconscious an' they couldn't bring him round an' had to send him to hospital, an' he gave her a beltin' too then married a wimpy blonde, but he died in jail anyway because the guy went deaf after the beating, an' my granddad an' great-granddad also liked a drink an' their places were a right mess an' for a time they worked for Baron Königsvater, the guy whose Jewish dad used to hawk tapes an' laces around the villages, but the emperor elevated him, so he lived in a manor house an' kept horses, an' he had white stables for 'em an' mirrors on the wall so the horses could see 'emselves an' think there were twice as many of 'em an' boost their appetites, an' his son for a change married an impoverished actress, which caused his old man to have a stroke, an' we used to get tan an' timber from there, an' we had to speak in German with him, an' he'd been batman to Archduke Eugen,[18] an' he'd served several famous *Deutschmeister*s,[19] it's an apostolic order that goes about in robes an' the sod were six foot tall an' handsome, an' another such were Prince Liechtenstein,[20] who held over a hundred estates, but joined some together to make ninety-nine to avoid paying tax an' he died of cancer of the genitals an' they fitted him with a tube, then the doctors cut it off an' replaced it with the tube, stupendously rich an' a real good-looker he was, but a poor beggar in that regard, an' the girl he told about things were wide-eyed an' completely dumbfounded, An' how do you know all that? – an' at the Plumlov estate the maid-of-all-work was washing the floor an' he came in from the forest looking like a gamekeeper, feather in hat, an' the maid yelled Christ, man, d'you have to traipse across the wet floor like that? – an' he begged her to forgive him an' then the steward showed up an' started berating her an' wanted her sacked, but Liechtenstein said no, the woman had been quite right, an' the archbishop, he were a right devil where women were concerned, had ladies he used to visit until the head forester shot an' injured him, an' he had one lad locked in the cellar for stealing cherries an' one baggage gnawed a hole in his back, so they kicked him off his throne an' he moved to Switzerland – call that an archbishop! – worse than a navvy an' that's why my dad didn't like him an' were always rowing with my mum, an' the girls around, their heads are full of daft ideas, like why I'm not married an' so when am I going to get married, but education, they've no head for that, chopped straw for brains, one'll say Oh, if only I could get married, I'd be a lady, an' another time she'll say Ah, I'm too scared, that's the fact of the matter, but Dáša's educated an' well-read an' she's constantly surprised at where I get all my knowledge about marriage an' existence from, for some people marriage means a lot, sort of legalised prostitution it is, as Mr

Batista's book says, then if he doesn't like her an' she doesn't like him, it amounts to nothing, but a pretty face an' a trim frame are the guarantee of marital bliss an' you, my lass, before you give your beloved your hand, get to know him, because in the home you'll get to know him at once, but at the dance hall not even after a year, an' he exhorts men to rein in their passion, a man can be married an' can easily get a girl on the side, but that costs money an' isn't to be recommended, because it can often lead to bloodshed, an' the worst in that regard are sultans, they've got lots of women an' each one is differently constituted, one can put up with a lot, another not, an' marriage is fine until infidelity creeps in, an' then if I get lucky with some pretty girl, I can't be certain an' nor can she, an' what's worse are the conditions that govern how we live, like Božena Němcová, clever woman, that, wrote all sorts of compositions and short stories an' she married a revenue officer an' was destitute, an' to survive they set up a rag an' bone shop an' then they lived better, but with just her art things hadn't been so good, though they did improve in the end, she were good-looking an' few could match her, where's the hope for a silly goose that hangs onto her mother's apron strings, what can she know about what a happy marriage is, not even popes an' kings had that much luck, relationships got pretty messy because of it or they'd murder each other according to how single-minded they were, an' if a man has the gift of the gab, things shape up quite differently, especially if she says Don't come near me, I'm a bag o' nerves today, he has to speak with feeling, to the best of his ability, an' girls get illusions about being everywhere an' doing everything the same as before they got married, it needs discipline to listen to each other, an' when the lying starts there's no way of knowing, a wedding, that's always easily done and dusted, the fun, the boozing, the music, but for a whole lifetime? – with some folks it goes as they want it to, all he thinks about is sleeping with her, good old Czech sex, but with the ideal couple there's a plan to be followed, but that can also fail, even when the greatest care is taken, if she gets the urge an' is all fired up an' excited an' then he yields, but there are exceptions in marriage where it's not love, but as it says in Mr Batista's book, a burst of passion or a passing fancy, when there are no kids, it doesn't matter much, but as soon as there are, that puts the kibosh on it an' he can't even go out an' buy underpants, an' if there are lots of kids an' they're going hungry, that's often when the shooting starts, I explained all that to her, an' she replied loftily, I couldn't have put it like that, so I tell her again, I see it all around, marriages where she says, Darling, you deserve a brick in the teeth, I'd gladly bash your head in with a hoe, or where he says, Sweetheart, you slut, you're a drunken slob, I'll split your kisser with a well-aimed hook, an' that's how marriage gets really odious an' ideals get a bit wobbly, there has to be constant equilibrium, but as soon as one side starts doing what it wants, that's it, he might just have a one-off with some other bird an' disaster strikes, or she goes an' tells someone an' makes a big deal of his sin, that's the big worry about marriage, an' Dáša came right out an' said I'd shoot him an' that'd be that, an' someone might say, marriage, okay you just give it a go, it's not like some barmaid who sticks her wotsit out for a hundred crowns, an' then doesn't even know she's had the guy an' that he's still around somewhere, it's rather gloomy, the quickie an' the forgetting, girls always ask Does he drink, an' Is he the boozy type, an' Is he a womaniser? – sure is, the old biddies will tell her, an' she takes it as gospel an' it's over, but once someone does nab something, a pretty woman, other guys soon come after her an' that takes the shine off intercourse, gloomily she said I know, you lot only like them unmarried an' young, but I jumped right in, an' no red-heads or not the wrong side of the menopause like you, an' there was that meeting on a train, and as soon as another passenger started talking to her, she sat away from him, an' in Prague she told me, old gasbag that she is, he were a right good-looker, like a horse trader, an' he got nowhere with her because he were married, but to me she said Dear oh dear, come an' sit next to me an' sing Balalaika an' go for top C, an' the old biddies just stared, a real fine lady an' me, an' she were afraid of soldiers, I'm scared of them, they're always drunk, but they'd have rogered her anyway before the ticket inspector arrived an' I couldn't have done anything, so for the sake of propriety I said, there's still me! – an' one boy an' a girl had locked themselves in the next compartment an' the guard hammered on the door an' they were having a right old ding-dong an' then they opened the door an' got arrested an' it caused an outrage, but they were blissfully happy an' said it didn't matter, we had a great time, and the guard and the station master could only envy them that bliss on the bench, but a case was made of it, or again, in Pardubice, I'd changed trains and a beautiful young lady came an' sat next to me, a beautiful coat across her arm with silk lining, an' she says Hold my coat for me, will you, I need to pop and get something an' she didn't come back, an' I was at a loss what to do with it, an' the train was headed for Nymburk an' she didn't show up again till Osek an' she took it from me an' said thank you an' nothing happened between us, then there was that time when it nearly did, while I was on military service, with the girl ticket collector, they wore peaked caps back then, pretty as a picture, like Miss Sýkora, an' I was leaving Steinbruck an' the dispatcher had said There's no stopping trains, take the express, I went an' stood on the end platform an' a door opens an' Say, soldier boy, come in here, but I says It's second class, Don't mind that, come in, an' I went an' stood by the window an' looked out onto the countryside an' she offered me an Egyptian cigarette, an' in comes this bloke, bearded an' with a pipe an' knapsack an' she tells him You belong in third, this is second class, and she asks me Are you single? And no girlfriend? How come? – an' I said I was going home from the front an' she rubbed knees with me an' that really turned me on, then someone else entered the compartment an' I hadn't the guts to face a ticking off for lewd behaviour, so I couldn't do anything but act the gentleman, then she said: When we reach Vienna, we can go out on the town, but at the Northern Line she just fluttered her hankie at me and that was the end of it, though I'd been lucky to get into conversation with a woman like that an' get given cigarettes, when in the army the women could be a real pain, especially the Polish ones, one was a teacher an' she climbed into my bed an' asked why I was so fidgety as I lay there naked an' tingling all over, an' the staff RMO came in an' roared at her, scram, get out of that bed, you slut, you trollop, an' so she just asked me what I'd like, cigarettes? – an' she brought me some an' she was quite happy-go-lucky, liked men better than food, girls in bars would tell me the same thing, Just like you men, they'd say, we also only think about people we like, otherwise it's just for money, an' she told me straight off, I wouldn't mind snacking on you, lad, an' old Švec overheard her an' he called the waiter over to pay, an' the cops said You've got what it takes, sir! – but priests now, damn 'em, they see fornication in everything, that's when one man uses more than one woman and vice versa, an' there's nothing anyone can do about it, Christ preferred drawing pictures in the sand, but it's just nature, when two see each other an' fancy each other, they get together, an' then how many priests have had plenty of women, and emperors and popes, and monks, given that the poor sods are supposed to be cut off from all that, here's a man an' here's a woman an' desire gums them together an' the village priest can blather away for all he's worth, an' when they get married, they don't love each other anymore an' Batista's advice is that they should be most particular about hygiene an' not go switching partners, so what's best is he one woman, she one man, an' that they be strong, otherwise there's no escaping infection, when she's having her period, that's the best time for getting infected an' spreading it far an' wide, an' it can be gonorrhoea an' syphilitic ulcers, blood poisoning an' diphtheria an' that's catastrophic, an' the doctors keep giving injections till it's over, or the bloke commits suicide, others might shoot or hang themselves even before they make it to hospital, an' to crown it all some folk even find it funny an' have a good laugh, but everyone has to look after their health an' be their own doctor

Knowing how to do things, what suits best, there's a weakness in every nation, so anyone, if you want to go somewhere, go, if you don't, don't, but then you're to blame for the consequences, in the army it's different, once you've been recruited, you have to do it and there's no gainsaying, at best you can have a good time an' make friends, because at any moment you can become deceased, and then May's the most wonderful time, and so we'd slacken off and enjoy the countryside and see some shows, which used to be banned, but those were different times, when rallies were broken up by troops or the cops, it got blamed on reactionaries alias imperialists, and then came unemployment while these days there aren't people enough, because they keep thinking up new things where previously it didn't matter a shit, now they're planting forests and factories until some committee decides the trees are dry or in a mess and so they have to be cut down again, and canals and fire stations and official buildings, in the past you had the pub and the patrons peed outside and the beer was tapped just inside the door, but now your pubs have high ceilings and concreted toilets and modern taprooms, no one bothered about that kind of thing in the past, but at least there was booze an' salami an' all that aplenty, while in today's pubs there's bugger all, an' if they do have something, it's rationed, only water's freely available, or they charge for it an' that takes all the taste away, an' there's more an' more people an' work likewise, in the past people were driven to suicide, they'd sleep on the floor an' had nothing to heat the house with, today everyone's got just enough, an' when they get married, they only get divorced again, though in the past it was seen as shameful, an' shopkeepers will still diddle you even today, when there were manoeuvres, the Emperor showed up with Albrecht,[21] that were his uncle, an' no one were allowed anywhere near in case someone killed him, an' he went about with two squadrons of dragoons, but when the archbishop came, the local priest drummed up all the veterans, an' the fire brigade an' the Orels[22] would turn out an' there'd be gun salutes, a great do all round, huge numbers, an' people didn't cause trouble an' they enjoyed it an' old biddies would gossip about it, then the Social Democrats started poking around an' caused dissent, an' people weren't used to it an' couldn't take it, the National Socialists[23] were rich an' sided with the People's Party an' there was one Sunday, then Corpus Christi an' mum went to church with Marie an' I made the soup, I didn't go, not interested, even then I knew it was all humbug, me being a regular reader of *Světozor*[24] an' novels, an' suddenly it went dark an' there was a thunderstorm an' time an' again the lightning conductor took a hit, an' the church tower an' one ball of lightning, kind of pale it was, ran down into the loft an' knocked the organist out, an' the old biddies took fright an' went to join the priest in the vestry, but nothing at all happened to the firemen outside even though they were standing by their appliances, an' the priest kicked the old biddies' arses for them an' cursed the verger for letting them in when he were wearing only a shift, an' panic broke out 'cos they thought the roof were caving in, an' as an altar boy was tugging away at the sanctus bell, he snapped the wire an' it came down an' hit people on the head, an' the old biddies was rolling about on the ground an' screaming an' the verger were having a quiet tipple, peppermint liqueur it were, nice, an' the priest looked round from the altar, asking the verger to pass him the censer 'cos its moment in the mass had arrived, then he had him add three teaspoons of incense to it an' then incensed the whole church with resin all the way from Africa somewhere – we should buy ourselves some an' make a little container with holes in an' a chain an' wave it about – an' the verger was already pissed when he arrived, an' where have you been? an' he thought it better to take the censer from the altar boy, an' when they went out to the vestry, he pulled a face an' said Where've you been? an' the boy said at catechism, I had to take the goat, then baff! so hard that the blood spurted from his mouth an' from the verger's, So where were you when it was divine service? Only outside, Don't you know you're supposed to be assisting me an' handing me the censer, you'd rather sit about drinking spirits? and baff! he punched him so hard with his knuckles that he were left rolling about on the ground an' that were the last time he crossed himself an' praised God an' he became the best ever

Social Democrat, so walloping your verger might not pay off, at the altar, during Mass, things have to be just right, it's not like letting a loom get on wi' its ra-ta-ta ri-ta-ta an' going off for a quick tipple an' then for a pee, but a verger, he has to be like a pharmacist, everything just so an' at the right moment, there's all kinds of crazy employments call for exactitude, Pávek, now, he were a dab hand at making suits an' he had to oversee fittings and take measurements, which he also did at Kafka's in Vienna, an' he had green trousers an' a gold medal on his company sign, an' a certain general ordered a light-blue coat from him, to be ready by Corpus Christi, with a gold collar, an' the collar didn't suit an' the general's missus turned up an' Pávek personally an' old man Kafka, a nervous type, especially being a purveyor to the court, that speaks of art, not just craft, he grabbed the general by the arse an' out they flew into the hallway an' you could hear the ranting, It's suited thousands before you, so it'll suit you too, I've never sweated so much as when I were apprenticed to Buriánek, good bloke, but he liked his tipple, when he could afford it he'd treat himself to a liquorade an' turn on his wife, Christ, bitch, who are you to stop me, I don't stop you puffing away on a porcelain pipeful of Dragoon baccy, an' I honed my skills with Lojza, an' the piping is said to be pegged an' the welt stitched, an' the white edges a hair's breadth, an' as to a fitting for the Emperor an' God I took those patent leather shoes to the party chairman, lacquered jemimas they were, wedgies, an' they hadn't to have any creases an' had to have welt ribs like bits of string, an' they were properly stitched an' with a fine edge, he said, delighted, Well, if your work's always going to look like this, you'll be able to apply for a job at the Jew's factory, an' the fellow you were apprenticed to – you can crap in 'is hands, they're no good for anything else, tell him as much again, an' the Jew, gold pince-nez, dressed to the nines and reeking of Cologne, walked about wi' 'is book in 'is hand an' smoking a Cuban, like when you get to university, everyone's handpicked, everything goes down in the book an' he keeps comin' up wi' new patterns an' I'd be on tenterhooks an' he asked did I train under Buriánek that I were so good at makin' shoes, boss, over here! was it really you made those shoes? an' they were all on edge 'cos they had a lot of botched jobs, and where d'you get the leather, I bought it, let's say you did, but you trained under a bungler, so how is it? and you didn't do a stint anywhere to gain experience and so how many dozen of these fancy shoes can you do for us? an' they gave me so much goatskin and calfskin that I saved half of it, tossed it on the floor, but mind you don't miss your train, an' they were all blokes who 'ad what it takes, Sokols and musicians, they'd made it to Vienna an' so had I an' they were my ideals, I even made shoes for Karafiát, he had a big, ginger dog with a tail like an elephant's trunk, an' there were this woman, eating white sausage at the annual fair an' the dog leapt at her an' tore her lip off along with the sausage an' he stitched her lip up an' paid for the sausage, but his sister now, she were a real beauty, beautiful an' ever so slim, she'd tell me, sit there young man till the doctor gets here, he sported a goatee an' a black hat with a black gutter dent like a photographer an' he were a good bloke generally, but a bit feeble an' small an' a patriot, an' the shoes cost twelve florins, it's like the bakery business is shoemaking, you slide the product gently into the oven, really gently using a peel, like when you're playing billiards, an' the oven has to be kept clean an' you mustn't wet your fingers wi' spit when your handlin' bread rolls, if the overseer catches you 'e'll belt you one, an' if you go for a pee you 'ave to wash your hands afterwards 'cos the stuff's for sale, an' eaten by the best people an' a baker might pick 'is nose so 'e 'as to 'ave 'ands like driven snow, wi' shoemak-in' though you can even scratch your arse, it doesn't matter, but a butcher, 'e 'as to be quite fussy, ours 'ad a bandaged finger an' when he were stuffin' some sausages 'e skewered 'is bandage inside one of 'em, an' who got it? an RMO, so they closed 'im down with a fine an' the doctor threw up into 'is plate an' beer glass an' regretted the butcher weren't a soldier, so it's worth thinkin' twice before embarkin' on such a trade, but shoemakin', it's like musical composition, an' that's why composers also call 'emselves professionals, but I preferred to go places, be out an' about in the city, there you could just buy yourself a bread roll an' wash it down wi' water an' pop into various shops sellin' speciality stuff, people like 'is type can be quite fussy about their feet, 'e couldn't stand creases in 'is shoes, an' another one might say he wanted Derbys, open-laced an' with a decent heel, an' another Parisian loafers, an' if you mess 'em up, it's the end, but if they're good, they're just as likely to say, okay, I'll pay you when I've got the cash, an' time flies an' you're as pale as a clout, like a clockmaker fixing the spring inside a clock, that's how a shoemaker works, shoemaking can bring you to an early grave, an' she tells me I thought she were looking out of the window at the time, plenty of girls are pretty footloose, an' I could've killed her and ripped her guts out if God hadn't made me such a nice person, an' you can be as careful as you like an' it can still go wrong, an' it's not like a bit of fabric you can undo an' start again, taking a hatchet to it isn't going to help an' the customer won't cough up, claims it's a botched job, it was meant to look great, but this is junk, an' it's the same with clothes, they have to fit an' not be like something your godmother wears, she lay down on a blanket at the edge of the wood an' said you keep lookin' at my legs, so tell me what you think o' them, well they're nice, but that matters a lot less than that they should stay straight and she shouldn't be flat-footed! an' she was pig-pleased that I liked them an' I could do anything I wanted with her, she was all fired up an' used loads of lipstick, but her father told her if I see you with your gob all made up like that I'll smash yer face in, an' then there are all those odd cases like the guy who divorced his wife because with no clothes on she was like a corpse because she didn't know that a well-built frame is the guarantee of marital bliss, an' so you, if you weren't so beautiful, I wouldn't even say hello to you, let alone go out with you, so you fancy me, she said, but I'm not so pretty as that other one, then she regretted admitting she was jealous an' would you credit it, along came an even more beautiful one on a bike an' she tinkled her bell and I jumped up, well, sir, what are you doing here? she asked me, an' the pair of them glowered at each other, the bitches, an' I were afraid they might start fighting over me or do each other an injury, after she'd gone my one said, right, but she can't cook as well as me, but blokes don't care as long as a bird's good-lookin', one promised her a car in exchange for her body, but does he have it written all over him that he's like that? then she went on about not having the gall even to talk to married men, but you're single, trusting you's something different, an' who cooks for you?, us, of course, an' she came back, well, well, so your nephew can also cook? an' she leaned across an' said Why didn't you come yesterday? but the gate were locked an' I could've been taken for a burglar, so she said don't be silly! you're so proper, so come again, won't you? an' some 'ookers told me, you're doin' okay, you're careful wi' yer money, money must be why you don't 'ave a girl, an' I asked them how much an' one said a hundred an' another that she wouldn't do it for less than forty, so I thought it better to say I didn't have any money on me, but Vlasta nabbed me an' said we could do it for love so I swore that even that was too much for me, but she could play the piano an' told me, Get away wi' you, hot shot, I trusted you an' was sure you'd marry me, an' I comforted her by sayin' I would marry her but only if I were a millionaire, an' she started moaning about me going to the Grand after this seventeen-year-old, an' I said nothing, because it were true, but then I stopped going because those bitches can make life hell, there's no shortage of blokes, but dead on their feet, an' the girls wanted only temperament an' good conversation, an' that's why they got all dolled up, white dress with a black belt, lots of gold an' jewels an' silvery shoes like the Pope an' a ring on each hand, a necklace, hair all got up in curls an' ringlets, their pimps ordered wine an' liqueurs, an' the other girl, Zdenka was her name an' from Prague an' The Harp, an' there were also some dragoons from Milovice an' she kept pouring drinks for herself an' me until she wet herself an' threw up towards midnight, an' I tripped an' fell in the lobby at Havrdas' tavern an' I made the mistake of lightin' up a cheroot an' the cops brought me back on a cart like a roll of lino, Zdenka Malíková was her name an' she said we'd share a bed together, an' the officers said they'd never seen one like her, she was the town's crowning glory, an' there was the thing that happened at the Kolářs' tavern when Olánek stood on a table an' peed in an arc into people's beers, but they just grinned, otherwise he'd have whacked 'em one, she was kissing me an' Olánek was going crazy, when it comes to that Mozart fellow, that's high-flown stuff, an' she tried to put me at ease, forget all that stuff, it's high art, but you can get one over on me in this place, I've no head for refinement, leave that to those wiser than me, but I once met Olánek at the pub he'd rented, he were different back then, an' we got into a scrap over the Moravian bird 'e were after an' who didn't want 'im 'cos she didn't find 'im at all pleasant, an' she 'ad a go at me, that I were no better, but I tried to defend myself, 'e was the one latchin' on to me though I weren't at all minded to be friends with 'im, so she mellowed an' said well, now we're alone, you can do stuff wi' me, but only so no one can tell, so I told her how the best things a nation has are its artists, we're too simple to understand how they composed things an' found names for them, my mum was educated but she had to admit her misgivings, it's all about ability, an' the most highly regarded she thought was li'l old Strauss, who were pals wi' Schrammel an' said, when they showed him Mozart's *Jupiter*, that he couldn't understand it, with such a dense mass of hooks above an' below the line, it churned his stomach as he turned it over in 'is mind day an' night, an' there was this guy, totally pissed, and he says, it's nothing!, so I got up an' asked, Waitress, has this gentleman paid?, an' Get out, you cretin, I know nothing about Suk, just those desires an' longings of 'is, an' the guy left, otherwise he'd have got a knuckle sandwich between the eyes, an' I kept telling her all that stuff an' explained that an overture is like a preamble, but the way musicians do it, then comes the theme an' two kinds of refrain, that's where a composition peaks, after that it's downhill, the instrumental motifs come at the start though you can't tell what's what, but that's why they've got different names so people know what's to be played on what, Řepa, great expert as 'e were, 'is sergeant clouted 'im over the head with a trumpet an' the bandmaster, Bruno, tells 'im, Idiot, can't you see 'e's supposed to pause? don't you ever do that again! an' 'e wanted me to play the two-string bass for him, an' he ran a music school in Krč, an' then there's the patience an' will-power needed to grasp the science behind it an' slave away at it, to become a virtuoso, that takes a lot of studying, it don't come easy, an' in America it's the Blacks that do the music an' we're left asking is that democracy? they treat 'em like dirt, but they're good enough for music, an' in this country it's the gypsies who play the fiddle an' they don't get to chair the local council or become ministers, an' one lot stole a picture of the Virgin Mary, an' when the local copper came, beard like Elijah's, an' asked where they'd hidden it, they said they hadn't got it, an' when the cops made a search an' found it under the bed, the Gypsy woman screamed But we pray to 'er, but the cops hit her, over an' over again, because a copper can't have any finer feelings like the Elector of Saxony, otherwise they're a right shower, travellers they are, an' they steal cash an' clothes an' they love the violin, that's the way of it, people shouldn't leave things open, an' there's even weirder cases, like when I went to file a report they said Blimey, but you've been killed in action, an' I insisted I hadn't been an' they should check the address, that it wasn't me, an' then they said it was Antonín who were killed in action, so I jumped for joy, there you 'ave it, I'm Josef, an' the brighter ones said, Idiot, you should've kept your trap shut, once you're down as killed in action, you should go off on leave, but what makes it like theatre is when they tip you cues, it's nothing, but there's no standing in for a tenor, there's that super voice, you're on stage an' no one's up to it, least of all when you've had no practice, so it's no go, an' who's to remember all the different tunes, *The Merry Widow* an' *The Gypsy Baron*, an' not get 'em all mixed up, then there's *Libuše*, *The Land of Smiles*,[25] they call for such experts as Járinek and Blachut,[26] the girl herself told me, true enough, you couldn't play that part, an' anyway why do people keep preaching at me? an' that's also why director Romanovski said that girls need no prompting

to hurl themselves at a tenor, and *Baron Munchhausen*, real gimmicks there, like the contrivance for firing him up to the Moon, an' the eunuch played by Kunrt, only someone good at bandying words can play him, but the Gypsy Baron's horse, he'd have to be dragged inside the theatre without the risk of breakin' its legs an' losin' the theatre money, unless they put rags round its hooves an' brought 'im in this way, the way people enter, an' not through them narrow gaps, that way it'd hurt itself, an' carefully so as not to damage the stairs, Šafránek gets all on edge, if it were a dog, it'd be easier, but a horse is a clumsy beast when it comes to stairs an' the stage is quite small, you come on with 'im an' he might even take fright at the orchestra an' fall into the pit an' smash up the piano an' kill someone, an' the musicians themselves could get nervous an' hit all the wrong notes, an' it could break its legs, *Miss Venus*[27] is so much better, no 'orse needed there, an' she's an angel an' they pull 'er up on a rope an' down below the guy, in his tie an' tails, sings *Beautiful Venus from a heavenly land*, it's an American thing, *my little golden angel, come closer to me, you are the rose and the scent of jasmine*, then the chorus girls do a tap-dance an' they've got ostrich feathers in their hair an' nothin' on but knickers, all the beauties of Nymburk could play the part, except Žanina, she'd just spoil it, hoppin' about like a shitty chicken, but Kamilka, she's got a sense for the exotic, she'd have to train the others, an' she were listening all agape an' gormless, if they pay thirty crowns a time an' there's two-three performances, there'd be plenty of fags an' rum even for the girls an' soloists, the rest can make do with black coffee, but nothing for the assistants, they're young, they can learn things, Talich[28] 'imself said practice makes perfect an' he sent me a message to come along, he needed a hundred actors from the conservatoire, an' Járinek, he's a fabulous singer, but he's useless at acting, Gleich[29] an' Blachut are so much better, they're cut out for it, like Maria Theresa, great figure of a woman, 200 kilos an' very demanding, no man good enough for 'er, a thin woman, not so hairy, she's got finer feelings than any pig, an' when she's about to give birth, they give 'er a caesarean, they have to slice her open like butchers slicing open a heifer, an' the nobility were perverted 'cos they could afford it an' they had a sense for art an' culture, except they'd really mastered the art of confusing folk by throne an' altar, an' Batista taught us that the sexual instinct awakens with maturity, an' though she's no beauty, he loves her, an' that's real love, but anyone who just seeks out women for their beauty, that's passion, an' she asked me What are you studying to be, an' I said I was an appraiser of pretty women, an' Batista deals with that in his writings as well, then there are freaks, those as can't give birth or have intercourse, there's the poor bloke with a sheep's pizzle for a penis, then there's faggots an' the odd dyke, they can't consort with a man so a pair of 'em crawl all over each other like monkeys, or there's people nobody wants, an' that has all sorts of nasty consequences, an' they invigorate their nerves, as Batista says, wi' all sorts of liquids like wine vinegar, an' they can't satisfy each other, 'cos she might 'ave only half a female organ, a proper female organ bein' one as can take five inches, an' a man's should be at least twelve centimetres long, then there's the elect among men, the ones they call one-ball-willies, but their kids are sickly an' don't live long, they've got no artistic faculty, others 'ave got sour semen an' mucus, it's supposed to be sweet an' can be tested in labs, you can tell what it's like under a microscope, those fertile filaments, but when there's just green matter, it's sterile an' women say it's no bloody use, then there's kidney problems an' gall, an' so some people are no earthly use, men like that end up workin' as brickies or navvies an' thinkin' about their stupid member, on the other hand there's those God's gifts, the ones whose heads fill with a thousand thoughts and their bodies are all a-tingle, like when a young man spots a beautiful girl

Lukas the garrison inspector didn't hit people, or dish out punishments, though Zelikowsky, he was a right bastard, had the men thrashed and tied to trees, especially officers, so they'd know how things were meant to be when he came along on his horse an' started dishing out commands, in German of course, an' the army was to spread out in extended order or close order an' then in a nifty double assault line an' columns of twos an' form squares an' then scatter like sparrows an' then they had to come together again, form a nice square, an' the battalion had a thousand men an' there were those orders left face an' right face, whatever the general took into his head, he'd raise his sabre, pointing it upwards, an' the officers were supposed to know what he meant, an' he could bellow at sixteen companies at once, that's a lot of people an' each an' every marshal had to know what was what, the main thing was to win without losing too many men an' tricking the enemy so he didn't know where the reserves were, an' at sentry outposts, they were the best men, all lance corporals, but a lot of them never came back, a man can be captured because of his own inattention, but drumhead courts martial recognise no such thing and will just shoot him, an' on patrol things are even worse, trying to discover the enemy's strength an' what guns he's got, an' how can you know what's there in the woods?, but it's better just to lie low an' listen out for a cough or a sneeze, for this job men were picked according to what their mugs said about them, an' some parts were open plains, but mostly it was small hills an' woodland an' more open country, no water, an' if there was, then pioneers had to be phoned for to fetch pontoons, an' a mound raked up in front of you is your best protection against bullets, the school of war protects folk by teaching them how to look after 'emselves, they draw it on a blackboard, first at the edge of a wood, an' on the first days after a clash there's also lessons an' the officers keep calling out *Zu mir*, an' if anyone wants to go an' take a pee, he has to report it an' be back right away, an' then we went on foot along a road an' there were lengths of rail laid out an' ammunition an' wire an' the injured, an' one guy wouldn't stop boozing an' he got diarrhoea an' shat in a ditch, an' along comes a brigade, that's two regiments, an' the colonel hopped off his horse and hit the guy across the back with his sabre, roaring *Schweinhund, Schweinhund*, an' as time progressed worse an' worse things came to pass, one man bayoneted another, or shot him, an' folk got so weak that they dropped, an' what if the enemy had got dug in, an' how agitated the officers got when a battle started an' a company of Cossack cavalry blew in then spread about all over, our machine guns were useless an' everything was on fire an' trees were getting blown right out of the ground, all down to their seven-pounders, an' when they turned an' fled it stopped, it was pointless to waste ammunition, the only girls were at the command cadre in Cracow and Przemyśl, where there were taverns, but women weren't allowed at the front, medical orderlies would carry the injured into the woods using horses, so they'd be under cover, any whores were inside houses, if the guys had money, an' there'd be a peep-hole in the door an' if you looked through it, she'd open the door an' ask What are *you* after, soldier boy?, but back then they were cheap, all they wanted was some bread, so only men from the field kitchen or officers could go for it, so our lieutenant advised us to chat up girls privately, an' if you buy her something sweet, you'll get her at the third go, there was one said to me Come now, soldier boy, give me some bread, but I said, Here you are, eat it, miss, an' at the station I'd check out the people, in case there were an enemy in disguise, big red rubber stamp, an' one fellow gave me the slip, so I went looking for him, an' I sees him entering the cemetery next to the station, so I says What's this about? an' Where's your ID?, right, you're coming with me! an' the guy went pale as organdie an' the cops gave him a good kicking for daring to go about Cracow with no ID, I went off to the gunpowder magazine instead, an' then to guard an old railway truck at Split, next to the sea, and the ecrasite used for blowing up bridges an' ships, looks like flypaper or some powder from the chemist's, an' I dropped a fag-end having nodded off, an' there was no messing with the Bosnians, they'd not think twice about bashing you over the head with their rifle butt the minute you budged, an' among the rocks at Monte Grappa[30] they really let us have it, an' we dashed about in the night, tongues hanging out, an' there were such loud echoes among the rocks an' so to help me through it I smoked cheroots soaked in saffron an' I had to be careful not to get my fingers yellow, so I gnawed away at them till they started bleeding, a chap has to be a bit wily, like trying to hoodwink a pretty girl, blow her away an' bend her to his will, like our old mayor used to say, for money, any idiot can do it, but for free! an' I always started by being a bit subtle, like my officer advised, much more likely to keep her on board than threatening her with your bayonet, at the start I didn't say much, just kept an eye on her likes and dislikes, until she started saying what she liked herself, then I picked my moment an' suddenly she said she liked wine, so I told her I didn't, so she said What do you like then?, an' I said I just loved pretty girls, an' she said that made me a lousy bastard an' she went to hit me over the head with a bottle, when I was at the artillery barracks in Olomouc[31] there were a place I used to go to get raspberry juice an' there was a pretty lass working there called Cilinka, Cílka for short, an' the chaps would take their accordion there an' without bidding she'd say Can I dance with you, sir?, an' we'd barely got half-way an' she said I'm a widow, Go tidy up, Cilinka, an' she said I just want a dance then we can get together, you're a great dancer, but I said I couldn't, I had to go back on duty, an' next day we were on a course an' the lieutenant was telling us about girls, someone knocked at the door an' in came Cílka the waitress to ask if I could leave, so I got a pass an' was quite flushed at the honour an' she stuffed a hundred cigarettes in my pocket an' asked could I go to the theatre that evening, an' I said I had to be back by nine, but the lieutenant said I could go an' we went to the Urania, it was some Jewish play up there on the upper square, where the Hotel Goliath is an' the place on the corner, that's the opera house an' inside it's just like Prague, the same lights, domes, seats, an' the walls painted grey, red stripes an' smooth concrete on the steps down, an' the play, it was about how this fellow didn't want to offer Christ a roof over his head an' how in the rain an' snow he had to go about with his pack on his back an' he had a weird name, Ahasver, an' during it she squeezed my hand an' kept kissing me an' asking Do you love me?, an' Would you marry me?, I'd love to get married but don't have anyone, but I said I wasn't available 'cos of the army an' the state of matrimony still had no appeal for me, so we parted on good terms, with me about to leave again, an' we made our farewells under the arches an' she gave me more cigarettes, Egyptian, for the road, an' in Germany I wooed an' won this stunner called Anna Hering an' I lived in their attic an' she used to come up to visit me, an' if she saw I had some mates in, she went back downstairs an' said to wait for her at the Waldteich, she dressed in white, just how I like it, a broad hat with a ribbon an' with a little veil thing dangling from her hat down her back, a layered tulle skirt, an' pretty little white shoes an' she went on about whether she fancied me an' whether I fancied her, an' a band of army veterans came past, playing in people's yards an' she had her arm in mine an' the Germans all gawped an' I was twenty with hair like a girl's I couldn't get a comb through, my suit with dark stripes a centimetre apart, a white panama hat with a black ribbon an' a stick with a nickel knob, like what was fashionable back then, an' as we said good-bye at the station she kissed me an' said Come back again an' she wrote pink billet-doux to me at home an' while I was there her mum would bring milk up to me in the attic an' my boss's missus would say, in her odd German dialect, That's a pretty girl, an' she also took a shine to me, but the men were all shagging her, wherever they could, guys like that don't care, an' the boss, he had a thing for waitresses, that's the sort of vermin he was, and I also went with Yugoslav girls, but they're a bit quick to reach for a knife, an' there's also been a Hungarian girl in my life, they're a passionate lot, great, an' this lovely stripped naked, a big girl she was, an' quite a hit, all she had left on was her headband, glittering there in her hair, breasts out here an' suddenly she says Coo-ee, I can speak Czech, an' Show me, Czech boy, what kind of a man you are, an' at another time an' place there were Poles an' they'll spread in an instant, but they included more scrubbers than the others, and Austrian girls, bitches most of them, an' not up to much in bed, but the prettiest one I saw was a colonel's daughter in a red dress, an' she asked me, Have you got any bread, soldier boy?, an' if you have, you can spend the night here, an' I said, If I had any, I'd let you have it because you're so pretty, I know how terrible hunger is, but you're so pretty an' pure, though I couldn't stay anyway 'cos I need to find my post an' they're waiting for me there an' she turned an' all awkward said Mummy, this soldier boy's got such lovely blue eyes, an' there was that time when some Slovenian girls were sweeping the road an' having a good old moan, You can have anything you want, soldier boy, just give us some bread, an' I told them we'd won, we'd got the whole of Italy, including the Pope, an' prettiest of all were the nurses at Kolín, they'd all been teachers an' office workers, an' there they were, coming in to take my temperature an' they had white caps, white outfits and coats like the ladies in pharmacies, an' one said Which of these guys do you fancy, an' the other one said If I had to choose, then that one over there, an' that was me, after which she always came to see me an' brought me cigarettes an' the others nothing, an' she'd be back at four an' in the meantime I'd check what would be best, thought probably *Balalaika*,[32] it being so full of bright costumes an' real popular with men an' the general public, an' Járinek[33] was in it, with Kraus[34] an' Holzinger[35] as guards officers an' in among them were these dancing girls in tiny skirts an' Kraus was in the middle an' suddenly he claps his hands, that's what he does, an' *nichevo, nichevo* an' out comes the Tauber woman,[36] I've come to bid farewell, old girl, an' where are you going? where are you going? to St Peepeepeepetersburg, that's how good they are with words, an' you're going away an' leaving me with the kid? an' who'll get your money?, I'm keeping it, an' there's so many doors with peepholes in them there, blimey, it's beautiful, wonderful material, an' suddenly out comes Járinek an' he's got a balalaika, it's a like a mandolin, an' I've kissed so many beautiful women for God's placed true love in the heart of one who's loved Him, an' sing, balalaika, that sweetest song of mine,[37] an' he's under a purple light an' she comes an' asks him What is it, a balalaika?, an' he says You're a *kalamajka*[38] an' they clink glasses an' he chucks the glass, which might break, but the time may come that'll bring me someone who might give me their love, an' at the end that high C, none of the Hlahol crowd[39] or that Hálek[40] shower can get anywhere near it, they caterwaul like a cow giving birth, an' it was the czarina's wedding an' she was all made up to look good, an' a priest was at the wedding, an' that's why every actor has to have read and learned the play, that's the real knowledge, an' then there's the dancers' pace an' Holzinger wearing trousers with side stripes an' he's got a goblet in his hand an' he gives each of the chorus girls his blessing, like a parish priest, that'd please the Russians if we put it on for them, an' we need to have at least fifty people on stage for all the dancing and drum-banging an' other stuff, up to the grand finale when they shoot the chandelier down an' nothing happens to him, Járinek that is, an' that's what it's about, an' there's divorces, an' then they start another tune to keep the audience happy, an' the musicians have to know what, an' the chief ballerina'll be Kamilka an' Járinek's part will be played by Ruda, a first lieutenant in the army, larynx like a bull, an' Kamilka'll be

in a green dress with gold moths on it, she had pleurisy an'
not even doctors from New York could help, an' some folk
find that funny, an' that's art for you, for a time no one was
a patch on the Smolíková woman, she could bring her leg
up onto her shoulder from behind, an' that's why there's so
few of them, true artists, there's one kicks the bucket every
minute, or Christ, hungry an' a fisherman, the pharmacist's
eyes popped out of his head when I sang Dalibor with his
wife, she likes a laugh an' wanted to be noticed an' me to
teach her the splits, but I told her she'd give herself a hernia
an' have to wear a hernia belt, an' that's no joke for a bloke
when he feels a hernia belt on a woman's body, it's all nickel, an' cold, even freezing cold, it works if you're supple an'
have trained a lot, an' so Christ, otherwise known as Jesus,
did things that no one before him ever had, baptised Jew
that he was, sought the same justice as Gandhi, so there'd
be less lechery an' thievery in the world, an' for that he had
to suffer, John Huss was another as let himself get burnt at
the stake from sheer stubbornness, an' they wanted to booze
to their heart's content an' after that wedding Christ changed
the wine into water, prankster an' magician that he was, an'
for those who didn't believe in him he changed water into
wine, life was the same filthy mess back then as it is today,
even Caruso overdid it an' they gave him a silver tube to
drain the fluid an' all he could do was write out scores by
hand, but after that he only listened to singing on records,
as soon as he woke up he'd start writing, because the best
dreams come towards morning, but when you've been up
for a long time, you can't put them together, an' you mustn't

touch the ground much, because of the magnetism, an' old wives think that being creative is as easy as blowing your nose, so, get up there, you shitty old harridan, and sing, an' so we spent ages chatting about the Baron an' no one felt up to it, just me, 'cos just like the Indians I was preordained to get epilepsy, that knack they had for knowing where there's water, these days it'd be worth being an epileptic, an' those fakirs who plant a tree an' after an hour it's grown several metres tall like some illusion, brilliant trick, or walking the high wire, like that Chinaman could, an' he parachuted down with an umbrella, best acrobat in the world, no one's ever matched him since, or the Mexicans on their dapple-grey horses, but Christ, known as Jesus, he was fanatical about justice an' he grabbed a bullwhip an' lashed out left, right an' centre an' kicked people down steps an' he could fight easily as well as my mates Benda or Římský, an' they ran away 'cos in his house of prayer they had a cattle market an' taught that everyone should be true colleagues with their mates, an' they jingled their cash an' the cattle lowed, Římský didn't like unfairness either, the lieutenant didn't know him an' when he came to our company he were a right bastard dishing out punishments to everyone and roaring 'Tention! an' Římský was still fidgeting so the lieutenant flew across an' gave him a shove an' that was Římský's moment an' he grabbed the guy's sabre an' smashed it in two an' he walloped him one an' that was the end of him, an' the officers scarpered an' the ranks were jubilant, an' that's how thankless the world is an' people so different in nature, one's a doctor an' another does gardens or cleans bogs, back then another was a drunkard an' his wife played the whore by lying down in a ditch an' when some soldiers came past she'd call out if anyone wanted it they could have it, but she was so ugly that nobody bothered, an' others might shoot themselves or each other over some eyeful, an' there was one who let fifteen Russians have it one after another on the island till her thingy was like a squidgy bun an' then she made a habit of going to the Žofín,[41] where there's that House of Culture of the communists, an' she could sing like a pro, an' since the beginning of time half of all women are slags an' the other half are headed that way, yet some are quite refined an' haven't forgotten their education, but that kind have generally died young an' grief-stricken, or for love of Christ they don't marry, one said to me, Come, will you, an' hold him for me, an' I held him an' she straightened his bed for him, though these days I wouldn't be bothered with the guy, an' in the field hospital I was attended even by baronesses an' today it's all harlots, an' when I was there with a hernia the doctors came and with them this blonde an' they asked me, Do you still dance, sir?, an' I said, What does the young lady do?, an' they said We'll send her to you, she's bound to remember you, an' even at that age I made out to her I was an officer in the guards an' if I'd trained from childhood, today I'd have got myself in the papers, just like Christ also trained from childhood to be a doctor an' jurist an' magician, if he hadn't been, they'd never have recognised him as God, an' freethinkers hold it against the church that if he really was God, how come he consorted with a fallen woman, but he'd only been giving her a lesson in sexual health, like Batista, an' she, Mary Magdalene, though originally a scrubber, finally made it to sainthood an' she wiped his blood on the Cross with her hair an' she didn't betray him an' he, crucified, talked to her, he being of royal blood, his mother Mary 'ad him with some king an' Josef agreed to take him in an' give him an upbringing, he helped with the carpentering an' sawed planks an' beams an' knew how everything fitted together an' he only became famous later, our parish priest gave me a prize for knowing the catechism, a picture of Christ our Lord holding a chalice, red cape hemmed in gold, but the other lads only got a clip round the ear because they said that Holy Trinity was the sister of the Virgin Mary, we had to know all this stuff, who's the Father an' the Son' an' the Dove, that's pure spirit, so there's probably only one God, an' as for church services, they were bullshit too hard to understand an' because she didn't, one girl was sat by a priest with her bare arse on a stove an' for that he was sent to a monastery, her surname was Ulmanová an' there was a great hoo-ha over it, an' those girls stayed on the shelf till they died, no one wanted them 'cos they didn't know what the Holy Trinity was an' in their old age they grew sunflowers two metres tall an' with golden discs, an' so singers an' Smetana himself died of consumption or they have strokes from all the effort they put in, his work was endless, but ordinary folk are more given to loafing' about, playing cards or knockin' off birds, people like him think only of their honour, or take Ištván, who travelled all over an' listened to music an' said there's a lot of music in the air, but that he couldn't capture it, that's how he'd fantasise, an' that woman who fired a revolver, good-looking piece, but jealous, that's just the lot of composers, and the seamstresses from Picks' would call out to me Nice to see you, sir, and when will you be singing again and when will you swim under the boat again, like that time years back or when you jumped fully clothed an' with all the money into the Elbe an' almost drowned Jarmilka? they don't make 'em like that anymore, no Strauss or Kmoch,[42] no Smetana even, poor victim of a stupid nation as didn't understand 'im, especially 'is refrains an' pauses, 'cos most folk are idiots an' nothing's ever right for them, but when there's a war on an' they get stuck in concentration camps, then they start whinin' an' turn in on themselves more, but otherwise their main concern's findin' enough to eat, an' Comenius himself said that every school should have a cane an' we also had a hard time of it, like being forever up before a jury or beneath a scaffold, an' our teacher would bash our heads on the blackboard an' slash us across the snout with his cane an' the priest[43] a rotten bastard like Hitler, always caning us an' keeping us in after school, walked about bolt upright, he did, bowler in summer an' Cossack hat in winter, that were discipline Austrian style, an' then geometry an' what equals what till your brain started to creak, an' refracting rays that's to say physics, so I used to go off into the fields to study an' Jewish ladies used to be out there waiting for a star to rise, an' the Slovaks boozed non-stop, before one o' them went to church, he'd have a nip of something an' they really were bothersome, 'specially when there were a wedding an' they came trotting into the church with their accordion an' a supply of spirits an' tried to get the saints to join them in a dram, but the village priest, big guy with a nasty temper, he'd scream at them, Tatar trash, savage pigs, is that the way to enter the house of God?, beat it an' the wedding's off till tomorrow, an' he'd holler at the verger as well till he were totally brainfarted, you filching, boozy good-for-nothing, clear off home, I won't have you vergering any more 'cos you nick my plums in the graveyard an' guzzle the communion wine, but when the dancing started, it was all ribbons an' fisticuffs an' stabbings, that's their thing, on horseback from first thing, an' I used to dance with the bride in the middle of a circle, women queued up to dance wi' me, accused me of avoiding 'em an' they plied me wi' drinks, but at home, up in the hills, they were all ragtag an' riffraff, tended to die o' consumption an' decrepitude, the odd one might hang himself, but the best thing used to be when me and the mayor rode out wi' flags the day of the village pageant an' the forest were all hung about wi' flags an' the best sokols put on a show an' Karafiát gave a speech an' I'd be there with the Hudec girls an' one of 'em were mad about my dad an' both girls were real beauties, one became carnival queen an' her brother were a major in the sappers, giant of a fellow, but his brother were an idiot an' acted as his dogsbody, an' his father were a drunk an' served at Šibenik in Croatia, an' when he came home he'd got typhus an' he were oozing blood an' slept in an outhouse, it's infectious an' his mother packed him off to hospital in Olomouc an' the place had to be disinfected, an' he died there, an' when I went to see him he were already buried an' the gravedigger couldn't find him, didn't know where he was anymore, so he looked in his book an' found him somewhere over by the wall an' his mother said he were better off like that, he'd only ever been an embarrassment, an' so we went back home on foot an' we didn't eat an' we were sorry we hadn't seen him at least deceased, an' it was baking hot, it having happened in August, an' so I did a spell as a maltster on a hundred florins a month an' I came home wi' money an' clothes an' new underwear an' a fancy modern hat, Wow, look at him!, an' Where've you been all this time?, anyone else coming home from the wide, wide world looked as if a cow'd been munching on him, an' I cleared my debts an' we bought a cow from Ponikev, over by Prostějov, a Simmental, but white with like a blanket across her back, pretty horns she had, a real fine specimen, cost a hundred florins, but then we sold her to the butcher because she were barren, but the work, like in a prison camp, up day an' night on twelve-hour shifts, an' folk were worn to a shred an' died o' pneumonia, four thousand truckloads an' some exported as far as America, back then people didn't go on day trips much, just to the fields and forests, helping out on building sites or at sawmills an' lime works, hard graft for next to no reward, but at the maltings I slept in the warm an' there were shops everywhere an' trams an' I never once thought of home, just smoked the odd cheroot an' grew fat as a pig an' our uncle? that's a long story, he did better than any of us, started out barefoot an' carried his school books in a wicker basket, but in the army he made it to platoon sergeant an' he had beautiful handwriting, got a gold cross from the Emperor, honour where honour's due, an' gold braid an' a pickelhaube, metre eighty-five he was an' always up for a scrap, once heaved a whole pubful into the village pond, but that was only when he were single an' as a recruit, but once he got married, he were quite serious, married the daughter of a head forester an' built himself a house in Wallachia[44] an' kept thirty turkeys, the following year they wanted to make me platoon sergeant, but I didn't want it, the first lieutenant called me a malingerer, said there were nothing wrong wi' me, but he sent me off on leave, that's how well they thought of me, an' I spent some time with five different regiments, but as an instructor, never on guard duty, I just led the guards out then sat the watch out in the guardroom, I used to carry Majors Michochović an' Toner's sabres an' Captain Liška shouted to me to hurry up an' get moving so as not to miss my train, an' I didn't pay an' I idolised no one yet no one ever got the better of me, so many officers fell, but I marched on trusting and fearless, an' when I was on duty as guard commander, the general bowed to me, they don't give the job to idiots, an' the general's wife would ask, Soldier boy, have you got enough cigarettes? an' she tossed me some, but I couldn't pick them up 'cos some officers were passing, but after they'd gone I made a loop in a piece of string an' hooked them up, an' the general's wife asked the NCO when I'd be back on duty, an' one bastard of a general, Adamstal he was called, ugly as sin, face like a bandit, lashed out at anyone and everyone, 'specially at inspections, an' though I was careful he shouted at me anyway, an' when I told Dáša she was surprised at all the blood an' that I'd been rolling around, an' that the officers liked me because I was clean-shaven an' pinched at the waist like some maiden, polished belt like a cadet I had, 'specially when they went out looking for girls an' took me with them, an' when we were trying to seize some hill the captain withdrew his sabre an' yelled Hurraaah an' the Russians threw down their arms an' cried Austriaman, spare me! what a lark, the lads would say as they came back under cover, an' whatever I captured an' confiscated I passed on to the officers an' they'd give me cigarettes an' the other first lieutenant, his name was Kotýl, he said, How about a song, lads, *A farmer was taking his flour to the mill*, an' one rowdy started playing the accordion *An' every girl will let you have it, whoopee-yippee, whoopee-yippee*, an' he said I like it, the army, but not the bloody shitbag Poles, an' I reported Sir! an' he came back Quiet! you're exhausted, mind you don't trip, a real jokester he was, an' he gave me pastries, biscuits, an' next day Captain Kerner, another big fellow, said Fetch my horse an' I jumped on it an' he roared Forward march, About turn, an' we had to sing *Wieder Heimat* an' he tinkled his cane on his jackboots an' some girls were coming out of church, he shouted to leave the girls alone, but the girls thought it wiser to make a detour through the fields an' the generals were in their cars at the rear, Manteuffel[45] an' Herr von Roseneck,[46] in those days they had golden pickelhaubes with eagles on, not like today's upturned pisspots an' the first ones to attack Russia were Dankl[47] an' Auffenberg,[48] a right pair of pince-nez those two, an' the commander-in-chief was Conrad Hötzendorf,[49] an old guy, but good-looking an' he stood erect, his son fell at Horodenka,[50] in the marshes, just like our Ludvík did, he was an archduke,[51] meaning he was part of the imperial royal family, had a lamb round his neck, except the emperor had it head up while his was head down, an' the discipline, the platoon commander would yell You scruff! an' just for an untidy bed, but at the front they were okay, they didn't badger us 'cos they knew we'd shoot 'em, an' during an attack they paid us no attention at all, one turned white as a sheet at the sight of a bayonet, but I was rock-solid an' filled with heroism an' could stand up to as many as four enemy soldiers at a time, but how?, you hid behind a tree or bank an' picked 'em off one by one, they'd taught the Russians the same thing, so we lay in hiding opposite each other an' only idiots poked their 'eads up, If I fall, the platoon commander said, you take charge, an' I said Couldn't someone else do it?, I'd rather make a run for it, they're a useless bunch an' unreliable, but the NCO said, You've been lying here a long time, aren't you getting cramped? an' one guy wasn't watching what he was about an' copped it an' he just screamed Aargh-aargh-aargh…, it's quite a relief to get back to life, an' I don't want to go through anything so God-awful ever again

The main thing is that life is so nice and beautiful, the old dear said, Isn't your son thinking of getting wed, now the war's over an' peace all around an' all those girls, That idle bugger?, he couldn't be bothered to look after someone else, that's the fact of the matter, he's the kind most likely to end like that, one in the head, like Pushkin, an' that was the end of him an' his poems oozed out of his head an' I often wept for the ones I'd never read but merely thought, guessed at them from his mug an' his fabulous sideburns, like the Emperor when he was a kid, when he also did the odd painting, an' we said we'd also write the odd poem an' send it to Kamila, just a short one an' not up to much, an' flowers as well, till she asked if they'd be roses an' if I'd be giving her a nosegay out of love for her, she was pushing her bike along by the Elbe an' in the garden I told her out of the blue, I don't want to hold you up, an' I kissed her an' she said God, what are you doing, an' I said I really wasn't God, just a man, an' she laughed an' I was master of the situation an' so like a sucker I did take her some roses I'd picked in the night, an' the Mexicans an' Spaniards, they love singing in the night 'cos they're an idle bunch, only interested in horses an' spying on women an' playing the guitar an' chasing girls, an' Blanka, despite being so pretty, wanted to spend the evening with me, to see how it went, an' we sang songs an' larked about, even worse than what goes on in bars, an' she liked it when I danced solo in my underpants, then the girls made a right mess puking in the toilets, all those spirits an' wine, an' drunk out o' them large goblet things, no surprise then that in the toilets they'd tell me, Don't get married, man, an' do you need a pee?, an' they'd go to take my member out, or genitalia as Batista calls it, an' I'd say Do whatever the hell you like, an' the main thing in the world is understanding, there was one girl all sorts of riffraff came after, but I was the only one permitted to watch her take off her shoes and stockings, then she'd ask

What do you think of my legs? an' when we was alone, she'd lie down on the sofa an' say Come an' lie down, an' she were always laughing an' she'd ask Are you getting tingly yet, old man?, I wonder, what would Batista have to say about that?, an' I said Woah, isn't the mistress due, but she said Count your blessings, silly boy, that she ain't here yet, an' she'd writhe about on the sofa, so I stroked her legs, she'd a' been a pushover, just gaggin' for it she were, but it made me nervous, if it'd been outside, well maybe, but then she said When it's nice, we'll go to Eden, she was unpicking her blouse an' cut herself with the razor an' said Quick, bandage me up before I get blood poisoning, an' as I were bindin' her finger tight she said Pity I'm not as pretty as the other one, an' I cheered her up by saying she 'ad other charms, You're slim an' you've got gorgeous legs, I don't like ones wi' big bellies or calves like sacks, but she interrupted me, You keep saying you love me, but you haven't shown it yet, so I knew it was serious, which is why I said You'll keep going till some widower marries you, an' then we took the washing to the mangle an' on the way back we picked up some beer, declaring one's love isn't easy, some just bawl you out as a total idiot, or there was one I went out with one evening an' she broke into a run shouting I'm a wild one, you should try an' tame me a bit, an' I replied This is better than if you were more on the meek side, an' another time they came an' sat down an' What did you have for lunch? I asked, an' What'll your dress be like? an' eventually we got onto men, one havin' taken her fancy, it calls for some real gimmicks, bein' on your guard like a copper once a girl gets the itch, older ladies advised me, save your breath an' head for the woods, but you still 'ave to stay in control once you're aroused, those thousands of infatuated ideas, Marie had a septic womb an' appendix, so they cut 'er open, the letter's on the table, she'd been moanin' about it a year before, an' the doc told me You'll have to have an operation, old man, won't you make provision?, an' you, nurse, hurry up, we don't want 'im to die on us, 'e 'ad a mask on, you know, that white cap thing, an' suddenly there's this woman, askin' where her husband was, so the consultant grabbed 'er an' Scram, woman, an' he booted 'er up the backside to make 'er keep away from the theatre, it's the toughest job, messin' about wi' blood an' guts an' watchin' the clock an' stitchin' a bloke up again, an' with earphones in the whole time, an' people heal at different rates, but a jailbird couldn't care less, if it's been arranged through the court, they place 'im in the doctors' hands, but when it comes to you, they can only set about you once you sign to say so, reassuringly they say Just sign it, if you were to die on us, at least we can't be sued, an' people leave 'ere on crutches an' wi' no legs, an' they're glad an' they even turn back to look at the building, just to check they really 'ave made their escape, 'cos once you've been mashing up veins an' bones, there's always blood left nearby an' that's a right bind, it's like some old piece o' junk, you can keep mendin' it an' it's still a piece o' shit, like wi' cobblin', tightenin' an' stitchin' the edges right so it's all even an' the leather pieces all nicely lined up, an' you might just miss an' not cut round it so the edging's spot on, an' wi' girls, as my dad used to say, you 'ave to use your nous, an' mum would say if you're goin' to sleep wi' a bloke, each one's got 'is mind on summat different, I regret I was poorly, think o' the money I could've made by now, an' the archbishop used to grow black roses an' others 'ad dance studios, it were often on at the Grand Operetta, a girl might stand on one leg on 'is shoulder an' the best ones at that in civvy street were the tavern whores, they were up for a spot of artistry, an' I happened to be dancing a quadrille with the Navrátil girl an' they deliberately tripped us up an' she bungled it an' we were sent flying all the way under the table, an' Vlasta, like a statue an' a dried out willow tree she got up on a billiard table, nobody could match 'er, she might have been a scrubber, but virtuous girls can't hold a candle to 'er, she were crazy about me an' she played the piano beautifully, an' some Slovak girl poured lemonade down the back of my neck an' they made out she'd been peein' there, an' as I carried her round the room in time to the music she was wearin' silk underwear an' yet she wasn't up for it?, then she gave me a hundred crowns an' for safekeeping I put them inside my shoe an' Vlasta said Gimme the money, after all you did promise to marry me, an' she didn't find anything an' cooked for me for free, but with a silent smile she'd always say This'll cost you a night of sin an' then she got killed in a car, but Havrda said she'd already been with 'im an' that she was a nurse, that might be so, mostly is, an' she threw the ring at the miller's feet an' I bought her nothing an' she came right over to me an' said Why're you sittin' 'ere like a bitter mushroom?,[52] an so I grabbed her an' pushed her against the billiard table, an' the waiter came to help her an'

I kicked 'im an' he flew like a football an' then a gypsy girl, Silva-Tarrouca[53] used to go there, she said I'll scrub up an' we can go on a date, but I didn't go with her, she were the jealous type, an' she'd have put vitriol in my coffee, but one time on Žofín,[54] with Zdenička that was, she were a good-natured one, an' as soon as I got there it were all cuddles by the gramophone, an' they played all the greatest songs an' there could've been all sorts of crooks there, but out o' sight, the madam said That one really likes you, So bring 'er to me, Give me the price of a bottle of milk, would you?, but I said I didn't 'ave any money on me or the mood or the time, the one behind the bar in Poděbrady, she'd do it for a hundred an' fifty crowns, an' when we went there she said Treat yourself to a liqueur, sir, an' Jiráček 'ad a dance an' he were pissed an' flopped to the ground an' lay there like a castling calf, an' the conductor had 'em play *Balalaika* at my table, the Jew was playin' a chromatic accordion an' singin' *Anabella*, the song Kolář used to sing at the National Theatre, dah-dah, ta-dah-da dah-dah, tra-la-la-dee, what a tune, hell, you need to be relaxed for it an' drink eggs an' lemon tea, but a smoker with a cold could never sing it, that time I made a boo-boo an' said she weren't as allurin' as she 'ad been, an' she bopped me one in the mouth, so hard I snorted snot all over my shoes, an' she said, Call yourself an intellectual, you sexpot?, she came from over Kostomlaty way, an' at another visit this woman says Great body she's got, an' she lifted her skirt an' she 'ad a silvery suspender belt like the girls at the brothel, an' silvery pants, the blokes kept moanin' an' groanin' about 'er not even noticin' them, not even lookin' their way, but the girls would follow me all the way back to my quarters, to look at my pictures, Othello's Mistress, like where 'e's this Italian or Greek ruler an' she's Indian an' 'e's murderin' 'er for bein' unfaithful to 'im, an' the other paintin', it's the Virgin Mary, the poor thing's all fragmented an' covered in little fishes, it's a paintin' on glass that Vaňátko gave me once, they were both real beauties in those pictures, but we didn't dance at my billet, she just sat on the bed an' said I can't drink, I've got a lot of work to do an' it would make my head spin, but next time she comes on her own!, an' I gave them all sweets, it cost fourteen crowns an' I was quite happy to raise a dapper shot of the hard stuff an' then it rained, a gold-hemmed cloud came over an' it were black in the middle like a chimney, an' so I told the story of how Kaluža an' Halíř arrested Lecián[55] an' how the lad had been playin' with a coloured football an' asked the whys an' wherefores, an' when he was due to be hanged he told the judge he wouldn't be going to bed, 'cos he'd be getting plenty of sleep in hell, an' he told the hangman Wohlschleger[56] Get on with it, you've got cold hands, an' his heart kept beating' a full thirteen minutes after he was hanged an' girls used to put flowers on his grave, but anyway, where does it come from, this predilection for crime in a man, there's no great skill in killing someone or taking money, I can show myself anywhere an' I'm popular, but he, poor criminal sod, he has to stay hidden, but then even the most well-meaning state won't allow it, the needy man has to grovel to earn a few coppers, but he has to spend money too, then he starts borrowing an' eventually turns into a rogue an' he's got to pay alimony an' satisfy his passions an' then he scratches his head an' says What 'ave I done?, an' that's when you get tragedies, there's one who had two boys with the maid, one hanged himself an' the other's a little guy an' he's twenty an' he stammers an' can't tell the time, an' his dad bashed his head against the wall, an' the garden was the death of him, built a pump an' a wire fence an' couldn't pay the interest an' the savings bank sold it over his head, an' one time he were dying for a bite to eat an' he went an' ate the roux an' she did a runner an' left him, we could also get boozed up like zeppelins, but then turn to crime, an' the police would come an' say Right, sir, you're comin' with us, the shame an' disgrace of it, life's not worth livin' an' no woman's interested in you, not even my girl would talk to me, she'd grab me by the collar an' kick my arse, though as it is she treats me like a lover an' says when I've got time we'll go dancing together, an' what does it mean, dancing with a girl like that?, well it's an honour, 'specially when she's educated, an' Gruléšek, he were a character, but abandoned, completed an apprenticeship an' bought an estate, an' kept on educating himself an' his daughter, she married a judge, robes an' all, he made love to her in a dip in the lawn an' he called out to me How are you? What've you been up to?, an' at Corpus Christi he wore a tailcoat an' got all pally wi' the priest an' he also had a top hat an' the grandest house on the square, he'd been born to some old dear when she were single an' his foster father gave 'em all such a thrashing that they wound up in the icy cold in a spruce grove an' he all boozed up an' stuffed to the gills in bed, an' after a time he said

Mum, you can come, but not him, he can stay where he is, I often think about those spruces, an' then a fellow has to grow up by himself, an' Dáša said If I had a husband an' he came home stoned, I'll hit him, I'll shoot him, but then it was raining and a wind blowing an' so she didn't come, but she did send me a message that she liked getting posies an' I told her I liked getting cosy, an' I held my head an' listened to the voices of the young folk as they stabbed each other in the head, one got fifteen months, his snout cardinal red, an' they had a party in the pub, adding rum to their beers, an' when this bloke came out the baker's son stuck a knife in his head right up to the handle an' Freddie couldn't pull the knife out of his head so they called a doctor an' he helped him an' he were sensible for the rest of his life, but his love-sick daughter put a bullet through her brains, ugly as sin, she were, he'd always been unlucky an' the one who did it to him got two years, an' when he got out, the first thing he did was go to a barn dance an' they stabbed him in the throat, nicked his tongue in the process, an' the one who did it to him got thirteen months then became a gamekeeper, who can talk sense to one o' them? he'd stab you in a public square, 'specially as he were from a family where the dad had been inside, an' back then there were no pensions like now an' you could work till you dropped an' in the end the only thing left was nursing homes an' the alms house for dimwits, an' the girls say At least you'll get a rest, an' I won't hear of it, it's a waste of time, it'd be the death of me, a good thing I never got married, if I had to be in one o' them places I'd do away with myself, or the others, they say kids are a family's fortune, but that's only if they make something of themselves, like being an actor or a singer an' bringing fame to the family an' the country, or a wrestler, but there aren't many such an' they all have a hard time of it, can't give it up an' follow their heart or natural instincts, they have to keep at it an' mostly they die of consumption or insanity or something just as wasting, an' then there's inspiration, an' once a thing's composed, you can go off for a walk an' a snifter, but those moments while you're doing the composing an' coming over all faint an' weak at the knees an' can't go on, an' start doubting whether you've chosen the right path, but then when Járinek sings, you're over the moon, an' marital infidelity, that's another pain in the arse, she cheats on him no matter how hard he tries, whenever I tried it on with one an' she said she might do it for a thousand, though I don't try it on with married ladies or widows, but a virgin, as Batista had it, that's heaven, when we were just a kiss away an' she said No, a kiss has to be begged for, an' I said I've never sunk that low, an' then she wanted to go to the forest, 'cos scrubbers, they can be got anywhere, an' anyone can, but nice girls, they need a go-between, an' then two more bitches, even younger, showed up an' it were non-stop larking about, an' would I sang *Our love's a light that doesn't got out* to them an' then they prattled on like young magpies about a museum, something that couldn't be glued back together, fifteen thousand years BC, bones from some animal in the Šárka valley, an' I just told them that before the Great War, under old Austria, we weren't in the habit of climbing through windows to get girls an' force them into it, we were taught that by Colonel Zawada, a Pole who had seven horses shot from under him an' led thirty march battalions into war, he had the sound principle of not raping women in war, but those girls, they just laughed at me, Wow, you really are degenerate troops, we're not surprised you collapsed on all fronts, an' they giggled, an' the colonel had a German shepherd with him an' two artillery batteries, the forest were packed full o' troops an' he went an' blasted the whole forest to smithereens, an' for the tricky spots he brought heavy machine guns in as well an' he kept studying maps, an' me, just standing there, one biddy asked me where her son was, but when he spotted it he hopped off his horse an' yelled No tokin' to vomen, you sonofabitch an' don' get distracted, an' he kicked the woman in the arse an' the entire guard had to come running out, fifty blokes, an' when he came back from the battlefield he had a great big star an' a gold collar, an' he were always in his office an' bossing us about till my ears started stinging, an' he had us polishing our weapons at gone midnight an' he also kept a close eye on us, taking us by the chin to check whether we'd shaved, an' at three it were time for a coffee an' at five to go out, the bugler started first an' then the drummer an' the officers were darting about with their sabres, an' when they discharged me I felt like I'd been reborn, an' when I was six I saw a railway for the first time an' my dad said They're lettin' off steam, stay back, an' the station master as well, Better keep the kid back from the line, an' Wichterle an' Kovařík in Prostějov,[57] they had a villa an' never stopped building onto it, inlaid with black marble an' gold inscriptions, not even the archbishop's got one like it, all gnomes an' birds an' rocks, benches, deers an' serpents an' roses on them, stakes wi' domes on top an' the quartz glinted like diamonds, an' they just ordinary old dodderers, Smetana were another toiler an' no great gent, a poor guy doing his level best to improve the spiritual life of his stupid compatriots, he were a saint like Dvořák, he also had his basinful of troubles, an' yet he worked his way up from butcher's apprentice to genius an' the brain inside his head bubbled away, 'specially when they wanted tunes pleasing to the ear, so such folk spend whole nights agonising while the rest just spend their time on the bottle or asleep, then there's Strauss, a real expert that one, screwed his scores up he did an' tossed 'em on the fire, it's supposed to make parents happy when a son dies famous, but most are just shirkers who get by, or there's Havlíček or John Huss, he still believed in God, not Havlíček though, the cops hauled him off, an' the shame an' trouble with women at first, then he ran across Juliánka an' she understood what he were about an' were glad an' she herself were educated, an' because he spoke the truth an' defended the truth the cops came an' Juliánka were heartbroken an' 'er dad, though he were fond of the bottle, Havlíček spoke highly of him, an' if anyone ignored the truth he were just stupid, yeah, if anyone knew it today an' were brave enough to resist the forces of reaction.., but because he were a bright lad he used a lot of Latin, that was one hell of a thing, *Ever since I've known your 'eart, Juliánka of mine, it was a star I'd come to know,*[58] an' even schoolgirls have stopped an' wept as I tearfully recite this into the dark sand, but he had no truck with Jesus, though he were no less strict morally speaking, an' priests sleep with their housekeepers anyway, but these days I happily get by on *kontušovka*[59] or rum, an' it's good for the chest an' the old-fashioned rheumatism people used to get after a chill, an' my dad advised If you did pair off with one, you'd have to love her right or she'd breeze off with some other waiter, if you don't keep them happy they go looking for some other heart, an' if you're on your beam-ends, go easy on her, but when there's money, go for it, they were up to no good, an' when I showed up she went straight for it an' What does the young lady do?, an' I said She's in dramatics an' I have to go now, but the lady said Oh nonono, if you won't take it amiss I'll pour you a drop of cognac, an' I promised I'd also take a little part in the play an' we were sitting in this magnificent room, like at the Pope's place, an' she said she'd sell me some bedroom furniture if I meant to marry the girl an' when I told her she said she already had some furniture an' she didn't like pale colours so I'd better not buy it, but all women bother about is stupid stuff to do with love, an' if something happens to one of them, she just starts hollerin', the first boots I made were for Crown Prince Charles,[60] when old Franz died he mounted the throne, he were married to Princess Zita of Parma an' they had eight kids an' the oldest were called Otto an' after the war 'e went to Spain an' he had something wrong with his blood an' she gave him some, but it were no good so he died, mostly Charles were pissed an' he fell in the Danube an' got dragged back out by pioneers, an' when 'e were visitin' the injured in Kostroma he gave his brother an orange an' some lemonade, an' fags to the soldiers, an' Wilhelm,[61] he were a bastard an' came from a line of pirates, an' back then they wore pickelhaubes, they looked like those little turrets on a kitchen dresser an' brass-tipped an' 'is aide were that famous bigwig,[62] such a sensitive guy that all the girls gave into 'im, an' as I were telling 'er about that she were busy daubing 'er lips in front of the mirror an' the trees were shaking about an' tapping at the window like it weren't an unfamiliar wind

But you can buy her a present and all will be okay, but we won't go far, it's raining and windy, but she'd twist it anyway, she told me don't worry, I'll always give you a call, so I'd take her to a vernal island, she does like a stroll, an' if the other one saw her out of the window she'd have an awful lot to say about it, it's been so long since we had a wind like this, when it comes it can blow for a week on end, I was sat in my room an' my feet were freezing cold, I made a spot of tea an' went out, it's ridiculous a wind like that, starts blowing the other way on Sunday an' a gale can last three days, there's just no knowing, by the sea it's utterly insane, an' as for breakers, a wave as high as our house can reach the road an' a boat can go flying an' tossing about an' stones landing all over the road, that's a sea storm for you!, it can even overturn railway trucks an' carry people out to sea an' even their donkeys as they make their way back from their vine-yards, it throws up great columns like towers, casting a mighty pyramid up into the air, an' such poverty an' star-vation that we were left eating dead fish out of the muck an' the army went begging from house to house, my first lieutenant would scrape the last bits of maize from the cauldron an' he *was* a first lieutenant, an' the submachine gun hadn't been invented yet, that came later, when roof tiles flew an' windows got knocked out an' women an' kids crying all over the place an' we were heroes, we were outnumbered fourfold by the Russians an' we chased them, heroes be damned, we were just as shit-scared as the others an' then heavy cannon joined in an' meadows an' cornfields were all ablaze, lucky I didn't get burned to a cinder, an' so I was resting on duty in that old jail, an' the Jew put on 'is fine lacquered belt an' a suit an' the Jews always stuck together, but he were supposed to polish his weapon an' he gave me a florin to extract his cleaning rod that he'd got jammed in his haste, an' off he went into town to chase the girls an' NCO Brčul showed up, all two metres of 'im, not a bad guy, but if he ever got pissed off he'd blow his top, an' he said what d'you think you're doin' wi' that gun an' where's that Jew?, I says he's gone into town, an' Freiherr von Bucherer had banned that kind of thing, having urged the officers to stop the men loafing about the town, an' he lay down in my bunk an' the Jew's were still empty, I stood beneath the little barred window an' waited till midnight when the Jew came back an' the Bosnian leapt up an' shouted who told you to go wanderin' about the town?, an' he belted him one, wallop, an' the Jew-boy lay sprawled on the floor in his fancy suit an' lacquered belt an' he had to go out all covered in blood an' when I went to relieve him I couldn't find him in the windy yard so I woke the duty watch an' we found him in a corner swinging, sticking out of the branches, 'cos o' that wind blowing in from the sea, an' when Major Michochović were dolin' out our pay, he had the money on his table held down with pebbles so the wind wouldn't carry it away an' he warned us right off not to go out an' drink the lot away but to buy useful gear such as skin cream, thread, buttons, an' the countryside were really nice, romantic like around Jerusalem, the odd tree, sallow or olive, an' roads leading uphill, always needing to be repaired with the wind blowing like that, the locals live on fish an' oatcakes an' they're like skeletons, vineyards hard as concrete an' at first it's impossible to get through to Poles, one Dalmatian girl showed me some hovels where the people had starved to death, an' at the spot there were a miserable little grove an' the sky were a gorgeous blue an' she were grazing sheep just like in a painting an' she asked if I were single, arid pastureland it was, an' our men were traipsing across it with their weapons, making themselves scarce under fire from partisans, an' the locals were shaking mulberries down, white, insipid, sweet, the trees were full of mulberries, there was a shortage of aircraft mechanics, but everyone said it wasn't something they knew anything about, an' we chucked grenades, you whip the cord out an' you can miscount an' there's trouble, when the sarge was training us he had a replica an' taught us about its parts an' how to count to twelve, an' when he went to the toilet some lout swapped it for a real one an' then we were practising naming the parts an' counting to twelve an' bang! it demolished the room an' his guts were all hanging out, they're like tripe sausage, an' it's got this bit o' string an' all the time you're one foot in the grave an' the other in the sickbay, Oskar Henek, the chap who enlisted for Štokava, shot himself an' one Pole shot himself in the leg out of desperation, an' there were all them training sessions an' each time something different, who's a commander an' what the different insignia are, an' when I went off to find some girls, I'd dress up, pale-blue tunic, black trousers wi' red braid an' a bayonet polished an' nickel-plated an' even a cap with a gold stripe, an' in Cracow we went to the third bridge an' it were all Polish an' Hungarian girls, Romanians, Germans and Jewesses, soldiers would often carve the place up an' the trollops would beat it, an' by the time the military police showed up we'd be gone, out there girls dance naked on tabletops an' in the field hospital they had nuns an' when they were bandaging me up one told another get out, you messy thing, an' they promised me frankfurters if I'd help dry the dishes, then the doc turned up an' what are you doin' here?, beat it!, an' one time I were on a divan with another girl an' she said don't be shy, touch me up, don't be such a silly, I'm quite clean, but I were tired an' when some patrons came they called for her an' she didn't go an' her boss an' the hotel owner begged her not to mess things up, an' at Žlábeks' one gave me a cheroot an' they poured out some wine an' Come an' look at the new girls, have a good look, an' the new one said I'm Eva an' I said pity I'm not Adam, an' some mechanical device led me by the hand up to a cubby-hole an' there were a dog in there, big as a calf, yellow, heavier-built than even our Bora, an' he jumped on my back, an' as I tried to escape, it did it again an' I were minded to jump out o' the window, but it were on the first floor, meantime she'd stripped off an' lay down, the little tart, on the green sofa an' what? is this gonna work or not? an' she grabbed me an' ripped off all my fly buttons an' again I were minded to jump out of the window an' the dog were growlin' so I lay down on top of her for the first time in my life an' she said you don't 'ave to pay, you get a student discount, but she did first check me out to see I didn't 'ave some disease, she were Moravian, from somewhere out Přerov way, an' so when a woman doesn't fancy a guy it's pointless, but it can be a bit irksome, which is why you have to take feroman-TX like artists, who've got a brain the size of a washin'-up bowl, an' a brain like that 'as to be grey an' full o' grooves an' folds, all wavy inside the head, an' it's there in them spirals that ideas are born, but where there isn't much brain, what' there's just crap, if I could've gone to university, though some studies are a bit woeful, take Edison, or whoever it was invented radio, or your Mozart or Strauss, no one in the world's a patch on those two, their stuff's still bein' played all over the world, all folk want is bits by Mozart or Strauss, if I 'adn't been sick since I were a kid, an' they were always torturin' me wi' medicines, if I'd been fit an' well, I wouldn't 'ave ended up stuck in the brewery, but when your eyes an' mind are done for, all grand ideas wither an' fade, but I've always wondered anyway about the right way to see things, but as I went on it got less, I couldn't really grasp it, but what did my favourite Kunrt say? the most beautiful woman is no match for the most famous of men, Albach Retty[63] was no match for

Járinek when 'e sang that song at the National House – *Land of Smiles*, or *shin-shon*, that's Chinese, but the young lady didn't know that, an' it would take a lot of effort, an' plenty of folk go mad trying, all artists, an' when they want to improve on a thing an' do what hasn't been done before, it drives them crazy, people play an' like only what they already know, but your artist, trying ever so hard to come up with something, suddenly his brain goes to pot with the effort an' there's nothing anyone can do to set it right, even that famous symphonist István dragged a chandelier down on himself in despair 'cos he couldn't get it right an' do something that hadn't been done before, or Edison, when he meant to invent the gramophone, to find stuff that hadn't been before an' wasn't even known about, an' where it might be an' how to work it up, fifty pupils didn't have a clue about it, for three days he sat on his high stool so the earth wouldn't disturb him, an' for three days he didn't go to bed so as not to lose track of the idea in his sleep, as a lad he had only one set of clothes an' was no better off than Truman an' Roosevelt, an' that's why he had a little china stool under his feet, so many desensitising currents come up through the earth, an' it was just then that he were to get married an' his wife came to get him, but he were dead-tired 'cos of all that science, an' if he'd let up he wouldn't have got it all together, two little cylinders opposite each other an' two little tubes in the ears, then he thought better of it an' invented that black disc, but at first you did have to put it in your ears, after he died an' they examined his brain, they found it filled a small bowl an' was all grooves and folds,

which is why it's in a museum, an' she stood in front of
a mirror daubing her lips and said where'll you take me, sir?
so we went out into the May countryside an' I bought her
some sweets an' she was as happy as a little kid an' squeezed
my hand

or: A contribution on the Renaissance
as compiled jointly with my Uncle Josef

If one of Christ's pals had been Římský, the celebrated baker Římský, who kicked a whore's false leg an' snapped it in two an' gave some cops such a thrashing that they needed medical attention, then things would be better. Long before Christ, the same idea was shared by the European Renaissance, Sophocles, Themistocles, Socrates, Mozart and Goethe, the quest for a refinement of emotion and libertinism. But Christ studied among old Jews, did his translations of the Old Testament, a huge guy 'e were, 'andsome, one as knew 'ow to handle women until the rest was all envious of him, like Martha, thou art careful an' troubled about many things,[1] he'd talk to any man an' any woman an' Martha were a gossip an' he didn't like that, because he were a doctor an' professor, a great mind an' a great scholar, an epileptic, otherwise they wouldn't have recognised him as a king and a god. Let someone try that, acting the martyr for the sake of love, an' not be a tinkling cymbal?[2] The trouble it takes to teach an idiot geography, geometry, sometimes the teacher don't get it either. And suddenly it's like He, out of the blue, has come an' seen that this world 'asn't got itself educated to this day! It's like when you're a student or apprentice. Does everybody 'ave it written in the stars that they're purveyors to the court? An' on top o' that being a purveyor of love, 'aving everyone 'ang on till his death, through great obstacles an' hard times an' hunger an' sickness, 'aving 'em work each according to his powers an' abilities, an' also instilling all that in every idiot near an' dear to him, no pope or archbishop ever managed even half an idea of what it is to go barefoot about the world an' sleep in a stable, with just a bit o' bread an' water, it's terrible, that, an' for a chap not to sin even in his thoughts among all that vermin, there's few as are up to it, apart from Christ himself, an' those high-falutin', supernatural ideas he had, they were what broke him. An' what *is* God? Someone tell me that! Like them missionaries, no fornication, no dirty goings-on with kids present, an' no consorting with more than one woman, in the army, too, they give you your orders before coffee-time, that it's drill tomorrow an' physical jerks, an' mind you've got your rifle polished, an' if it weren't, the captain would summon the sergeant, one guy shows up, coat covered in blood, got pissed somewhere, the major's sittin' on his stallion an' has everyone searched, an' then comes trouble. So Christ is also responsible for his cohort, he'll also wind up sittin' on his little donkey in front of the Almighty an' surveyin' his imbecile flock an' then there'll be no excuses, none of your sorry, guv, I didn't 'ave the time, Christ'll 'aul him out, kick 'im around a bit an' give 'im a sock in the teeth an' they won't feed 'im an' they'll even lock 'im up, 'cos in the end even an emperor will fly off the handle. Then try governing nations according to the European renaissance! I've put ladies to the test, to see which one likes what. With one it's a new dress, one a ring, or another the passion flower of love. Yeah, an' I'd like a million! I was just larking about an' all those bitches, except the passion flower, declared they'd go barefoot all the way to Prague to find me... An' so missionaries go criss-crossing the world, wearin' black kaftans, their chins not like Elijah, but shaven clean, a silk rope doubled at the waist, rosary like what you see Capuchins with, an' birettas on their heads, not like a parish priest, but three-cornered like an archbishop's, a massive crucifix 'ere with a gold Christ, an' they used to go around fulminatin' the whole time about love, not 'ow to hug a girl, but like when some poor fellow's short of a thing, one who's got more than enough should let 'im 'ave some. That's real love, not doin' somersaults on a sofa, for if you gained the whole world, it profits not,[3] there's just that pure soul, an' the renaissance has to cultivate that from infancy. Free-thinkers often badgered 'em wi' monkeys an' fishes, but that were just biological and psychological fantasising. A free-thinker asked: Where did the first chicken come from? An egg of course! the missionary bellowed back. An' so they spent the next two hours shouting at each other till they agreed that egg an' chicken are both God, an invisible spirit, an' that Eve were seduced by a doctor of medicine, like Havlíček[4] taught us, an' isn't it odd that Adam were made of mud an' Eve of a bone, but where on earth's the chicken then, an' where's the egg? An' so missionaries got the odd clip around the ear for their gloss on the cosmos, not even Christ 'ad a bash at that one, let alone any piddlin' pope or silly little archbishop. We can't believe things that are impossible, even Christ taught that, an' anything that's done without conviction is bullshit an' to 'ave a spirit is to 'ave a sound brain an' sound blood, an' once that goes, you've 'ad it. There's just the good deeds you left behind, but if you can't control yourself, then it's goodbye, you're not a human, you can't go about hittin' people an' swearin' at 'em, that's so ill-mannered, an' nobody's helped by mass murders. After all, the world's a big place an' can feed twice as many people, so what's the big deal if I eat my fill? An' if there's a little extra bit o' lovin'? What bliss it is when a twenty-five-year-old he runs into a twenty-year-old she, it's like a flower openin', but old folk, that's just two wax figurines, corpses, it's only the young, the first ones, as the writers of the Renaissance tell us, an' wi' oldies, that's just wishful thinkin' an' just the gift of givin' an' of loving everything, as a substitute for lovin' lasses. An' there's the acrimony that causes distress, like over who's the better-lookin', or 'ad an education, an' over this one's bein' the daughter of a monarch an' the other's a dollar princess,[5] an' whether that fellow's a writer or an editor. It's that wretch nature that set people against one another an' it drove Jesus crazy. Wearin' clothes, that's the rule in colder climes, but where it's hot they go naked an' in places like that there's no lechery like wi' people who wear clothes, it tickles people's fancy, she don't know what he looks like, but folk with no clothes on don't even notice each other, an' among nations that go about naked there's a lot less pickpocketin'. An' so all things are governed by control of the emotions and passions and debauchery. Wee Mozart or the writer Goethe, they can't fly off the handle like some carter an' yell: "Young lady, you can kiss my…!" Instead they get a grip an' write a little poem or a little tune an' send it to 'er with a bunch o' flowers as is right an' proper. That's your European Re-

naissance, but Christ 'as no part in it, because it isn't enough for 'im. 'E wants everything an' that's 'is weakness. If only 'e could be pals wi' Římský the baker, a chap who sought justice by wreckin' pubs an' demolishin' 'is cell, door an' all, an' beatin' the livin' daylights out of prison wardens, 'im as they 'ad to spray water in 'is eyes wi' a fire hose.

A SCHIZOPHRENIC GOSPEL

Dedicated to my seventy-year-old muse,
my Uncle Pepin

As the old Jewish merchant was getting together a selection of brushes and Kobas padlocks for me he told me, without stopping what he was doing, that there was this parish where Jesus Christ was born in order to save the world again. And with each sentence he looked at me through the thick lenses of his spectacles to see from my eyes whether he really could have been born. So...[1]

Out in one suburb there lived a man called Joseph, who spent evening after evening not taking a girl to the pictures, but assembling an old has-been of a car, which he imagined he was converting into a luxury limousine.

You'd think that, having successfully completed the task, he'd be jubilant at being able to take Mary out for a drive, but not a bit of it. He was looking forward to something going wrong with it and the chance to start over again.[2]

This being the way of it, he also imagined heaven as one vast meadow filled with scrap cars, where each new arrival was given the tools with which to spend eternity assembling whatever took his fancy.

Miss Mary, with whom he had a thing going, loved going for rides in leafy places, but with Joseph forever doing things to the body of his car, and hardly ever to hers, she got bored and let herself be shamelessly groped by the Holy Spirit, and so she started writing poetry in secret.

But epileptic prophets and the law had stipulated something different. In the diary in which she kept a record of her periods, there was a day that didn't get ticked off and her pencil waited for another ten days because she thought she might have caught cold in the damn' shed.

On the twelfth day, Mary opened the door and saw only Joseph's legs; the rest of him was under a car.

She sat down on a pile of brake disks and said: "Sorry, Joe, you'll have to come with me to get some injections. I'm up the duff and I don't want to keep it." And Joseph replied: "Half a mo', I just need to tighten these brakes."

And so the virgin went for her injections, and when the Holy Spirit saw the trouble he'd caused, he abandoned the girl so that holy writ might come to pass.

Nine months later, baby Jesus was born, though initially he'd been nearly shaken from the tree of life because Mary kept jumping from ladders and doing somersaults as she tried desperately to miscarry.

And she was unhappy, because the practical Joseph just wasn't having it that the Holy Spirit could have fitted his girl-friend with a baby without her having slept with him once.

When Jesus was still a kid, he attended school in Libeň, and in his satchel he had his packed lunch and his books and his mind was on silly things. Once, geometry and physics having failed to tell him what the Teaching of all Teachings and the Art of all Arts were, the teacher stood him face to the wall and banged his hooter against it crying: "So you refuse to study? You want to be a disgrace to the great Marx-Lenin?"

And the young Jesus had his first caning, because only now are all nations taught according to the Teacher of All Nations, John Amos Comenius, that the rod should always be to hand.

When the RI teacher came in, he, having had *The Internationale* sung, asked: "What, young Jesus, is the Silesian Trinity?"[3]

So Jesus, still not quite with it after that first caning, said: "Saint Trinity was the sister of the Virgin Mary."

And he got another beating, with a piece of rubber tubing on the soles of his feet, after the dictum of the teacher of all nations, who is particularly worshipped today throughout Eastern Europe, that a piece of rubber tubing should always be to hand.

For quite a while longer the re-educated chaplain fulminated at Jesus as he wept: "You capitalist monstrosity, that didn't come from your head, you must be in league with the Vatican."

It was only later that afternoon, after he'd recovered, that Jesus found himself a stick, took his halo off and made it into a hoop, then went charging up and down by the Rokytka,[4] where the boys were having their baptism of booze and, the little pricks, bashing the bishop in the bushes.

When he grew up, all the beautiful women settled like flies on his lips, and they all had a single wish: that the lad die nice and close to their entrails, covered only by beautiful shapes and a triumphant smile.

But young Jesus hadn't yet developed the urge to go about on all fours, because he'd read Mr Batista's screed on sexual health,[5] about boys not sticking their penises either in the holes in axe-heads, or in oil lamp chimneys, because such episodes lead only to grief.

Instead he preferred to carry a frozen twig of eternity between his teeth until little green flames flared from his nose and a tiny purple tongue of flame wavered above his straw hat. And of course he hung his wings about with bricks to stave off delirium. When he lay down on the grass, no one tried to stop him being an assemblage of previous lives. He had an exact recollection of having been nitrogen, phosphorus, iron and water and he initially felt it was impossible to think up anything that he wasn't himself made of. And an amiable sniffing about reigned over all things, as in epilepsy.

However, while young Jesus was meditating in the grass, secretaries general were lacquering his lace-up sandals in anticipation and curling his hair with tongs and cutting the cloth for the most elegant of togs just so that he'd get involved for once.

Suddenly young Jesus sat bolt upright and saw a tree with coelenterates, marsupials, cetaceans, mammals and prophets perched on its branches and Someone sitting at the top of the pyramid, bathing his feet in the heart of man.

At that moment young Jesus felt that everything had frozen inside his brain and that nothing else existed but infinite love and that he had been sent to create out of his hoop an acceptable idea.

So there and then he did his first miracle. When some wedding guests wanted a drink, he changed wine into water for them, and they almost beat him to death.

After this incident his pals set him up with a butcher's wife to cure, because she drank a lot and so was squandering her husband's substance.[6]

So young Jesus set off for the address and lo! The butcher's wife was lying plastered on the couch. He said: "Madame, there is a commandment against drunkenness. Why do you spend the money that your husband keeps aside for improving his business?"

And the butcher's wife snapped back: "Improving? What? The business? Ha-ha! It goes on women. And gin. So I do it as well. And they'll go an' nationalise us anyway."

And she lay her head on the desk and knocked the ink bottle over. And young Jesus persisted: "Where do you keep the drink, missus?

With her eyes she indicated a small cupboard, and when he opened it he was struck dumb by the beauty of the shapes and names and contents. "So this is the muck you drink! Ugh!"

But out of the blue he recalled a quotation from Scripture: *Weep with those who weep and rejoice with those who rejoice.*[7] So for the sake of appearances he came out with: "That looks pretty good, fetch me a mug, would you?"

So the butcher's wife gave young Jesus a guided tour of her bar, they drank from the aforementioned mug and he was soon the worse for wear, because he'd never had a drink in his life.

And he picked up some scissors from the desk: "Right, let's perform that old Bohemian ceremony of hair shearing." And he snipped off the end of her free-flowing locks.[8] After another half-hour the butcher's wife cut young Jesus' hair off and they found it terribly funny. Then she lay down and fell asleep and the mutilated Jesus went outside, where the butcher was waiting for him: "So, has she come to her senses?" But young Jesus got the wrong end of the stick and said: "She did, but then she fell asleep. I don't know, I really don't, but this nation is certainly not going the way of Masaryk and Beneš."

And he burbled on down the street, with a sensation as if his bones had had brass wires woven into them. By the war memorial he fell into a swoon.

Some kids who were playing there with a handcart, loaded him onto it, cut some birch wands and performed a grand entrance with him. All the way they rang doorbells and cried: "Come and see, we're carrying young Jesus, pissed. Come and see!"

As they carried him up the steps to the house they were laughing so much that they dropped him several times on the concrete tiles.

After that young Jesus used to go the Haláneks' gin palace,[9] because of his pals. Nearby, on a corner of Lily

Lane, he met a little Jewish girl called Magdalen[10] and fell in love with her.

He would go to the bread shop with her, and to the hairdresser's and on the way they would chat: "Do you think, lord, that the world is built on sex and sex alone, as Freud would have it?"

And young Jesus, in order to balance out any dialectical discord, told her about his halo.

At the time, her eyes were iris-coloured in the daytime and forget-me-not by the light of the moon, her mouth was strawberry in the light and violet by night, her cheeks pansy in the early evening and clove pink in sunlight, her breasts were mallow in her bodice and peony in the bath. And her sex organ? Saffron in bloom in a meadow and overripe redcurrant in the sheets, though young Jesus hasn't even kissed her yet.

One day, clutching his halo instead of his straw hat, he asked the little Jewish girl: "Do you love me, Magdalen?" And she replied: "I will when you stop being crazy." And she was thinking of a car.

But young Jesus persisted: "Do you have, Miss, even a little bit of the love your clansman Christ talked about?" And she replied: "Oh yes, though that's why we crucified him. But once no one wants me anymore, I'll come and sleep with you."

And young Jesus, having swallowed that wire, kept worming: "But how will you want to sleep with me with no flowers, no poetry? If you love me at all, be my wife." But she replied: "Only after death."

And she left, heading up the stairs, past dead water lilies and the half-dead young Jesus, who, though he didn't want much, did want everything, and so nothing."

After this debacle he preferred to go to the Kuchynkas' dance hall;[11] he wasn't a dancer, he just sat under the horse chestnuts, doing the accounts for that Someone in whose name more than a hundred million people had already been murdered.

He lay his head on the marble tabletop and fretted about ways to save people from the scrap yard. His mind was so one-track over it that his pals had agreed among themselves: "He needs a girlfriend, that's all it is."

But he was thinking that the sword that starts out in the mind will inevitably turn into a real one and inevitably red blood will flow.

And the marble tabletop turned into a chopping block or altar, and that Someone appeared to him, not in the form of a carrier pigeon, but in the form of a false leg that had sunk through a cloud. And the false leg was covered in dried blood and covered in rust as if it had been lying in Tertiary marshland. A voice perfumed with affliction spoke: "Ah, that is my son, who seemed so good in my sight."[12]

After he came out of his stupor, young Jesus saw that his friends had stopped dancing. To them he said: "This religion thing is driving me mad." And his pals replied: "You bet. Or you could have yourself secretly sewn into a cow's hide and let yourself be re-rogered by a bull."

The day after these voices and visions, young Jesus hopped on his bike and rode to St Cath's[13] for a consultation. When he arrived, he glanced up at the ceiling and said: "Right, I'm here." And he entered and the door clicked to behind him and instead of door handles all that remained were little ears, and there was no way of going back.

Two men were just dislocating a man's arms and he was bellowing: "You whore, you whore, you're turning into a slut."

A woman in white was kneeling on the floor, her face red. Before the two men chucked the roaring patient out, they said: "Things are surely going to go badly for you one day, doctor." But she responded: "You don't say! He thought he was talking to his wife." But by then the door had closed again.

Young Jesus cried out joyfully: "There they are!" And picking up his spectacles he went on: "And, doctor, miss, I've had a certain Someone talking to me, but in a way that makes me think it's God himself." The doctor said: "He talks to patients of mine as well. But what does he try to get you to do?" And young Jesus said: "To save the world, and he said I seemed so good in his sight." And he unkinked the ribbon round his straw hat.

The young lady doctor narrowed her eyes: "You know what? Get married instead, or start keeping some nice little geese, because if you start heeding those voices, we'll come to get you, us or State Security." And she expelled some smoke through her nose.

Young Jesus cried: "No, no, no. I have to follow them. But Miss, I hear plenty more of those voices, a whole confusion of them. Could you do me an analysis and tell me which is the right one?"

"Well, even if I knew how, I'd go right out and buy a notebook and write out my own voice, because I also get voices and don't know which is the right one," the young lady doctor burst out laughing. "Look, Vincent[14] didn't ask any doctors either. I expect it's here, and here."

And she tapped young Jesus on his straw hat and on his wallet, and he felt very, very small.

Then she opened a drawer, took out a photo and said: "Look, this is a handsome student of medicine with plaits. He was also visited by voices going on about the equality of all men. But after a time – straitjacket. And after six months? Notice the bent back here, the elongated arms, the sunken jaws. A clearly visible transition to the chimpanzee. And this is how he looked at the end – but I won't show you that. It's quite distressing to see a man crawling on all fours, especially a handsome one who thought that he'd set up a quite simple, free world, filled with friendship and love. Promise me it would be better for us to meet on the scaffold than here, where everything tends to be out of joint."

Young Jesus said: "Well I'll be on my way. Goodbye." And he strode over to the door, but the young lady doctor had to unlock it for him. "Goodbye, sir."

"Goodbye, goodbye," young Jesus repeated. Out by the gate he clapped his hand to his forehead: "The bike!" And he returned to the passage where he'd left his cycle.

As he rode down Štěpánská Street, boys shouted after him: "Stop, stop!" And as young Jesus applied the brakes, one of the boys told him: "Your chain needs pumping up, sir!"

There was that holiday when they took a trip on a pleasure steamer on Mácha Lake[15] and his pals kept playing fab hits on the gramophone and they were feeling swell.

But young Jesus was mindful of distractions from the true path, which is why he said: "Beware the leaven of the Pharisees." His friends replied: "You mean because we've brought no bread?[16] Right, if there isn't any we can buy some." And young Jesus felt sad because they weren't poets and didn't know what a metaphor was. But since he believed it was never too late, he recited: "A man that is an householder went out early in the morning to hire labourers…"[17] but before he'd even finished the first verse tourists were already taking flight, because vineyards had been nationalised and young Jesus was an agent provocateur. And his pals were also alarmed: "Master, whiz off, whiz off, let's not end up in the nick."

And he lay down on a bench below deck and listened to the drive shafts quaking fervently as if it were only among them that the Holy Spirit dwelt. He shaped his ticket into a dove of peace and whoosh! He'd thrown it out through a porthole into the blue air.

After they docked and evening had arrived, young Jesus went up on a hilltop and did a spot of automatic writing and then analysed it. As he knelt there, a halo formed on him and he almost caused a forest fire.

People out on sailing boats thought someone up there was cooking on a primus stove or that there was a swarm of fireflies. But he lay there in the soil worried sick, because people didn't give a damn about anything.

And he didn't go back down even for the night. He remained inside a nearby chapel, where, having removed the flowers and candles, he lay down on the altar. As he lay there, he raised one foot and set the eternal light swinging with the tip of his tiny shoe, so transforming the chapel into a red pendulum clock.

The chapel really was so small that when he stretched he got whitewash on both his soles and his hair. So he lay there in silence, wondering who to ascribe that chorus of bloodied corpses to. And not knowing who to or what for or why, he fell asleep, like unto his own image.

When he awoke, the eternal light had come to a standstill and sunlight was streaming through the window. Then he heard a shout and two peasant women ran out of the chapel crying: "A miracle, a miracle." But that day young Jesus saw no merit in advertising, so he quickly put the flowers and candles back where they belonged, straightened the altar cloth and ran down the hill.

In the night, as they lay in a hotel bed, two of the friends were musing: "Since you're such a wag, young Jesus, fix it so that after death we can be right next to you, because you're fun to be with."

But young Jesus said: "No go, that's fixed by the other guy." And he pointed one finger upwards. Then his friends all pounced on him: "So are you just the doorman or errand boy at that place where you work?"

Young Jesus said nothing, because that was indeed more or less how things stood, if not quite right. Instead he pulled his blanket up over him and fell asleep.

Towards midnight his friends woke him: "Master, listen, there must be some impropriety going on in the room next door." And indeed, you could hear someone next door groaning and moaning in sensual delight. "Master, go there and do something about it, we've been putting up with it for an hour already."

"And so I will," and young Jesus hopped out of bed, and, just as he was, went and knocked on the door, twice. As he was about to knock a third time, the door opened and a bearded stove fitter appeared in the doorway and smashed young Jesus in the face with his fist. And young Jesus, though he would have liked to say something, turned and fled back towards his own modest quarters, receiving at every step a biff from the begrimed stove fitter's big toe.

As he seized the door handle, he discovered that his friends had locked the door. And kicks and curses and gobs of spit rained down on young Jesus and he, like St Wenceslas, still held onto the handle, crying: "Lord, if thou be willing, remove this cup from me."[18]

After a while there was a click in the lock and the half-dead young Jesus collapsed among his friends, who were half-alive from laughing and out-prattled one another: "Some path of thorns, eh? You got to give it to him, our agent of the kingdom certainly has a way with people."

And young Jesus climbed onto a chair and inspected his bruises in the mirror above the washbasin. He said: "If only the guy had cut his nails! And I say, verily I say unto you: Cast ye not your pearls before swine."[19]

And he cooled his backside in fresh water while his friends thought up some pretty decent metaphors for his predicament.

When they got back from that quite promising excursion, there was a heat wave and they would go swimming below Libeň Bridge, at the spot where there are those two boats half under water and another two moored to the bank. The friends were having fun banging the cable with sticks and were gleeful when a woman's head poked out of a porthole: "Bastards, quit banging the cable, will you? It goes grouching right through the boat."

"Grouching right through the boat? Exactly what we were hoping for," the bathers burst out laughing and jumped into the water, where dead rats, leaves and other such were floating about.

They bought a washing line, made a knot in it and one at a time they swam off holding the line. The rest held the other end and ran with it across the fish hatcheries while the swimmer's head dug into the surface and created a fan shape. And so they took turns and even young Jesus got a taste of what it's like to have your eyes hooded with water. As dusk descended, some workmen also came down to the river. And young Jesus said: "I shall go and speak to them."

He went and stood next to the houseboat down whose chimney the lads were in the habit of defecating, and said: "As the in-thing among the Indians used to be finding a pathway through life by which to reach nirvana, so the in-thing in our own age is work as a means to transforming this world into one in which man would no longer be exploited by man, except through the class struggle and the *Herrenvolk* doctrine. But tell me, my friends, what will you take with you to your iron and steel processing plants and down your mines and back up again? Love, love, love and the humility with which it is so much easier to beat the norms they set us and the troubles that beset us. Verily, I say unto you: in the times to come, the most menial tasks shall be performed by those with a university education, and this shall be the supreme order, for only in this way can the evil and the filth of the world be diminished. So we shall end up where we began. With the beggardom of the ancient Indians, but enhanced with humility and love. Thus through work and in work doth man attain identity with his own self and the rest of the world."

And young Jesus had spoken and he gestured like this with his hand towards the storm clouds. But by then the workmen had long been in the water and they shouted to him: "You can shove all that where the sun doesn't shine. Hearing about work gives us backache, like in the cinema, by the end of the day we've had as much as we can take."

And they banged the cable until the shaggy head came flying out of the porthole and shook its fist at them: "Bastards, quit banging the cable, will you? It goes grouching right through the boat." "Grouching right through the boat?

That's exactly what we were after." And they jumped into the water with the lads. Only young Jesus stayed out of the water now. He was woeful unto death, for his wet trunks were clammily cold.

He watched two women hauling an old man out of the fish restaurant, trying in vain to get his seized-up joints moving. He saw the old boy's legs and head flopping all over the place, like a dead bird who'll never be got to fly again. Then they sat him in a wicker armchair, placed a small table in front of him and on the table a book, and every so often they'd come and turn the page for him, because the old man was keener to live now than when he was young.

Young Jesus wanted to say something nice to him, but the women waved him away, pecking at their foreheads with one finger to indicate that it was pointless.

One afternoon, young Jesus started pining for a girl in the asylum, and when he went to see her, she wasn't there.

He went out into the grounds and sat down on a bench, near where a man with a briefcase and a moustache was standing, holding forth to some women: "If people, through a mere chink, came upon the true face of truth, they'd all go crazy. That's how powerful the truth is." At that point young Jesus nearly jumped out of his skin: one woman had sprung to her feet and shouted: "So what's the truth that prevails? What are all those sly inscriptions on the John Huss memorial?[20] Within the Party I also told the truth, and if it weren't for the madhouse, they'd have locked me up. Ho, ho, ho, ho, the truth prevails!"

And the wretched woman ran down the path, beating her blouse and still calling out: "The truth prevails, the truth prevails." But the patients shook their heads to the effect that it doesn't.

Only one woman said nothing. She was ready to leave, with her face mournful and confused, her coat and her case, with no idea where she was going and how and when. She gave off an aura of futility and fatigue, and young Jesus concluded that the people here had either too much of something, or on the contrary too little.

Having risen to his feet, he then passed a beautiful lady in a blue coat, looking as if she were off to take a nap in another dream-world. Taken by her beauty, he spoke to her: "Where are you going, Miss?"

And she replied: "Do you see that tall tree over there? That's where my beloved hanged himself, he wrote me a whole suitcaseful of *I love you, I love you, a million times over I love you and a hundred million times*. But I wasn't listening and so he hanged himself, but only after he'd tied this whole suitcase of poems to a rope next to him, so all through that windy night it kept banging against the tree trunk, like that axe in the Czech fairy tale.[21]

And she turned into an avenue to hold a requiem and young Jesus followed her. He passed a motionless, glum-looking man, who then turned, yanked a small table off the tree to which it was screwed with tremendous force, and hit young Jesus over the head with it from behind, uttering with gravity: "And this has been sent to you by the Archangel Gabriel."[22]

By the time young Jesus was released from the hospital, it was the first full moon after the vernal equinox, so he went back to his small home town to be screened.[23] When his turn came, the council of scribes and Pharisees asked him: "Tell us, Jesus, what would you do if someone came to you and tried to get you to tear up your Trade Unions Council ID card?"

Young Jesus replied: "If that someone were a functionary, or the secretary himself, I would do it, as a matter of union discipline. But true faith lives in the heart and carries one over every obstacle."[24]

They were lost in wonder and asked a second question: "If we gave you a rifle and sent you into the forest to stand guard, would you go?"

Young Jesus replied: "If there were no one there, why shouldn't I? But if the enemy were lying there with machine guns, would you go with me? For woe to him who causeth a public nuisance."

And the scribes and Pharisees wondered at his wisdom and put to him a third question: "If someone came to you and said a revolution was in progress, would you fire on us?"

Young Jesus replied: "I'd buy the Party newspaper, and if it offered no guidance, I would make enquiries at the secretariat, because a man is more than all sacrifices."[25]

And all those about him wondered at his fealty and so they gave him one extra question: "Now pay attention, young Jesus, careful now: Who was the Christ?"

Then young Jesus, to reassure himself as to how low things had sunk, replied: "The Christ was the one who, if he were alive today, would surely have joined the party that is so dear to us."

At which point the council and the people could no longer contain themselves and they rose and clapped their hands and young Jesus also clapped his hands, because through his mouth the Teaching of all Teachings had spoken and the Art of all Arts, except the heart of Jesus.

That evening, downcast and weary, he spent the first night in ages at his mother's. But in the night, after it had all sunk in, he was moved several times to try and hang himself, so his mother even had to go to the toilet with him.

Early one morning, he went for a walk by the waters of the Elbe and he watched fishermen dorsal-hooking live fish so that, as bait, their suffering would endure.

The lame past lay behind him and nowhere was there a footprint into which he might match the sole of his own shoe. He was alone. And he could help no one, though he fain would, and he could speak to no one, though he fain would. Like a lone, single individual he was digging out a pathway to his own self and hence to Someone and Something and Nothing. Through a narrow gateway, with his cohorts, to meet the angels whom men of iron shall duly kiss into reality. But who will wish to look willingly upon himself and behold his figure crumbling away?

Who can stand the sight of highly polished golden calves, as if the ancients hadn't said long ago: "Know thyself, that is what thou art, the gods are you and it is the violent who enter the Kingdom." And as he walked, his voice cried out: "All of you, who think that all great men, if they were with you today, would happily knock about with you in T-shirts and beneath your banners, go and have a pee! Popes, secretaries general, may they shave all your fingers with a pencil sharpener, for you yourselves enter not, you just whet your knives against seeming madmen, fictitious criminals and the new-born babes who give you the slip in their invisible shirts." Thus cried the young Jesus and falling face-down in the earth, he had a fit in the enlightenment of which he saw the earth as it was, doomed to destruction, because God was what he had done and what others had been doing.

After a time, running across one of the friends from whom he had split, he told him: "Go in peace and be not alarmed. From today, if you want to be my friends, nothing can befall you except death by firing squad."

Whereupon one pal filled his pants with gravy and the cocks crowed, because he happened to be called Peter and he also happened to leave for good.

Which is why the late Pope, né Pacci,[26] hung on till the age of ninety-two, went climbing in the Alps and buddied up to the Emperor at Ischl, where the Tyroleans yodelled to them to the sound of zithers.

When this Holy Father was dying, they, on the advice of an English doctor, put a seventeen-year-old girl in bed with him, but he died anyway, because he no longer got that tingling, though nothing could have happened to him except the eternal life of which he was so scared.

Today's Pope, he's rather keen on dollars, and his pals seek the advice of capitalists and they can't abide communists.

Which is why he strolls about the Vatican in silk, like a ballerina.

The day before his death, which is in infinity, young Jesus thought up, and so had, the following dream – as a reward to himself, mankind and above all his friends:

At the Holešovice abattoir, he and the twelve had each knocked back two litres of beef blood and quickly boarded a packed tram, where suddenly all thirteen of them started puking a blood-and-mucus cocktail into the laps and faces of the people and one another. Whereupon, for the first time in his life, young Jesus started shouting: "This is my blessing and my recompense." And the people leapt in beautiful arcs from the Holešovice embankment straight into the river, and they retched and, for once in their lives, they longed to be purged formally.

The following day, as men from the tramways department were cleaning the tram of its knee-deep layer of sick, they had to divert an arm of the Vltava to the spot so that the mess could be borne away by the current, in just the way that Hercules, that handsome Greek, had been smart enough to contrive things.[27]

And the cleaners were so bemused at the wonderful sight that, hands clapped to the back of their necks, they vomited their modest company lunches into their caps to cries of: "If only Salvador Dalì could be here now!"[28]

Someone in the heights was splitting his sides laughing and dabbling his feet in the heart of young Jesus, which looked outwardly like the face of a superannuated, deaf-mute child.

End of Chapter 1.[29]

I/

Summer is marked by Uncle Pepin's wearing two pairs of trousers. In winter he wears three. When people realise, as summer draws to a close, that uncle is triple-trousered, they say: "We're in for a hard winter!" Dad frequently ticks him off because of the trousers, saying he'll lose his robustness, but Uncle Pepin protests: "It won't do any good anyway, Mr Hanka was robust enough an' he got kicked by a horse." That evening, at my parents' behest, I moved in with him to teach him the right way of doing things. I told him: "Look, Uncle, it's really not very nice, is it, going to bed with your clothes on." But he replied: "Suppose there was a fire?" I wasn't giving up: "And isn't it unhygienic?" But Uncle said: "Suppose I need to pop out in the night to get some cigarettes?" In the end I did succeed in persuading him to try removing at least one pair of trousers. After we'd gone to bed, Uncle Pepin began pacing the cellar (we lived in the cellar) and saying out loud: "What a fool, what an idiot, what an ass, so well educated and yet 'is brain's totally flimsy." I leapt up: "Who's an ass?" But Uncle Pepin replied: "Who? That twit from the brewery." And he crawled into my bed, scratched himself, clicked his tongue, then he kept getting up again, opening cupboards, chopping wood and practising top C. In the morning, the worse for lack of sleep, I asked him: "What do you eat, Uncle?" And he, fresh as a daisy, showed me the pot in which he kept his ersatz coffee boiling until he poured some hot water into a mug.

Then he'd add more ground chicory and keep it going. That day I'd boiled some potatoes and made a garlic sauce and grilled some salami. I poured the sauce over the potatoes and salami and asked him: "Well? How do you like it?" Uncle Pepin replied: "Well, if you like them, potatoes." I pressed on: "Potatoes, but what about that brilliant sauce and the salami?" To which he said: "Well, if you like it, why shouldn't you make it for yourself. They make it for the archbishop as well. But at the front we often didn't get even this." In short, by the end of December I was also sleeping in my clothes, and also in three pairs of trousers. Because what if there really was a fire? Or what if *I* wanted to pop out at midnight for some cigarettes? And why bother cooking? We keep boiling the chicory down till it thickens, then we add some more and keep it going, we eat a bit of bread and drink a spot of brandy. We spend all day in bed like a couple of puppies and tell each other how fond we are of each other: "Bohušek, I love you more than Slavek!" And I, at the mere thought that Uncle Pepin might die, start to cry in advance. Then we lark about all night and talk all about popes, emperors and girls. When Mum and Dad found out, they said: "You're just pigs, the pair of you!"

11/

Since then, Uncle Pepin has come to us for lunch. It's midday, Sunday, and Uncle nowhere to be seen. "Where's the idiot got to?" Dad's losing his temper. Mum says: "You'll see, this is how it'll end one day; he won't come because he'll

be lying chin up somewhere." I say: "I'll go and fetch him."
In some alarm, I cycle to the hovel where he lives, open the
door, go down to the cellar, fling that door open and would
you believe it! There's Uncle Pepin standing contented by
the window, a box of matches in his hand and a cigarette
between his lips; he takes out a match and seeing that he's
holding it by the end you strike, puts it back in the box,
turns the box round, opens it again, takes a match out and
only now strikes it, looking at me as if I'm not even there.
I get cross: "Christ! You stupid! Why haven't you come
for lunch, we'd got to thinking you could be dead!" Uncle
puffs away and says: "I've had an awful lot to do since this
morning, lad. I had to chop some wood!" In the corner I can
see a few bits of wood and shout at him: "That can't have
taken more than a quarter of an hour!" Uncle Pepin stares
out of the window and says: "An' I had to break some coal!"
I look in the scuttle and groan: "That much could be done
in another quarter hour." At this point Uncle Pepin sticks
the dead match back in its box and apologises: "All right,
but the postman'll be bringing my money on Tuesday." In
the end, half-crazy, I get my serene uncle to the lunch table.
Innocently, he asks my mother: "Sister-in-law, have you got
any cigarettes?" And Mum, afraid he was going to dun her
for some, snaps back: "No!" Then from his waistcoat Uncle
takes a cigarette with gold edging and says courteously:
"Have this one, it's really good." After lunch Grandma,
who's been reading the paper, asks: "This Montgomery
chap, is he Russian?" And Uncle replies: "Yes, he is, Gran,

you can tell from the name." Then Grandma reads on and again looks up: "Look Frank was executed and now he's popped up in Spain?"[1] And Uncle, all heart, explains: "He broke away, Gran, an' now he's creating havoc there." Then he starts talking to the cats: "So my little teddylings, do you fancy a trip to Korea? Wouldn't you get lost there in slippers? While we, bloody bourgeois, are falling asleep."

III/

Today, 21 January 1952, Uncle came home from town, beaming hugely. "Stalin's dead!" He'd heard it on the municipal public address system and Muscovite Járinek[2] had sung him a requiem, canonical hours. Everyone took fright, but I, who knew that Uncle called Willi Forst Lili Ford and Dean Acheson Ess Echon, and instead of asphalt said aursfalt, instead of motorbike mobortike and instead of Marxism marsism, asked him for safety's sake, "Uncle, wasn't it Lenin they said had died?" And Uncle said: "Sure, and Božena Němcová as well." And as if nothing had happened, he started telling about old man Choorchill lighting a cigar and flying about the world with his Fulton address and the Russkies going crazy about it. "And in America some guy called Schmitt has invented the microphone and something else, or something of the kind, used for curing cancer by means of a bladder, when you can't tell one cell from another. I hear people going about telling one another the news: Stalin's dead. An' it was on the town public address system and Muscovite Járinek sang him a requiem." I says: "Uncle, can you hear what you've started? You'll get yourself put away." But Uncle Pepin went on: "Poor dead Frank, the emperor, great guy, though he drank himself to death, died in the toilet he did." I shouted: "But Stalin isn't dead!" Whereupon Uncle put Dad's glasses on, though he's got the eyes of a lynx, and scours the paper, scouring, scouring until he points triumphantly to one sentence in Gottwald's[3] address: "Lenin, he's the Stalin of our times!" He sets the glasses aside and whispers to me with a faint smile: "That's the school of the freethinkers, the school of Havlíček,"[4] and in evidence of his own enlightenment, he claps his hand so hard to his forehead that tears spring to my eyes.

A FEBRUARY STORY

1

As soon as snow started to fall, Uncle Pepin wound his scarf around his chin and ears and developed toothache, because he was supposed to clear the snow from around the house. When he heard me coming down the stairs, he switched off the radio and hopped into bed.... I went in and, sure enough, Uncle Pepin had the blanket pulled up right over his head and he was moaning. I shouted savagely: "Uncle! Snow! Look sharp, grab a shovel and let's get to it!" But Uncle just edged back the blanket and chattered through his teeth: "Here, here, oowowowow, Jeeze! It's been killin' me ever since the last snow, it started with a blast of cold when I was clearing the snow!" I said: "Clothes off and we'll see!" And I got all the ointments and drops from the first-aid cupboard and started rubbing Uncle's teeth with Expeler camphor oil, that stuff with the anchor trademark,[1] on top of that a layer of stiff haemorrhoid ointment and a generous dose of black rheumatism ointment to round it off all the way up to his ears. I looked at Uncle's neck – filthy. I said: "Why don't you ever wash, for God's sake?" But Uncle Pepin protested: "Oh, no, no, no. Anything but that! It's not healthy when you've got toothache. And anyway, now I've got this ointment on! And I had a wash when I got shaved!" I said: "And when was that?" And he said Thursday. And now it was Sunday and the snow was coming down. I said: "So wrap your head in your scarf and have done with it! Let's get cracking!" But Uncle went on moaning: "But all

I've got is slippers, and they'll get wet!" And I lamented in turn: "See, ever since Christmas I've been telling you to buy some shoes, but it's always been 'too wet', or 'there's a frost', or 'spring's round the corner anyway'..." At which point he interrupted me: "I *would* buy some shoes, but the shops are closed today. And we've got no running water." I shot into the corridor and indeed, the water wasn't running. I went back to him and advised: "All you need is a few handfuls of snow and you'll have plenty of water!" And Uncle shouted back: "Idiot, snow's cold, and even if I heat it up, how can I use it on my teeth? Even river water would be better than that!" And so I rejoiced: "Okay, that's a brilliant idea, so grab something to put it in and get down to the river." Uncle got out of bed, picked up a tiny pint pot and opened the door. I yelled: "Stop! Where are you going with that pot? That measly little pot?" And Uncle replied in all earnest: "To the river for some water, I'll have a bath since you're so keen on the idea." And off he went, and I was left screaming, banging my head on the wall and lamenting: "I don't believe it, I'll kill him and we'll have peace at last!" After I'd calmed down I was left standing by the window like an idiot, saliva dribbling down my lapel, and unable to think clearly with the pain. No sign of Uncle. A thought flitted across my mind: "Christ, what if he's slipped off the chute into the water and drowned?" And, just as I was, I ran out into the snow, bare-headed, I ran and got cramp. But from a distance I could see Uncle standing on the stony bank with his little pot. I hopped across to him and bellowed: "Muttonhead, why are you standing here like that? Why don't you come back?" But he turned to face me with his black-greased mouth: "Was it me who sent me here? Was it me who wanted a bath?" I yelled, so loud that people on the bridge turned to see: "But what are you standing here gawping at?" And quite calmly Uncle Pepin replied: "I've got one foot caught in the rocks and can't move!" And indeed: his shoe had got in among the rocks and I had to pull, keep pulling, like in that fairy tale about the turnip, until finally it was out. Uncle bent his ghastly blackened face down to me. I was also horrified by those trousers that he'd inherited from someone whose legs must have been so crooked that they'd been measured with a crooked tape. And I was knocked for six when Uncle whispered to me: "And you're lucky, you idiot, that the water didn't rise, otherwise I'd have got drowned an' all because you're so pernickety!" And that really got up my nose! And I said to myself: "Now it's my turn!" And in honeyed tones I said: "Now you can laugh, let's forget the snow and grab a sledge instead and go sledging on the hill above Šafařík's mill…" And Uncle Pepin roared: "Just look at him, the silly ass!" And he exposed me to the whole town… "Sledging! Ha-bloody-ha! And the insurance company manager will see me and they'll take my pension away for playing silly buggers about town!" But I carried on gleefully: "Okay, so we won't go sledging, but I've got two pairs of skates at home so we can go to Remanence[2] and we can skate there hand in hand and whirl in rings and do somersaults… maybe Žaninka will be skating there as well…" Then Uncle lunged at me, his teeth had stopped playing up and he threatened me with his fist: "Do you know what a knuckle sandwich between the eyes is? Žanina? That crappy old maid, whirling in rings? There's no dog as would even cock a leg against her, and me, handsome devil that I am, I'm supposed to fancy her? She walks like a chicken that's shat itself, or like she's got an udder between her legs! Make rings, at best she should have one in her nose. I'd give her a kick in the pants!" And I, afire with vengeance, went mercilessly on: "But she told me what a nice little pair of pyjamas she's started sewing and how she'd like to have a baby with you following Mr Batista's manual, and hop! how she joined you in bed..." And Uncle started roaring like crazy: "An' I gave 'er a kick up the arse! She wants a kid? Pigs might fly – she's well past the menopause! Sour seed or mucus!" And I, sensing that I'd calmed down, that I was now lord of his toothache, went on: "But she told me you kissed her on the eyes in your pad, so I get this idea that you'll give her your pension and go back to cobbling in the evenings..." And Uncle Pepin started shrieking again till he was nearly hoarse: "Bollocks! Leather's dear, they've stopped selling it and there's no money to be made anyway!" Then I finished him off: "But there *would* be money to be made, she'd harness up the dog of a Sunday, she said, and you'd drive out to the fields and dig..." At which point Uncle lunged at a boat tied up by the bank, pounded the poor thing with his fists and did like this to himself with his hands: "I'd yank her innards out like this... fifty-year-old hag that she is..." And I pressed home: "And how old are you, Uncle Pepin?" He stood there and said nothing. I repeated the question: "How old are you?

Well?" And Uncle whispered: "I'll be seventy this year!" Then with a woeful look on his face he said: "If it weren't you, Bohušek, I'd give you such a knuckle sandwich that your teeth would come shooting out of your arse." I said: "So there you have it, get your pot and we'll go and have that wash, then we'll clear away the snow and this evening we'll go and see Auntie Milada and old man Kocián in Prague."

It's Sunday, outside the silent snow is falling and no teeth are aching.

11/

Before we set off, Mum kept trying to put Uncle off: "Don't go anywhere, stay sat on your arse at home, save up for your funeral, and what are you going to do there, it's not like they're expecting you." Uncle nodded, but after she left the room he shook his head: "These parents of yours, they're like little kids… you an' me, we'll also take a trip to Budapest together, to Vienna…" I said: "Come on, let me see what you've got in the way of clothes." And as I opened the wardrobe in the cellar, mould and moths flew out to meet me. I said: "How about this greenish suit and the white hat with the snap brims?" But Uncle yelled back: "Certainly not. I'll wear that when I accompany a young lady to a spa at the height of summer! The trash we're going to see can make do with this striped suit, like what engineers wear, the fancy tie old mother Zakouřilová gave me, and this imperial greatcoat!" And again it was my turn to shout: "An' a cow's tail in your hand! – no, it's unbecoming, you have to wear a decent tie and pin the high jump medal that Grandad won for his team onto it, that'll cause a riot with the women!" And Uncle, relishing the idea, said: "Yippee, I'll be like a privy counsellor, a diplomat, a merry widow!" So I got him dressed, having first spent half an hour bashing at the clothes in the breeze, though clouds of dust still rose from them. Uncle's enthusiasm grew and grew: "No, no, don't clean 'em up too much, you might do some damage, the emperor only wore things dapper-clean when he went to confession." Then he had the bright idea of perhaps wearing a pince-nez, so people would think he was a professor. I shouted: "Not that, that won't do, those purple mittens and your yellow hiking boots are a much better idea..." He turned to me in surprise: "They're not hiking boots, they're Paris-cut cowhide loafers!" And I went on: "Heels and edges adorned with circular stitching!" And Uncle, in a low voice, as if he'd gone mad, whispered: "What edges? What circular stitching? What *are* you on about? D'you fancy yourself as an artisan in Vienna? D'you know what the chairman of the association would tell you?" And I actually recoiled when he whispered what the chairman would say. But then I yapped: "Get dressed! Get dressed! The train's in an hour!" And then Uncle Pepin announced that he couldn't find his citizen's ID card. So we opened the cupboards and started a search, it was time to leave for the train. I said plaintively: "Where've you put it? Where've you put it, you idiot, where are you going?" And Uncle calmly suggested we should prop the new cupboards up with planks so the undersides wouldn't get wet. I shouted: "The train leaves in half an hour and we're to waste time messing about with cupboards!" At last I found the ID card among some photos of girls and we hared off to the station. The train was already there and Uncle asked: "Shall we buy some fags for the journey?" But my head was already cracking up, I grabbed him by the hand and like two mental patients we ran onto the platform and into the train. And we were on our way. I said nothing, just staring at him reproachfully, as if it were thanks to me that we'd made it. Uncle said: "It's no big deal. There'd be another one!" I waved that away and silently asked myself why we were actually making this trip. Why I was taking him with me. Nothing but bother. And I goggled at the passing country-side, I knew every inch of it, yet I was looking out on it as if seeing it for the first time, even making myself interested in it, if only not to have to think about the jaunt we were on. Then we went into a compartment where some other pas-sengers were seated and a bespectacled woman was reading a newspaper. Uncle Pepin removed his greatcoat, then his ordinary coat and it became apparent that his shirt was torn. I shushed him with a finger to my lips because the woman was reading *Rudé právo*.[3] Uncle – how like him! – asked aloud: "What! Oh, I get it, *Rudé právo*. Yeah, as if I hadn't noticed. She might inform on us!" So I settled down, having first got Uncle back into his coat, and smiled amiably at the reading woman, as if to say we'd only been joking. The lady leaned towards her neighbour: "There's no denying it, the Russians really are clever." But Uncle took it upon himself to reply on behalf of the other lady: "Rubbish, the place is a total shambles. During the war Freiherr von Wucherer[4] said: 'Another hundred thousand like you an' we'll chase the Russians out beyond the Urals!' And today? Missus, have you any idea what Austrian discipline is? Do you know where we'd chase the Russians to today? You can have no idea! Freiherr von Wucherer, old Red-nose, turned up on his stallion and his lieutenants knelt down before him, and the mere sight of the owner of his regiment gave half of us constipation!" And Uncle Pepin waved a dismissive hand and I got this sense of my brain being tin-plated or stuffed with tinfoil. I tried to save the situation and so I said: "He means the Czarist Russians!" And I gave Uncle a wink, but he just went on: "No, no, we could drive today's Russians out beyond the Volga if only we had a hundred Austrian divisions! Hurrah! *Vorwärts!*"[5] I said: "Don't you need a pee, Uncle?" And uncle said he did. Once out in the corridor I begged him: "God have mercy on us! – leave off, will you? Or we'll both be buggered! That woman's doing her nut!" And Uncle replied: "But what was it Master John Huss taught us? What was it that got 'im burnt at the stake? And what about Jesus Christ an' Havlíček, victims of a stupid people as 'ad forgotten to stick to the truth?" I roared back at him: "All right, you're right, so let's both go to the stake, onwards and upwards and ever bolder towards a happy future!" And I undid his flies and he said: "The world needs martyrs!" In resignation I said: "Okay, I can just see the blazing crown above my head! Though a halo would suit us better. Here, let me do you up again." And when we got back to the compartment, Uncle asked the reader of *Rudé Právo*: "I say, Missus, in which assault line would you like to be advancing on Russia?"

And so at Čelákovice we concurred in the belief that old Austria had been the best thing in the world in every regard. And at Horní Počernice Uncle Pepin gave a rendering from the play with songs called *Nine Canaries*,[6] bellowing it out like a right-hand pair-cow, and people came in from other compartments and congratulated Uncle and me, saying how lucky the world was to have us. When we alighted in Prague, Uncle gave everyone a kiss and the woman who'd been reading said: "What a man, what a man!" As we stood alone on the tram stop island Uncle Pepin said: "We made the poor sods happy, put on a good show for 'em, eh? What d'you reckon?" But I was just looking around in case we'd been followed by the secret police with handcuffs and an arrest warrant.

III/

Every day I'm up at quarter to four and I travel to work at the Kladno iron and steel works. I get back at half past three in the afternoon. I asked my uncle to light the stove so it will be cosy and warm before I get in. From early morning Uncle will have been piling on whole shovelfuls, adding wood from old dye barrels for good measure. Each veneer has a different colour and Uncle Pepin, as he saws them up, invariably gets different colours all over his hands, then he touches his neck, his fancy collar, his forehead and he rubs his eyes, so that when I come home I think I'm seeing not my uncle, but a parrot. Then it's so hot that the sweat pours off us, but Uncle revels in it: "I've been stoking non-stop like an engine driver just so you'll be warm." If my bus is late, uncle gets his coat and waits at the tram stop, daubed like a moon-eyed parrot, so when I first catch sight of him from the tram I think something awful must have happened. But he's only come, he says, because he was afraid I'd copped it. And it *is* a wonderful feeling to know someone's afraid for you, that you mean something to someone, that someone's really worried on your account. You breathe a lot easier. He's also quick to tell me how people spot his wonderful suit and that collar, but I detect something else as I walk along with him – that people are positively alarmed at the sight of his garish phiz. Then we enter the house, uncle's bought a bottle of rum and immediately offers me some: "Have a drink, you're knackered!" We make some coffee and I make to pour some rum into Uncle's, but he takes the bottle from me and dribbles only the tiniest bit in: "See? Like at the pharmacy." Then he suggests we go out. I always want him to have a wash. So, in his overcoat, he washes under the tap, using just two fingers. After one day of his staying with me I'm already feeling so feeble that I don't even shout at him, and the jabbing sensation inside my head has also passed. I always drop off into a dull sort of sleep and only wake up as he's leaving. He's forever telling me stories, all the time, but I can't bear to listen because it brings back the aforementioned headache. I might say the odd: "That's peculiar", "And is that really how it was?" or "Such things do happen," And for the rest I'm half-asleep. What's really odd is that at home he never talks about politics, saying: "What's the point?" But the minute we get on a tram he'll launch into some woman who's knocked him with her bag: "Get out o' the way, you old hag, this isn't Korea!" And if a car passes him he'll shout: "Bastard, if I'd got a hand grenade, it'd be comin' your way right now!" And he's always wanting to buy flowers and to go and see girls he knew twenty-five years back. Like Bobina at The Harp, or Vlasta who he says works at Vašat's caff. But I tell him, look, they'll be in the poorhouse by now, if not dead, it's been such an age. But he only gets it once we're actually at Vašat's, flowers in hand, in front of some old dear sitting at a silvery cash register. Uncle twiddles his thumbs in embarrassment and asks her: "Don't you remember that time when you asked me: 'Do you want children?' An' I told you: 'Yes, but made of sugar'?" And the old lady shakes her head, she doesn't remember. "And don't you remember, missus, calling me a sex maniac and hitting me over the head with a bottle?" And the old lady tinkles the cash register and shakes her head, smiling. So we leave Wenceslas Square and I feel sorry for Uncle Pepin. But he's not thinking about it. Or rather doesn't want to think about it, or maybe he can't bring himself to think about it? Who knows? Instead he starts rambling on about Mariahilfe, the Ringtheater, Burgtheater and the Stephansdom.[7] "That thing with Vlasta, that was the last straw!" So I take my Uncle Pepin to the theatre to see *Marianna, the Mother of the Regiment*.[8] While I take a stroll alone, to recover. So I walk and I wait, but by half past eight I'm already missing him. I wait amid the stream of people until I spot him. Looking like Arthur Schopenhauer. When he sees me, he elbows his way through the throng yelling at the women: "You should sit on your arses at home an' not go spoilin' other people's fun! Best place for you lot's the front line, with Captain Hovorka pokin' at you with 'is sabre!" And with a gleeful expression on his face he tells me what he's just seen. And I, though I've seen the play myself, can only moan and groan: "You don't say!" Uncle goes on about Vlasta Burian[9] prancing around in the uniform of a pontifical guardsman, exchanging salutes with the soldiers and Marjánka supplying the pontifical guard with booze and feeling sorry for herself. And he claims Vlasta Burian had said: "Don't you worry about it, Marianna!" and that they then all went off and sang songs with the pope.

I'm almost asleep and Uncle Pepin is still waffling on about how lucky it would be to be an epileptic, then says something in praise of the select order of one-ball-willies and falls asleep. He tugs the blanket over his face, so the minute he drops off I wake up. I can hear an awful racket coming from beneath two blankets – like when someone's being strangled…, then a death rattle, like a voice struggling to break through a layer of tripe. I jump up: "That's it, you pig!" I put the light on, whip the blankets off him and make him swear not to cover himself up again if he wanted God's mercy. But he just looks at me and tells me: "No, you shouldn't drink so much coffee with rum, it's not for the weak an' feeble. You should drink more entorhermetic[10] and entrahimatic[11] infusions an' when it comes to wine, only feromantochiol."[12] "Good God, Good God…," I mutter under my breath, stuffing my ears with soft bread…, "what a pig…" and I fall asleep with Vlasta Burian walking round and round my bed in the uniform of a pontifical guard.

As the Atom Prince[1] was dressing for work the clock showed quarter to six. He hung his apron on his pendulum grinder and passed through the gate out of the grinding shop into the early morning sun.

The open hearth furnaces of the Poldi iron and steel works were gushing white smoke and workers were streaming along every road around, each to their own daily grind. The Prince approached the baths of the unsheltered pickling plant, where a huge figure of a man kept emerging out of the green fumes of hydrochloric acid before vanishing again.

"Hi, Vindy,[2] g'morning!"

But Vindy was busily sweeping the scale from pickled billets and muttering to himself.

"Hello there, Vindy…"

Vindy straightened up and said: "Isn't it weird the way that stupid whippersnapper Nezval[3] drags the hierarchy of heaven into his poems?"

The Prince stared into the green scum round the edges of the baths.

"I need a favour, Vindy…"

But Vindy smacked the baths with his wet gloves:

"Could he be a Jew? How dare he go stealing from art galleries! To me he seems to carry a whiff of the synagogue of the Antichrist! There's a poem where he writes that his birth was attended by the Archangel Gabriel! Since he doesn't believe in him, why does the silly ass drag him into it?"

The Atom Prince leaned in towards the flat surface of the hydrochloric acid and saw himself in it. He had curly hair and a German Afrika Corps forage cap perched perkily on top of it.

"I say, Vindy, you won't tell on me... there's a female convict here at the plant, about thirty she is, with freckles, a redhead, I've spoken to her once... only once and I think she's here for political reasons."

Vindy brandished his fist in the general direction of Prague and shouted:

"It looks as if it's up to be me to defeat the shadow of freemasonry! I'll write a poem and call it... *How Bruder Viktor Ahrenstein carved a cube by proxy*!"

The Atom Prince stared fondly at Vindy: he liked it when Vindy's scribbler spirit floated like this above the fumes of hydrochloric acid.

He said: "She's called Rosetka and she's here, lock-me-up, lock-me-down. I spotted her by the crucible furnace, having a snack of tea and bread, when I was going to the billet store... and as I rode past the women convicts on my spoil truck I deliberately derailed it. She was sitting with her back to me and I had a crowbar to lever the wheel back onto the rail... and I whispered... 'Do you have your cuppa before or after dessert?'... And she, Vindy, like talking to another convict woman, she says... 'I wouldn't mind eating a bit of dry bread on its own, if only I were out of here...' I said in a low voice... 'What's your name?...' And the other woman replied by saying to my one... 'Rosetka, how beautiful the sky is today!...' A prison guard was standing by the crucible, watching, but seeing nothing... I'm wondering, Vindy, could I be wrong in thinking she's Jewish?"

Vindy heaved himself out of the pickling bath, leaned against it in the posture of a count and said: "Yes, I dunno, but I reckon so. Yesterday I wrote... 'The thoughts of Isaak Jakob Mautner as he sits in the office of his Náchod headquarters'[4]... I expect that's the way of it!" He cleared his throat.

"In the Spring of 1830, one Mauthner, a Galician Ashkenazi Jew, arrived in Náchod and said: 'That building over there is going to be mine!' In 1832 Mauthner the burgher said: 'That cotton mill over there is going to be mine!' In 1839 Mauthner the factory-owner said to himself: 'I've got five mills and I want to have nine!' And thus was born the concern that was Mauthner Mills Co., the concern of an industrial magnate with no coat of arms and no traditions, a magnate who, as he passed his realm on to his sons, did not anticipate that his sons would shroud themselves in a mantle of joint-stock anonymity... and so he certainly could not have anticipated that in the red press of the proletariat his sons would be labelled leaders of..."

The Prince leaned over and scooped up a handful of the silent green scum and listened as it quietly ticked away in his fingers and gently ate his skin.

He said: "This stuff, Vindy, it's as thick as a beef soup... But I went on to ask the backs of the convict women... 'Do you need anything?' And the other one answered for her... 'She needs a bloke, a decent bloke's what she needs.' I continued levering the truck up and continued whispering...

'Do you need anything?...' And Rosetka whispered in a different direction... 'Come to steelworks number two canteen at one o'clock and pretend to be having a cup of tea in the corner...' Why not write this down, Vindy?"

Vindy put his brush down and said: "I've also got to write something about Chaplin! He gets on my Christian wick! A millionaire, every five years he boots his wife out and gets himself an even younger one... Today his sixth, raped into having three kids... but our Jewish millionaire is still playing poor old Charlie... everything that surrounds him is awful and evil... All around him nothing but evil people... only Charlie, he alone in the whole wide world, is striving for true love. The spirit of the synagogue wafts from Chaplin, too, and I'm going to take a close look at him."[5]

The Atom Prince was watching him, and at the far end of the ironworks a hundred-ton drop hammer gave a mighty whoof that made the whole earth shake and sent a white, listless cloud up into the blue air.

He said: "That'd also be nice! Then after I got the truck back on the rails, I heard Rosetka say to the girl she was sitting with: '... Well I wouldn't... me, when I catch a little beetle or spider behind a wire screen, I carefully tap it out sort of to show Fate that it might sort of care to be kinder to me...' Will you write this up, Vindy?"

"I will... the story's ringing inside my soul... I will write it out, it's going to be called... *In the embrace of a beautiful Jewess*... I'll write it up, then once she's out and falls in love with a man who knows nothing about her... I'll put a little boat trip in it... she'll say... 'I only like the most ordinary things now…' and he'll start having a go at her… 'Looking at you, I'd say you're starting to fall apart… the other day you lost a tooth… you've had your hair dyed, and a kidney removed…' And she'll fish a snapped carnation out of the river and say… 'I wonder who threw this carnation in the water?'"

Vindy voiced the question so earnestly that the Prince whispered:

"I don't know…"

"No, not you… it was her asking… and then, out of the blue, quite casually, the Jewess says… 'It was around the end of the war and they were taking us to Oranienburg, a whole trainload of women, and somewhere around Hoyerswerda the Yanks shot up the engine, strafed the train as well and all the SS fled. We scattered into the forest and I was slightly injured… as you put it, it was probably the result of me sleeping with blokes in grassy clearings!'"

"I never told her anything of the sort…" The Prince pointed to himself.

"It's part of the story… 'and we dug ourselves into the fallen needles beneath the branches of the spruce trees… then we heard the dogs and SS-men… but they didn't find us. We stayed there the next day as well, and when we thought we were going to die, we heard some Czech voices… They were Czechs, they'd been repairing the railway track… that evening they dug us out and I was taken off to their camp, where they hid me under a bed. When the front came closer, one of them, Pepík he was called, loaded me onto a little cart and hauled me all the way to Bautzen… I still couldn't walk… my wound was festering…'

"'In Bautzen we waited till the front passed and the Russians gave us a pony and so we reached Georgswalde. There they took the horse from us and Pepík carted me all the way to Česká Lípa, where I was taken in hand by the Red Cross... and I never saw Pepík again... I waited, but he never came... But isn't it a lovely day today?'"[6]

"How right you are, Vindy, a sky worthy of Italy!" said the Prince, looking up.

"No, no, that's said by the Jewish girl, and she carries on pulling the carnation along in the cold water..."

"Vindy...," said the Prince, feeling slightly awkward. "You know, I'm a bit of a degenerate, good hearted, but a bit too cocky... ever so slightly mad. I've occasionally made fun of you..."

"Me? I've nothing to forgive anyone for, nobody's ever done anything to me... they couldn't!" said Vindy, picking up his brush again and scouring some more scale off the steel.

Hundreds of thousands of sparks flared in the windows of the grinding shop. The Prince ran along the planks, turned round at the gate, but Vindy had quite disappeared in the fumes of hydrochloric acid, those greenish fumes.

Around half past nine, one grinder after another fell silent and the operatives raised their visors, undid their aprons and sat down to have a snack.

Kudla said: "Well, Major, how about it?"

And the Major sat down on a crate and said: "Okay, Kudla, but you mustn't leave me looking unshorn!"

Kudla flapped out a scruffy piece of calico, printed with

all sorts of kids' toys, held it in place round the Major's neck with a bit of string and reassured him:

"Trust me... we'll just go for an American cut... I say, guys, my brother-in-law told me they caught a rat among the furnaces... the slaggy sent us to the tool shed to get some petrol. Then they doused it, set fire to it and let it go... ran the whole length of the trough it did, like a rocket..."

So spake Kudla and he ran the clippers into his hair.

"Christ, don't overdo it!"

"I know what I'm doing! Just layerin' it. You don't want it pokin' up at the back, like this retard here..."

He pointed his clippers towards the Atom Prince, who just pulled a face:

"Look, scrawny, leave my shaggy locks out of it... but what sort of barebones tale of a rat was that? Now me, when I was on the open hearths, we also caught one in a trap. But! We put it in the charging box and the crane operator drove it right up to the furnace. It had just been tapped, so it was open and hungry... and I opened the box and the rat, seeing the hole at the far side of the furnace, scuttled right through it... We ran round to the other side... and I took my hat off to the rat... It was lying there, dead, its paws all charred... but! It had seen a chance and had taken it!"

The Major extricated a hand from under the drape and howled:

"Kudla, spare a thought, don't take too much off, I don't want to end up looking like a bloody Prussian!"

"I know what I'm doing – it's gonna look just fine! It'll all come just right, leave it to me! Eh, Johnny?"

Johnny gulped down his salami.

"Sure. But I only ever get my hair cut at Hairdressers for the Young. There's one there, he's French, Theodor Olivieri, and he's a great guy. Ask anyone, they'll all tell you he's ace. Drainpipes, an A-line coat and on Sundays he wears a kind of stetson. But he wouldn't say a word to you... it's only for me he does exactly the cut I want. Waves, and at the end he'll ask... 'Would sir care for eau de Cologne or violet water?'"

Johnny removed his cap and showed everyone, especially Italian Boy, just how wonderful his waves were, waves such as they only do at Hairdressers for the Young and only for Johnny.

Italian Boy started to lilt:

"I've had enough... I'm going home... So depressing here. Such a lovely girl, I said to her... I'd like to give you a kiss, Miss... and she... so would they all... I said I'll wait for you outside the gate... But she said she didn't have time... I said, so how about this evening?... but she said she needed an early night because she had to be up first thing. So I gave her a rose at least," said Italian Boy and, lying there on his back, carried on eating his bread roll and salami.

Atom Prince jumped to his feet:

"Things really are going downhill where girls are concerned! Like yesterday, I was sitting at the bar in the Baroko, dressed to the nines, one leg across the other to give a good view of my striped socks and dinky shoes – I'm rather particular where they're concerned because I've got small feet, and next to me, sitting on a bar stool, was this woman. I said: 'May I treat you to a glass, Miss?' She ran an expert eye over me and ordered an egg-flip. As we clinked glasses I said: 'You've got gorgeous tits, Miss!' She spluttered and said: 'Do mind your manners!' And I asked her: 'How much would you want to have your fence knocked down?' She played dumb: 'What did you say?' I said: 'For what financial contribution would you be willing to let yourself be tumbled and stuffed!' And would you believe it, she walked off! I know her, and how she makes her living... Truth is, women like a nice bit of chit-chat before, during and after..."

"You're talking bollocks," Coffee-boy grumbled.

"No, he's not...," said Kudla, brandishing his clippers.

"That shitbag kid o' mine, he's the same. Came in and said: 'Get this, dad, we rigged the drop hammer to stop exactly two millimetres above my nose.' I said: 'Don't tell me you lay down under it, did you?' 'I did, dad, but it's real scary, up there the hammer looks tiny, then when it crashes down to two millimetres from your nose, your whole world goes black.' I told him: 'You shitbag, why did you lie down under it, why?' 'For the thrill of it, dad!' 'I'll give you thrill, you shitbag!'" – And Kudla brandished the clippers at the Prince.[7]

But the Prince waved it aside:

"Give it a rest, the curtain's coming down. I say, Palmiero, you know I've no idea how you came to be here?"

"Aha," said Italian Boy and folded his hands behind his head. "I used to kip out on public benches. One day, I was lying there like that in a park, in Turin..., and I heard someone walking around me..., opened my eyes and there's someone kneeling beside me. I sat up and by the light of a streetlamp saw another Italian, just like me. I asked him: 'What are you doing here?' And he pointed to the newspaper I had covering me, and he said: 'My name's Ampolino and I've just been reading off you this notice that they're hiring men to go and work in Czechoslovakia.' And there you have it, me and Ampolino, we've been here for four years, but really and truly, there's nothing doing... Back home, girls don't work and in the evening they're all sex and singing... *ó suol beato... ove sorridere volle il creato...*"[8]

Italian Boy sang softly and Johnny whooped with delight:

"That's Kučera's Hawaiian guitar ensemble![9] *Lacrimas negras*![10] Oh my! They were to play it at the Winter Stadium, but because it was so cold, in August, it was moved to the People's Palace... and I tell you, it was packed out... packed out! So me an' the lads, we stacked three tables on top of each other to get a better view, an' just as Kučera struck up *Para Vigo me voy*,[11] one table leg broke an' I was sent flying an' landed on top of this woman an' she yelled... He-e-e-lp... an' I fainted." "Keep your head down." That was Kudla pushing the Major's head back where he needed it.

"So, Johnny, you say you fainted? You poor little mite, and what would you have said to someone like Scavenger Bird?" Kudla gave a cruel laugh.

"At our hospital there was one they'd nicknamed Scavenger Bird: when I first came there, the lads told me to promise him a snifter and in return he'd eat his dinner with a corpse..."

"Hell, Kudla, there's a ridge here at the back! Get rid of it, will you...!"

"I've told you, stop worrying, it's gonna look just fine! So I paid the old screamer, the lads locked the closet and fetched a nice, mellow corpse, the Bird sat it on his lap and the lads tied the dead guy's hands to Scavenger Bird's, set some goulash down before them and they really did it... They had their dinner together... What would say to that, Johnny?"

"Cripes! I'd have express trains going round inside my head, my washing lines would start getting jumbled up and I'd end up in Beřkovice[12] with my head between electrode pads..." – Johnny motioned with his head and shifted his hands to his knees.

Frenchie had finished eating, he wrapped his knife in his napkin and said: "So, Palmiero, go, pack it in and just leave. You don't have to stay. I also thought that coming here might bring me luck, so after twenty years I came back, to the place where I'd lived when I was a kid. Came back... they'd chucked me out really, me being a bit of a leftie. It's obvious, as a miner you can't lean any way but left, but here I'm to the right for a change... Where am I going to get chucked out to next?"

He sank into a reverie.

"So, if I do get the nagging urge, I'll go, and keep going, in France they'll put me away for a time and then I can start living again... not that life here's that bad, but it's sort of nicer to die in a world of wine,[13] and that's something people over there are good at..."

"Or could I be getting too old and it just seems that way to me? Ah, well! I say, Kudla, tell us some more about corpses!"

Kudla turned in his genteel way to the Major:

"Pomade on it?... Or just some lotion?"

"Lotion," said the Major bitterly, paralysed at the prospect of seeing himself in the mirror for the first time.

Kudla smiled. "After an autopsy, a cadaver has a little tag tied to its big toe with string. We used to collect cadavers in a van... But doesn't this make a good scalp massage as well, eh? It's some I've got left over, original stuff from Procházka of Prague... So we used to drive out to Ruzyně with them, along with the guy from our office and all the paperwork, he'd turn the tags so he could read them and check them against his inventory. By then the van would be backed up into the morgue and one time the guys said: 'Mr Schörner, sir, there's another one still on the chopping-up table over there!' So Mr Schörner went to see and suddenly the corpse did a salute like this, hand to forehead."

Kudla executed a salute with a ghastly grin on his face, like a wax figurine.

"And Mr Schörner knocked my coffin lid off with his foot, flung his arms out, fell across the coffin, his papers flying all over the place, but the guys just laughed. 'Mr Schörner, sir, don't be scared, it's what she does...' And in the van they tugged on a string and the corpse saluted again... Parting same side as usual?"

"My head feels cold!"

"Don't worry... So we'll do you the kind of parting old Fairbanks[14] used to have, okay?"

"Erm, okay." Atom Prince smirked, because he'd always been jealous of Kudla.

"Last Sunday I was fumbling about starkers with my neighbour... also starkers. An' I said to her, 'What would you do, ma'am, if I hanged myself here?' – An' I took a picture down and my tie off, made a loop in it, stuck my head through and just for the hell of it stuck my tongue out. An' guess what she did! She got a knife an' went to cut me down, almost cut my throat, she did..."

Kudla's eyes flashed: "I can pee you two bucketfuls a day of tall tales like that. Beat that if you can!"

Prince bristled: "Is that aimed at me?"

Kudla turned to the grinders:

"If the cap fits... But guys, here's one calamity that actually happened. Strašnice Crematorium. Me. And an attendant at the crem called Olda Tůma... And what do we two have in common? Once a month we'd go and buy daphnia together. And why? To put in the aquarium... for the fish."

"So there was this one time I was going down the steps, looking out for Olda, but the supervisor couldn't tell me where he was... He was looking up, waiting for the little light to start flashing, the red light that tells him a coffin's on the way down... Through the wall I could hear them singing *Bohemia the beautiful, Bohemia of mine...*[15] I pressed him: 'Boss, where *is* Olda Tůma?' But the light came on... and the coffin descended... landing on some runner things... I'd often seen it before, Olda had shown it to me... The supervisor took some tongs, suddenly turned towards me, pointed to the coffin he was holding with the tongs and roared: 'This is your mate Olda Tůma!' Believe me, with that I fair shot off to get the daphnia!"

Kudla untied his apron, flapped it out and said:

"There you are, Major, a picture of perfection!"

But Major was fingering the ridges and was dubious: "Let's hope..."

The Prince said stiffly:

"I think I might get married... I'll marry my cousin, a country wench... but very gentle! Last time I stayed there, she played me some Ravel, but I just sat there trying hard to think up dirty tricks to play on my fifty-five-year-old aunt..."

"Who's he talking to? Has he gone mad?" Kudla pointed over his shoulder towards the Prince.

"As far as I know, your mother wanted to chuck you out; pity she didn't, you thirty-year-old pipsqueak!"

Prince stood up for himself:

"As if happens, I'm okay at home now. Mother's got this date she goes to football matches with so he doesn't get cheated in the club caff... he's a bit soft in the head... but Mother? She hasn't lost her edge. The other day she got undressed and I was lurking in the background... her chemise was ripped and, believe me, there isn't a girl who wouldn't be proud of a pair of jugs like hers..."

Kudla was putting his apron back on, the others likewise. And Kudla was mocking: "Who's he talking to? What's anyone done to him? Who's he getting back at? Where's the life in what he's saying? That's bilge, Prince!"

And Kudla grinned, raised his hand in salute and launched into a spiel in an alien voice:

"A military cortège, men, is a serious business, no laughing matter... The duty officer details six men of the same size, not one tall one, one short one, like here recently, so the deceased doesn't get shaken about inside the coffin. Then he details two more to dig the grave. Soft soil – one regular day's work, stony soil – two... And if the dead soldier had been a Christian the duty officer details someone to carry a cross, but the cross must have its ribbons fluttering even if the guy carrying it has to blow at them! Because a military cortège really is a serious business, no laughing matter... Before the burial the officer in command commands: 'Cortège detail! Face... the rear wheels of the hearse! At the double, march! And no grinning next to the hearse! Or I'll have you locked up!' The army band comes to a halt by the cemetery wall to play a fanfare. So the grave has to have been dug well in advance! Not like last time, when the cortège turned into the cemetery to find the blokes with pickaxes only just clambering out of the grave! I'll have you locked up!... Because a military cortège, it's a serious business, no laughing matter..."

Kudla dropped his salute... "That's how the captain taught us winos army regs..."

He pulled his goggles back down over his eyes, pressed the start button and once the disk was at full revs, brought the handles down under his armpits and lowered it onto the steel billet to take out a crack or sliver. And he splattered out a long comet-tail of sparks. So one grinder after another roared into life, showering long tails of sparks onto the men's boots and into their aprons in various shades of red according to the kind of steel they were grinding...

Someone slid back the grinding shop door and shouted into the dust and gloom and lamps:

"There's a film crew here. You're to go and have yourselves filmed!"

Johnny, whose grinder was by the entrance, stopped his machine and went from one man to the next bellowing in their ears: "We're to go and have ourselves filmed!"

So they stopped their machines and went outside the grinding shop, blinking in the sunlight and hawking up and spitting out great gobbets of black stuff.

The overseer, who'd once been a grinder-operator himself, but whose work now consisted in running about with files and posters, pointed across the rail tracks:

"There's a film crew here, from Newsreel..."

And, full of his own importance, he scuttled off to a works council meeting.

"Greetings, comrades!" That was the young man in a corduroy anorak.

"Look, for the next issue we need a group of steelworkers having a lively discussion about the situation in Korea... Over there by those two trucks of ingots would be a good spot, what d'you reckon?" This last was addressed to another young fellow wearing an Australian beret and carrying a shoulder-mounted camera.

"Should be okay… it's in sunlight…"

"Good!" said the anchor in the anorak.

"Some of you could have clambered on top of the ingots… and you could be studying a map… and… The ones down below could appear to be reading *Rudé právo*."

Atom Prince pulled his curly hair tight under his Rommel cap[16] and smirked:

"Let's hope it's not going to be another like last time, when the radio news did theirs… hustle and bustle in the steelworks! Tee-hee!"

He grinned.

"What was that then?" the anchor asked.

"Oh nothing… we were already in the bathhouse, the works was silent, but the reporter said: 'You, miss, climb up into your crane cab and drive it up and down a few times…' So she drove it up and down, the radio minions began dropping buckets and bits of rail and empty chromium and vanadium barrels onto a steel plate, the reporter held his microphone up to it, then he started gushing to the listeners about the hustle and bustle in the steelworks, where everyone busts their guts to a hundred and twenty per cent. Tee-hee-hee!" And he grinned.

"But that's a purely technical thing! The main thing was to capture the idea… surely you see that? Does this train here travel up and down all the time? Make for a good backdrop, don't you reckon? Churns out some great smoke."

"No it doesn't travel up and down the whole time…," Kudla remarked politely.

"Pity… so come the other side of the track… This won't

take long and you'll soon be able to see yourselves in the cinema... We're calling it Tea Break at the Factory..."

"Ho, ho! Tea break? But we've already had ours!"

"What harm can it do? You can charge it to us. Buy some salami and a bread roll all round... – What d'you reckon?" the anchor asked the cameraman.

"Should be okay..., but where's the canteen?"

"Here, just round the corner," Kudla pointed and he looked uneasy.

"Good, I'll go, meanwhile you see how it might go out here," said the anchor and stepped across the tracks.

"So, Johnny, what about you and your women?" the Prince asked.

"What? You'd be surprised! At the Blue Star I cut quite a caper with one... wherever she went, I followed, I even followed her into the ladies. And her husband took it amiss and gave me a smack in the face to remember him by. Like this! Said I'd taken her knickers down!"

The cameraman adjusted his camera and waited while they hauled Johnny up onto the ingots... then he said: "This way will do just nicely... I can pan it..."

"And you're saying you hadn't taken her knickers down?" the Prince asked, taking the map from the film guy.

"I hadn't... but I did just get my hands on them, but Christ, what a fuss... People get so edgy. I got another smack in the face in Prague once..." Johnny swung on his feet.

"If you wouldn't mind... you up there, be looking at the map...," the film guy growled into his camera.

But Johnny was still full of his story:

"I'd gone to Prague to buy some records. Kučera and his band. And in Košíře I called in at the Green Tree, the band was in fine fettle, an' there was this pretty girl at one table, I goes over to her, bows and says: 'May I have the pleasure, miss?' and to her fellow: 'Okay, mate?' But he comes at me like so-o-o… 'Sling yer 'ook, dickhead!' An' I says: 'What was that?' An' 'e says it again: 'Sling yer 'ook!' I bows and tells the girl: 'Forgive me, ma'am, I'm gonna have to teach your friend a lesson!'

"An' I tells the guy: 'An' you, shitbag, come outside, let's 'ave this out properly!'"

"So we went outside and he floored me in one go! Quite a stroke of luck I didn't have the Kučera records with me, otherwise he and his band would've been in smithereens… And that, guys, is what happened in Prague, to me!"

Johnny pointed a finger at himself.

"Me, for whose benefit the Sylvians start playing the minute I enter the People's Palace in Kladno… and their drummer, Jarda Votava, he's a star turn, when he really gets into his stride, his drumsticks go flying off into the audience!"

The grinder men laughed, but Johnny was all in earnest:

"Look, you sack o' pricks, what are you laughing at?"

Johnny was offended, but he happened to glance across the tracks towards the annealing shops… Suddenly he stood bolt upright. He'd spotted something wrong. The blokes there had come running out, hands clapped to their heads.

"Something's happened!" he said, pointing towards the forges.

The grinders all hopped down and ran to the spot, but Johnny remained rooted to the spot... He sat down heavily and watched the mêlée by the gate, where they were all looking down at the same spot... Something was lying there in the gateway and a few of the men were trying to crowbar something pretty heavy out of the way... by which time it was obvious to Johnny that some human disaster had happened, he knew the kind of confusion that broke out if a grinding disk snapped, making mincemeat of the entire machine, whipping the handles out from under your armpits... leaving the operative with a broken leg or slashed eyebrows...

Someone ran passed the truck Johnny was sitting on shouting: "An ingot's landed on top of someone!"

Prince jumped down and grabbed him by the shoulder: "How did it happen?"

The man who'd seen death pointed behind him: "The crane's grabbers got an ingot by its arse and... brought him down!"

"Maybe it won't be too...," said the cameraman.

The Prince smirked: "Don't talk crap... even from this distance I can tell it was a thirty-six... an' that weighs a ton and a quarter!"

And from his vantage point Johnny could now see them bringing a barrel-chested man out into the sunlight. And as they brought him along the tracks, Johnny saw blood mixed with the white powder of his crushed dentures streaming from the man's mouth. Then someone shouted at all and sundry: "Why are you standing about? Nothing better to do? Get back to your jobs!"

But all and sundry – they each of them saw in that body their own potential selves.

"Who is it?" the grinders asked Coffee-boy.

"They said he's called Machač an' he's from Rozdělov – an' he's got two kids." Coffee-boy was trying to get his breath back.

Kudla said: "Well, lads, I'd like to know which of you's got the guts to go an' tell his family. When my dad came home from the night shift, Mum, as soon as she heard the gate click, made his coffee an' set the mug an' some bread on a chair. An' as he took his boots off, he'd start eating, then he got washed an' dressed... an' went off to play cards at the Blue Star... I'd take him his lunch there. Then when he came in in the afternoon, he'd just lie down on the floor, straighten up an' go to his next shift. He was always on nights. Then one day the gate clicked, she made his coffee an' set the mug on the chair... but Dad didn't come in... after it had all gone cold, she went out and Dad's pipe invaded the sitting room... the only thing left of him... He'd been buried in a rock fall and his mates had come to tell us... They just deposited his pipe and fled."

"Comrades...," said the cameraman. "Believe me, this has been a bit of a shock for me too, but we do still need to get to Chomutov..."

Having said that, he and the anchor started passing round rolls and slices of salami.

"Do get back up there, I won't keep you long," the anchor said apologetically.

Atom Prince called out provocatively:

"Say, Johnny, you went to the football on Sunday! Come on, tell us how it went!"

"Great match, believe me! In the second half, three of the Teplice team flattened our Majer, but Messrs Fous and Linhart gave Teplice such a hard time that they tried to do for the umpire... And Draganiola and Kokštejn got carried off, but otherwise it were a great game! Kuchler's eye's still got a bulge like this even today!"[17]

"Comrades, please, do hold this newspaper and look as if you're reading it!" said the cameraman and set his face against his camera.

Then the camera began to whirr and Johnny cried out with glee:

"But before they mashed up Kokštejn, he'd given 'em a couple o' right maulings... what a treat that was, your ladyship!"

Johnny bent down to the group on the ground and did a pencil drawing in the margin of *Rudé právo*... a crossbar and two posts.

"So... and this cross here, that's one of the Teplice fullbacks and this one's the other... this cross, that's the Teplice halfback... and Kokštejn's here... But what do you think he did?"

"How would we know..."

And Johnny put the paper down and let go of the ingot, speared Kokštejn with his pencil, then dribbled to his own zesty commentary:

"He got the ball... spun past the half, did a postage stamp pirouette past the fullback, one more little zip and from the six-yard box shunted the ball under the bar..."

While Johnny was getting carried away, the anchor was reading aloud the notes that would be heard the following week in the main cinemas in Prague:

"Any time now, Pusan will fall. All you imperialists, give up now and go jump in the sea..."

"That's enough for now, Bob... let's just do a medium close-up from up there by the map... you get up there, I'll hold the camera for you..."

In all innocence, Atom Prince asked Johnny:

"Why did the army let you go?"

"Why? Because they pissed me off!"

"And why did they piss you off?"

"Because they kept pushing me around. All the time... the get down and stand up and sleeping in a tent when it rained. So eventually I grabbed a sub-machine gun and sprayed everything with it and one shot went right through the platoon sergeant's ear..."

"That was after, Johnny, but what about the time you released that artillery piece?"[18]

"Oh, that! That was at Jičín, on a Sunday, I wanted the sergeant to be pleased with me, so outside, by that gun, I got him to show me the ins and outs of it... And the sarge was tickled pink to have someone show some interest... and then I unchocked the gun and it rolled off through the gate and hurtled down the avenue towards Jičín... people had to jump out of the way. And then during some manoeuvres at night I tossed some part of my assault rifle and the men were sent out to search for it, so in the end Professor Henner had been right when he told my mother I wasn't cut out for the army and never would be... So they dismissed me, stamped my army ID card and sent me on my way..."

Johnny was in his element and the camera was whirring away behind his ear.

"And what was the second goal like?" the Prince was curious to know.

"You mean you haven't heard? Everyone else in Kladno knows – the papers have been full of it... so see this!"

Johnny took his pencil out and drew two posts and a crossbar on the map the Prince had shoved in front of him. And he jubilated:

"These are the Teplice fullbacks, and here's Kokštejn!"

He drew two crosses by the Pusan fortress, then drew his pencil, as Kokštejn, quickly and surely between the fullbacks and stood alone in front of the goalie...

And the camera purred on and the anchor read from his notebook: "The whole of Korea will be liberated from the capitalist yoke. It is only through our labours that we can show our solidarity and swill the steel of peace down the gullets of the imperialists..."

"An' he flicked it past him...," said the Prince.

"All done. Thank you...," said the anchorman.

And Johnny hopped down and ran towards the grinding shop gate, found some chalk and showed that the gate, the whole gate, was the Teplice goalmouth and Johnny himself was Kokštejn.

"No fancy work, no whacking it in, on the contrary. On the contrary! The goalie took a full-length dive, but Kokštejn dodged out of the way…"

Johnny gently drew the invisible, but, for him, so very visible ball to him with his instep and, as he fell onto his back, he cried:

"And like that, almost in a somersault…"

Johnny landed on his back and scissored the ball into the top corner of the goal.

From the other side someone dashed the gate open. And through it came the black-coated works manager.

"What are looking for, Johnny, there on the ground?"

Johnny sprang to his feet. He took out his chalk and drew on the gate: "Just so's you know, boss, these are the Teplice fullbacks, and here's Kokštejn…"

"Give it a rest, Johnny… You've already done me the same drawing in the office…," he said and proceeded to the canteen for some soup.

Kudla sidled up to the Prince and whispered: "You're a brick… thing is… I've got kids…"

It was nearly one o'clock as the Prince ambled into the canteen. The talk and general racket was so loud that anyone trying to speak had to shout. It was hot and the steelworkers were knocking back beer by the lakeful. The cleaners and tea ladies were sitting at a long pewter-topped table and from the telling glances they were exchanging they were having great fun with one young woman, who was comical for how nothing was sacred to her: any beans she didn't know, she couldn't spill... so... she spoke only the unvarnished truth.[1]

"What else could I do? Right now I'm helping out with the oxy-fuel cutters, 'cos I've got little Jaroušek to feed!"

"An' what about his dad, big Jaroušek?" said one of the old women, feigning curiosity.

"That idiot? 'E went off an' married some cow an' got 'er up the duff in no time, like 'e did me. But I'll tell you this for nothing, Jaroušek's comin' crawlin' back... yep!"

And the Prince had no idea what the wasted womenfolk found so funny. So he stood there, leaning in a corner by the pewter countertop, on which stood two pails of black coffee and a number of small glass jars that had once contained mustard.

The door opened and in stormed a man in a real fury, his blue goggles held to his hat with wire, and he roared, actually outroaring the entire canteen:

"Who d'you think's gonna clear away those anticorrosion pigs for you?"

A gaunt man, absolutely dripping sweat, wiped his face with his whole hand and said wearily: "Was I supposed to get hold of a crane somewhere? There's no woman, no crane driver attached to number twenty, guv!"

"What's that?" the foreman bellowed.

"There's no crane free!" the workman bellowed back.

"So you should've brought the jib truck in to deal wi' them pigs!"

"It was in use, with a load of chill mould batchers!"

"So you should have waited!"

"Waited, waited! It's all very well for you to talk about waiting! Right now it's carting rebars off into storage!"

"So get back there and carry on waiting!" The foreman shook the workman physically, but just then a bell rang... three hammer strokes on a bell.

"Well...? Boss! There's arc furnace S about to run a test! So we've had it for now...," the smelter relaxed and savoured a good swig of beer.

The Prince helped himself to a scoop of the brownish liquid and still failed to understand why the old biddies were so gleeful at the young woman's agitation:

"That's what it's come to... a packed bus an' 'im, wi' that pregnant cow of 'is, standing behind me. One prat from our place shouted to me... 'So, Jarmila, what's your husband up to?' An' I 'ollered back the length of the bus: 'Screw a husband like that! An' I mean it!' An' I tell you, ladies, the entire bus were gobsmacked!"

At that moment Rosetka entered the canteen. She headed bashfully straight for the corner, tipped a bucketful of spoons into the sink, turned on the tap and listened to the water.

The Prince poured his coffee away and took his time rinsing the glass.

"What's new in the outside world?" she whispered and picked up one spoon.

He slowly poured a coffee and whispered: "The Americans in Korea have landed in the bolshies' rear… and they've suspended MacArthur… Pity, that! He wanted to drop an atom bomb wherever might have taken his fancy. To knock out China…," he said, smiling cheerfully.

She stood there with the spoon. "And that would have made you happy?"

"Me? – And how! I dream of little else…"

"And what if there were people down below?"

"People, exactly… lots of people… the more the merrier," said the Prince, laughing, and he sipped his coffee.

Rosetka started busily cleaning the spoon.

The Prince said, in a whisper and giggling blissfully:

"The West Germans are going to get an army. For now just a *Grenzschutzwaffe*…,[2] but headed by Guderian.[3] Mannteufel…[4] A pair of go-getters…"

Rosetka tossed the spoon in the sink.

"How did Zátopek[5] do in the five kilometres at the Olympics," she asked, hoarsely.

Staring into the corner, the Prince said: "Churchill's address at Fulton was a wake-up call for Europe! Thinking just of defence for now… but later things'll start from a position of strength… probably with Eisenhower at the helm…"

"How *did* Zátopek do in the five kilometres?" she asked again, her eyes flashing angrily.

"Oh, him? He had us guessing. The bus was struck dumb. A national disaster... pity!" And the Prince spat a bit of chicory from the corner of his mouth.

"He lost...?"

"It was just as we all wanted! He won that race of the century... But do you know who's likely to become president in America?"

"But *how* did Zátopek do...?" she said, dropping three nicely scoured spoons into the bucket.

"How... it was a close-run thing... at first Schade[6] stuck out in front, then came Pirie[7] and Chataway,[8] for a brief moment the great Gaston Reiff[9] shone out... After the eighth lap it got very hairy. Gaston gave up and Zátopek started doing his breakaways and at the last lap even Mimoun[10] came through, but in the end it was Zátopek who won, in an Olympic record time... A disaster, like I said, not a word passed in the bus next morning... But they've done a hydrogen bomb test in the Pacific... a thousand times more powerful than the basic one...," said the Prince, but the young woman, to the delight of the men as well, was now shrieking for all to hear:

"And that cow of 'is sent me a message, d'you know what it said? She said... When I pop I'll leave it outside the bitch's door... meaning me, 'cos since I get a child allowance for one bastard already, as she said, I can take on the other one as well..."

Suddenly Rosetka whispered: "If no one's watching, look at me…"

He held his glass up against the light and picked more bits of chicory out with his finger… he shifted his gaze and looked into her face. She was pale, earnest, quite different from the day before.

"How old do you think I am?" she whispered nervously.

The Prince wanted to say thirty-two, but spotting the long crease about her mouth he said: "Twenty-nine."

She whispered: "I'm twenty-six… Yesterday we finished unloading a whole train of Swedish ore… they brought it in wagons with the markings of the American Zone, so don't talk to me about America… I couldn't care less about… But are you human?"

"Possibly…," the Prince said, now somewhat ill at ease.

"That's good enough… so, wait for me tomorrow morning at quarter to six in the drawing plant… by the clock, I'll be there, tidying up in the tool store… and don't be scared. Bring me some cigarettes… as many as you can…"

"You smoke?"

"No… it's not for me… the girls…"

"And what can I bring you?"

"A bar of chocolate…"

"How much longer have you got here?"

"Three years…"

"Hm, that's ages…"

"Too right, but there's to be an amnesty sometime, so I'll be going home…"

"Amnesty... I can imagine the whores and petty thieves going... but you?"

"What do you take *me* for?"

"I can guess at a glance... You're political..."

"Certainly not... at the next amnesty I'll be going home... definitely..."

"I thought... Sorry, no offence! Okay, *das ist gut*, I'll bring you some fags... definitely... and a whole packet of chocolate... and Zátopek went on to win a great 10 kilometres... and then a glorious marathon... I'll definitely be waiting for you in the morning..."

"I wonder... and... once I'm out of this place, we can go out on the razzle together... Look, I have to get going... have to...," she whispered into the sink, having scrubbed the spoons to the brightest silver several times over.

She smiled and quietly departed in her burlap skirt and white linen bodice.

The Prince watched as she headed out through the door; before she closed it, she glanced back at him and gave a nod with her eyes.

Only then did the Prince register himself standing there in the canteen among all those human voices and the clink of glasses. And again that young voice was giving vent to its indignation, shouting... and anyone who was listening looked as if they were listening to something ever so funny...

"... an' so, comin' off shift I stops 'im and says, get this, you blitherin' idiot, you can tell how well I'm lookin' after your kid, spotless, 'e is... an' that stupid cow o' yours, she's been puttin' it about that little Jaroušek's gonna die on me an' you aren't gonna pay nothing! But Jaroušek's alive an' very well! An' he's gonna live an' 'e's gonna pee all over that bitch o' yours' feet! An' would you believe it, I musta struck a nerve, 'cos 'e went right out an' bought the lad some sweets... An' more than that I can't tell you...," she added and smiled a happy smile.

The Prince glanced up at the clock. Bath-time! And the foreman crashed into him in the doorway and shouted:

"I bet you forgot to add some crude iron to the smelting charge, eh?"

And one of the smelters replied into his tin pot:

"There weren't none..."

"But you must have put something in, surely!" The fore-man threw up his hands.

"Sure... moulds!" said the smelter.

"Moulds, moulds! But they're past it!" the foreman wailed and turned to some of the other men, bellowing and pointing a finger:

"And you, water-babies, drink up... an' jump to it! Open-hearth number eight's gettin' the squitters!"[11]

THE GABRIEL EXPLOSION

A short story

He opened the iron door, he bent, I passed through. Then he opened the wooden door, and thus did I enter his stable. It was a partitioned loft area with the ceiling plastered, there was a little dormer and the ceiling sloped steeply downward following the angle of the roof... I grew concerned: "Oops, I'm treading on your picture..." But he said gruffly: "Don't worry... it's a carpet..." Having got used to the half-light, I saw that the picture consisted of a woman lying legs apart and a naked, exultant man about to mount her... He, no less gruffly: "Don't worry... that's my mother and her pook-ie..." And then he began explaining the pressed plants on the chimney breast, some mournful leaves stuck on a sheet of card, placed opposite each other in a regular pattern, like green swallows flying down to the ground... It was only then that I looked about me and was delighted, depressed and beatific: "So that's where you sleep?" And where the ceiling sloped steeply downward lay a pile of glass wool and on it a blanket, on the blanket a smaller ribbed blanket, on the smaller blanket a sheet of canvas... I veered too close under the roof and with a bonk! sank into the glass wool, which gave out a loud scratchy sound... I sat there motionless, but my heartbeat rustled quietly through the glass wool... There was no desk, all his writing stuff lay about the floor, his drawing things... nearby an oil lamp with a black chimney, and light struggling in through the dormer window, with a myriad minuscule filaments of glass wool dancing in it...

the room became otherworldly... it was far too like out-houses, a knacker's yard... something could have happened... Vladimír[1] had stuck his head outside, onto the roof, and I could hear his voice coming in from out: "Last night, through here and like this, I was looking into people's bathrooms, their homes... into people..." Then he drew his head back inside and collapsed to his knees, opened a ledger with a network of blue lines and started writing crazily... I said: "You can't write like this, when it's below zero... and drawing's surely out of the question..." Whereupon Vladimír raised his right foreleg into the light and with a blink of his fingers said: "I've got that sorted, I just engage different muscles, turn and turn about..." To myself I said: "What a star...," and I stood up and the glass wool noisily erased the imprint of my buttocks... I rose on tiptoe to the dormer window and said: "How can it be that Bambino used to walk down there without meeting you... and yet!... You did use to go to the Malvaz!..."[2] And the quadruped Vladimír carried on writing with his right foreleg... He said: "Yes, we did use to meet there, me, Reegen, Bouše... Krauer..."[3] And I chipped in: "... and I saw you there, I did! You'd be sitting by the gramophone, changing the records... plotting... and back then I was smitten with a Jewish girl with a green ribbon...[4] troubled by Liliová Street... the house with the double-twisted snake... the old ladies, little dogs... The passageway into the Klementinum... Eros spattered with lime, and back then Halánek's[5] was still open..." Vladimír picked up where he'd left off, but still writing: "... or we'd meet by the little fishes[6] on Old Town Square..." Which got me quite excited: "I used to wash in that fountain with the fishes every day, first thing, before I dashed for my bus... just after four... in the morning..." At which point Vladimír stopped writing and rolled over onto his side: "My hand's started to ache... those places, they're our stomping ground... We used to hold séances there... there's still an outline of Rotbauer[7] in Karlova Street... There we got the evening crowd so wild that people started leaping up the walls... using a stick they picked out patches and showed what they were seeing in them... mediaeval... their eyes popped out of their heads and they screamed... we herded them from lamppost to lamppost and drummed our ideas into them... Krauer, Reegen..." Vladimír leapt up onto his hind legs and withdrew a photo from a mountain of paper... He pricked one youngster's eyes with his pencil: "That's Reegen... only ever at night... cigarettes, beer and he'd just sit and stare... all through the night... at one stage he and the lads would sleep in a disused greenhouse belonging to the manor house on Slav Island... he kept some blankets in the middle of the greenhouse and caught up on his sleep there... his living dream... but now he's got TB..." Vladimír crossed to the dormer window... the afternoon sun chopped his head off... I said: "Move in with us, you can share with the carpenter's mate and you'll be comfortable enough, you'll be able to write and paint... we'll put on exhibitions and suchlike..." But the headless Vladimír said gruffly: "But I'll still keep this set-up... it's pretty nifty... you know the stuff I've already written up... I'm working on interplanetary competition... a letter and report for Professor Vondráček… vice-chancellors and editors… that innovative idea of a shovel with a ring attached… let the bastards know there's no escaping explosionalism… even the things at Altamira[8] arose by association…" And picking up a pencil, he started turning a stain into a female bison… "A blotch like that… just needs finishing off…" I objected: "That's fine, but it's just the start of something, it's too passive… after that you need to drive it home… a picture… and there you have it, critics, take it or leave it…" Vladimír's head wasn't going to stop now: "Maybe, but I'm after something else… when I'm out sketching in the street, people give themselves up to me, they come up of their own accord… ask questions… then they make their confessions… I unleash what's inside them, the same thing that the Surrealists sought as individuals and covertly, in secret, nothing to see, not a sound to hear… out in the street everyone brings back their childhood cupboard… they pump blood into their imagination… we turn the street into a picture gallery… on an outside wall a Rembrandt gains vibrancy… because it's shaped by the observer's associations… then it actually becomes the observer's own picture…" I objected: "But then not only a wall… but everything, anything, anyhow… even a landscape can be transmuted by association… what about the poet?… and then there was that school in Germany where the kids were taught to see anything in anything…" The head on the roof paused, then took off again: "But we'll burn galleries down! Terrorise people! We'll herd them into drawing classes and teach them… make it compulsory… everyone shall be an artist… It's all a matter of how you go about it…" And poking his head back inside the loft he went on: "And we shall be the dictators! We'll lock 'em up! Chop their heads off! Where's the helping them if they don't want what's good for them? We have to get tough with them!..." I objected, squatting on my haunches: "Okay, you'll dictate what's to be... But somehow or other you have to pick up on the past... after all, that's what the Surrealists were after... art to be done by all..." But Vladimír raised the last toe on his foreleg and said: "All that stuff the Surrealists had in books I've got here in my little finger... and then people today, they've no live experience, they just wallow in and rehash formulae that did once have life in them... so let them come out into the street with me... into the squares... You understand, surely, I'm not going to wait until some future accords me recognition... I'll be dead by then... I want it now, today... to engage people right here and now... with the people inside people... you send your *Bambino* to five friends and that's it... until maybe one day... but by then you'll have been missed..." I interrupted Vladimír's flow: "But surely you have to pin down things that'll buck the trend... people will leave the streets... and then indoors... what indoors?... something that's inside them all the time... fluorspar, apatite, feldspar... woman, apple, friendship... ten commandments... and transgression and regression..." Vladimír said: "So how about it? Come on, let's go out in the street! Right!" He got a stepladder out of one corner, a board and a sheet of paper: "And you take those paints there... that little bottle of turps..." I begged him: "Let me carry the steps, I'd like people to think I'm a painter..." And

we left the attic and stairs behind us... then the house, and
the streets came forward to meet us and the streets closed in
behind us... At the corner of Týnská Street and Old Town
Square I said: "That bell up there once came loose while it
was being rung and it shot down through the roof... the
house is now called Bell House... I used to live here... third
window... that's where the Bambino di Praga lived..."
Vladimír pointed to the John Huss[9] monument: "Once
a mad woman was climbing up that... first onto Huss's finger, then on top of his head... The fire brigade showed up...
ha, it was so sad and magnificent... and over there, on that
wall... no, that one!, I sketched things out all over it and
people really did think it was damaged frescoes... they did
see the things I'd hinted at in those blotches..." We went
past the little fishes, the New Town Hall... along by the wall
of the Klementinum and onwards to the river... I was quite
keyed up and started again: "Down there on the waterfront
there was a knot of people... I went down and lo and behold... there was a naked woman washed up by the waves
onto the sand... she'd probably been lying beneath the weir
in the hard water, the water helped preserve her, fish and
crayfish had chewed at her arms, face, fingers and insteps...
but now she was lying on her side on the bank as if sunbathing... the spotless white of her limescale-coated side and
chest... People were fascinated... as if fishermen had tipped
the Venus de Milo out of their nets... over there, Vladimír,
do you see that Art Nouveau building?... not that one... the
third along... I was walking past as they brought someone
out... a blood-soaked sheet about the neck... she was said

to be an Austrian officer's widow who'd cut her throat... disenchanted with life... used a razor so her head tipped back like a suitcase lid... in an alcove... I went back there and made my own the little rococo room she used to sit in... the screen she undressed behind... the small carpet with its blood-soaked corner... then down these steps to Kampa Island, past the rowing boats... Eduard Terrace... the Sova Mills... along under the chestnut trees... Blanka's footpath... and Vladimír, just look at that sluice!... then there below the Smetana Museum, and I walked barefoot along the weir to the sluice... that's where I used to go swimming, reading... one afternoon I heard: 'Help!' I jumped into the water... and over there, onto that stretch of waterfront, we hauled out two young men... and the doctor couldn't help them either... they lay there under the overhanging trees and they were dead... their mothers horrified... and the people... then a black car, the undertakers jumped out, touched their caps with one finger: 'Hi!'... backed the hearse up and took out two black coffins... tipped the lids back... one took a body by the arms, the other the legs... then that dull wet horrific thud... the lids... and I made my way home, sad... and that time at the foundry, endless disasters... grinders might crack... machines blown sky-high... one with his leg smashed in two... one with his eyebrows ripped open... I went home and got out my Perkeo typewriter and wrote... all night... and day... I didn't go to work... I was afraid of death... and so I wrote *Bambino di Praga*... in an aura of deathly death..." We went beneath the Bridge Tower and I noticed that Vladimír was walking with the innocent gait of a goat kid, giving way at the knees, and the location distorted his face... On the square in Malá Strana he stopped beneath the arcade, set up the stepladder, then the board on the ladder, silently opened the paints and approached a pillar: "So this part here!... What do you reckon it is?" I said: "A banal moonscape with a lake and a meadow and a bull grazing on it!" As he mixed the turps Vladimír said: "So be it!" And he started painting with his right foreleg... A pretty girl came along in a saddle-shoulder coat and high heels... and she stopped and stared. I went up to her and said: "Come closer, Miss, and tell me what you think." And she said: "What's that man painting?" I said: "That blotch there is what's inspired the painter to paint!..." And I went over to the wall and sketched out with my finger: "See this moon here? See this bull? See this lake?..." And the girl nodded with her chin and squeaked: "Oh dear me! I've never even noticed!" I rubbed my hands: "So you do see it, and all that, and much more besides, you can evoke yourself... so when you go along a street all on your lonesome, you can have fun with the blotches and patches on the wall plaster... like when you're lying in the grass with your boyfriend and guessing what this or that cloud reminds you of... look here, Miss, what do you think this mark might be?" But the girl just shook her head in token of her ignorance. I ploughed on: "Just look closely..." And I ran my pencil round the patch. At which the girl clapped one hand to her mouth and squeaked: "Who'd have thought it – it's a girl reading a novel!" I said: "There you have it! This patch is now yours, take it with you and know this: you will now never be bored... in the blotches on walls and the cracks in them you'll be able to see whatsoever you will... something to help kill the time or revelations of your most secret wishes..." And the girl said a puzzled thank you and left. Meanwhile a little huddle of people was watching Vladimír at work. It hadn't got through to them why he would fix his gaze on the wall and then start painting... they hadn't made the connection... I went back to the wall and sure enough... now they could see the bull, see the moon, see the lake... But one little fellow with his cap pulled down over his eyes suddenly declared: "I'm seeing something else altogether, I can see a map of Europe!" And he hopped over to the wall and marked out what he was seeing with one finger. I said: "There you have it... Vladimír, do paint the gentleman's map for him..." And Vladimír overpainted his moonscape and did the map... Another onlooker saw barn owls and baboons in it... So Vladimír painted some barn owls and baboons into the same picture... and people started recalling their childhoods and seemed to me to be yielding to fever... obsession... passion... They now numbered twenty or thirty, so the policeman on point duty came over and sermonised over their heads: "Step back away from the traffic, please..." And off he went back to the crossroads in his nice white sleeves. Then a man in intellectual spectacles stepped out of the huddle and wondered: "But art... this can't be art! Art has to be something beautiful, perfect, something that is greater than us, knocks the stuffing out of us..." I tried to explain: "You have to understand that this is the pre-lyrical stage, this isn't a result but what goes before a picture… the initial chaos out of which… But the good man persisted: "So this isn't art then. It's a subjective clue… everyone sees it differently." I said: "But we all see an apple differently, or an event, our whole life… it's obvious this isn't a resultant…" At which point Vladimír turned and said tersely: "Bur it is, it's is the resultant image of how I've been affected!" And I kept silent, although I knew that Vladimír was teasing the bespectacled onlooker and I hesitated, because what was in front of Vladimír was no longer a picture, more a kind of tuning-up leading to a symphony… Then three men showed up and the one wearing an English trench coat asked scornfully: "What on earth's this you're painting?" And the great crowd, spread out all the way to the roadway, fell silent. Vladimír turned as we turn from sleep to reality and calmly said: "Nothing." And the man hissed like a true inquisitor: "So… while people are committed to building socialism, this man here is creating NOTHING…" And Vladimír repeated audibly: "Yes, nothing." And he went back to painting some kind of spotted dog seized by a spotted typhoid fever… And I was overcome with anxiety… because he was painting it over the barn owls and baboons and maps and all that on top of the moonscape. And the man in the trench coat screeched: "I wonder if you've ever come across a certain Courbet…" Whereupon I went close up to his coat and shouted: "Of course!" The man, looking about his friends and the crowd, voiced aloud: "Well, well, the backroom boy! The adjutant!…" But I shouted back: "We know him all right! And we also know that Monet was vilified in the name of Courbet, and Cézanne was vilified in the name of Monet and Picasso in the name of Cézanne! We know that anything done here and now is vilified in the name of what's been done before! It's just your putrid brain that doesn't get it!" And I stepped up close to the man and we stared into each other's eyes... mesmerising each other... Then he hopped back and declared in loathing: "Who are you? I could catch something nasty from you!" And over his head his bespectacled friend howled: "This is a fascist provocation of the working people! The police should be sent for!" Things were getting a bit hairy... the crowd sat up and took notice... and Vladimír finished painting his grue-some picture. I said: "Look, folks, that's utter rubbish! Look at my hands!..." and I showed the crowd my calluses... "And let them show you their dinky hands!... Us here, this paint-er and me, we travel daily to work in the Kladno steelworks and in the evenings, instead of resting, we stake our lives. Why, do you suppose? Here... this is my ID card... here's his..." A bearded workman stepped out of the crowd and pointed to Vladimír: "I've seen him here twice before and I listen to what he says... he's right... I've often thought of my wardrobe and could never figure where the owls and bats came from and he explained it perfectly well... while paint-ing these walls..." But the man in the trench coat insisted: "Rubbish, their intentions lie elsewhere... they're fascists, this is fascist degenerate art!" And from beyond the crowd and over its heads the traffic cop took a look and warned: "Right, gentlemen, one last time, or I'll start taking notes!..." It was alarming, those three wanted to get us detained. Then a man with a parting surfaced from the crowd and took our part: "No, I've been listening... it's all wrong, leave off and go your ways, I'm the editor of a Moravian monthly for teachers... these lads are innocent... go about your business, all of you, be sensible and you two, pack your stuff up... goodness, this is no way to solve problems..." And he came right over to us, while the man in the trench coat rolled his sleeve back past his wristwatch and declared, surveying those present: "People... at six forty-five and ten seconds precisely these artist gentlemen have revealed to you – Nothing..." And they crossed to the pavement opposite, from where they kept a hostile watch on us... The crowd broke up... Vladimír folded his easel... striding along in the roadway came E. F. Burian in a floral, bee-decked waistcoat and a huge ribbon... We set off and the editor spoke: "I'll put this in our paper, it'll make a nice article, but you must approach things from a slightly scholarly angle... if you let me have your addresses I'll send you copies when it comes out..." As we walked back across Charles' Bridge, Vladimír unpinned the picture and hurled it into the black waters... We just leaned over and it did a white zigzag down... I noticed Vladimír's hands and the journalist almost made to jump after it. He mumbled: "Why d'you do that?" Vladimír said: "Why bother keeping it...?" And the vault of heaven over Prague made a beautiful evening...

MADE IN CZECHOSLOVAKIA

A short story

I /

1) The doctor combing his hair and inspecting the comb against the light to see how much hair he's combed out. "I've started falling apart slowly."

2) The bearded Bondy[1] resting on the sofa. A bottle stands on the carpet. Bondy's legs are concealed under his loden coat. The ghastly noise of waste pipes travels through the house.

3) Bondy leaps to his feet and listens closely. "What's that?"

4) The doctor switches on the radio and the little green window lights up – "What? The house has crapped itself."

5) The beardie in long johns stands, leaning close to the wall and listening to the sound plopping through the house. "Holy shit, that's quite a turn!"

And he pulls on his trousers. "Doc, have you got some paper? My wretched discharge…"

6) The Doctor hands Bondy a thin sheet of paper covered in writing. "In this house we wipe our bottoms with poems." And Bondy slowly empties the bottle of vodka.

7) The eye gleams green and a tenor accompanied by an orchestra is singing divinely: *Niemand liebt dich wie ich al-*

lein...[2] Bondy finishes off the bottle and the laces that tie up his artificial leg, which is hanging from the ceiling, dangle about the crown of his head.[3] "I'd like to believe that whenever I hear music like that lines of verse will come flooding in..."

8) "You may remember, Bondy, that right now someone is waiting for someone... possibly..."

9) Several flimsies fluttering constantly in the draught from the window frame. "Oh, oh, that time in the jug in Vienna... mountains of stuff to eat... I'm tearing up some newspaper to roll a ciggie... tear off a bit and read: *Záviš executed...*"[4]

10) Heavy snow falling outside and a little gypsy girl standing out in the yard, a doll in her hand, dressed exactly like the girl herself. A tenor accompanied by an orchestra continues singing: *Lieber Freund, was gibt es mit den Sternen...*[5]

II/
1) The Doctor and Bondy going out. The gypsy girl with the doll smiles at them, turns, and in her embarrassment flicks one leg, then stands on the spot, legs crossed. "You know, the best thing would have been for his mother to have had him taken to St Cath's."[6]

2) Out in the street, Bondy and the Doctor stop next to a Communist Party glass-fronted cabinet with that poster showing crossed telegraph wires and the legend *Do you know*

these cronies? "Who'd have thought it... Pure Salvador Dalì! With Vladimír things are also reaching the point of paranoia... those letters... Dear Professor and lecturers... letters to vice-chancellors, editorial offices and then that poem... *Heda went to meet her father, picking kingcups on the way...* each word on a separate page..."

3) A broken bed lying on the bank of a stream. "Do you know how Vladimír's dad died? Fell into his potty, and when they picked him up, he said: 'Jaroušek, brush your teeth every day...' and he died."

4) A blackbird sitting on a stone, it hops off and bathes in the water. "This whole age we live in is paranoid... Bondy, have you seen in the newsreels that Soviet children's opera about the dear little stork?"

5) The Doctor raises his arms, makes them into wings and steps onto an upturned boat. "A little Soviet stork flew to Egypt... and the animals made the Russian guest welcome..."

6) Bondy standing on the bank, looking puzzled, strokes his beard... behind him, it looks as if a train has trickled into one ear and is now trickling out of the other. "But the wicked British imperialists disturbed the peace of Egypt."

7) The Doctor leaping up and down, performing confused animals, turning and running away, dropping onto all fours.

"And a little black boy bursts onto the scene, falls, his black mother likewise and the English beat them with a cowhide."

8) The Doctor lashing out at the air, trampling, destroying. Bondy rubs his whiskers... he's startled. "Holy shit, that's quite a turn!"

9) The Doctor twitches his head backwards, stuffs his fists in his mouth in utter horror. "This is what Young Pioneers[7] sitting in an auditorium look like." Then he waves both arms and jumps off the boat. "But the dear little Soviet stork won't let the little black boy go, no it won't!"

10) Bondy splitting his sides laughing. "Ha, ha, ha!" The Doctor, using sign lnaguage, chases someone out of the boat. "Shoo, shoo, shoo!" Then he claps his hands and shouts gleefully: "That's how Young Pioneers cheer from their seats."

11) The Doctor scoops air into his hands and hides it under his wings. "And the dear little Soviet stork took the little black boy with it to its own country and there the Young Pioneers gave him a neck scarf and danced a quadrille with him."

12) The Doctor sets his arms akimbo and starts tap-dancing – heel, toe, whole foot; Bondy is lying on the ground, groaning: "Stop it, for God's sake, stop!"

13) The friends congratulate each other and walk on, following the stream. They stop by a fence on which is a picture, in a child's hand, of a herring picked clean, an arrow and the inscription: *Fišer*. "Vladimír ought to get here quick to take a photo of this."

14) The two walking on past an outdoor restaurant, a pile of chairs, fallen leaves and snow... Lying on a frozen surface is a folding bed. "Wouldn't it be something, Bondy, if we opened that bed out and lay down on it naked with just our hands clasped and our genitals poking upwards..."

15) "He[8] taps on my door one morning and asks me through the wood: 'Are you still in the land of the living, Doc? I had a misgiving last night that you'd slashed your wrists!' So I check to see if I'm in a pool of blood, because the bastard is good at predictions. I say through the wall: 'No!' and collapse between my sheets, and he calls back: 'Just an idea I had.'"

16) "Or he might take out that fiddle of his and start playing and sing as he plays. Then he'll switch to the mandolin and quite without warning he'll scream till my blood runs cold: 'Hehehehehe!' And through the wall he informs me that he's just invented suicide. He'll rig a sword up in his little room, lock the door and swallow the key, switch the contraption on and it'll chop him into little pieces... And in the next room he'll start triumphantly playing his fiddle until my brain feels as if it's having nails hammered into it..."

17) A snow-covered hillock with a bare-headed gypsy boy standing on it, staring down on his friends as they pass by. "Or he might come in, I'm in bed reading and he raises his arms: 'What are you doing, lying there? What are you waiting for? Why don't you go and mix with the populace?' And he screams over me: 'Hehehehehe! And I've already got thousands of bits of evidence, thousands of people know about me, but what about you, poor slob, and your anal froth?' And he looks at me in my duvet as at some repulsive beast. And again he shrieks: 'Hehehehehe! And French radio has reported that the main trend in art in this country is explosionalism.'[9] And he marches off and I come out in a mortal sweat."

18) "Or he'll start spelling it out to me: 'I'd raise you up high along with the rack I'd have stretched you out on, high above a pond, and I'd lower you into the water until bubbles appeared and out again, all day long, taking care you didn't die on me... or even better: I'd toss you into a canal, cover you up to the waist in calcium carbide and in due course, when you wetted yourself, you'd catch fire and burn to death. One helluva torch! Hehehehehe!'"

19) Bondy is overwhelmed by these images. "Oh dear, of dear! And I have to poke about with a pin, or dig about the streets with my finger like this, to look for it, and there's so much of it. And what makes it worse, it's brilliant! Real turns they are!"

20) A lorry drives up onto the bank and tips a load of refuse over. The driver gets out and shovels up the spillage. "But how can we force him to paint? To make sure there'll be some actual artefacts?"

21) Some decrepit old men and women burying themselves in the refuse, eagerly combing through the junk, the bits of wood, coke, scraps of metal, rags, paper. "You know, Bondy, I reckon he'll be more of a poet! He *is* a poet!"

22) The friends standing next to the footpath, next to the footpath a handcart, next to that a dog of sorts, and next to the dog an old lady packing rags into a sack. "Stick him in the madhouse! That's my idea, to the madhouse with him! He might pull himself together in there an' then start working... not likely, but this tip here an' those old folk... a perfect image of the capitalist world..."

23) The old lady removes the dog's muzzle and the gypsy girl throws him some bread. "Tomorrow he's got to go an' get himself a sick note an' I'm going with him. An' you, Doctor, you do your damndest to talk him out of that letter-writing crap an' get him back to work, such a great talent, deary me! If he shows the specialist only a tenth of the stuff he's churned out, they'll give him six months off with his nerves... an' he'll be able to draw, paint, write."

24) Heavy snow falling, flakes settling on Bondy's bushy whiskers, but Bondy's being a bit sentimental. "You know,

when they let Záviš see his wife for the last time, they were like seeing each other for the very first time and falling in love. He declared his love for her and she swore to be faithful, and how she'd go about things after they were married... But Vladimír? With that social complex of his? The most conscientious bureaucrat in the republic? And that's why he got bundled into a car and carted off!"

25) The friends returning. The gypsy lad still standing on the embankment, looking down. "When my brother showed up, he told me the convicts remembered seeing in the morgue, next to a woman's body, two naked men's bodies as well..."

26) On the frozen surface a broken folding bed. "Who chucked that there? Some lads!" Bondy picks up a stone and throws it onto the ice. A hole, a plop, the water spills over. Snow is falling thicker and thicker.

27) Bondy and the Doctor are passed by an empty cart pulled by a snow-covered man, a snow-covered woman and a snow-covered girl. "She'll be a pretty lass one day."

28) Beneath a waterfall, a blackbird bathing among the old pots and a rusty cooker. "That's the age we live in!" Behind – tracks in the snow; in front – snow falling thick and fast. The friends merge into the blizzard.

1) Visible through the glass wall of the hallway of a suburban coffee house, a gypsy girl, who takes a gypsy youth's hat from him, plants it in her own hair and looks at herself in the mirror of a weighing machine. "You know, I'm sort of abandoned, alone, these days."

2) The gypsy girl with the hat is dancing in the hallway with the gypsy lad, they stop and he explains the dance steps to her. "I go to Medek's place,[10] start warming up a bit, but his wife's already home, she keeps opening the door and looking at me reproachfully. So I have to go back outside..."

3) The gypsy girl steps up to the glass wall and presses her little nose against it. The Doctor hops up and gives her a kiss through the glass. "So get married."

4) The girl spits, steps onto the weighing machine again and looks at herself in the mirror. "You know, if someone knew me only from *Prager Leben*,[11] they'd think I must cut quite a figure, but I'm not like that anymore, I'm getting more and more soulful... If I did get married, I'd go out and meet her on her way back and we'd talk about poetry... she might afford to keep me... or I might find a job for a few hours... Medek says marriage only comes into its own after two-three years... but above all, I wouldn't be alone..."

5) A stray dog running about in an entry-way, sniffing at a corner, and when Bondy makes to touch it, it runs away.

"Look here, Bondy... marriage, marriage... marriage to a woman who'll stick with you... her relations will badger her, she'll lose heart and then you *will* be alone... without illusions... right now you're alone, but otherwise... then you'll be alone forever."

6) The friends standing outside a florist's bearing the legend: *Cut flowers from cold storage*. "You know... my mother jumped from a window... I can't stop thinking about it... so I've always got a kind of tiny insurance on me... phenobarbitone... I keep it here in this pocket... see... or you could get out more?... there you could at least shout, but here, and never see a single poem published?"

7) "All well and good, but on the other hand, if you leave the country, you'll lose the language as well, its finer points... you'll have to translate your daydreams... you'll lose any motifs of your homeland... and if you come back, you'll be an alien..."

8) Bondy smiling with insight, gazing at an asparagus fern, a cyclamen. "So what's to be done? Just record events... and live with no idea to follow?... Myself, I don't know anymore..."

9) The friends arm-in-arm, coming out of a passage. They stop in front of an illuminated sign: *Goat-brand Premium Lager from Velké Popovice*. "Hopeless! I've spent Vladimír's money, and the beekeepers' petty cash. Today, young Bondy, we're destitute."

10) Bondy squats down and tries to lure the stray dog back, but it flees once more. "But I don't have the tram fare. All I've got is one crown. But I did see one on the carpet at your place…"

11) A Jewish girl standing outside the Kovomat[12] ironmonger's, a prosthetic for a leg. Seen from the side, she's looking at the trams, cars, trucks, people, but without taking them in. A lady comes out of the shop, offers the girl her arm and the girl drags her artificial leg into the stream of people. "Bondy, I could love her, love her all my life, she could well need me, I'd be happy… I'd stop writing…"

12) The Doctor takes two crowns out of his pocket. "Here's your tram fare." He stares into the crowd. "Thinking about it, I'd give her my legs and have hers. With my legs she could run about and dance… and with hers I'd stay indoors and write, and the job centre would stop pestering me… I'd just stay indoors and write…"

13) The friends reach the tram stop traffic island, two young lads are there, wearing bolo ties and Budapester shoes and one of them keeps taking out a little brush and giving his swish footwear a meticulous once-over. One of them gets carried away: "Great things are going to happen today… Armstrong[13] on the trumpet with jazz accompaniment… tradada pumpum… tradada pumpum…" The other interrupts him scornfully: "You're a hundred years behind the times, pal! The modern configuration's completely different…

electric banjo, electric guitar… electric keyboard to do the percussion and tss tss tss tss and a cornet doing its stuff in the background ta ta tata ta…" A number thirteen approaches and Bondy jumps aboard. "And say hello to Vladimír!"

14) Bondy settling into the tram and waving his chubby paw. Some young lads standing on the end platform, crooning away to themselves: *tss, tss, tss, tradada ompapa, tss, tss…*, tapping their feet and getting carried away as if moonstruck. The Doctor waves, the Doctor watches until the thirteen disappears. And it's snowing heavily, ever so heavily, again.

BLITZKRIEG

A news flash[1]

I/

Summer wasn't yet over and Vladimír[2] had popped across to Malá Strana. He set his stepladder next to a moss-grown wall, on the steps a drawing board and paper and on the paper he sketched Egon Bondy[3] after one of the patches on the wall. Half an hour later Bouše[4] showed up, set up his own steps behind Boudník and sketched Vladimír sketching Egon and thereby the patch as well. Another half hour later Dočekal[5] ambled up, set his steps up behind Bouše and started sketching Bouše sketching Vladimír sketching Egon Bondy, the patch that had happened by, pulling total realism along by a string. The delighted little Egon asked Dočekal: "What's that your painting?" And the kindly Dočekal said quite truly that he was painting Bouše painting Vladimír painting the patch. Whereupon Egon, though he might have swooned with pride, commanded: "Send that explosionalist patch a smack in the face!" And having given the kindly Dočekal a smack, he left, looking smug. The kindly Dočekal passed the smack on to Bouše, Bouše passed it on to Vladimír, who, with a jubilant cry of Hehehehe!, gave the patch such a smack that to this day he has his right hand in a bandage. But before the bearded Bondy reached home, lo and behold! His right cheek had swollen up. Ever since, he has threatened Vladimír with publishing future explosionalist artefacts in the *Midnight Series*,[6] which scares Vladimír.

Some time later, Egon and Vladimír were on their way from
The Two Old Ladies.[7] Vladimír was getting carried away in
his explosionalist manner: "We want to turn patchy and
crumbling walls into picture galleries." But Bondy voiced
his opposition in broken Russian with an admixture of
German words: "Yay, yay, ja, ja!" Then Vladimír stopped by
the wall of the Klementinum and yelled: "Look!" And he
stood stock-still in front of a patch: "Look, this bit looks as if
someone's standing here, the chest, shoulders, that defamiliarising expression on the face!" And to make better sense of
it, he took a carpenter's pencil and traced out the figure and
its finer details... "See, it's like this hand is holding a cigarette, see the smoke!..." But then the patch moved and its
free hand, as yet untouched by the carpenter's pencil, gave
Vladimír such a smack in the teeth that he fell down, since
what had been standing there was a real baker's apprentice,
waiting for his girl, who'd failed to show. Vladimír scrabbled
around on all fours for his glasses, muttering to himself:
"I must be mad!" But the greatest living poet bellowed like
a rutting stag: "Ho, ho, I knew it! Long live Total Realism!"
And having given Vladimír a protectoral pat on the shoulder... the friends returned to The Malvaz.[8]

III/

One night, before they went their separate ways, Bondy and
Vladimír went to get themselves a last jug[9] of Velké Popovice
Premium, because it was going up to midnight, when the
pub closed... As they were making their way back to 24 Na

Hrázi Street,[10] Vladimír said in his devilish way: "This stain looks like our door!" And his eyes lit up... The scornful Bondy laughed and said: "Rubbish! We total realists aren't easily fooled!" And he walked smartly through the door, which was, however, a genuine stain. Vladimír yelled in triumph: "Yet it does move![11] And yet explosionalism does live and have its being!..." Then as he doused his broken nose under the tap, Bondy snuffled: "I must be mad!" And he ran outside to give the faithless door a sound kicking. Vladimír, thinking Bondy had gone outside to throw up, as was his wont, followed him out and wondered why he was kicking the wall. Then the Doctor came out and said: "Why are you kicking the door, chaps? You've woken the whole house!..." Since that time, signs and arrows have led tourists to the little house in Libeň. But at night, the Doctor thinks it wiser to lead his guests on a rope, like a party of climbers. The Doctor does indeed lead his guests thus, but mumbling to himself, just to play safe: "I must be mad!"

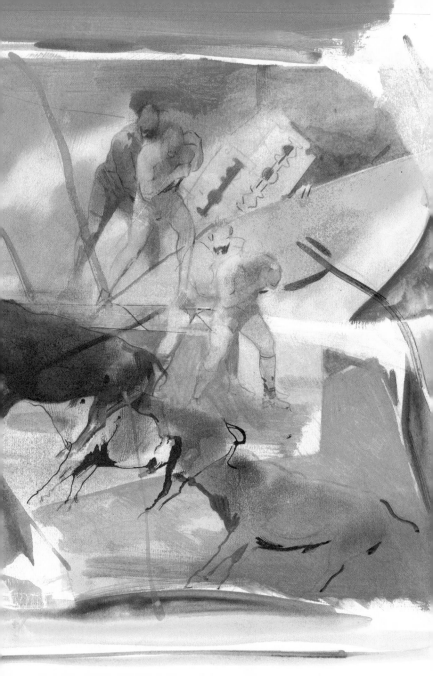

1/

It was quite fun at The Two Cats.[1] I was sitting right opposite the door and the waiter brought me my next pint bearing it high over the heads of the other patrons.

Sitting opposite me was a giant of a man and the beer glass within his paws was so small as to be entirely hidden.

"Everybody's got something they love, haven't they?" he said for perhaps the thirtieth time. But when he looked round, into the eyes of his neighbours, they'd all heard it, but none rose to the bait. So it was left to me to smile back at him.

He walked round the corner of the table, sat down on a vacant chair and held his glass guiltily in both hands. He had a drink and set the empty glass down.

"Surely, everybody's got something they love..." And he laid a heavy arm round my neck, like a sack of cement.

I looked him straight in the eye and inside his rough skull I saw two skylarks rising, attached to strings.[2]

"What do you love? Tell me, go on."

"Love? There are people and things I love, just like any-body else has," I said.

"All right, so tell me what *you* love best."

"My piano."

He spread both arms wide and whooped for all in the Two Cats to hear: "See! And with these two hands I'll move your piano out for you, just so's you'll see how sensitive they are!"

The waiter swung another beer down and duly marked it on the beer mat. My neighbour's beer mat was already looking like a kid's drawing of the sun. The waiter said heartlessly: "You're not the only one here, mate, I don't want you bothering others!"

But the man wasn't listening, in tears he was scrutinising his huge hands, as if seeing them for the first time.

"Just look at these humane little hands of a removal man! They're serious stuff, if you could just see them carrying other people's things gingerly down from floor to floor, with so much tender loving care. And what floor do you live on?"

"Fourth."

"So you really must move! If only to appreciate the sheer knack of it."

"But I'm not minded to move!"

"Oh, do move, I only want you to see how careful I am. Everybody's got something they love and me, like a pussy cat I'll get it from one house to another for them. He put his arm round my neck again and his beer gleamed, just as if he'd taken his hand from round a lantern.

I sipped my beer. "But, my good friend, I have a place to live, I'm happy with where and how I live, so where's the point?"

"Okay, how about this? I'll move the piano downstairs for you, then move it back up. And I won't charge you. All I want is for you to see how careful I am with other people's belongings."

In desperation I looked up and there in the doorway

stood a waiter from the Lucerna bar, Kolečko, who I'd done a stint with at the Kladno steelworks, and he called across: "Golly, what are you doing here? Are you free? You *are* free! Let me treat you! But not here, this place is a pain, no fun at all, let's go somewhere else!"

I rose to go, but the removal man tried to talk me out of it: "Stay here, don't leave me, we were just about to get on to actual removals."

I looked him in the eyes and saw in each of them ten tankards piled one on top of the other, threatening to go tumbling down at any moment.

"That's my friend over there."

And stepping over chairs, beer mat in hand, I made it across to Kolečko. We shook hands, and I stood back to get a better look at a man I'd only ever seen in dungarees. This time he had a coat slung casually over his shoulder, looking slick, his hair greased, and prematurely aged.

He took my beer mat and shoved it in the waiter's pocket, the waiter leaning back as if he were holding eight beers in each hand. Kolečko told him – loud enough for the entire pub to hear: "Chalk it up to me, Venda. I'll see you straight tomorrow!"

Once we were outside, he hooked a familiar arm into mine. Ahead of us, bouncing their sticks on the pavement, were two blind accordionists, roaring drunk. They had their arms linked high up by the armpit, like when kids play at angels, and their accordion looked from behind like a cow's skull coated in phosphorus. As we passed them, giving them a respectfully wide berth, the blind giants were whispering to each other and crushing each other's arm with their own: "Right now I'd like to drag you off somewhere and smash your little hands, break your little legs, gouge out your little eyes and bite off your little ears…" And the other, or maybe he was the first, reciprocated the sweet nothings: "I wouldn't do anything to you either, though I might just torturytorture you ever so slightly to death…"

Standing by the wall of the Pinkas Tavern,[3] a handful of patrons were finishing off their last beers. From the open doorway we could see the waiters gathering up glasses, tidying beer mats away, untying and folding their dirty aprons. They said hello to Kolečko, but he turned left, into the kitchen, where the portly manager's lips were moving as he counted the money without stopping.

"Hi boss, two large brandies when you've got a mo."

With a nod the boss indicated that he'd seen and heard us, but he went on counting the banknotes in his fingers, like a rotary press.

I settled down at the clean kitchen table, right next to the patent bread-slicer.

Opposite me sat a black-suited man with a mournful, tormented face that seemed to be suspended from the triple rings under both eyes, which weren't visible. But he was focussed on amusing himself with the reflection of his red wine, which skittered about the table top according to how he moved his glass.

The boss completed his accounts, stretched and yawned.

"So you're acquainted with the bard Kolečko, are you?"

He opened a little cupboard, poured out two brandies and set them down on the table.

The man, still fixated on the reflection of his red wine, which he chased all the way to the edge of the table, asked: "Where's the water? The asses have gone and drunk it!... Just an idea, boss: would there happen to be a bit of your nice goulash left?"

Kolečko appeared in the doorway with a glass of brandy between his fingers and he clinked it with another glass of brandy held by a hand poking out of the darkness. Then the hand, in a white puff sleeve, vanished and the sound of someone retreating along the corridor could be heard, following by a door banging.

The boss wiped the sweat from his brow with his hand and said: "There's no goulash left. The kind folk have eaten it all."

The man jiggled his rings by way of acknowledgement, topped up his wine from a little jug and went back to watching as the garnet-coloured shadow on the table made the bright speck in the middle move.

Kolečko sat astride a chair and twirled his glass in his fingers like a tiny chandelier.

"So, how've you been?"

"They stitched my head together and I had a crack in the back of my skull,[4] all in the cause of making our homeland even more beautiful and with no artist's eye having even an inkling of it...," I said with a smile.

"Stitched it together? Get that one down you, and, boss, give us another!"

I tossed off the brandy and, as I brought my head back down, the triple rings were bearing aloft, the way a water spout does, the beautiful eyes of the man with the red wine mirror resting between his fingers. The rings under his eyes put me in mind of the ring gripped by Wenceslas as he was being murdered.[5]

"And when they stitched you together, did it hurt?" the boss asked, setting a tray with the glasses on down onto the table. I gushed with a quiet, happy laugh:

"No, the doctor took his scissors, cut my hair off and Lie down on that table over there, and I says, Sure, are we going to do some darning?, and the doctor says, Yes, we'll do some darning, then he threw a cloth over my face and I says, This is what they do to bullocks at the abattoir! The doctor says to the nurse, Hand me the scissors and penicillin, and What do they do to bullocks at the abattoir? I could feel them snipping at something inside the wound and I says They put a cloth over the bullocks' eyes! and the blood ran down towards my ears, then the doctor says, Hand me a needle, nurse, and Why do they put a cloth over bullocks' eyes?"

Kolečko and the boss knocked their glasses back and the boss touched my arm: "Go on, drink up! This round's on me!"

But Kolečko took it amiss: "No, boss, that's an insult, I invited you, today it's my treat!"

The boss fetched a bottle with a nickel spout and drizzled a thin stream of brandy into the glasses as if urinating.

The boss said: "So why do they put a cloth over bullocks' eyes! Well?"

"I told him, gently: So they can't see that far worse things are about to be done to them, then I could feel myself gripping the edge of the table the entire time the needle was insinuating itself into my skin and pulling it together, like a football being stitched, then the doctor says, And what worse things happen to bullocks at the abattoir? And I says to him Death..." I smiled, stood up and clapped Kolečko on the back: "And after the doctor snipped off the last little knot he said, Right, bullock, that's you darned! But Jirka Huml, the guy you used to work with, he's dead now..."

"You don't say!"

"'Fraid so! In the storehouse, that hellhole, a threeton truckload of steel rods overturned on him, swept him against a wall, but some of the billets were poking out and spiked him in the back, about ten centimetres deep, Jirka kept his cool, telling them what to do, Come on, lads, help me, help me, lads, lift them away, one at a time, but don't use the crane, or I'll be crushed for good, so we spent ninety minutes heaving the heavy billets away, and only then did we hook the truck onto the crane, gave the driver the nod and one guy hooked Huml under the arms and pulled him out. Even next morning in hospital he could tell his wife to get off home, it was nothing, but by evening he was dead, his kidneys torn away...," I said sadly.

Kolečko, who'd had his collar bone smashed by an iron bar when he was working at the same place, jumped to his feet: "Let's drink, bottoms up! And I'm paying, boss!"

The boss clapped the back of his hand across his yawning mouth, then he rose and we all raised our brandy glasses towards the ceiling light until they melted away. And we tipped our heads back and the glasses made contact with our lips.

Kolečko went over to the till, rested one shoe on the step and waved a 1000-crown about. The boss, his backed turned to me and headless, calculated the tab on a strip of paper.

The man opposite me, eyes down, was playing with his glass of wine again and talking to himself: "Concentrate harder. You're focussed on it. Now you've got it. And say it, quickly. What I'm afraid of, Marion."

The boss completed his calculations, stuck his pencil behind his ear, which I couldn't see, then he placed his hand on the counter and his ring gleamed next to a bowl full of little coloured slips of glass.

The man stood up, raised his glass and, as he finished his drink, the red reflection ran from the table to the wall, where it flickered for as long as it took to shrink and shrink before slipping after the wine into the man's guts. Then he set the white scratchy shadow of the glass down on the table along with the glass itself and went out to the boss and asked: "Marion, what does this man love?... Think hard again. You know as well. You're also given to calling it out. Open your mouth. Now!"

The boss raised his fleshy head and turned:

"No, doctor, we'll sort it out tomorrow, right now I'm dog-tired, good night, gents, good night."

We all three went out into the night. Jungmann's[6] legs were still paralysed and he was still sitting there in his wheelchair.

Two pairs of high-spirited girls crossed from Jungmann Street to Jungmann Square. As they passed us, laughing, one of them: "Watch it, there's a drain here." She glanced at the head waiter from the Lucerna and, her calf flashing through the split in her skirt, she stepped over the grid.

Kolečko took it personally: "Who are you calling a drain, you slags?"

But the pairs, chattering away noisily as they crossed the silent square, receded into the distance towards Wenceslas Square.

Kolečko stared after them, even after they'd passed out of sight:

"Those birds come to our bar, they do it for three or four hundred... I can have any of them for nothing!"

The man with the triple circles under his eyes had sobered up:

"I've known these girls since I was a kid, not these ones exactly, but others like them.[7] At Teta or Ara they were getting two hundred and fifty crowns a month, so they had to pick up some extra on the side! Never mind the young ones, that was okay, but whenever I saw the older, godforsaken poor things selling themselves at Těšnov, in the park next to Denis Station,[8] at Invalidovna... at Šenfloks', by Kučeras' and at the Old Lady tavern, ugh. Then those streams of people heading for the flophouses in Kobylisy, or to Krejcárek, to the Jews' Furnace park, the brickworks at Libeň, as they streamed passed ours of an evening my sister would always scream, 'Something has to be done for those people, it has to be,' we were well-off, so we could afford to be generous and we would give them something, but today my sister denies ever having said anything of the sort."

I said: "But today, girls working at Perla, the White Swan[9] and other places, they're paid less than two thousand and they also need to make a bit more on the side, except today you can't tell the difference between a decent woman and a whore, just go to the Carioca,[10] or the Barok, an office worker there offered to do it for five hundred…"

The man shook his circles: "That's true, but believe me, back then they were to be pitied, but this lot are just despicable."

I exclaimed: "But living hand-to-mouth…"

The man looked my way a second time, bowed solemnly to me and introduced himself: "For twenty-two years I've been a general practitioner having to deal with venereal diseases."

Kolečko, who all this had completely passed by, suggested: "Come to the Lucerna, Doctor, I'll keep a table for you, just phone ahead, ask for head waiter Kolečko, the show that's on right now's called 'Three Hours of Laughter' with Fanda Mrázek,[11] Gollová[12] and Ruda Princ!"[13] Our venereal disease doctor raised his eyes to the heavens and asked: "Marion, what's a stellar constellation?"

And, shoulders hunched, he left.

Alone, the statue of the revivalist Josef Jungmann reared up towards the sky in his electric chair.

2

Next to the window, three men were playing cards. One bald ancient in tiny glasses remarked: "That seven's a stinker!"

"Trump!" "And overtrump!" "And what was that about the seven?" "Stuff your seven!" And as they were settling up, the coins clinked so loud that the blind girl fished a ticket out of her pocket, flourished it towards the door and said: "The ticket inspector's on his way."

The young man sitting next to her ran his hand across his face and, not knowing what to say, waited for the girl to realise, having heard the sound again, that it was just coins. Disappointed, she popped the ticket back in her pocket and sighed: "I get it..."

Baldy laid his cards down on the briefcase balancing on three pairs of knees, withdrew his false teeth from his pocket and said with a smile: "I need to put my gnashers in so I can gab better..." He rubbed the teeth on his sleeve, glugged them into his mouth and snapped it shut, picked his cards up, read them and, as he declared his hand, announced: "Balls like a badger's!"[14] Since no one wanted to go for a higher contract, he said: "Good card, bad card!" and reshuffled.

The blind girl opened her little bag and enquired: "Are the lights on?" The young man grew uneasy: "Yes, they are, but..." She interrupted him: "So let me show you what I was like when I still had my sight..."

And she passed him a photo, just missing his hands.

He redirected his fingers towards hers, took the photo and examined it. Then he said: "But there's something odd about the eyes... What a lovely name, Lída!"

She folded her hands between her knees and made herself wafer-thin:

"That happened when I was unsticking her from the album – I jabbed her eye. Thing is, I've been jabbed at ever since I was little, lost my mother at four, and you know how it goes, my stepmother gave her own kids chocolates, but to me she said: 'Your dad can buy some for you…' So I'd run off to the cemetery, or creep into a corner and cry: 'Mummy, Mummy, if you were here, I'm sure you'd give me some…'"

The old boy in specs flung a card at the briefcase and said: "There's one neat little trump for you to make a bit of a splash!" And he raked the cards together.

The blind girl half-turned to the young man and he felt as if she could see him. Diffidently he asked: "Tell me, Lída, how did it happen?"

As if having expected the question she replied quickly: "I used to love croissants and as you know, there's nowhere that sells them at tram termini. So I always begged my driver to wait a minute. One time I'd popped into Vacínova Street to buy some and a motorbike ran into me. I don't remember more than that. In the afternoon, a policeman told me I'd nearly had it, but I asked him: 'Where's my pouch with the money?' But the doctor pushed me back into bed: 'Lie down, lie down, you've got a cracked skull.' I said: 'But there's nothing the matter with me. Let me get back to my tram, the number five's waiting for me at Palmovka, but it waited six weeks for me; I did want to go to work, the state needed my services, so I had to be seen by a board, the girl in front of me was a ninety-nine per cent invalid. The chairman of the board says: 'It doesn't look that serious, she's so young and pretty.' But the doctor who was there with him, says: 'Remove your hair, Miss.' And she took her wig off and her head was quite bare and from behind I could see a large silver plate on top of her skull. She'd been working somewhere in Stalingrad and a lathe had wormed its way into her hair... Quite something, eh?" The young man glanced at her hands clasped below her knee and, looking up, noticed for the first time that the blind girl sported a communist badge in her lapel. He asked her: "And how did you fare?" She looked in the direction of his voice, unclasped her knees and pointed at herself: "Me? I told them I was off to work, back then I saw things in comradely terms, but now I'm like anybody else... Back then I told them: 'They need me, they do, I must get back to my tram,' but eventually I had a breakdown, my hands couldn't hold anything and somehow my optic nerve got trapped. Maybe an operation will help one day. Or is that just them trying to make me feel better?"

And the train clattered over a bridge. After it had passed back into the silence of the night, Lída listened awhile and said: "We're just passing the cemetery at Čelákovice, aren't we?"

He leaned towards the window, blocking the players' view of their cards, and indeed, there were a little lights here and there among the desolate headstones.

She asked: "My mum was born in 1904. How old would she be now?"

Settling back down with her, he said: "Forty-eight."

She lapsed into a daydream and again clasped her knees in her hands, forming a heart shape: "So little? What a young mum I'd have... Ah, well! At least she wouldn't see me with no eyes. Give me the photo."

The young man steered the portrait towards her fingers and she placed it back in her little bag, having located it on her other hip.

And she went on: "Too bad, but we've had some right-royal carnage. There was that number one that flew into the co-op in Vršovice, all the way to the counter! Or my own smash-up on the fourteen in Charles Square. And after my motorbike thing they wanted to put me on night watch at the tram depot, but not likely! Spend the night wandering among deserted trams with no people – horrors! They keep staring at you, all red and with that blue light shining down on them! Scary! And me there all on my lonesome? Ugh! But how it was with that fourteen, it started to roll back down the hill, travelling backwards. Lucky there wasn't another one behind us, or there'd be no meat shortage – we had a whole class of school kids on board. They were screaming all the way so I says to their teacher: 'Miss, tell your kids to behave!' But she says: 'You'll just have to put up with it, I've been a teacher for twenty years!' So we carried on travelling backwards, gathering speed, I tried sanding the track, the teacher jumped off and bang!, several of the kids with her, the rest were terrified into silence. But we did manage to stop it at the foot of the next hill. Then there was that trailer car off a number eight! Going up to four o'clock in the morning and it broke away from the depot and beetled off towards Prašný Most, then at a gallop towards Špejchar with some guys from the depot chasing after it in a car, but they didn't manage to jump onto it. The road goes slightly uphill past the Sparta ground, but our number eight trailer was having none of it, oh no! It went sailing past and hippety-hop down the hill till it derailed on Strossmayer Square, knocked over a phone box and nobody got hurt at all!"

With a smile on her face, the blind Lída was relishing her exciting past.

The bald ancient said: "We had a great game last night. The funeral guy, picked him up and carried him, me and Pepík. I had soup, a schnitzel, a glass of stout and coffee, and every now and then I popped out to the kitchen for a snifter."

The young man, puzzled, was cracking his knuckles.

The girl Lída suddenly remembered: "I'd been through a shock like that previously, in Berlin. The air-raid sirens were going off, I grabbed my suitcases and ran to the bunker, but suddenly something told me: 'Lie down in the ditch!' So I did and stuff started coming down all round. When it stopped, I got up and I couldn't see the bunker any more. Next to it there'd been some horse chestnuts in bloom, but now the leaves had all gone, and the flowers, just the bare branches, like in winter, and the odd rag here and there. Then my hands started shaking, I dropped my cases and was rooted to the spot. Obvious really, Berlin all ablaze, a bath hanging out here, there in a house sliced in two with a table set for dinner and the corners of the tablecloth blowing in the draught. And all the dead bodies I saw! Have you seen the film Far from Moscow?"[15]

The young man replied hollowly: "Yes."

With a smile she said, getting quite carried away: "Why did that Tamara Makarova not marry the agronomist at the end? I'd have wished her as much from the bottom of my heart. But no! Though it did happen in The Village Doctor.[16] I remember! I saw it twice. The first time, right after the newsreel, the lights went up and they announced that any members of the people's militia who happened to be in the cinema should return immediately to their bases, and I saw it again last year and I was in the militia myself, but believe me, in wartime I'd much rather be a nurse, I'm also Catholic, first as a little kid my father had me crossed off, but when he died and I was in an orphanage for a while, the nuns re-enrolled me. Do you understand what I'm saying?"

The young man gulped several times and said: "I do, I do."

And she went on with her confidences: "And these days it's got so bad, the way folk are deserting the trams. We had 14,000 women trained up, but 12,000 of them have already handed in their notice, because they can't do it, the ride, the rocky ride, is bad for their ovaries. I did my best to talk them round, saying how the state needed them, but they left anyway and after four years of it I could tell it wasn't doing me any good either, and the doctor told me I'd also got something wrong with me inside. Now I remember! Gensdorf it was called. A factory 5×5 kilometres square, but the Americans drew a black circle round it and made quick work of it and in the evening a list was drawn up of who'd come back. That day there were sixteen missing. The day before Marunka had told me: "Something's going to happen, you'll see! Give my love to Mum and Dad!" And the lasses in the sleeping quarters said: "You're like a mother to us, Lída!" because before the air raid I'd wrapped rags round their ears so their eardrums wouldn't burst. I was shaking all over, then I went outside, then back in again and kept waiting for Marunka to come back, but by night-time she hadn't, I lay on my bunk, staring at her little suitcase on top of the wardrobe, then I got up, locked it away inside the wardrobe and lay down again, then I packed everything up, took Marunka's suitcase with me as well and went off down the concrete path into the smoke and there my arms started to shake and bang! went the cases onto the ground! The camp commandant, a German woman, found me, she woke the girls and they tied me up in a blanket because I was thrashing about so much. And you know what? Yesterday, for the first time in my life, I bought some lipstick."

And she turned and puckered her lips towards the young man. Then, still in that posture, she lapsed into thought and said: "Isn't this the descent into Hloubětín?"

The three men packed away their cards and counted their money and the train was tossing sparks and the city lights behind it. For all he wanted to, the young man was quite unable to utter a single word.

Having groped about briefly, she laid her hand on his and whispered: "Some people from the sanatorium will be waiting for me at the station. Take me to them, will you?

And how about this: Come and see me there sometime and we can go dancing! I learned to dance last year at the home. Before, when I went to dancing classes, or to some do, I saw the girls had their mothers with them and I'd burst into tears and run away, but now I can dance, and I've even bought that lipstick. I'll take your arm onto the floor and when we dance you'll take the lead. So how about it?"

The young man, numb and scared witless, suddenly stiffened his resolve and said: "All right, I will come for you, this Saturday, on Saturday, around three in the afternoon…" And he gave her fingers a squeeze. And the more lights there were, the broader the smile on Lida's face…[17]

3/

Two women elbowed their way into the compartment, one helped the other off with her back pack and then they took up seats next to the window.

A man, drunk and old before his time, greeted them: "Hello, my good Catholic girls, say, are you off to the convention?" However, they didn't reply, as if they were returning from a funeral somewhere, a rustic November funeral, so muddied they were and in soaking wet, twenty-year-old, off-the-peg clothes.

The elder of the two fished out a pair of bible-reader's spectacles, hooked them with a bony finger behind a strand of her grey hair, opened a tiny book and started reading aloud to the younger woman, whose still fresh and unfeigned tears mingled with the rain from her hair and face.

An off-duty engine driver, travelling on his subsidised

ticket as a railway employee, was staring out through the window into the mournful, rain-sodden landscape, where joyless people were topping sugar beet with sickles. The young man next to him was gazing in sheer delight at his new, mustard-coloured shoes and holding between his fingers the knot of his bolo tie, running them down to its tip and whipping it out from under his coat.

Then a loud noise, and the Košice express shot through the station, the wet blue sides of the carriages relieved by the willow-brown of the dining car, a brown smudge no bigger at that speed than a door standing still.

The engine driver took from his waistcoat a huge Roskopf Patent pocket watch, which flooded the compartment with its ticking, and remarked: "What did I say?"

And the soaked old lady read in a croaking voice: "All was quiet inside the manor house. Outside it was a beautiful warm night. The moon and thousands of stars sailed across the firmament. Vilma opened the door leading onto the terrace. 'The Baron,' she cried out in alarm."

And the younger, drooping head wept on.

Then the train moved off, the buffers steadied the motion and the rain bore down on the metal roof.

The young man pinched the creases on his trousers, propped a learned finger against his temple and said: "And so I acknowledged that I was a subtenant of Mr Jiří Drahota, but that he no longer lived there. The official asked me who, then, I was actually subletting from. I told me truly, if against myself, that it was Mr Boudnik, but that he'd moved out as well."

The engine driver folded his red hands and looked out painfully from under his cap at the young man, who lost his composure and stared down at the ground.

"'Stop there, Baron!' cried Vilma. 'Those words are unbecoming of you, Baron, remember that you are married and I am a poor girl who has nought but her honour!...' 'Vilma!' he cried, 'love does not diminish honour and knows neither poverty, nor class. You, Vilma, must be mine, even if the whole of Hell should conspire against us!'"

The prematurely aged, but drunk man stood up straight in his corner, cheered and beat his breast: "I've got it! Progress is assured by those who've been executed! They had to nail him to the cross, and if they hadn't, he just wouldn't have been! There'd have been no Jesus!" But the man endowed thus with vision started to choke and collapsed into his corner, and the young man, his finger savouring his tie, could go on: "Then the official wormed it out of me that it's actually a factory flat, the place I live in, and he phoned the regional authorities on account of my milk, and kept nodding his head and saying 'Yes, yes, yes,' then he hung up and said 'No, it won't do, you have to get your milk at the factory and if they don't sell it there, you still have an inalienable right to it.'"

"'Do you receive visits from married men at night, dressed like that? And I trusted you!' And the baroness's eyes flashed thunderbolts at Vilma and her husband. 'So the baron here is your sweetheart?'" the old lady stuttered and the old man, exhaling fumes of absinthe all over the compartment, threw up his hands: "That's the thing, they execute one, then another, a tenth, a hundredth! Then as they're executing the thousandth, they assure themselves: 'Aha, there must be something in it.' So in the name of all those who they've executed, they amend their dogma. That's how progress comes into it!"

And that kindly man stared at one single spot, like a pig struck three times with a mallet.

The door slid open and the comely ticket inspector entered; she probably hadn't been on the railways long, because her manner was amiable as she asked: "Has anyone new boarded the train?"

The old lady, her reading thus interrupted, testily tendered two tickets, then clip! clip! and she went back to croaking her way down the page. Before the ticket inspector got her image trapped in the closing door the drunk said: "You're like that pussy cat on chocolate bars, all you're missing is the ribbon round your neck!" She closed the door and said: "That would never do – the boys could find me too easily," and, smiling, she bore her sweet little face away, her carroty hair neatly rolled up under her enchanting cap.

"Half-way through the wedding feast Vilma began feeling faint. She tottered and would have fallen if her husband the head forester hadn't caught her. The baroness fetched some drops and sent for the estate's doctor."

And the truth-telling young man completed his tale: "I told the official they didn't sell milk at the factory and I couldn't drink an inalienable right, so I'd have to buy my milk in town, I said, but that's too far and they wouldn't let me off work, so the official advised me to get my milk in the first village outside Prague, perhaps Ďáblice, only an hour on foot, or I could take the train to Horní Počernice."

The engine driver spat and yielded to his sense of outrage: "Blimey, mate, you're a good 'un! I couldn't keep my cool like you, I fly off the handle at the slightest provocation. One time my fireman made me so mad that I slung him off the train while it was moving!"

Slapping his thighs, the drunk shouted: "But the Alexandrian School! And they were out by only a few metres. Let them try measuring the world's diameter with sticks today! There's no such thing as progress! There isn't!" And, happy now, he wrapped himself in his coat where it hung – and ripped the loop it was hanging from.

"'Vilma, do you deny it? You've taken poison!' 'I'm happy, Baroness, who's fault is it?' 'Yes, Vilma, only today, dear great and noble soul, have I come to understand the sacrifice you have made for my marriage.' And shortly thereafter Vilma died. She had kept her word and been true to her Václav to the last."

The young man added under his breath: "I'm just so disposed to love the truth, that's my problem, so when the official finally told me he'd be sending the housing committee to my flat as, he said, an undeclared accommodation unit, I was so enraged that out in the corridor I smashed the milk jug."

The engine driver had stopped listening. He got an apple from his little case, eagerly polished it on his sleeve and subjected it to a close scrutiny, sank his teeth into it and with an audible crunch tore off half of the fragrant flesh. A spray of sweet droplets shot from the corner of his mouth.

"The death knell rang out over the manor. Vilma dead!...

"... Then a loud bang came from the grounds beneath her window." With tears streaming the younger woman removed her face from her hands and cried: "Stop, Mother, stop! Take pity, don't read any more!" And she clasped the old lady round the neck and each wept into the other. "Oh, Mother, Mother, why don't they write such beautiful books anymore? Why? Don't read to the end, it's heartbreaking! So, Vilma dies? I guessed as much from the outset!"

The old lady slid her head down from her daughter's shoulder and, having wiped away her tears, surveyed her fellow passengers and said aloud: "Any minute now and it'll be Nymburk."

The engine driver, off-duty and travelling on his subsidised ticket as a railway employee, stopped chewing: "What Nymburk?"

As she shut the little book the old lady said: "Nymburk nad Labem, of course, but we're going on as far as Jičíněves."

The engine driver threw down his apple stalk and nudged his cap to the back of his head: "But you're not heading for Nymburk, this train's for Prague, next stop Kyje!"

The women's crumpled faces froze.

"Show me your tickets," said the engine driver.

"Good God, woman! Really? What time did you set out?"

"Half past five this morning from Prague."

"I get it," the engine driver surmised. "You took the slow train to Brno, and the guard told you to change at Poříčany and wait for the Jičín train, which was behind yours. Right?"

"Yes, sir!" the ladies acknowledged fearfully.

"So you went and sat in the waiting room and read your book about the baroness and when the platform assistant called it out, you scampered onto the first train you saw, just so's you could carry on reading, am I right?"

"Yes, oh dear lord, goodness me!"

"Pretty grim!" the engine driver exclaimed. "You know what you two deserve? You pair of ninnies? To have your skirts lifted and be given a good whack on your bare backsides!"

The young man fingered the knot of his tie, unbuttoned his jacket and said: "If you don't mind my saying so, it looks as if the ticket lady punched their returns."

"Show me," the engine driver roared.

"Upon my soul! Quick, get off right now, this is Kyje, and wait for a train here!"

The women hauled their bags down, struggled through the door and jumped off the train just as it began to move.

The engine driver dropped the window and called back to them: "But it won't do you much good! You'll have to buy new tickets. Your train crew's going to be from Třebová, and they're a merciless bunch!" He pulled the window back up, almost snapping the strap. Then he flopped back down and closed his eyes.

The prematurely careworn old man stood in the middle of the compartment and snapped back one finger after another: "Who have I sworn allegiance to so far? The Emperor Franz Joseph, Emperor Charles, presidents Masaryk, Beneš, Hácha, Tiso, then Beneš again, and Gottwald. That's eight potentates I've sworn allegiance to!" He rolled his eyes and waving his ninth finger before the closed eyes of the engine driver, said: "I wonder who'll be next!"

The well-mannered young man, fearful lest the old boy step on his mustard-coloured shoes, pushed him back into the corner: "Pull yourself together, father, pull yourself together!"

The engine driver opened his eyes, then his little case and took out another beautiful apple, wiped it on his sleeve and sank his teeth into it. With the apple still between his teeth, he took out his timepiece and was almost gleeful: "We've caught up with the timetable, I wouldn't mind betting it's Panenka driving." And he glanced at the station signboard – Libeň.

The young man rose, looked himself over, wet his fingers, ran them from top to bottom down his trouser creases and gave a happy laugh.

The drunken, prematurely aged man in the corner burbled into his coat: "Jesus at school... Lenin at school... Jesus in the desert... Lenin in the desert... Jesus' grave in Jerusalem... Lenin's grave in Moscow. Isn't it amazing how alike these religions are?"

"They gave me a pass so I hopped on the express, and when I got home in the night and unlocked the flat, there was no one there."

"How many kilometres is it?"

"A hundred and ninety. The concierge's light was still on, so I knocked to see if she knew anything. And as the door opened, I saw our Miluška asleep on the sofa. So I asked: 'What's happened?' And the concierge let on that my missus had left the child with her and gone off to a masked ball. And how far do you have to travel?"

"Two hundred and twenty-six. But isn't Miluška only seven months old?"

"That's the point. Six, actually! But I shouldn't have gone home unannounced. I meant to surprise her, and now…"

"I'd have grabbed an axe and beaten her to death!"

"Me too, at that first moment I wanted to chuck all her stuff out of the window and not let her back in, but what to do with the kid? I've got no one and in a few hours I had to set off back to my unit. And then, my old lady's got a really cute wotsit."

"But I'd have grabbed an axe and beaten her to death! And when did she come in?"

"Not till around one-thirty. I waited outside the house and just after one-thirty I spotted her at the corner, and she wasn't alone. When they reached the street light by the house, that paramour of hers did a runner and she was rooted to the spot, saying nothing, all hung about with sequins and her mask quivering in her hand."

"I'd have thrown myself at her and beaten her to death on the spot! But what did she have to say for herself? What, if anything?"

"Nothing, nothing at all, I couldn't get a word out of her, and she couldn't move. First I had to carry Miluška upstairs, then her. All night she lay there with her eyes open, like a statue, and it was only as I was leaving around midday that she shed a few tears. Anyway, I think this must be Lysá."

"Right, this is where we get off, but I'd have taken an axe to her!"

"Are you sure you haven't left anything in the dark?"

"No, nothing, but I'd have given her such a working-over that she'd make the acquaintance of Christ!"

– – – –

"I'm glad there's a seat free, girls, after a Sunday like this I'm worn to a shred. And do you live in that dodgy part of town?"

"You mean Žižkov? Goodness no! We've lived in Košíře ever since we got married."

"Say, girls, wouldn't it be just great if the train stopped right outside our house."

"Not half. But you're so posh, I see the point, it'd suit you down to the ground, but I'd be happy enough if just my bed would come rolling up to meet me at the station, I'm bushed! But where do you actually live, Zdena? Nad Kavalírkou? Na Zvonářce?"

"Even further than that! My bloke, when he was running after me, he'd tell my little sister a fairytale about a prince, meaning him, who used to court a princess, meaning me, and how they got married and lived happily ever after. I told him: 'I'll give you that, you're a prince right enough, but above all one with money, especially living at Hliník!'"

"So you live that far away! Dear me, that's some distance you have to travel. But such is life, right? What do you think, Mančinka, has the cat got your tongue?"

"Me? I couldn't care less about anything these days. I'm happy enough living in Bílina, I've got a decent wage and above all nobody pesters me."

"But Mančinka, you won't be able to see much of your man like that. So far away!"

"That's why! I go wherever I want with whoever I want and other blokes at least treat you better, at least they talk to you, and buy you flowers."

"But it's your husband that's away in the army!"

"What husband? I put my foot wrong there! He's worse than the others! I won't be coming back. I wanted to tell him how the lad's growing up, what needs arranging, but he, eyes popping, just hauled me off upstairs to his room like some whore, didn't even let me get undressed, so I was still in my coat... Ugh! Don't talk to me about husbands, I didn't get a wink of sleep, so at least I'll have a good kip now. There, and now I'm asleep!"

"You're weird, Mančinka! Sleep on! But how come your bloke's been put away for so long, Zdena?"

"He was half a day late getting back. Our little girl fell ill, so I wrote him to come right away, but they wouldn't let him out. Then she got a bit better, so I put her back in the nursery. Then one evening I brought her home and by morning she was dead, in her pram. I looked at her that morning and she was completely dead."

"And your man?"

"I sent him a telegram and they did let him out. When he saw our little girl in her little coffin he said: 'Hasn't she grown! Even if she was alive, she wouldn't recognise me now.'"

"Is that all?"

"Then he was late getting back, so they locked him up, took away his bootlaces and belt so he wouldn't hang himself. What a thing! Let him come and see his kid alive, oh no, but in her coffin, that's all right! They couldn't care less. But never mind, he was out today, actually just for the evening, so we went to a hotel, and where did you spend the night?"

"One of his mates lent us his room at Milovice, so that's where we were. I'd really been looking forward to it, but lying there in somebody's else's bed, it was really quite off-putting. Anyway, he'll be back home a year from now and everything'll be fine and dandy. I was always a bit of a giddy-goat, I liked to go dancing, that was my thing, dancing, but I'll survive for now. I'm a wife. But I'm really feeling sleepy. Shall we have a snooze? We're still only just past Čelákovice!"

"Sure, I can hardly keep my eyes open either. Hold my hand and lean against Mančinka, there you are..."

And I'm still staring out of the window into the dark January night. Only the large rectangle of the adjacent carriage is lighting up the snowfields, platelayers' huts, meadows, fields... constantly tied to the speed of the train. Flocks of partridges have forgotten the massacres of autumn, so they probably think it's safe to fly down to the trackside and people will toss them something, as if there's a rule that says that man is the measure of all things. I'm sitting next to the carriage window and looking straight ahead at the silhouettes of three young mothers, barely out of girlhood, and when the lights from a station land on their laps, I can see that their hands are linked. I watch those human hands, just as, outside Lysá, I had stared into the gloom at two young soldiers, who were seated opposite each other and were also holding hands...

Eventually I plucked up the courage to ask the slumped figure: "Headache?" And from out of a fold of its spring coat a face rose up and in the blue light of the lamp I saw a girl's face, a tortured human face with wrinkles that stretched, like a pair of moustaches, along the line of her mouth. A hand slipped out of a sleeve and tapped one finger against her chest: "I've got a pain here…!" Tenderly I asked: "So it's your airways?" And the wrinkle-cut mouth smiled: "Not really… For two months they haven't known what to do with me. My heart! ECGs show everything's normal, but I've got a chestful of gunge that keeps churning irregularly… My endocrine system's also affected and they give me injections in my thyroid…." And her trembling fingers fished a cigarette out of her handbag, and as she went to light it, her hand shook so badly that she kept missing. In the blue gloom a dear little ember kindled. The girl threw back her head and puffed out some glass wool against the blue light. Her hair had slipped down over her shoulders and now she began to speak in a low voice: "At first we all came out in these pimply welts, and then this heart… I work with toxins, packing salts of iodine." Then I asked mischievously: "And what about that cigarette?" The girl hissed: "It's the only thing the doctor allows me…" I rubbed my hands. "And where are you going?" She tossed her head back and her hair spilled back into the hood of her coat and the cigarette described a treble clef, ending between her lips, then she filled her lungs with smoke until her sunken cheeks turned

red. And the next words rolled out amid the smoke: "Where am I going?... To the National Health Institute... My own case, well, it's pretty clear, I've had it, so it seems, but what about the other girls?... The ones still working?... We work with toxins constantly and we get no milk ration or any other benefit... and even if we meet our target by a hundred and forty per cent, we still get less than three thousand... tphut, tphut!" She spurted a speck of tobacco from her upper lip. And I stared out of the window and the train seemed to be passing vast acres of waving corn and I also caught the whiff of oilseed rape in bloom. On one bend the moon crossed from one corner to the corner opposite as I flattened myself against the window and said: "Yes... it is corn... Three thousand gross, you say?... And yes, it is rape!" There was satisfaction in my exclamation. The girl breathed out a long party horn of smoke and suddenly rolled up her sleeve: "Yes, three thousand gross... And look! We're covered in these and they itch till you draw blood... Previously I worked, or rather was made to work, in the rubber industry... working with sulphur at vulcanisation sites, wearing a mask, admittedly, but I still got burned. When I arrived home my mother would say: 'I'm glad you get out in the sun...' And now I'm being treated for my heart at Poděbrady... they tell me it's hopeless, but who knows? Chance might step in, mightn't it? Or God?... Do you smoke?" But I wasn't hearing, so fixed were my thoughts on something else. Then I gave myself a shake and read inside my brain what had been said. "Oh, yes, I do smoke..." and I smiled at her affectionately. With a backwards flip she tipped some cigarettes into the palm of her hand: "Please, take one." I did take one and judged from the feel: "Aha... Chesterfield!" Having lit my own and hers, I could feel her nails twitching and digging into my little finger. Then I also realised that the train had stopped after several previous stops and that it had taken till now for me to realise the fact. I also remembered that the clock of the Špork family château[1] had been striking. And having thought about it and counted the strokes, hearing them again in replay... I made it eleven. I struck a match and it lit up both our faces and we watched each other closely like pointers on scales. I said: "It was eleven o'clock at Lysá..." But she, greedily inhaling the smoke, replied more to herself: "You'll say it's not possible... And yet... And yet today there are kids being treated in Poděbrady for angina... While there, I've met groups of apprentice miners... they get it from the work they do, not the actual work, but the fear of the things that happen in mines... rock-falls, water bubbling up and pit props cracking... and the odd accident... the legends of accidents past... If an apprentice were down there with his fellows, well maybe... but on his own... A child'll walk through a forest at midnight with stouter heart if his father's there too... And suddenly, angina!" She was quite taken by the word and laughed so hard that she started to choke. Suddenly she paled, froze and then slowly, holding the burning cigarette in her free hand, sank, fingers clasped to her heart. Lower and lower she went right down towards her knees, across which her platinum hair flopped. The ember of the cigarette was all that moved. I felt my brain being gone over with a wire brush and the pain came back. I pushed one hand inside my shirt and straightened the bandage on my shoulder, then wiped my fingers on my handkerchief and again I had that crackling sensation at my temples and the itchy sting of an inflamed nerve. In a hollow tone I asked: "Can I do anything to help?" But touching her knees, the girl's lips merely repeated: "It's nothing, it's nothing, it's nothing…" I stood up, then sat back down, and got up again. After a moment she flicked her hair back up and once more I saw her deathly pale features: "That's better!…" And her lips sought the cigarette and the cigarette sought her lips. Once more the ember brightened and exhaling more smoke she said: "On top of everything else, I used to have complexes. As soon as I saw a razor, a knife, a sickle or scythe, I came out in a cold sweat to the point of fainting. In my automatic writing the doctor found things* that he then explained to me and the anxiety and fainting stopped."

* In our village there was this family of madmen who called themselves the Counts Coloredo. They would only ever correspond with dukes, and if they wanted to go somewhere by train, they demanded the directors of the railway company supply them with a parlour car. We kids used to enjoy shouting from the nearby woods: 'Count Coloredo, in a year and a day we'll have you up before the court of Heaven…' Then one of the crazies came charging out with a scythe and ran after us. In my terror I tripped and fell and the madman didn't spot me, though the scythe swung past just inches above my head. The boys climbed into a loft and the madman hacked at the ladder with his scythe. Some people ran up, a straightjacket, and I fainted. I was five years old…

I didn't even wait for her to finish but burst out: "That's all wrong, a sickness doesn't pass with its being explained, it's with the explanation that it begins... the method gets applied to everything until the doctor hits on something he can't explain. And that's where true human sickness begins... A sense of guilt... And what is a human being?... A cleft! The thing is, Miss, I'm..." At which point her hunched-down figure catapulted itself upwards, describing some brutal lines with the cigarette: "No, no, no, no! Not a word more! What do I care? I'll jump out of the train!" And so she stood there, describing fantastical non-stop flashes in the air with her cigarette to the point where I went quite numb. I watched her float back down onto her seat and suck herself back to her cigarette and she again billowed her words through the smoke: "... Yes, yes, everything comes back... Like when you forget a suitcase somewhere, deliberately, and years later they bring it back to you... the original case, fresh, undiminished... Horrors!" And she stared off into the distance. I found my tongue: "... Yes and today that's the very cost of holding on to all the things that make human life worth living... Otherwise living wouldn't be possible... Shall we depart? What boots it? What's there to regret? And so farewell! But until the measure of all things is retaken, the things upon which man and his liberty stand, there can be no living for me, or for you, or for society... And... and... And who are you?" Whereupon the girl, not altering the direction of her gaze, rested one elbow on her knee, drew her hair back from her forehead and held that thinker's pose: "Who am I?... A young woman!... A one-time medical student turned editor with an information service turned jailbird in Pankrác for fourteen months turned translator of medical books turned packer of salts of iodine and now a wreck… one of many… nothing special, a girl who's got only two and a half million blood cells and who knows what lies ahead… Ah, thank goodness, the outskirts of Prague at last!" With satisfaction she stared out of the window. "Pity I studied medicine. But here's Prague now and I love Prague, see the first constellations of streetlights, the first tattoos on the body of the city…" I had an upsurge of emotion: "You must let me have your address, I'll write to you!" The young woman shook her hair and spread her fingers wide into two fans: "You mustn't even think of it! No, no! That's the last thing I need! I honestly don't want to know about you… You can see how ill I am and such things are for the well…" So I pleaded, quietly: "How about a short walk by the river?" And I watched as her fingers searched her handbag for another cigarette. She said: "An Alsatian puppy will do for that…" I pleaded again: "Say yes!" At which she nodded a token agreement, but said: "No!" I raised my voice: "Really not?" And the young woman shook her head from side to side, from ear to ear and said: "Yes! I do really mean no!" Then she turned grave: "… But promise me one thing, I beg just one thing of you, a single wish…" I started to melt: "Yes?" Then with a childlike smile as she slipped a cigarette between her lips she said: "Yes, give me a light!" In exasperation I reached for a box of matches, struck one and held it between my palms. The young woman leant towards it and the flicker spilled across her wretched features. I had an urge to set fire to her soft hair, but thought better of it and in the glow of that matchlight I etched her dear face on my memory for all time. I stamped out the match and looked through the window. Yes, we were at the former vineyards. I rose slowly and bent down to her: "This is where I get off... I wish you all the very best of health and happiness, and au revoir!" She blew aside the smoke and, keeping her shaking hand in mine, babbled: "Best of health? But yes, I accept... And happiness? Likewise... but not au revoir, au not-revoir, not goodbye, 'bye for good!" Suddenly she seemed to have caught the sound of something, she tipped her head in attention and cried, beguiled: "And we've had it!" The train was slowing to a stop. Next I ripped my hand from hers and hit the young woman in the face as hard as I could and stared, bewildered, at what I'd just done to her, stared into her face that hadn't even flinched, though black blood had spurted from her nose. I turned and lumbered beneath the blue light across to the door. I turned for one final image and saw the young woman stroking her childlike face and pitying herself out loud: "Poor little, poor little, poor little thing..." I sprinted down the corridor, alighted and heaved the metal door with such violence that it snapped shut of its own accord.

The station master stopped swinging on his chair, stared into one corner of the office, then shook his head as if to release whatever water was making his ears ring. Behind me I heard the train guard shift his feet and heave a deep sigh.

Finally the station master collected himself and repeated in a strange voice: "So dispatcher Lambora gave the order: 'Go forward, driver, there's something wrong somewhere, so brake slightly as you reach the station and check if there isn't a train stuck by the warning post...'" And glooming his eyebrows he gave his own dispatcher a look of such severity that the latter slowly froze under his stare.

As always, whenever I've told this tale, I waited for the station master to finish agonising over the idea. And as always the station master asked in funereal tones: "D'you know what I'd do with a dispatcher like that, me, as his station master?" I said as I always did, perhaps for the tenth time of telling the same people the same thing: "I don't know. I really don't!" The station master rose to his feet, went red in the face, waved a threatening fist at the past, grabbed the chair by the back rest and banged it on the ground, shouting: "I'd have him hauled away in chains! Straight to the slammer with a criminal of his sort!"

And with his arms folded he passed through the half-light cast by the green lampshade to the wall, where he hammered at the blackboard with both fists and moaned: "To the slammer, straight to the slammer! That's what I'd do!" The dispatcher went over to the block station and cleared the arrival track, then he pressed the lever down and shouted down the megaphone to the signal box: "Set track three for train 6363!" And he looked up to face me and out of the blue asked: "And how was it with you and Inspector Vodička?" The station master slowly rejoined us, pushed the chair back with his boot and sat astride it, chewing a finger nail. Looking into his haggard features, I said: "We were on a traffic-handling course in Hradec Králové, on the second floor of the station building.[1]

"And if we needed a pee, we had to go downstairs into the station, because the second-floor urinal was blocked with matchsticks tossed there by the dispatchers. But I went into the one we were barred from, undid my flies and peed to my heart's content, I was still mid-pee when some chap took me by the sleeve and asked menacingly: "What are you doing here?" I said: "As you can see, I'm having a slash!" But he kept on: "But why here, where you're not allowed?" I turned and, just for luck, aimed some at the tip of his shoe and said: "I just felt like it." And he roared back at me: "And do you know who I am?" As I shook out the last drops I said: "Haven't a clue!" And he threw up his hands and screamed: "I'll have you know I'm Inspector Vodička!" Calmly I returned: "So go and have a good moan to the fifth tap in the washroom, or... go cry to the headmaster!" But he shouted: "What? Inspector Vodička and cry to the headmaster?"

And as always, whenever I told this tale, I didn't get to finish it. As always, the station master swung his leg across the chair and guffawed, bore his spluttering, asthmatic cough away into the corner and gave his inspectoral stripes a good shake. Then as he came back, he wiped away the tears of laughter and worked violently at restoring his crumpled features with his fingers.

The dispatcher picked up his torch and went out onto the platform and before long a goods train rattled the window panes. It was only then that I realised that the bell had indeed rung and the train had been reported to the next station. I even re-counted mentally the bell's pleasing rings and saw out there in the dark the look-out men lowering the barriers to the cracked tones of a bell, gathering up their flags and disappearing into the dark, then as the train passed by them they stood to attention and saluted even though no one could see them, no one could possibly have seen them. Then seeing the red tail-light and satisfied that the train had passed through in its entirety, with their lamp at their feet they raised the barriers like winding up a bucket from a well. The train guard opened his little case, fished a slice of salami from its paper wrapping, tipped his head back and dropped it into his mouth, the station master went back to straddling his chair and then asked, in expectant innocence: "And how was it with those two trains entering a single-track station at the same time?" I feigned surprise, though I'd told the tale many times before: "How do you mean, two entering?"

And the dispatcher came back in from the platform, bringing with him a detectable whiff of air, sat down and reported to the next station: "Train 6363 passed through at seven fifty-nine." And he entered it in the book, then got up, crossed to the block station, pressed the lever and cleared the track. As he took his seat he reminded me: "You know, when we were on that course together!" And he looked softly at me. I said: "Oh that! We were on this course and Inspector Chmelař asked the whole class if it was at all possible to have two simultaneous arrivals. I put my hand up and said: 'It is, but you have to be on the platform and take care the trains don't run into each other.' And the inspector cupped one ear the better to hear, and asked, into the deathly hush: 'And where have you done it like that?' I replied, unflustered: 'Dobrovice, where I'm from.' At which the inspector stood up and, right there in Hradec, started threatening our dear little station all those miles away: 'I knew they played silly buggers there! But this! I'm gonna give 'em a piece o' my mind over this, damn their eyeballs!"

And as always, whenever I looked at the station master, I saw him looking paralysed. Eyes narrowed so as to savour the monstrous image to the full. He spluttered repeatedly and, as always, asked sadly, absently: "And you really did that with the trains?" I reassured him, with my hand on my heart: "Honestly." "But not with expresses, surely?" "No, only goods and slow passenger trains. And only if they happened to meet at our station. We had a clear view in both directions. All the way to Nepřevázka and Voděrady." But the station master was liking it less and less: "I can't get my head round it. It's terrible, dreadful!"

He got up again and ambled about in the gloom. I said: "Right, sir, I'm off out again. I'll wait on the platform." But he took my hands in his and pushed me back down on my chair: "Do stop fussing! Your train's nowhere near yet. Stay and tell us about the time you welcomed operations manager Podaný to Dobrovice along with the railways CEO."

I registered surprise: "Welcomed?" And the station master said: "Come on, you know, how you'd been on a training course and your station master was just sickening for his promotion to inspector, and how his office was all upholstery, carpets, potted palms, and a huge sofa that the dispatcher from Sadská who used to do turns with you ripped with some girl on night duty." I pretended to be even more surprised: "What sofa?" And the dispatcher, leaning across the glass table top, took over: "How the station master flew about the office doing his nut: 'The bastard's ripped my Austrian sofa! Ripped the waxed canvas cover!'" I remembered: "He's right, he was quite a lad, that dispatcher. There was another time he brought a bird in, got drunk with her and sent her to sleep naked in the store-room. It was summer and the bird ripped open a duvet, poured glue all over herself then rolled about in the feathers, and in the morning, with people on their way to work, she ran up and down the platform with the feathers stuck all over her. Or, wow, that thing he and the station handyman did to the telegraph girl! They were on night duty and getting bored, so without warning they grabbed the telegraphist, hitched up her skirt and printed all the station's rubber stamps all over her thighs and backside, but she told on them at home and that led to disciplinary proceedings. Restricting her personal freedom. But what happened then, station master?"

Amazingly, the station master practically had it off pat: "There was a break around midday, truants were off for

a beer and the phone went. You picked up the receiver to be told by Mladá Boleslav that a motor inspection trolley was on its way. You asked: 'Who's on board?' And the voice on the line said: 'Only the district permanent way inspector.' So you set the signal and through the window saw that your resident big cheese, the station master, had come out by the rear door in an old uniform and hatless to attend to his pigeons. To clean the pigeon loft. Just like that."

I stood up, leaned against the edge of the table and asked in a tone of surprise: "And what did I do next?"

The station master started rocking happily on his chair: "And then squatting down by the stove, you were playing with the cat and her kittens, tickling her under the chin, when someone entered the office and came and stood right behind you..."

I looked from the dispatcher to the station master and back and fed them the next line: "And what did the guy standing behind me suddenly say? What did he say?"

The dispatcher, kneeling on a chair with his torso reflected in the glass tabletop, took over: "The man said: 'That's a funny way to spend your time on duty!' But you went on stroking the pussycat's chin and said: 'Well, it's only to while away the time.' So the man walked nervously up and down the office and started up again: 'And what does the instruction manual say about it?' And you said: 'But that only gives broad outlines, nothing specific.' And the man, now in a roar: 'And do you have any idea who you're talking to?'"

And mid-rock the station master interrupted his dispatcher: "You put your hand under the cat's tummy, stood up and turned to face him: 'I don't, sir, because sir hasn't introduced himself.'"

By way of explanation I added: "Thing is, people were always coming into the office. From the refinery, or just to pass the time of day, but what happened next, I can't wait to hear."

The station master swung his leg, crossed to the spot under the light, gave me a sudden cold look and said: "'I'm operations manager Podaný!'" And tearing his eyes away from me, he clasped his hands together and shouted across to the train guard: "Jesus! Everybody used to quake in their boots in the presence of Podaný. Ex-Austrian army officer!"

The guard clicked his teeth: "I know the guy, I know him! But what happened next?"

The station master's eyes flashed: "So you stood up straight, touched your hair in salute and he bellowed: 'Put that cat down!' And he tore it from you and hurled it towards the stove. And then he screamed: 'Where are the others?'" The dispatcher halted the station master with a raised hand and took up the story: "At that point, the door opened and I came in with three beers in each hand. I set them down on the telegraph desk and presented myself. Mr Podaný paused and gave the beers a long stare, as if seeing the like for the very first time. Then he pulled a face and said: 'What does the instruction manual say about drinking on duty? And where's your station master? Where is he?' Then the trackside door opened and, but station master, you take it from here..." and the dispatcher left with a smile and went to clear the arrivals track.

Filled with malicious delight, the station master took up the story: "The trackside door opened and in came the station master covered top to toe in pigeon shit, without his cap and with his shirt open at the neck. And as he presented himself, a little bit of down on his lip kept rising and falling and once he'd made his report it floated gently to the ground and the tabby kittens leapt at it. Operations manager Podaný went closer and closer towards the station master until they could almost sniff at each other like dogs, until Mr Podaný said ever so sweetly: 'I thought this was a railway station, but do you know, station master, what it really is?' And he bellowed: 'An alehouse, a total shambles!' And outside, in the motor inspection trolley, the railway CEO was waiting." And as the station master told the tale, I saw him turning pale, he even sat back down on his chair and for a moment held his head in his hands as if the whole thing had happened to him.

I hopped lightly down off the table, for the moment had come for me to round off the story that I'd told a dozen times before: "Then they left, the station master remained standing on the platform, in a uniform rendered unfit to be seen by his pigeons, while he had a brand new one hanging in his locker. Then he stormed back into the office and whined: 'Why didn't somebody warn me? Bastards, why didn't you tell me?'" So I said what happened next. "He rang Mladá Boleslav, and there they were over the moon – they were in the habit of doing things to rattle others up and down the line. We reported to Luštěnice that it was only the district permanent way inspector on the way, but that was no help to the station master; he locked himself in his office among all that fine upholstery, carpets and potted palms and spent the entire afternoon sitting at his desk, muttering non-stop: 'My inspector's stripes are down the pan, my stripes are down the pan.' But isn't that my train being signalled?"

The station master had simmered down and was smiling silently. He turned to me and asked: "So, wouldn't you like your old job back?" I said: "I would, as I sit here, right now, on the spot. I do miss it and it's a pity I left." But I could see that the station master would be happy with anything at all, just not that. He stood up, held both my hands tight for some time and almost begging, said: "You're welcome to look in any time, whenever your train's late, just stop by. Or pop in any evening and we can have another nice long chat."

As always, I was amazed: "What? The same again?"

He place one arm round my neck and, holding it there, assured me, with not a hint of jesting in his eyes: "Yes, the same again, nothing but the same over and over again. I can never hear it too often!"

The dispatcher slotted the departure sign into place, gave me a gentle knock with his green lamp and said: "Here's your train now."

A CHRISTENING

The car's engine had been picking up nicely through the deep dark forest and sucking in the fuel with all the more relish and even took the rise quite smartly. And once more the headlights were sniffing at the deep, russety, leafy forest. Then suddenly, out of the ditch and onto the roadway, hopped a doe. She stood legs apart, staring helplessly into the lights.

At that moment the parish priest caught the smell of grassy glades and scorched pines and In vain, Soul of Christ, give me thy blessing! There, up ahead, beneath the small oak tree, he used to wait for deer with his finger firmly and mercilessly on the trigger, and, Body of Christ, in vain preserve me! At another time a pheasant might have lumbered into flight, a tiny forward shift with the rifle and down the bloodied bird would fall, bouncing off one branch onto the next, and, Thou, blood of Christ, in vain inflame me, thou, water from Christ's flank, cleanse me in vain!

And in the selfsame flash of his mind the priest weighed up the cost of getting his mudguard hammered back into shape, and perhaps a smashed headlight replaced, and now he could see the doe quite close up. Decision taken and mind made up, he gripped the steering wheel, turned to take it on his right wing, nearly shot out of his seat with the impact, then fell back and braked. He put the engine in neutral, shifted the gear lever into reverse and, craning round to see through the rear window, backed away. And in the diffuse glare of his left headlight he saw the broken body of the deer, beating the air with its tiny front hooves.

He switched off, opened the door and hopped lightly out of the car, but then came back, lifted out the little case containing his liturgical paraphernalia, grabbed the heavy starting handle, trotted down into the ditch and, having judged the distance, hurled himself onto the beast and pressed it down into the fallen leaves with his whole bodyweight, because he knew that with one strike of its hoof it would cut him open to the bone, even through his clothes. In its anguish, the doe gathered its strength and rolled over several times with a violence that surprised him. But he held on tight, gripping its gulping throat hard and pressing it back down into the wet leaves with his whole torso and both legs. And with a new surge the doe again rolled this way and that, taking the priest with it, but he renewed his grip, gripped the animal by the throat and clamped the twitching flesh between his knees as if he were playing some living, fantastical cello. A moment or so having passed and sensing the animal's strength fading, he released his right hand, scrabbled in the leaves for the starting handle and hit the doe's skull with all his might, then once more, then the body slackened, jerked again like a woman making love, until finally the priest could hear beneath him the loud, but weakening beat of the animal's heart.

He carefully let go, adopted a kneeling position and hauled himself up onto his feet, then he bent down again, picked the doe up by all four of its legs and with a mighty lunge threw it up next to the car's tyres, he picked up the starting handle and scrambled out of the ditch onto the road, then finally put his case of liturgical paraphernalia back in place. He opened a rear door, gently picked the doe up, turned and, like putting a baby to bed, laid it down behind the front seats.

He shut the door, walked round the car and, God be praised, the wing wasn't too badly dented. The headlight, though, was a goner. Ah well, he mused, contented. One headlight will have to do, plus my fog light. He sank deep into his seat, pressed the starter and the engine sprang into life as if just waiting for it. He depressed the clutch pedal, shifted into first, touched the accelerator and, barely realising it, passed into second, then third. He pondered: if only, in his headlights, he'd seen a fiery cross poking from the doe's head, he'd have stopped. But as he'd begun to storm up the hill in the depth of the forest, he pursued the thought, he'd have hit it at full speed anyway, even in the knowledge that he was about to kill the Son of God, because once the animal was down and he, bare-headed, kneeling to disembowel it with his hunting knife, then bringing a spruce twig down to drive into its still warm flesh, this was all that was left to him in this world, all he had to hope for, believe in. Then oh, Suffering of Christ, in vain give me strength, then, Christ, in vain conceal me in Thy wounds, I am a heathen, I am sounding brass.

At the bend next to the Nine Crosses, he slowed and remembered how, but three hours previously, he had stood in his black vestment with a red chalice on his breast, surveying all those who had come to the funeral, quite capable of casting the widow into the open grave, as if it had been her fault that her husband had hanged himself in a shop window. He had stood over the grave and, having finished telling the sorry tale of the pregnant Leah,[2] he'd surveyed the scene and pointed at the eyes of all of them: "If there is any among you here that is without sin, including me, let him cast the first stone at this woman."

And now again he sensed the agitation of the outraged people at the funeral. And his one headlight lit up the first four-metre-tall cross, then the second, one after another until the ninth pinged into his brain through the corner of his eye.

That must have been a dreadful business, half a century back, a spurned suitor had waited with some friends and hatchets in a thicket, and as the wedding party made its way back, they'd hacked all nine to death in their carriages. The priest dropped his gaze, glanced at his little phosphorescent hands then back at the grainy surface of the road. I do hope I'm not going to be late for the christening.

At that moment something stirred within him, he braked and as he looked behind him he heard the stunned doe come round, shoot to its feet and he felt her cold muzzle touching his ear. And then he heard what he'd always feared. One front, razor-sharp hoof sliced several times into the seat's leather cover. He stopped the car, turned right round this time and saw two feverish eyes. He quickly reached under his little case, gripped the starting handle once more, knelt on his seat and cautiously, so as not to rip the fabric on the ceiling, stunned the doe again with a curling blow. He quickly opened the door, angrily swung himself out, whipped open the rear door and, from the side, aimed several more blows, shattering the doe's skull. He groped and felt the fragments of bone, slammed the door, put the starting handle away under the case with his liturgical paraphernalia, and sank heavily back into his seat.

When he entered the hallway, he was met by the young father who, half-way towards him, stopped and cried out: "Goodness, Father, what's happened to you?" Only then did he look down at his clothes and saw they were covered in blood and mud.

And his face was mirrored in the horrified features of the handsome father. The priest pulled himself together: "It's nothing, I ran over a hare, so it'll be the blood, and then I had to change a tyre. So, young man, put me somewhere where I can tidy up."

He took the young man by the arm, but the latter squirmed away, then opened the door to a closet, entered the dark space and having switched on the light, stood in one corner.

The priest entered the mirror and with something like satisfaction took a good look at his wild and bloody face. He said: "Don't worry, I must have put my hand to my face!" And he turned and asked: "Bring me some water, will you, Brother?"

The young father flicked his curls back out of his eyes and mumbled: "But there's some here." And he picked up a pitcher and tinkled some water into the stone basin.

The priest removed his coat without a word, rolled up his sleeves and gave his hairy arms a good soaping. Without pausing as he rubbed his frothy fingers, he half-turned: "And how are things with your marriage?" And he looked straight into the young husband's eyes.

He flinched. He dropped his gaze and his curls flopped down as far as his eyebrows. He tossed them back and whispered: "I'd thought, Father, that I'd become someone else, that something would happen, but…"

Now bent over the basin, the priest let the water trickle through his fingers; "What 'but'?"

And the curly-headed young man lamented: "But nothing happened. It's like I've buried myself. They won't even let me play ice hockey anymore, I'm not allowed to do anything and I really enjoyed…" He fixed the priest with his sorrowful eyes and added with a grin: "It's like if they banned you from carrying a hunting rifle."

The priest scooped some water into his hands and pressed it to his wrinkled face. He soaped his hands and rubbed his face. The young man stepped forward and touched the bloodstains with his finger. "Here's some more, Father, on your ear, and more again round the back of your neck!"

Finally the priest lifted his wet face and asked: "All right now?" And the young lad touched his cheek, turned it this way and that and said: "Clean as a whistle." And he handed the priest the towel. As he dried himself, the priest spoke earnestly to the young man: "Are you a sportsman? Won't you be going off on military service soon? Never ask anyone about anything, only yourself. After all, lad, they'll be opening an artificial ice rink in the town this autumn, you'll be able to go and train and play there. You've got a mind

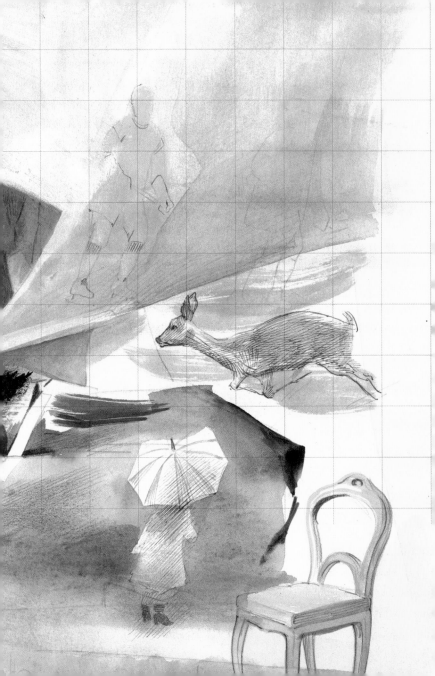

of your own, surely!" The young father rallied, but shook his locks once again: "They won't let me go anywhere. I've grown so flabby! I wanted to have some drainpipe trousers and a fancy jacket made, but they said that now I was married I had to have some wide trousers made and a discreet jacket. I bought a fabulous hat, a Stevenson, absolutely brilliant, but it stays in the wardrobe. And my wife went and put dark polish on my yellow shoes, inlaid with white stripes. If you could only see, Father, what I have to put up with! They're good to me, but I don't have a smidgen of liberty. It's like I've died since I got married…" And his tears dripped to the floor.

The priest angrily cast the towel aside, took the young dad in his great big hands and shook him like a moneybox: "You must – keep telling yourself, I must, I must! And take no notice of her parents! Jesus Mary, you've got your whole life ahead of you!"

But the young man shook his locks right under the priest's chin: "No hope, they're stronger than me. My whole life's been ruined!" And he suddenly looked at the priest in such a way that the latter crossed over to the window.

"But Father, you can't possibly go in with your clothes in that state!" the young father said, clapping his hands together. And the priest remembered the christening: "You know what, I'll get changed in here. You join the guests inside and let them know I'm here, and have the women get some luke-warm water ready, so the baby's head doesn't catch cold!"

The young father having left, the priest took a cloth and started cleaning the blood and mud off his clothes. But he felt even uncleaner than he had been before. He tossed the rag aside, opened the door and listened. Just subdued talk coming from the rooms. He shot down the hall and slipped out into the yard. He unlocked the car, took his little case out, quietly re-locked it and made it back along the poorly lit passage into the closet.

He opened his case and pulled on his black, flowing vestment, did up the buttons and, facing the mirror, tidied the collar with both hands and pulled the crinkled red chalice down over his chest. Then with his head slightly raised and that well-rehearsed vacuous expression on his face, he left the closet, paused, returned and switched the light off.

He entered the room looking soulful and cried, with his arms flung wide: "Good evening, my sisters and brothers, good evening!" And he proffered his hands all round like some Indian deity and there was not an eye that did not look down beneath his eagle gaze. He began to apologise: "I'm a little late." And pointing like a connoisseur at the bottles of wine on the table, he said: "Enjoy yourselves while the father and I make up an altar in the next room."

The curly-locked young father ran into the next room and switched on the lights. The priest followed him in calmly, holding his wide, floor-length skirts in his right hand. And he closed the door carefully behind him. So it was here there'd been a wedding six months ago, but also here that ten years ago an old lady had lain in her coffin, tiny, dried up, only just covered in skin. He said: "So, brother, we'll make a little altar on this big table. Pop next door and get some geraniums." He clapped one hand to his forehead:

"And fetch the little case with my liturgical equipment from the closet!"

After the young man left, he paced the room with the red chalice on his bosom, trying to work out how much the doe was actually going to cost him. The broken headlight, the torn seat covers, his ruined clothes. Hm. And it was here on this chair that that unpleasantness had befallen him at the hastily prepared wedding. Jokes were being told, and each time his turn came, he told one about some madman. Then a woman had risen from this very chair, pressed her hankie to her eyes and she'd run out. He asked the man of the house: "What's up? What's wrong with her, not local, is she?" "A fortnight ago they put her husband away in an asylum, she went to see him yesterday, he was sweeping up the autumn leaves and loading them onto a cart, but the wind kept blowing them back all over the yard." An unpleasant business, most unpleasant, but who could have known? That's just it, we so often commit evil and we can't even help it, oh, whited sepulchre, you do keep committing evil, just now and again...

And the young father came back in, carrying the geraniums and the little case dangling from one finger. The priest carefully closed the door and made his decision: "We'll push this big table aside, and you say nothing to anyone, just get your skate blades sharpened."

But the young dad placed both hands on the smaller table and said under his breath: "I shall get them sharpened, but I'd rather we had the altar on this small table."

From his little case the priest took a nickel-plated Christ and set it down in the middle of the large table. He paused for thought, looking at the sofa: "Let's get rid of that doll, so. And this is where the guests will sit, we'll set the various chairs in a row and remember this: once you lose your own self, you're done for!" He took two cut-glass candlesticks from his little case, stuck candles in them and stood them next to Christ. "Right, and now pass me the geraniums. Along this side of the table we'll have the godparents, the mother and you." And he added confidentially: "Christ also pursued his own goals and ignored whatever his relatives might think. Stiffen thy sinews, my lad, stiffen thy sinews!"

But the curly-headed father stood crestfallen next to the little table and pleaded: "Father, let's move everything here; this really is far better suited."

The priest lit the candles, turned, casually blowing out the match: "And why?" Then he took out a little cut-glass jug, held it up to the light and declared with satisfaction: "I've bought this new. Nice handiwork, eh? But you have to play ice hockey, you must, you must, you were always the best, so you must!"

The young man's face disappeared beneath his drooping curls: "It *is* lovely handiwork, I *will* play ice hockey, but don't have the altar there, I've…" The priest held the ends of his richly embroidered stole between his fingers, then stretched out his arms and tossed the stole down his back, tightened it round his neck and let the ends hang free alongside his arms: "Now fetch some warm water and remember, games aren't a sin and you're still young!"

The young man went over to the altar and glancing at the nickel-plated Christ gabbled: "Father, on that table, before we were married, I, no we… we… where Christ is, that's where her hair was and here at the corner, right where the jug is, was her…"

The priest stroked the corners of his stole: "So we really should transfer it!" And he fixed the embarrassed new dad with his gaze. But then his sharp eyes guessed: "But what's gone on on the little table? Surely not there as well?"

The young dad tossed his locks back with one swift move and said firmly: "There too, but only once."

The priest made up his mind: "So, we'll leave things as they are. It's all just symbolic anyway, even that lukewarm water is a symbol, all rituals are symbols, but…" He squeezed the dad's elbow: "But only your life is for real, which is why you must play and not make of life just another symbol… So now run and get that lukewarm water and have the guests come in. Let the baby be brought in by its godfather. And let the christening begin…"

A fine, dreary drizzle had started coming down; I thought it better to cross over to the side where the billboards were and, as always, I read with care what was on new at the various cinemas – new posters with the old illusion that one Friday I might actually see something on offer that appealed to me. Suddenly an old, rasping voice asked me: "Excuse me, I can't see high enough, would you mind telling me what's on at the Humanity today?" I stood on tiptoe and read: "Lighthouse, Eden, Moscow, Friendship… The Humanity, you say?" "Yes, the Humanity, it's the one closest to where I live, I'm just this old pensioner you see before you, see?" "Ah, found it! So today they're showing a great love drama, *Be Expecting Me…*" "Mmm, that might do. A drama! I bet it's an English film!" "No, sir, it's a Russian production." At which the pensioner angrily raised his walking stick, waved it about in the air and shouted: "Well, they can expect me there for all they like! The old lady an' I, we'd rather stay in and read a cheap paperback, see?" He gave a wink of his wily eyes and merged into the rainy crowd. I crossed back to the other side of the street, entered a pub and remembered passing a queue waiting in the rain, for what though? I didn't know. With my thumb and forefinger I indicated to the waiter that I'd like a large one. And what else can she want from me? I ran my eyes anxiously along the shelves with their bottles standing to attention, then I looked long at the crusty leather coat of an old man who had raised a tiny shot glass with his red hand, downed his liqueur in one go

and with his bowler-hatted head thrown back was waiting for the last drop. And yet, as always, the moment I saw her, I'd head straight to her, after all that's happened, I'd still fly towards her. This time I'd said You can sleep on my brass bed, just don't let them take it, for the love of God, don't let them take it, it doesn't matter one bit, its father is the one that brings it up. The old man had finished his drink and was grumbling with his exhilarated eyes: "In the days of old Austria?[1] For twelve thousand florins you could get a farm with six cows and three pairs of horses." That day, pale, so very pale, she had borne her glazed eyes down the stairs and I'd said What's the matter, for Christ's sake, tell me what's wrong with you. She just blathered, Home quick, grab a cab, I'm all right now, but get me home quick, I'm okay, just get me home quick. I had a drink, still attached to the rim of the old man's bowler, a halo in black, then my eyes slipped down to the chauffeur's coat he had on, with under that an old grease-stained dress suit, and even further down his shoes, crossed, and no less wrinkled than his face. He was muttering away and the cigarette stuck to his lower lip bobbed about: "And when I went to buy a horse? Quite a horse you could have for a hundred and fifty florins," by now he was shouting, "an' then, pal, you could get a good heifer for eighty! An' if relations gave me a crown, then for a few coppers I could go to the circus, but as a little lad I wasn't allowed to spend the rest!" I'd waited for her again on Arbes Square, but she played the stranger, like who was I waiting for, to which I... that I was only... but she, she didn't have the time, and Stop pestering me! I said, Well let me at least... but she said Get lost, suppose someone were to see me with you. The old boy's head had sunk down and his face was hidden from me by his bowler, the cigarette had fallen to the filthy floor and smoke rose silently from it, twirling about the old man's trouser leg like dried-up ivy curled round a statue. She'd hopped off the tram and I'd gone after her with Here you are, and in turn I hopped off and saw that she'd unwrapped the dinky American gloves, Now who in the world has hands that they'd look good on? She'd stood there as if I'd placed a bomb in her hands. But it was time to go. I left thirty crowns on the bar counter, reached for the door handle and yanked the door open. The old boy raised his bowler and: "Is it still raining?" and I replied for my own benefit: "It is, and it's good that it's raining, at least I don't have to visit my old woman's grave in the cemetery." Through the glass of the closing door I saw the waiter standing with what looked like a broken neck, holding a shot glass to his lips and savouring the green liqueur as if he were blowing a miniature trumpet. And the dreary drizzle was still coming down. I crossed back to the posters and, as always, read by the light of a street lamp the old programmes on today's new posters, quite free of any illusion that one Friday I might actually see things on offer that appealed to me. Then with my first glance into the distance I could tell that it was her approaching. Three more street lights to go, two... Jaunty and ironic even in her gait, like the kind of Moldavian gypsy girl over which Polish magnates used to shoot one another. At the Humanity cinema they'd begun showing the great love drama, *Be Expecting Me*.

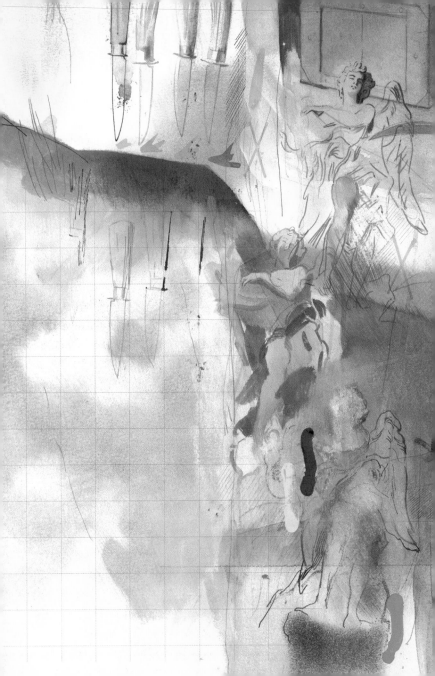

She, drowning waist-deep in toys, with big eyes, as big as my mouth, and with an impeccable apricot complexion, I'm a shop assistant on eighteen hundred a month, with no interest in the job, with eyes as big as her mouth, with an impeccable apricot complexion, she's a shop assistant, with no interest in the job,[1] if you don't like it you can leave, an exasperated old lady is applying her shrivelled lips to a child's mouth organ to see if it plays, over a customer's shoulder I saw him as he was, saw him come in, *I* saw *her* seeing me as I was, seeing me come just to see her, him to see me, for a precious image, I frightened the eyes out of me, came out from behind the counter and stood there, all different shapes, my legs slightly impaired for walking, she stood there facing me, all different shapes, I stood facing him just as I was, touched his hand, I touched her hand and the hands squeezed each other, I said to him: "Goodness, what brings you here?", but words failed him, words failed me, in the sight of all I stroked his cheek, I don't care what the gossipmongers spread around the shop, she stroked my cheek and so I whispered: "Nothing in particular, I just came to tell you I'm...", the old woman surfaced and croaked: "I'll take this mouth organ, miss," I stepped up to her counter and picked up the toys she was selling, he picked up the toys I sell, I gave the woman her change and now I'm standing beneath his gaze again, she's standing right there beneath me and whispering to me: "I *told* you not to leave, so why did you go there?", but I couldn't tell her I couldn't go walking about the town where she'd said: "No," oh, God, she's so beautiful, so young, so full of charm, I'd told him: "If back then you'd done something to me, hit me, been nasty to me, but I can't help coming to see you, and you will write to me again, won't you?", but how could I have done something to you, hit you and been nasty to you?, but you must come, I will write, I let my eyes slip down to the little flaxen-haired girl with a scooter, she was surveying the dolls, which one do you like? this one?, so you have it to remember me by, and I stroked her little fair head and sensed that I should go, my eyes having closed about me like water, and in turn I picked out a little musical box and said to him: "And here's something for *you* to remember me by," it was the first time she gave me something to remember her by, I paid for the doll, she was standing by the till, I was standing by the till and I turned the handle with my beautiful hand and the silvery device opened up, I received my change and a touch from her warm hand, I touched his hand and gave him his change, but customers were thronging round the toys, "so, bye for now, I have to go," I said, tormented, I said to him: "And you won't even give me your hand?", but I was already heading, stricken, for the steps and could hear her pure voice beating at my back, "no, madam, I'm sorry, this pram comes in beige only," I wonder, will the silly man look back? I didn't look back, I didn't look back, the gossipmongers are going to have a field day...

"Have you been waiting long?" – "Oh, no matter, I see the way people are buying apples, or I get to thinking…" "You also do some thinking! Duh!" – "Yes, how nice it used to be here on Arbes Square, when it used to be flowers they sold and the like." – "Really? You've got quite a talent for observation, you should have joined the police. What's left of it now?" – "Nothing. At least some of the pubs still have their good old names. Isn't it so much nicer to agree to meet at The Two Red Hearts than at catering facility no. 357?" – "Isn't there a nice smell of pine needles here?" – "And you're looking a bit down in the mouth!" – "I tell you, in the run-up to Christmas the shops could give you a nervous breakdown." – "But you're still looking beautiful!" – "Well, well, you put on a good show, but what are our womenfolk doing?" – "Womenfolk? I get you! They keep tidying up after me, shifting the furniture about and now they even cook for me." – "Like what?" – "Potato dumplings! But I had to go chasing all over Libeň to find some loose potatoes and only got some at the top end, by the Cross. I was so mad I stopped for a snifter at The Old Double Base."[1] – "Get away!" – "But as soon as I got home with the potatoes, she sent me back out for a quarter-kilo of lard, to have them soaked in it. The ignominy was too much, so I called in at Hausman's tavern…"[2] – "But you were never a one to drink, were you?" – "But what really got my goat was the poppy seed. In not one of the Brotherhood[3] shops did they have a grinder…" – "So where did you stop that time?" – "At The

King Přemysl, but then one concierge did let me grind it. And after all that my old lady wanted me to say how good they were, but I was so knackered, said the wrong thing and little wifie burst into tears, and so to placate her I scrubbed the floor." – "And then straight to bed?" – "Oh, no, that's only for after a wedding. But so as to clean under the bed as well, I borrowed a dog on the pretext of taking it for a walk, then kept throwing a tennis ball under the bed until it swept all the dust out with its coat, then we went for a walk up to Castle Top,[4] there she wrung her hands, lay her head on my shoulder and whispered how wonderful it'll be once I'm sixty and lose any carnal desires." – "Ah, you men, you poor things!" – "Yes, yes, and then the dog ran off somewhere and I blew all my fuses in terror, because if anything happened to the dog, its mistress would have cut my throat, but the dog was already back home." – "And then?" – "Then I had to let myself be led by the hand and was chafing at the bit so badly we decided to go and see a love story at the cinema to clear the air. But the film they were showing, *Story of a Young Couple*[5] it was, was so ideological that it set me right back on my feet and I made straight for the exit." – "There's a thing!!" – "Yes, yes, but what's your father up to these days?" – "He sold all his stamps at a bazaar. He'd been expecting a pogrom after the trial, but they didn't catch up with him, others carried the can. Today the stamps would be worth ten times as much. But at least Dad's got nothing left." – "He had a factory, didn't he?" – "The Germans took that from him, and now this lot..." – "Why didn't he flee the country?" – "That's our folk all over! They couldn't imagine not seeing their piffling factory again, so they stayed. Thirty-one relatives on my dad's side got done in at Auschwitz and all because they couldn't part with their property in time."[6] – "That's terrible. And how did your father survive?" – "Didn't I ever tell you? One February, they shoved them all out of a carriage somewhere near Česká Třebová, stood them all up by the cemetery wall and raked them with gunfire. My dad, being so short, fell down with the ones who been shot and after the Germans left, he climbed over the wall and burrowed his way under a pile of withered old funeral wreaths, and the next night he set off. He got picked up by some alien visitors, Germans from somewhere in Pomerania, Dad pulled out his gold teeth and gave them to them and then they drove him all the way to Chlumec, where he was kept in hiding by some carpenter right up to the revolution..."[7] – "That's..." – "What d'you mean, That's? But there was that time when there'd been a fresh fall of snow here on the embankment and you and I had crossed from the Rudolfinum and you told me I'd got sincere eyes. Remember?" – "How could I forget? No one had been across the snow before us so there were only our footprints behind us." – "Have you any idea how happy I used to be back then? And have you any idea at all how glad I was to lay my head against your coat? It had such a nice tobacco smell!" – "Yes, tobacco, but... What's your sister doing now? Does she still have that slight limp?" – "She's married, happily so. Up to last year she kept waiting for her man, but he didn't come." – "Who?" – "This is something I'm sure I haven't told you before. Well, as the war was coming to an

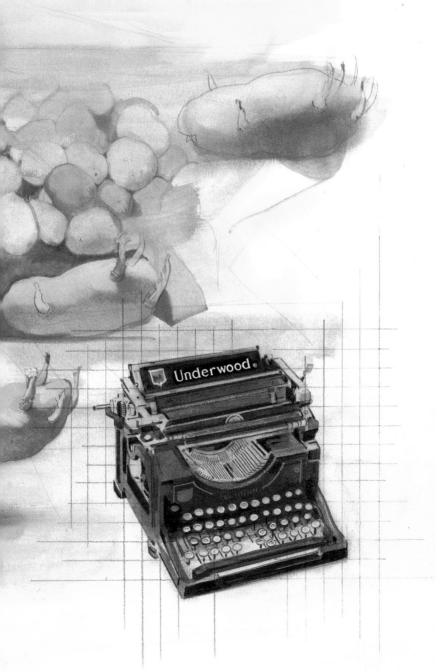

end, they were taking my sister and others to Oranienburg and somewhere near Hoyerswerda their train was shot up by the Americans, the train crew fled and the women scattered into the woods. My sister got a shrapnel wound in her leg, so she and another one buried themselves in pine needles, then they heard some dogs and SS men near their hiding place under the branches of a spruce tree, but they didn't find them. They stayed there for two days. Just as they'd begun to think they'd had it, they heard some Czech voices." – "Good lord!" – "So they piped up and two workmen, Czechs, who'd been repairing the railway line, dug them out, took them by night to the camp and hid them under a bed there. As the front drew closer, one Czech got a handcart and dragged my sister all the way to Bautzen, where they waited in a cellar till the battlefront passed them by. Then the Russians gave them a pony, then took it away again, but the Czech man, Joe was his name, hauled her all the way to Česká Lípa, where the Red Cross took charge of her." – "And what became of Joe?" – "Nothing. My sister kept saying he'd come for her, that Joe was her Prince Charming, but he never did.[8] So last year she got married, she wants children." – "So you're fairly happy at home?" – "Ever since my dad sold his stamps and we've nothing to our name but our bare hands, yes, we're happy." – "And you personally?" – "Me? After all my mother and I went through at Theresienstadt, my only pleasures are little things. Like seeing you." – "Hm." – "Look in on us sometime before Christmas Eve, all right? And when spring comes, promise you'll take me out in a boat again!" – "I will come, but why

432

the boat in the spring?" – "You can row and I'll dabble my fingers in the river, all right?" – "All right." – "So! Here I am!" Once they'd touched cheeks in good Old Testament style, she heeled it. Then he watched her diminishing down the corridor of the Art Nouveau house. Before she went through the swing doors he noticed that her figure was entirely made up of swanlike curves. The glazed swing doors shattered the image. As their swing slowed he saw her shoe part company with the stair. He stayed staring at the vacant door until a black-clad old lady came out, holding the leaves of the door steady, and a black dog came shuffling out into the evening to sniff devoutly at a lamp post. He gave the animal a scratch and asked it: "What are you getting for Christmas, me old mutt?" The old lady, sprayed by the hissing light of the gas lamp, said: "A sausage! But this Christmas will be a sad time for us!", then she added in a whisper: "I took Whoopy to the doctor and the doctor said that Whoopy's got a tumour, prostate, and he's going to die…" She turned her face up to the light to reveal her death mask and croaked: "When my daughter comes to see us for the festive season, we'll take him to a different doctor, in case the first one's got it wrong." And her voice contained a glimmer of light. He gathered that the old lady was expecting him to say something. Brightly and with conviction he said: "I'm sure the first one did get it wrong, just look, your doggie's looking good, a picture of health!" The old lady smiled, shook her head like a horse straining at the bridle and slipped into the farther dark with a comical tread. For a while now the dog had given up sniffing the wall. From the unnatural tone of the voices he had sensed that the talk was of him and that he would probably die soon. He started to bark and ran off after the old lady into the gloom.

She was standing at the window and looking down… The branches of the trees reached up level with her, to the first floor, and with every gust of the breeze its twigs tinkled against the glass… She was looking down, it was that time when the institution's patients took their constitutional in the grounds, but she wasn't seeing people, just afflictions promenading hither and yon.

"What are you looking at, Missus Mona?"

"Ah, Erni, you're here? I'd forgotten. Have you finished writing? Come and see, I don't like the look of that Bondy fellow,[1] not one bit… Juvenile paranoia's a nasty business, we're forever back to the start with it… so it strikes me that a few months from now that nice lad won't be able to be let out on his own… he'll suddenly get a black mark and start regressing back into a monkey…"

"But doesn't he look like that normally?"

"What would you know, Erni… but I'll show you some photos and you'll see just how fast he goes downhill…"

… said Mona, and so she walked across to the safe, rummaging in the pockets of her white coat for the key. But when she reached it, she clapped a hand to her forehead:

"Even my mind's starting to play up… I've gone and left the key at home… but tell me, Erni: where were you all night the day before yesterday?"

"Where… but I've told you once already. I slept in the hut in the garden…"

"Come off it... You and fall asleep! I know you fell asleep, but where?"

"In the little hut in the garden..."

"Or you spent the night with some woman...? Eh? You do realise I'm supposed to report such matters to the Criminal Investigation Department, don't you?"

"But Mona, I really did drop off in the hut in the garden... but you just said you'd left the key of the safe at home. Let me show you something... now... Have you got hairpin?"

"Yes, but what for?"

"You're about to see something no one's ever seen before... within three minutes I'll have the safe open."

"Well I'll believe that when I see it..."

She opened a drawer and handed Erni a hairpin. Then she sat down on a chair and watched with curiosity as his long fingers straightened the hairpin, then bent it, slid it into the lock, pulled it back out and bent it again.

"Just so you know, there's nobody in the country as good at this as I am. You have to have a delicacy and precision of feeling in your fingers, like the best surgeons who operate on joints or the brain..."

... said Erni, and he slipped the hairpin back in the lock following several more adjustments.

"Put simply, the knack comes from how my nerve ends go right into the hairpin... like a piece of wire, it's an extension of my spinal cord... but it's only any good for little locks like this one! With a modern safe you need an electric drill and a jemmy... You should have seen the fabulous kit I used to have, almost surgical... made of the toughest steel... tungsten steel, but silver-plated..."

"I've only noticed just now what nice hands you've got, Erni."

"Of course... how can anyone play the piano or violin with horrible hands? But it does have its disadvantages, having the kind of golden touch that I have! Sometimes your hands even work against you..."

"Like how?"

"Like this, Mona... sorry, Missus... Any safe that's been done over will have been done over in its own particular way, and I've known plenty of great cracksmen and they all left a bit of themselves in every safe they ever cracked... a kind of visiting card... Criminologists faced with a cracked safe leaf through their minds and look for the M.O. and the mastermind behind it..."

"You don't say!"

"Yes... they can tell almost immediately whether it's the handiwork of a layman or a dusty..."

"What's a dusty?"

"Dusties – dusty millers? That's just your common-or-garden hacks... the kind who crack safes from the back, tip everything out on the floor, and get ash and the lining stuff all over themselves and leave grubby marks everywhere... But I was never like that. I used to leave my safes all spick and span... But then they'd come straight after me... my style was..."

"So they had you right away?"

"Only once in ten years or so! More important than doing a safe is creating an alibi... I think we've got it... I can feel it in my fingers... Yes, the final hurdle. But you mustn't get the wrong idea! I was never a Dědek or a Lecián![2] I'd never handle a revolver... I was always more the aesthete... There, didn't I tell you?"

"You've done it..."

He turned, still holding the hairpin in one hand, and performed a ritual opening of the armour-plated door with his free hand.

"Bingo!"

He rubbed his hands together, but Mona said sadly:

"You're wasted here, Erni, it's a great shame... but that can't be helped, can it now? You've just proved to me that you are who you are. A debonair criminal and for me also a..."

"Just say it, Missus Mona... it's there in your eyes, so I know..."

"What can you know?"

"I always know things, I have this special sense, so I know pretty much everything..."

"Aren't you overestimating yourself?"

"You know very well I'm not... What's the time? Four, one minute to four... so it's been exactly a hundred and one days, twenty-three hours and now... seven seconds since they brought me here from the fortress at Terezín[3] and since you examined me... How could you tell there wasn't – and isn't – anything wrong with me?"

"Well... they do say I'm pretty good at what I do... and how could you tell there's something the matter with me?"

"From your eyes... Mona... and the furrows on your forehead and from your mouth..."

"All right, now see here, Erni... we've started something and we've gone too far to make fools of ourselves now... I'll continue sending fortnightly reports to Terezín to confirm that you're still what you made yourself out to be... a dangerous manic depressive... but how much longer will I be able to keep the game going?"

"I'll leave that to you... but believe me, Mona, even if they let me out of prison, there's nowhere I'd rather go than here... to carry on typing up your interviews with the patients... I'd carry on repairing fridges for you here, and faulty calculators... I'd carry on opening things you've mislaid the keys to... if only you'd known me in civilian life! Even in Terezín I used to put my prison trousers under the mattress to keep them creased..."

"Erni, you're a real scoundrel, you know... and I believe every word you say... That's the worst thing about it... my hair's already turning so very grey, but..."

She gestured dismissively with her hand.

"Look, Erni, how much of your sentence is there left?"

"I've done three years."

"How many to go?"

"Another two... and I'll be on tenterhooks the whole time... does it bother you that I call you just plain Mona?"

"Not really... and I not Mrs anymore either..."

"Divorced?"

"No..."

"Separated?"

"Not that either…"

"So widowed… I'm sorry…"

"It's all gone now, Erni… little more than dreaming a dream… I'm more the widow of my own illusion than of my husband… I used to have more zest, I had some go in me and thought everything could be changed by science, that a damaged mind was like a mangled bicycle… my husband was a manic depressive even before I married him… but I took it into my head to marry my patient and use him to prove the worth of science… and science proved to be worth a lot…"

"Did he get cured? Or rather, did you cure…"

"Yes, science proved a great deal… one day, I unlocked the door of the flat and my husband was hanging from the chandelier, so what I'd been treating others for now others have been treating me for here… six months, but I'm back to my old self, Erni, as you can see…"

"Yes, I can… but are you going to show me those photos… there…?"

"You don't want to see them… there's no point anyway… a curly-headed schoolboy at first, you might be thinking some American high-jumper… but half-way through the file the arms have grown longer and the jaw's started to sag… and by the end he's the bell-ringer at St Mary's… something that's still a bit of a rookie… but how long did you say you've got left on those tenterhooks?"

"Two years, Mona…"

"Hm… two years?… Humph… almost an eternity looking ahead, but like a moment when you look back on it…

we'll see... Erni, this is starting to make me feel a little tired..."

"Yes, I can tell... I really was about to go, goodbye, Mona..."

"Goodbye then and we'll carry on writing tomorrow morning..."

Late in the afternoon, just before the doctors' rounds, Monika went for her customary walk in the grounds. Having come out of her room and locked the door, she met a female patient in the corridor who might well have been waiting there just to tell her tearfully:

"Doctor, doctor, there's a stork clattering inside my belly... and doctor, tell me the whole truth, what does that language mean?"

"What language, Angela dear?"

"The language of the birds..."

"And what do they say to you, Angela?"

"I've been hearing them again... They say, it's syphilis, you must get treatment..."

"Come, come, Angela, where could you have caught anything of the kind... where on earth? Is it signs you hear, or actual speech?"

"Speech, doctor... I can hear it right now, saying: 'Are your eyes well?'"

"And what else do you hear, Angela?"

"They tell me Sleep... sleep... sleep..."

"So you'd better take a nap... I'll write you a prescription later and the birds will go to bed..."

"But the bird voices tell me... 'Sleep! You're an idiot...'"

The girl pointed behind her.

"Look, Angela, that's enough! I'm the one to know what's what... you're a little overwrought... I'll give you a pill and afterwards you'll see the birds going off to bed in the branches..."

She stroked the girl's flowing hair, then unlocked and carefully closed the door. Then she ran down the stairs and out into the grounds.

The wind was bending the branches of the hundred-year-old trees and the air was filled with the groaning of timber. So Monika, in her high heels, walked all the way to the far end, almost to the high wall, and there she sat down on a bench out of the wind.

"God almighty, what have I got myself into? Goodness, I'm a doctor and I'm harbouring a criminal for an illness he doesn't have, but that he successfully fooled them with at Fort Terezín... but where was he that night? The CID has already phoned once to say Erni'd been seen on Wenceslas Square at gone ten o'clock... when was that? A month ago... in a light suit, and I said at the time there must be some mistake, a purely coincidental likeness..."

... Monika whispered to herself, and she wanted to light a cigarette, but couldn't raise her arm. She could well imagine Erni actually walking about Wenceslas Square a month back... just as he'd spent the night before last outside the institution... She could see it, but if she were to imagine picking the phone up and reporting Erni's disappearance to the CID... Monika found that even if she summoned up all the voices from every corner of her soul... she could never do it.

"Can't be helped...," she whispered to herself and listened to the wind having its way, brutally, but symphonically, with the treetops, and she looked back at her institution with all its lights on, and with a slight shift of her vision she saw it was the trees at rest and the whole building lurching from side to side... She raised her eyes to the cloudless sky and it was the same with the stars... the constellations just as tipsy as the brightly lit asylum... the whole surrounded by a four-metre-high wall... "... there'll be Walter there in the corridor looking in his pocket for his glasses, in a pocket he doesn't have, for glasses he doesn't have either... so he can read the notice on his thigh... on a thigh where there is no notice, and the alcoholic Mrs Rozkošná will say, next time I have her in front of me, 'Doctor, the furniture, when I fix my eyes on it... even the furniture's dying...' and 'Doctor, you're getting old, growing older and older, and even more, now you're a skeleton and all those around you are death's heads,' and by the next window old Mrs Choděrová will tell me she had her confirmation today, Mr Klouček will tell me his face has completely changed shape overnight, and the one who keeps staring at the window pane will insist he can see his dearly beloved in it... Then there's the Mráčková girl, a fine arts student, who craps in her bed every night and scrabbles about in it with her hands, and when I ask her why she does it, she'll say 'Because I didn't want to and it was the only way I could salvage my freedom'... and for his part, Mr Bondy will point jubilantly at the patch on the wall… 'Doctor, I can see a beautiful panther here…', and I'll tell him 'So what's with the beak and the tuft on its head?' and he'll correct himself… 'Sorry, sorry, so it's a parrot or a crested lark…' Mrs Malá will still be wailing over the waste paper basket, crying that her canaries have flown because someone has stolen her roof… that old soak Kudlaba will greet me with 'You took your time, waiter… set up the billiard table and fetch me a stonking great rum…'"

Monika rose to her feet, drew her coat more tightly around her, and as she came out of the sheltered spot a huge gust gave her short-cropped hair a good shake… she quickly made her way back… hurrying, but, as always, passing beneath the mighty oak that clanked as it fought back against the onslaught of the wind, she was thinking, as always, of that patient of hers who for years now had been writing up his life's work, dozens of notebooks, until one night he escaped… "…it was just such a night as this…,"she was thinking, "we searched and called out…" it wasn't till nearly midnight when the wind really got up and the wardens heard knocking in the crown of this tree… they'd shone their torches… and as the wind blew, the writer stood out against the branches… and next to him hung his suitcase, the case he'd been banging at the branches with… as they lowered the patient down a rope, it was a bit like a Descent from the Cross… and then they cut the suitcase down as well… it dropped from branch to branch, hit the ground and got smashed… "One o'clock was just striking on the asylum clock tower… as I shone my torch inside the case…" there were ten kilos of exercise books densely covered in one and the same sentence:

I love you, I love you, I love you, I love you...

A seething anthill of I love you's.

After the doctors had done their rounds, Monika went down the long corridor, stopped at door number ten and knocked... and again. Then she depressed the door handle, entered and closed the door behind her, not with a handle this side, but a button to press.

"My apologies, but I did knock, twice..."

Monika was stuttering.

"I'll sit down, if I may."

Having said as much, she did, opposite a woman who was still quite young, barefoot and smoking.

"Do you smoke, Eva? Excellent, keep up the good work..."

... said Monika, but she could see she was wasting her breath, because the patient couldn't be bothered to flick her ash into the ashtray and her jacket and skirt were covered in it.

"How've you been sleeping?"

"... you know what, I'll bring you some Dormiral, it doesn't affect the heart one bit..."

... said Monika, but the patient was engrossed in the smoke twirling up from her fingers.

"I know... sometimes life makes no sense at all, sometimes a heart can pay a hundred thousand crowns for a single slice of bread... but believe me, Eva, I'd love to help you... if only you'd say something, at least tell me something... How am I to get through to you?"

... Monika asked, but it was more asking herself... for

now the patient hadn't a single reason to step back along the fragile bridge that still linked her to the world.

"I know... sometimes there's no wish to live, not at all... not a single reason to tread the earth... though there would be a reason, but only if things were the way we'd like them to be..."

... said Monika... but nary a flutter stirred in the woman's face...

"So, what's to be done?"

"You're an educated woman, so how might you demonstrate your fealty to the earth since you're condemned to having your being and living on it...?"

But the patient just went on smoking... the only thing she held on to was still that cigarette.

"You're a married woman... so there might be a reason... after all, your husband... and I know him well... I'm sure Karel needs you..."

Monika had her ears pricked, but not a rustle came from the pretty face...

"And there are those two children..., Eva, listen, you're a mother when all's said and done... and as a mother you can relive in your daughter the same girlhood... that you had yourself all those years ago..."

The patient stubbed out her cigarette and made to light another... Monika thought she was about to say something... She spat a speck of tobacco off her lip and again filled her lungs with smoke... and again watched apathetically as it twirled up from her fingers... as they rested on the arm of her chair.

"Have you no more feelings at all from the idea of seeing the sun, a meadow full of flowers... or even a bunch of roses? The intimacy of home? Music, theatre, clothes... all those little things that add something to the life of a woman and mother?"

But the patient tossed the cigarette aside, swung up from her chair and made a dash for the door... but the handle was missing. So with the hand that still bore plasters round her wrist she pointed at the door and:

"Get out!"

"You want to drive me away, Eva?"

"Get out!"

"Eva..., sit down, calm down..."

"Get out!"

Monika lumbered to her feet, shrugged, unlocked the door and, in the doorway, said: "I'm going... but Eva, believe me, all I want is to help you back on your feet a bit... more like having a chat between friends... woman to woman... but if that's the way you want it."

"Get out!"

She stamped her bare feet, she, Eva, a lawyer's wife, whom they'd taken to the surgical clinic of the hospital on Charles Square with a slashed wrist... and then brought here, to the institution.

Monika left and clicked the door shut against the still pointing hand. She stood there a moment, staring at the gloss-painted door panels, trying to get the drift... but she lacked the key. So she stood there, one voice inside her was saying 'Leave her... leave her at the mercy of Fate, slip her that knife again...' and another voice urged 'do everything, everything to make that knife disappear...' they were voices... but Monika knew that she still knew nothing and that she was rather in awe of this woman, who'd rather block her brain than admit something that was... but that she profoundly wished wasn't...

During the morning, when the porter phoned Monika to tell her that some gentlemen from CID would like to speak to her, she said:

"Have them come up..."

And she could tell at once.

After they'd come in and introduced themselves, she offered them armchairs, but only the superintendant sat down. The inspector walked about the room, paused at the window and looked down, into the grounds of the institution.

"It's odd...," he said.

"... that the grounds of all asylums are so much of a muchness! That van Gogh guy got it spot on...[4] but before I forget: Doctor, where was Erni between Wednesday and Thursday?"

... he enquired, but was looking down to where two inmates were sweeping up the falling leaves... leaves that the wind kept snatching from their shovels, so not much was getting tipped into their barrow, and if it was, the wind only got hold of it again.

"Where would he have been... here... at the institution, but we couldn't find him all night... he slept in a hut in the garden..."

"That's what he said, right?"

"Yes… I did send out a search party…"

"In a hut in the garden… that one there, where the vegetable plots start?"

"Yes."

The inspector turned and addressed the superintendant:

"Get some men and have that hut searched…"

"Sir!"

And the superintendant left the room… The inspector went back to the window and looked down: there was a woman standing there next to a bench, her scarf was blowing in the breeze, she had her coat over one arm and a parcel in her hand.

"There's one of yours wanting to leave… or has she just arrived?"

… he asked, and Monika knew at once.

"She's a patient… a melancholic alcoholic, it's just her thing, she packs her clothes and when she reaches that bench… there's nowhere else for her to go… so she comes back… it gets her out of doors…"

"Hm… but now explain to me how on the 15th of September at ten p.m. Erni was out of doors as far away as Wenceslas Square?"

"It's a mystery to me… inspector… at eight p.m. the patients are back in their wards and my duty ends with the doctors' rounds… unless I'm on nights. But we do have warders, guards… and then there's a very high wall…"

"Wall, wall, wall! To Erni, any wall's a piddling little fence!"

The inspector squared his arms, straightened his back and looked back down into the grounds.

"I can quite believe it... I'm sure Erni liked it here! I'd also like it... did you know, I attend your public lectures? Psychoanalysis is a bit like what I do, getting a man to shed his skin... though it only works with those who aren't in the know... you'll get nothing out of Erni... he only responds to facts, solid facts... I know he's done twelve safes, but I had him jailed for only two; you see, I've had the honour of knowing Erni for twenty years..."

... said the inspector and re-focussed his eyes. The superintendant was just coming out of the hut and carrying something like a light-coloured suit...

"Aha!"

The inspector rubbed his hands in glee.

"The thing is, during the night from Wednesday to Thursday a certain large company in Brno had its safe broken into... yesterday I saw it for myself and believe that the only person capable of doing it is Erni, and that little hut in the garden... that might give us the clue we're after..."

"Are you sure you're not mistaken, Inspector?"

Monika was on edge.

"Let's imagine that Erni was over the wall at eight... a fast car could have got him to Brno in two and a half hours... cracking the safe wouldn't have taken him more than two hours... that's half past ten, half past eleven, by half past twelve he'd be done and could easily have been back here by five... then a good night's sleep in the garden hut..."

... said the inspector and he crossed to the door and opened it and Monika saw the superintendant bringing back a covert cloth suit slung over his arm and a raglan, which he then placed on the table.

"And where are the boots?"

"This is all we've found so far, Inspector, it was behind an old wardrobe..."

"Keep looking... the boots are more important... do a thorough search... You take charge! And have five men comb the garden, inch by inch... there could be some silver gear buried somewhere!"

"Sir!"

And the inspector quickly departed.

"So what do you say to that, Doctor?"

"I see what I see, here on the table... but how much was taken?"

"Four hundred thousand... but yesterday we collared a group of eleven youngsters... Car thefts... but imagine, Doctor! They only stole Tatraplans,[5] but not with a view to making money... They had a garage where they took the cars apart and used Tatraplan parts to furnish their flats. Seats with tyres screwed on at the side... and they had armchairs, the four doors set in the wall complete with ash-trays, the steering wheel erected in the middle like a table, and each of them had one wall adorned with an instrument panel... carburettors as flower vases... a whole engine block in lieu of a statue... so eleven Tatraplans they stole, then furnished their rooms... romantics, just lads... but where's Erni now?"

"Right now he'll be in hydrotherapy..."

"Right, I'll go and take a look at him... by the way, Doctor, three years ago some warders of yours tried to steal Bedřich Smetana's[6] medical records... the last fortnight before his death... I wouldn't mind coming by and taking a look at them... might I, just a peek? You know... to see how one might appreciate his music differently and in greater depth."

"By all means... give me a call... for my own part, I'd like to ask you about certain facts when crime seems akin to an infirmity... those records are now kept in the main safe, it's terrible reading and not meant for public consumption... like the last years of the composer's journal... I've seen and read it... you can already tell from the diaries the way he was headed that led him to wind up here..."

"What a way, what a way to go..."

... said the superintendant and returned yet again to the window and looked down... But he could see nothing, because he'd become bitterly engrossed... then he said dolefully: "Van Gogh shot himself – probably sensed how he might have ended up... and a good thing he did. But! I almost forgot: That night, did your people also search the hut in the garden?"

Monika rallied.

"No... to the best of my knowledge, when I asked them and made that very point, they said no, they'd forgotten to."

"A-ha... that's unfortunate... un-for-tu-nate! Bother! If we can't turn up more, Erni could get away with it... at best we'll have enough to charge him with leaving the building without permission... Damn! Damn!"

The inspector turned and smashed one fist into his other open hand...

"Too bad! I'll go and get Erni... we can complete the formalities later, after the whole case has been investigated... I'll go and wait for him!"

... said the inspector and left the office... And Monika remained seated there, looking at the covert cloth suit tossed across the table top... she knew Erni had done it, but she began praying silently that they'd find nothing more in the gardens...

Then there was a knock at the door and she said: "Come in!"

And in the doorway stood a warder with the patient whose answers yesterday had still been being typed up by Erni...

"Come and sit down, Mr Bondy... let's continue where we left off..."

... said Monika, offering a chair to the handsome young man, who shyly took it.

Monika opened a drawer, took out the papers, sat at the typewriter and said:

"So yesterday we got as far as... *and so I could smell where the dead human flesh was.* I see, Mr Bondy, that you were born in twenty-four, what is your most abiding impression of the Reich?"

"Brunswick... not the bombing raid, but three days later... the burned-out city and a boy roller-skating along the road leading to it... with a can of milk..."

"Hang on... roller-skating... with a can of milk. Good... Are you still getting headaches?"

"Not really... it's more like my head's blocked up, or my brain's plastered over, just now and again, when there's a change in the weather, there's these three nails that drive right into the heart of my head..."

"Good... right into the heart of your head... How long were you unconscious following the fit?"

"No, it wasn't that, it was more I was lying there with this feeling of my brain being being squashed down into the bottom half of my skull..."

"Yes... brain, and...?"

"And then I was filled with a whirring noise that went with a feeling that my blood was being crammed into my legs by its own centrifugal force..."

"Yes... Mr Bondy, crammed into my legs... a little slower if you wouldn't mind... I can't type as fast as Erni... there. And what did the outer world seem like?"

"It was like I was seeing trees and flowers for the first time... and it was hard finding names and it was hard to believe that the houses were in the ground..."

"... houses were in the ground... done! Listen, Mr Bondy, you express yourself brilliantly, do you write perhaps?"

"Well yes... but only the odd study. Like I wrote one little piece: 'How I taught my cat association, so that in a small stain she would see a clothes moth and go for it with her paw...'"

"And go for it with her paw... And?"

"Then there was: 'How I used a tethered balloon to make a tomcat look at himself in a mirror…'"

"Look at himself in a mirror… And?"

"Then I wrote a short study 'On the effect of the environment, smoking and mirrors on how marriages are concluded between persons having similar facial features'…"

"… between persons having similar facial features… got that… now Mr Bondy, what were your feelings when you tripped and split your lip… You know… when you had that fit…"

"I seemed to be surrounded by a circle of bellowing organs, Doctor, and in the gaps I could hear angels singing…"

"In the gaps angels singing… What was your sex life like before you came here?"

"Nothing much, I'm practically a virgin still… it could never work out… I did try, but it felt as if I was being watched by people through a partly drawn-back curtain… once out in the country, in a cottage… very nearly… but the chickens the other side of the fence started clucking and a woman's voice was calling… come chick-chick chick…!"

"Slower… and a woman's voice was calling… come chick-chick chick… and have you been in love, or not?"

"Utterly… but I felt like as if I wasn't athletic enough… so day after day I went for a run round the Olšany cemeteries and cleaned my teeth… every Sunday I got all dressed up and took the train to Křivoklát, that was where her parents lived, and I wandered about the village and past their house, but never exchanged a word with her… just saw her…"

"... past their house, but never... well, I think I've got enough, Mr Bondy... if at some stage I need it, these accounts of yours, for a book I'm contemplating, would that bother you?"

"Goodness no... on the contrary, I'm glad I can tell you everything..."

"Well, thank you, and I see your split lip has completely healed..."

Monika stood up... she gave Mr Bondy her hand and nodded to the warder that he could take the patient back. Then she slowly filed the typed pages away and heaved a deep sigh.

Shortly after, the inspector and superintendant came in and with the experienced eye of a psychiatrist she could tell that they'd found nothing.

The superintendant picked up the suit and coat and the inspector said: "We'll be taking Erni... and please, in your own interest, add to all Erni's records an account of that night from Wednesday to Thursday and send it all to Terezín... The responsibility is yours... not for his disappearance, but for not reporting it..."

The inspector touched his hat and was about to go when Monika asked:

"Where is Erni?"

"Outside the door here..."

"Might I ask him about it myself?"

"By all means..."

The inspector opened the door and Monika saw Erni standing next to the banister, closely surrounded by a number of policemen.

"Erni... your doctor's got something to say to you. Come here."

... said the inspector and went out into the corridor with the superintendant.

When Erni came in and closed the door behind him, Monika stepped up close to him and whispered:

"Where did you put your tools?"

He whispered:

"Here... in your bottom drawer..."

"Oh, yes... but Erni, will you write to me?"

"I will... every quarter you'll get a postcard with greetings and best wishes from Erni."

"Say something nice to me, Erni..."

"Good bye, Mona... and what will you say to me?"

"Good bye... and au revoir, when you've completed those two years on tenterhooks..."

After they took Erni away, Monika suddenly had an image of Eva flash before her. She found the name, and the phone number, and dialled...

"Hello, is that Dr Hrůza?"

"Yes, speaking..."

"Hello, Karel.... this is Monika Helceletová..."

"Well I never... and how are you keeping, Mona?"

"So-so... but Karel, I need to speak to you... could you..."

"No, quite impossible... I don't have the time... imagine this, Mona, I'm acting for a group of fourteen spiritualists... for three weeks I've been reading spiritualist literature and I just can't make head or tail of it..."

"Look, you can stop that, Karel... you're really serious about Eva, right? But never mind us, that was just a thing between students... but things really are dreadful with Eva... I'm afraid..."

"But Monika, I know... but there's really nothing to be done about it... I reckon you'll find this case of mine more interesting... the way I see it, only the mediums will come out of it unscathed... that's a fact, even according to Pavlov[7]... but the twelve who listened to them, they were in full command of their senses... yes, and they asked about political realities... in advance, right... What do you think?"

"Nothing... only that ever since Eva was brought here she hasn't spoken a word and we have to force-feed her... she just smokes like a chimney... listen, Karel, this is just an idea I've had... I can't find the key to her... Might she not have been unlucky in love... yes? So it would be a good thing if you told me about it, perhaps over a coffee sometime..."

"Sorry, but no... look, Monika, I'm not going to travel anywhere anymore, understand... the thing you want, I did it long ago... with Eva I've exhausted every remedy, yes, even including my own honour, not just as a husband, but also as a man... So hold your horses! Eva's been cheating on me for six years with a tram driver...!"

"Who?"

"A tram driver, quite a looker of course, something like Gabin,[8] a tram driver nonetheless... are you there, Monika? So what about it..."

"Listen, Karel, couldn't we... it really is serious..."

"I know what you're going to tell me, but hold on, sit down, so as you know... I, a lawyer, I've knelt down in front of this bloke and begged him not to wreck at least my domestic harmony and to stop cheating on me with my wife, but he said Get out! Again I tell him and beg him, she only slashed her wrist because of you, go and look at her, say something to her... I can rehearse it with you, but do say something nice to her... but he just showed me the door and said Get out... Mona, are you there? Mona!"

ONE ORDINARY DAY

A short story

Lift the receiver, if the party being called responds, press the button and speak, so I pressed the button and recognised Šárka[1] at once.

"Šárka sweetie, is Daddy in? Get him to come to the phone!"

But the child's voice trilled: "No-no, Daddy isn't in, he's disappeared, he's gone, Daddy's got lost..."

I adopted a more severe tone: "Don't be silly and fetch Daddy, he's still in bed, go and have a look, it's still only half past seven..."

"All right, I'll go..."

"Run along, lassie, run along!"

And I stood there in the broken glass-sided box, stroking the chain to which the receiver was attached, these days everything in the world is attached, tied down, shut away, roads are allowed to be used, or they're not, spitting on the floor is banned, as is smoking, talking politics in the pub, leaning out of windows, getting too close or standing too far back, likewise changing your job, writing and thinking in a different way, making fires and dropping litter is also prohibited...

"Hello, yes, I'm here! What's going on?" I shouted into the receiver: "Have you heard, Karel? No? Right, come straight round to my place, yes, mine, I'm going to get an injection and I'll be right back. See you!"

Replace the receiver, so I replaced the receiver and went back out into the still free air, it hasn't been banned yet or rationed, or only on the open market. Though something like an air tax could be introduced, I mused as I strode along Sokolovo Avenue, people were already queuing up outside greengrocers', like sorry little funeral cortèges... and I turned into the corridor, up the stairs to the dim first floor, then into the waiting room full of patients sitting and standing, some waiting for the dental outpatients department, some for the doctor's surgery, though they were all in a gloom so deep that anyone coming in from the street had to stop and wait a moment before he got used to the half-light, some arrivals put out their arms and groped those already present, only when a door of one of the clinics opened was the light that issued forth so strong that it blinded like vitriol, like large headlights in the depth of night, after which the darkness of the waiting room seemed even darker.

"It's terrible how few doctors there are, forty per cent of them are said to be in the army," a voice came out of the darkness.

"My nephew, he's also a doctor, got hauled off on manoeuvres and he wrote saying he'd got nothing to do, and that when he got bored he'd ask the boss doctor: 'Major, sir, let me grind some coffee for you, so I'll have done at least something today, okay?'" another voice added.

"While we could spend the whole day gawping at nothing in here," said a third.

"I've heard," someone else said, and his voice seemed to be coming from right down on the floor, "that at Vinohrady, when a doc at the health centre enters his consulting room, he's got so many people waiting that he opens the waiting room door and calls out: Who's got 'flu? Right, ladies first! And they all go piling in, so first he counts them, then he lays the same number of scrips on his desk, then bangs his rubber stamp on them the same number of times, does one as a specimen then signs them all one after the other. Then back to the door and: And now men with 'flu! And he does it all over again!"

The door opened, and in the rush of light a nurse in white and dazzling spectacles called out: "Next three women here for an injection!"

And with the three women a thickset gypsy, his neck wound round with a white towel, wormed his way in and over to the couch with its white waxed-linen cover. The door closed and the medical instruments gleamed as what the brain had just recorded lingered on inside it. And the door opened again and the patients could see that the waiting room was packed, and the nurse was steering the recalcitrant gypsy back out and the indignant voice of the doctor was ordering him from the room and the gypsy was shouting in his priceless patois: "Zounds, Jeeze! Gypsy's a working man, he come first. He got a sore throat, his poor little leg bad!"

And when the door shut, the gypsy sat on the ground and pounded the floor with his fists, shouting: "Zounds, Jeeze!"

Voices out of the dark tried to make him see sense: "You'll just have to wait a few minutes more. It's women wanting injections that go in first."

But the gypsy was tearing his hair out and throwing the tufts up against the dim light coming through the window and going on about being a working man.

Then the door to the dental surgery opened and out came the white-coated dentist, his coat flapping and filling the waiting room with light and the smell of anaesthetic tinctures, and he tapped on the consulting room door, it opened a chink then the nurse let the dentist in, and again all the patients squinted as the light came flooding down to their feet. Then the three women came out, the gypsy rose and slipped through the closing door into the consulting room and closed it behind him. And again came the enraged voice of the doctor, the rasping voice of the gypsy, followed by the even louder voice of the enraged doctor, and then the door flew open and all the patients jumped, and the ones who were seated sat bolt upright and the gypsy's shadow fell across the waiting room floor, the bandage round his neck had come loose so it looked as if his neck was wound round with a sheet, and the doctor was pushing the gypsy and, having shoved him out, he closed the door, and the gypsy sat back down on the floor and pounded it with his fists and tore his hair out and tossed it in the air. Then the dentist came back out, crossed the waiting room and entered his own clinic.

I said to the gypsy: "That's also a doctor, a throat specialist."

And crawling on all fours the gypsy followed the dentist into his consulting room and all the patients had their ears pricked, but not a sound came, no shouting, no swearing, no voices growing ever louder and ever more exasperated. Just silence. Then through the padded door they did hear the dentist saying: "Well, my son, what's the matter?" And the gypsy's rasping voice: "It hurt here, doctor." The nurse opened the door, carrying some files, and through the door they could see the gypsy pointing into his mouth and the dentist pushing him down into his chair, then picking up his forceps and saying: "Come, come now, it's a good thing you came…," and the door of the dental surgery closed, the nurse passed through the gloom and knocked on the adjacent door. And at that instant a fiendish shriek came from the dental surgery, a long drawn-out, articulated shriek.

"Some people have kinked roots, it can cause a hole in your palate and even go as far as your septum," one of the patients said.

"And they had to tie me to the ceiling by the feet and knock my teeth out with a mallet, that's how weird my roots were," said another out of the darkness.

Then the door to the dental surgery flew open and the dentist was dragging the gypsy with his dental forceps, the gypsy was clacking like a death rattle, several patients fell over, the dentist's white coat having brought so much light into the waiting room, the gypsy grabbed hold of the flowerless flower stand with both hands, but the dentist's firm grip kept tugging at the forceps and the gypsy's tooth as its owner still held on to the flower stand, and the tooth wouldn't give, so the dentist hauled the gypsy back inside his clinic, flower stand and all. And after the door closed, the gypsy gave out one last shriek and all went silent inside.

I removed my cap, went quietly out into the corridor, turned the key in the washroom door, entered and from there into the toilet, I stood there quietly in the dark, holding the bolt with one finger and listening through the crack in the door. The gypsy came out of the dental surgery, holding his face and whimpering quietly, and then he asked the patients: "Where the one with cap, was sitting there..." And after a moment during which I broke into a sweat, the ever-so-faint whimper set off down the stairs... the door to the dental surgery opened, the dentist came into the washroom, washed his hands and as he was drying them on a towel he smiled and muttered to himself: "That'll teach you to come plaguing doctors..."

And after the dentist left, I went back out into the cool of the corridor, chucked my cap down the light well, I'm not having that injection today, unless after lunch maybe, and I'll come in a different hat and coat... And on the way back home I was thinking of IT. I've cleared everything up and burned it. If they came, I'd – what would I? – I'd go with them, I'd have to go with them, then there'd be ages on remand, no walks, no sunlight. Then the trial, jail, how long would I get? Two, three? Five, ten years? And hard labour in the mines, quarries, heavy industry? Ultimately I have to reckon with it, though I consider myself a citizen of this state and have nothing against it. Just the freedom of speech thing, just the writing, just the thinking, just the chatting to friends. They'd have to cut a bit of my brain out so I couldn't think and love or hate the way I do. No, I can't love them, even though I do render unto Caesar what is theirs, and I've rendered and will render what is mine unto me, God and man. But that's the very thing they don't want, they want me to render everything, all my thoughts, my innermost secrets, everything, all that's human, all that's God's unto Caesar. And yet, what about my life? I won't be back in some other age, and I do want to live, enjoy my life, even surrounded by injunctions to do this and not do that, life to which no one has a right but me, life for which no one is responsible but me. And my disappointments and my pleasures must be without Caesar, he can make do with eight hours of hard graft, accidents, death and compulsory attendance at extra masses. I can't love them, I can't go forward with them, though I wish them no harm, I don't like them, my mind has told me not to, and just as I breathe this air, so I need to think and live my thinking, and if unable to think and live in my own way, I'd die as from lack of air... And turning off into Brethren Lane from Sacrifice Street I told myself that everything, despite all that, everything was good, everything except me. It's been others who've brought me to my own self, they and their endeavours have carved out of me a being in mine own image, an image quite different from the one I wanted to have... everything is good, everything except me, I've done too little with myself, I could have done much more, it's because of all the things in the world that I have my own self closest at hand. The rest might land me in jail, but even that's for people, even there there are people and events and things in readiness solely for me, for them to apply the pressure to crack the kernel me out of the shell me.

469

And at the point where Brethren Lane meets Weir Lane at a right angle, Karel crossed those few metres, slightly hunched and, despite the warmth, wearing gloves, a purple neck-scarf and a trench coat that hung off him like a shroud, like a Franciscan's habit.

"Hi!" I called out.

He turned. I said: "Fancy meeting you, eh?"

He rubbed his rheumaticky hands together: "What's up?"

I went slowly across to join him and said: "Get this, yesterday, boom, boom and Václav Černý[2] got banged up."

Karel leaned back against the wall: "Christ! An' I had a dream last night about water an' that always…," he couldn't finish and gasped, then he closed his eyes and took a deep breath.

"Yes, yes," I said, "they searched all through his library, anywhere where he kept books, took everything away, him included, and his desk. Did he have anything of yours?"

He raised one arm and let it drop: "Damn! Anything of mine, even just reading it gets you life, let alone… Hell, why did I want to become a scribbler? Why didn't my mother drop me head down on the paving, or why did my dad let me land on the sheet that time, then I wouldn't be here today… let's just hope Václav was a bit careful and kept my versididdles in a safe place… Have you got any valerian drops for my head?"

"Sorry, mate, I haven't," I said and we mounted the steps into the yard, then up to the passageway, I unlocked the door and opened a window.

I said: "Quite the opposite! Professor Černý has always been grossly negligent, criminally negligent, and get this, he's never stopped believing that this year, whatever year it happens to be, that that year it would all come to an end and he'd start publishing his *Critical Monthly* again..."[3]

Karel collapsed onto a chair, his hands dangling to the floor: "So he's been hoping to publish *Critical Monthly*?"

"Yep," I said, "he's been an awful optimist, when his students told him in January '48 that things were looking bad and could he let them have their doctorates there and then and not on the due date in a month's time, Dr Černý told 'em not to worry, if anything did happen they'd get their titles when things got back to normal, *doctores sub auspiciis*...[4]

"Terrible, that, *sub auspiciis*," said Karel with a grimace.

"Yep, every year, an' it's been four years now, he's said that before the leaves fall it'll all change again, but when someone said in the spring that the change wouldn't come till around Christmas, the prof stopped talking to him, 'cos he wasn't quite sure if it would come on the twenty-fourth or twenty-sixth of November that year, but that his journal would be able to come out as a Christmas special..."

This news finished Karel off. He stood up and cried: "Optimists, they're the undoing of nations. If Hitler hadn't been an optimist I'm sure he wouldn't have blundered into a war like that... and now me at home, cripes, my father-in-law's gonna do his nut! If he commits some political stupidity, that's okay, he's a national hero, a martyr, but if I do, he starts hollerin': 'Stop, man, think about your family…' Jesus, this optimism, it's obscurantism… I should grab a cab and get home quick and hide my *Labyrinth of the World and Paradise of the Heart*, that thing I wrote sort of in anticipation! It would be bad enough if they found the latest *Letters and Postcards,* they'd even lock my dachshund up just 'cos he gets a mention![5] Give us a fag!"

As he was lighting it, the flame missed the cigarette several times.

I laughed: "Go on, set fire to everything!"

He exhaled the smoke: "Not likely! I'd never get anything down again, it'd be like I'd incinerated my own self, come on, it's my life's work, reality once gave itself up to me like a virgin, so me go and burn it! Hardly!"

I said: "So learn it all by heart, and then burn it!"

He drew in more smoke and said lachrymosely: "That's the soddin' tragedy of it. I can learn things, I know Eliot's *The Waste Land* by heart, but can't remember one jot or tittle of my own works, let alone a whole line. It's hopeless… Look at us, never satisfied with being regional poets, we wanted higher things, we wanted to get to Prague, and now we'll be laying down our lives, never ever to see our little collections of verse in a bookshop window."

I tried to console him: "Do stop fretting, my life's work's also at Professor Černý's, and I wanted even more from him, a critical appraisal and for him to put his name and address to it."

He let out a groan and started running about the room: "Oh God, it's all clear to me now, the cops are going to ask: 'Who were your friends?' and they'll come and get me, ouch, have you got any aspirins, this has all made my knee start playing up."

"No, I haven't," I said, "and Černý doesn't have your address and they'll never get anything out of him, the Gestapo didn't get a peep out of him,[6] or out of me for that matter."

He glanced at the sun above the rooftops: "Ain't bloody true. They inject you with something and you start talking and you even feel great at how well it's going. I've been looking into it, there's this poison stuff, something like psychoton,[7] but a thousand times more effective."

I said: "Do stop exaggerating, Černý mightn't even remember who you are, he'll have forgotten your name, and as for your *Labyrinth,* he'll have hidden it somewhere and forgotten where as well..."

"On the contrary, Václav has a very good memory, like a postman, he remembers things you told him years ago."

"That's not so good," I said, "though I've just remembered that that collection also contains a geographical reference, to National House in Nymburk..."

He cast me an infantile glance: "Your collection?"

"No, no, your *Labyrinth and Paradise of the Heart...*"

He groaned. "Oh yeah, I remember now, I rewrote it eight times, then another six times and hadn't remembered, but now I do and I'm scared. Ah well, if nothing else, the cops'll go to Nymburk and ask 'Who writes versididdles hereabouts?'. They'll say Hrabal and Marysko and they've got us, oh God, oh God, why hast Thou forsaken me?"

I said: "Forsaken *us*, but you have to be brave, if they haul me off, I won't say a thing, I don't recall a thing, I've given it up, I was working my way towards socialist realism and was hopeless at it, so I've given it all up, and that's what you have to say as well."

But Karel was shaking his head. "No way, fat chance. They ask you: 'Did you write this?' an' if you say: 'No,' then wallop an' a smack in the teeth, an' again, 'Did you write this?' Wallop an' another smack in the teeth. An' in the end they ask you; 'Did you write this?' an' you say 'Yes.' So they give you a bonus smack in the teeth for lying an' you fill your britches. Ach, if I were brave, but I'm scared, that's it, I'm scared, everybody's scared... I've just finished reading *The Light of Vitriol*, how they torture the convicted man an' end up trying to quarter him with horses, but the horses aren't up to it an' the executioner asks permission to cut through his inguinal tendons an' then it goes like a bomb... Your gothic man, he were used to that kind of thing, torture were pretty humdrum, but the mere idea of it leaves me prostrate... *these parts so shallow, with tracery ramparts, crooking a spire like a finger afar...*,[8] oh, why didn't we just stay in Nymburk writing drivel like that? Why? Tell me, why?"

He was shouting and yelling and waving his hands above his head.

Closing the window, I said: "Stop shouting, there's a *tenner*[9] lives up here, she's happy to eavesdrop, oh but never mind, shout away, closing the window won't do a scrap of good, she listens through a huge pot placed against the wall, that's how I eavesdrop on her as well... the number of times we say nothing and know full well we're eavesdropping on each other, our respective pots separated by nothing but the wall..."

Karel gazed into the far distance and spoke again: "You're right, there's no escaping anything, whatever you do nowadays, all roads lead to jail…"

I said: "Talk as loud as you like, but we have to act, look, I've burned stuff, hidden stuff, so now, where are you going to put your stuff?"

He pulled on his gloves and started thinking: "Yeah, where shall I put it? If I hide it at home in the woodshed, an' if the cops come, that's the first place they'll think of, that it's in the shed underneath the coal pile… or suppose I take it to Grandma's and hide it in her wardrobe? But then I wouldn't dare let on, because she gets scared in advance, she's already told me once, fixing me with a stare, never to leave anything there or they'd lock her up, and Granddad… My best bet is to leave it at the theatre under my locker![10] But once the cops learn I'm in the orchestra there, they'll go straight to the theatre and there – it's so obvious now – they'll head straight for my locker, because where else could I have put it? Or at my mother's place? She's scared of nothing, she'd use a medium to squirrel out where I'd hidden the *Labyrinth*, then she'd go about the city, showing it to passersby in the street an' boasting: "Look what a clever son I have, what a lovely thing he's written… and the cops would know all about it in no time…"

I said: "Okay, best keep parents out of it. Last time we were expecting a raid, my ma shoved those telling letters of yours somewhere in among the beer sales records and now she can't find them anywhere, the account books went back to the office and so they're still in hiding somewhere, waiting…"

Karel fell silent, smiling his enchantment: "So even my letters are lurking somewhere for the chance to turn against me!"

I said: "Possibly, latently, but now get a grip, we have to do everything possible, go through everything, clear out, burn stuff, have a good look around, where are my texts?" I opened the cupboard and ran my eye over the shelves from top to bottom: "There's nothing left here…"

Karel rose and surveyed the shelves: "And what's this? What's this red thing?"

I was taken aback: "Where? I've no idea!"

And Karel tugged at a corner of the thing and a five-metre Union Jack fell off the top shelf and rolled down on him, draping his head and shoulders, then unfurling and hanging majestically down to the floor. So Karel was left standing there like a statue waiting to be unveiled, completely smothered in the red, white and blue crosses of the British Empire.

We were both panic-stricken.

Karel spoke first, in an alien voice: "Boo boo boo boo boo! This is just the moment for the cops to show up, then the trifling matter of demanding to see our ID cards… and then: 'Preparing for the arrival of capitalists, you are under arrest for anti-state activity…'"

He disentangled himself from the flag, which slid to the floor.

In a hoarse voice I said: "I'd totally forgotten about this, we've got to hide it right away, it's the flag I found in a drawer when I was winding up that company, you know, Karel Harry Klofanda Praha Platejz,[11] I'd meant to have it dyed black and the girls to cut it up and make me some boxer shorts out of it."

Karel smiled his enchanted smile: "I can just imagine the cops falling for that one! To make boxers... but I'm ready to concede that fate has all the power needed to beat even our best endeavours, like in a classical tragedy. I'm gonna hide nothing, an' as for destroying my work, I don't have the nerve for that, so the best thing's gonna be if I tie it up with a black ribbon an' deliver it to police HQ myself, knock an' ask: 'Am I in the right place?' an' if they say yes, I'll say: 'These are my writings an' here's my address, or d'you know what, let me show you the key passages in *The Labyrinth of the World and the Paradise of the Heart* an' you can just keep me here.' That's what I'll do because you can never know what God has in store for those who love Him. We wanted to climb higher an' higher, an' that's how it's gonna be, the glory of being tried alongside a university prof, who will, in prison, grant us the title of Doctor of Letters, we'll be *Doctores litterarum sub auspiciis*. What more can the human heart desire?"

He rose, still smiling his enchanted smile: "So, Bohumil my lad, farewell, I'm off, I'm delighted you think we might share a cell, share a trial, share our forced labour, where we shall write our little poems an' stories for the benefit of the nearest brick wall..."

I said: "You're right."

And I spread the Union Jack across the made-up bed.

I said: "That's probably the one place they won't find it. But think of this: in Paris there's this landed gent who's been waiting over a quarter of a century for a revolution, he's reduced to driving a cab, but, like our Václav Černý, he's waiting for that turn for the better, and that he'll soon be able to publish his *Critical Monthly* once again."

Young Karel smoothed out the folds in the flag on the bed, growing ever more enchanted: "So now you can bring a beautiful girl home an' lay her right down on the bed here: just imagine what a boost it must give to a girl's heart, having beneath her the flag of the British Empire. Could anything more wonderful befall anyone?"

He turned in the doorway and added in a low tone with a finger placed conspiratorially to his lips: "I've got a little time to spare this afternoon, so I'll finish that poem to Konstantin Biebl,[12] it's only now that I have a clear view of the lad, dentist an' poet as he was... an' I'll spice it up a bit... This evening we're doing *The Bride of Messwina*."[13]

And out he went in his trench coat, stooping slightly and wearing his purple neck-scarf.

From the threshold I said: "I can tell that people in the front row of the dress circle and galleries are going to be looking down on you and thinking: That cellist there's playing with special feeling today... those beautiful tremolos!"

And a door flew open and on the threshold stood the tenner woman with a pot in her hand and she called out: "Do you know what the best place for hiding papers is? Stick your manuscripts in an empty pickle jar and bury it in the garden!"

Karel flung his arms in the air and called back: "Not a hope! If I went an' buried them, I'd never find them ever again! After war broke out, I buried a demijohn of plum brandy in what was only a tiny garden, an' I've never found it to this day! To police HQ!" he cried, pointing in the direction in which he thought Bartholomew Street lay.

I said: "We *shall* make our mark, Karel, I'm going to write a story about this, maybe my last, but after that we'll have become Doctors of Letters."

The tenner woman filled her pot from the outside tap and added:

"*Sub auspiciis.*"

NOTES

These notes are a limited selection of those included in the Czech source edition and additional ones thought desirable precisely for this English edition. They are given without specific attribution.

p. 9 WHY I WRITE?

This text first appeared in *samizdat* form as the afterword to *Životopis trochu jinak* (A slightly different kind of biography, Prague: Petlice, 1986), then as the first part of the eponymous section in *Život bez smokingu* (Life with no dinner jacket, Prague: Československý spisovatel, 1986), and in the Collected Works edition (*Sebrané spisy Bohumila Hrabala*), Vol. 12, pp. 274–278. The latter consists of 19 volumes which appeared between 1992 and 1997, and will be referred to below merely as the Collected Works.

1. Available to Hrabal in Czech translation since the early 1930s.
2. Available in Jaroslav Zaorálek's Czech translation of 1936, the same year in which the French original, *Mort à credit* appeared.
3. Nymburk is a town of some 15,000 inhabitants that lies 28 miles east of Prague and is intimately connected with the early part of Hrabal's life, not least for the brewery where he actually grew up and for the role it has played in the history of Czech railways – likewise relevant to Hrabal's life and works.
4. The universities were closed by the Nazis on November 17, 1939. Two years later, Czech émigré students and the British National Union of Students were jointly instrumental in having that date declared International Students' Day. The student rally marking the fiftieth anniversary of the closure, on that date in Prague in 1989, helped trigger the events later known as the Velvet Revolution.
5. Ladislav Klíma (1878–1928) was a Czech philosopher, writer, dramatist and exponent of Czech expressionism.
6. Libeň is an old industrial part of Prague 8, now forever associated with the time spent there by Hrabal and his circle of close friends, most notably the artist Valdimír Boudník.

7. Hrabal's favourite quotation from Lao Tse's (Lao Tzu, Laozi) *Tao Te Ching* (translated variously as *The Way and its Power*, *The Classic of the Way of Virtue*, and *The Law (or Canon) of Virtue and its Way*), available to Hrabal in a Czech translation by Rudolf Dvořák, published in 1920.
8. *Docta ignorantia* – 'learnèd ignorance', the term invented by the German philosopher and theologian Nicholas of Cusa (Nicolaus Cusanus, 1401–1464) to denote the condition of the human intellect in relation to God.

p. 19 THOSE RAPTUROUS RIFLEMEN

Hrabal's first ever short story. After numerous alterations it was first included in *Poupata* (Buds, Prague: Mladá fronta, 1970). The version translated here appeared in the Collected Works edition, Vol. 1, pp. 173–190, and is based on the original typescript dated 1945–1946.
1. 'Nuncius', the brand name of an imitation of the French Bénédictine liqueur.
2. The Nymburk firm of Wantoch brewed various spirits, most notably a widely reputed griotte. The company was founded by Ludwig Wantoch (1856– ?) in 1878.

p. 49 CAIN

This text is the first forerunner of *Carefully Watched Trains*, one of Hrabal's best-known works, thanks in great measure to the film version. There have been many variants, out of which the author (actually after the success of the *Trains*) created the 'Legenda o Kainovi' (The legend of Cain), published in *Morytáty a legendy* (Gory stories and legends). Hrabal confessed to being inspired by Goethe's *The Sorrows* (or *Sufferings*) *of Young Werther* and by Camus' *The Outsider* (or *Stranger*) (see the Collected Works edition, Vol. 2, p.233). The version used for the translation comes from the 1949 typescript *Židovský svícen* (Menorah) and was published in *Schizofrenické evangelium* (A schizophrenic gospel, Prague: Melantrich, 1990) and in Vol. 2 of the Collected Works (pp. 7–36).

1. Protectorate – referring to the period of the Second World War when most of Bohemia and Moravia (the western and central provinces of what had been Czechoslovakia) became a protectorate of Nazi Germany.
2. Hrabal studied at the Law Faculty of Charles University in Prague from October 1936. He took the exam in the history of law in February 1937, and in October 1939 he received his certificate for the successful completion of eight terms of study.
3. The terminus ultimately called Prague-Těšnov was demolished in 1978. In its lifetime it had had several names, including Prague-Vltava (Moldau) Station during the bulk of the German occupation (1940–45).
4. A pet name and historicising diminutive of 'Bohumil', hence an admission that the story has a basis in the author's own life.
5. A novel by Karolína Světlá (1830–99) published in 1868, celebrating the moral strength of the simple woman; most of her works hinge on strong female characters, and she is also seen widely as the initiator of the Czech 'rural novel' genre.
6. That is, the Saint's lance on his statue at the top end of Wenceslas Square in Prague.
7. An allusion to Genesis 4:15. – "And the Lord set a mark upon Cain, lest any finding him should kill him."
8. Zboží is the village east of Kostomlaty, half-way to Nymburk, now known, and so marked on maps, as Kamenné Zboží.

p. 97 **TRAPEZIUM NUMBER TWO**

Published in *Poupata* (Buds, Prague: Mladá fronta, 1970) and in the Collected Works, Vol. 2, pp. 37–41. The present translation is taken from the latter, which was based on the 1949 typescript collection *Židovský svícen* (Menorah).

Translator's note: The title has been left as in the original, for all its opaqueness. The text comes from the same source as 'The Feast of

Sts Philip and James' below, ordered later in the collection. However, if it, and the image therein of squares and rectangles turning into trapeziums during the character's momentary derangement had been written earlier, the offending window and the confusion of the character in this text perhaps explain why 'trapezium number two'.

1. *Habeš* (Abyssinia) and The Colony (*Kolonie* in Czech) are parts of Nymburk (see 'Why I write?', note 3), the latter a vast workers' housing complex.

p. 105 THE HOUSE THAT REFRESHED ITSELF IN A FLASH

Published in *Poupata* (Buds, Prague: Mladá fronta, 1970) and in the Collected Works, Vol. 2, pp. 42–47. The present translation is taken from the latter, which was based on the 1949 typescript collection *Židovský svícen* (Menorah).

1. A reference to René Crevel's (1900–35) 1926 novel, *La Mort difficile*, published in a Czech translation in 1929 (in English not until 1986), and described by Jean-Yves Alt as his 'best, least surrealist and most autobiographical novel' (http://culture-et-debats.over-blog.com/article-28595744.html). The phrase as book title and as an allusion recur throughout the story, with a final allusion in an untranslatable pun on the author's name in the last sentence (Cz. *krevel* = haematite), partially resolved by recourse to an anagram in the translation.

2. This section taken over into 'Cain', see p. 67.

p. 115 THE FEAST OF STS PHILIP AND JAMES

Published in *Poupata* (Buds, Prague: Mladá fronta, 1970) and in the Collected Works, Vol. 2, pp. 42–47. The present translation is taken from the latter, which was based on the 1949 typescript collection *Židovský svícen* (Menorah).

1. Referring to Frederick Winslow Taylor (1856–1915), American promoter of advances in the management of business and industry.

p. 125   **SCRIBES AND PHARISEES**

Published in *Poupata* (Buds, Prague: Mladá fronta, 1970) and in the Collected Works, Vol. 2, pp. 37–41. The present translation is taken from the latter, which was based on the 1949 typescript collection *Židovský svícen* (Menorah).

1. The story exploits Hrabal's experience as an insurance agent. He joined the Small Trades Old-age and Invalidity Fund as a controller on 16 Sept. 1946, and his career in insurance ended on 31 July 1947. This text is also Hrabal's first experiment with conveying the 'things people say' in the form of a monologue.
2. Matthew 5: 15: 'Neither do men light a candle, and put it under a bushel, but on a candlestick.'
3. Hrabal did actually have in his flat an object of the kind described.
4. Robert Desnos (1900–45), a French surrealist poet, arrested in 1944 by the Gestapo, imprisoned in turn at Fresnes, Compiègne, near Flöh in Saxony and in Theresianstadt (the Terezín holding camp on Czech soil). He lived to see the camp liberated, but died of typhus soon after.
5. The inventory of Hrabal's flat really did include a prosthesis.

p. 133   **NO ESCAPE**

Published in *Poupata* (Buds, Prague: Mladá fronta, 1970) and in the Collected Works, Vol. 2, pp. 37–41. The present translation is taken from the latter, which was based on the 1949 typescript collection *Židovský svícen* (Menorah).

p. 137   **THE GLORIOUS LEGEND OF WANTOCH**

Published in the Collected Works, Vol. 2, pp. 62–67 on the basis of the original typescript. The variant in *Poupata* (Buds, Prague: Mladá fronta, 1970) is later.

1. A(n obsolete) kind of therapy using pulses of 30–100 Hz to stimulate muscles.

2. Three (among very many) of the famous spas of Czechoslovakia.
3. The story is riddled with Old Tom Gin, still made to a popular 18th-century English recipe in a variety of places around the world; the title refers to Ludwig Wantoch's distillery in Nymburk.

p. 149   THE SUFFERINGS OF OLD WERTHER

This is the first time that Hrabal employed the uninterrupted narrative torrent of Uncle Pepin (Josef Hrabal, 1882–1967), who was always a great inspiration to his nephew. The text is the first variant of *Taneční hodiny pro starší a pokročilé* (translated by Michael Heim as Dancing lessons for the advanced in age). Uncle Pepin will reappear in the early *Lednová povídka* and *Únorová povídka* ('January Story' and 'February Story', herein pp. 265ff and 272ff), though he is accorded far greater space in the memoir novels *Postřižiny* and *Městečko, kde se zastavil čas* (translated by James Naughton as *Cutting it Short* and *The Little Town Where Time Stood Still*). *The Sufferings…* was first published privately in March 1988, to reappear subsequently in *Schizofrenické evangelium* (A schizophrenic gospel, Prague: Melantrich, 1990) and in the Collected Works, Vol. 2, pp. 71–124. The text here is translated from the latter, which is based on the typescript of *Poupata* (Buds, Prague: Mladá fronta, 1970).

The 'narrative torrent' dashes forward in fits and starts, switching without notice between two, three or four threads tangled together in the speaker's mind, creating all manner of hiatuses, ambiguities and the appearance of this or that thread's having got lost, only for it to surface half a page or more later. It also comes gushing in different versions of Czech, from something approaching, but never quite reaching, the standard language to various bursts in mid- to low colloquial language, some versions of which, especially those involving technical jargon, are heavily laden with Germanisms. These are not preserved in the translation, because there is no version of English similarly impacted, or impacted analogously by some other alien tongue.

01. The implied comparison is with Otokar Korbelář (1899–1976), an actor and director, and Zdeněk Štěpánek (1896–1968), actor, dramatist, director and scriptwriter and a key figure at the National Theatre in Prague.

02. N. Batista was the author of several popular works on a healthy sex life, writing in the early years of the twentieth century. His name will crop up several times more in this long narrative. Neither the World Wide Web nor the Czech National Library have any inkling what N. stands for.

03. Jaroslav (Jára) Pospíšil (1905–79), opera and operetta tenor and star of the 1930s, with 22 films, 4,600 opera performances and over 500 gramophone records to his credit. He is clearly deeply rooted in Pepin's memory and his name figures in a variety of hypocoristic forms throughout the narrative.

04. Antonín Holzinger (1891–1953), theatre and film actor and singer whose career was spread over seven of Prague's best-known theatre companies.

05. František Voborský (real name František Vohnout, 1913–80), actor and singer, whose career began with a company in Nymburk, Hrabal's home town. Like Holzinger, he had a long spell at the Grand Operetta in Prague.

06. Tomáš Baťa (1836–1972), the driving force behind the Czech multinational Bata Shoes.

07. Ferenc Futurista (real name František Fiala, 1891–1947), Czech actor and sculptor and one of the most popular comedians in the 1920s and 1930s.

08. Part of Nymburk.

09. Božena Němcová (1820–62), Czech writer, held to be the author of the first Czech novel, *Babička* (The Grandmother), a moralising story of country life. Her husband Josef Němec (1805–79) was a revenue officer.

10. A reference to the nineteenth-century Czech National Revival, which revived the language and saw an upsurge in literature.

11. Rudolf Bechyně (1881–1948), Czech journalist and politician, a native of Nymburk, between the wars a central figure among the Social Democrats, often holding a ministerial portfolio.

12. Karel Havlíček [Borovský] (1821–56), largely satirical poet and razor-sharp journalist, considered by many the progenitor of Czech journalism in the strict – *and* investigative – sense of the word.

13. Karel Havlíček's daughter was actually called Zdena.

14. Zdeněk Nejedlý (1878–1962), Czech historian, musicologist, literary historian and Communist politician, twice minister of education in the post-war years, with a break as minister of labour.

15. A battle fought in the Ukraine on 8–13 March 1918 between the Czecho-Slovak legions and a numerically superior German force. 145 legionnaires fell and *c*. 300 Germans.

16. Prof. Theodor Khon (1845–1915), the controversial seventh Archbishop of Olomouc, made to resign by the papal authorities, lived out his life at Ehrenhausen in Styria.

17. On the evidence of this text and a couple of hard-to-find references on the internet, it used to be possible to have an ex-fizzy drink bottle filled with spirits of one kind or another to take away after a session in the pub. Variants of the Czech word (*zódák*, as here, or *soďák*) are based on the German or Czech words for soda water and used colloquially for any *limonáda* – be that actual lemonade or some other fizzy drink ending in -ade in English, hence the neologism used in the translation.

18. Eugen of Austrian Teschen (1863–1954), a native of Židlochovice, an archduke in the Habsburg line, the son of Archduke Karl Ferdinand of Teschen and Archduchess Elisabeth of Austria. He commanded the Austrian troops in the First World War and was made Field Marshal in 1916. From 1894 to 1923 he was grand master of the Order of Teutonic Knights and upgraded one of the Order's seats, Bouzov Castle.

19. *Deutschmeister*, i.e. *Magister Germaniae*, the highest-ranking member of the Order of Teutonic Knights.

20. Prince Johann II von Liechtenstein (1840–1929), the capable administrator of the family estates in Austria, the Bohemian Lands and Liechtenstein, founder of hospitals and orphanages. For the employees of the Poštovná porcelain works he created a housing estate, he founded the first College of Forestry at Úsov and the School of Pomology and Viticulture at Vranov near Brno.

21. Albrecht von Habsburg (1845–95), the éminence grise at the Austrian court of Franz Joseph.

22. Orel (Eagle): This was the sports organisation set up by the Roman Catholics to counter the better known, left-wing Sokol (Falcon) movement, which had shown itself overtly anti-Catholic. Orel's roots lie in the setting up of a physical education division of the Union of Catholic Journeymen on 14 March 1896 in Prague. Orel has disappeared from the scene several times, most notably being banned under the Communist regime, but it has now re-emerged with sufficient vitality to have, for instance, its own football league. Its members are themselves called 'orels'.

23. Not to be confused with any later, similarly named party in Germany.

24. *Světozor*, a widely read, Czech illustrated magazine launched in 1834 by Pavel Josef Šafařík, taken over in 1899 by the Otto publishing house and published by them for over thirty years.

25. *The Merry Widow* (1905) and *The Land of Smiles* (1929), operettas by Franz Léhar; *Libuše* (1872, first performed at the Czech National Theatre in 1881), a grand opera by Bedřich Smetana; *The Gypsy Baron* (premiered 1885), an operetta by Johann Strauss the Younger.

26. Beno Blachut (1913–85), Czech operatic tenor.

27. *Miss Venus*, originally a German 'film operetta' of 1921, starring Ada Svedin and Charles Willy Kayser, dir. Ludwig Czerny, music by Jean Ailhout. During its projection the silent movie was accompanied by music and songs.

28. Václav Talich (1883–1961), a leading conductor, associated chiefly with the orchestra of the National Theatre and the Czech Philharmonic. In his younger years he had conducted the Ljubljana Symphony Orchestra, which oversaw operetta productions at the Slovenian Provincial Theatre.

29. Jaroslav Gleich (1900–76), opera and concert tenor, soloist at the National Theatre from 1927 to 1962.

30. A hill in Veneto, Italy, the scene of major fighting in 1917, culminating in and better known as the Second Battle of the Piave River in June 1918.

31. There is still a barracks on the site, *kasárna Hanácká*, and there is still a Goliath (*Goliáš*) restaurant opposite.

32. *Balalaika,* a 1936 musical show, set in Russia, initially staged at London's Adelphi Theatre, adapted from *The Great Hussar* (1933) by composer George Posford (1906–76) and lyricist Albert Eric Maschwitz (1901–69). It also became the basis of the eponymous 1939 American film starring Nelson Eddy and Ilona Massey.

33. See note 3.

34. Hugo Kraus (1894–1961), actor, singer and stage director with a hugely varied career. In 1929–45 he was at the Prague Grand Operetta, finally becoming its managing director.

35. See note 4.

36. Slávka (Jaroslava) Tauberová (1903–83), opera singer, dancer and film actress. After short spells at other theatres she became the star performer at the Grand Operetta (1929–39).

37. From a tango in Posford's *Balalaika*.

38. *kalamajka*, a Czech folk round dance. Rhymes with *balalaika*.

39. The Prague *Hlahol* male voice choir was founded in 1861, the women's choir in 1879. They survive as a mixed choir.

40. The Hálek Society is an amateur theatre group, one of whose stars was Marie Kiliánová, Hrabal's mother. It was founded in 1860 and is still going strong.

41. The Classicist, later neo-Renaissance palace, cultural centre and concert hall, on Slavonic Island in Prague, built in 1836–37.
42. František Kmoch (1848–1912), a renowned Kolín bandmaster and prolific composer of brass band music.
43. I.e. in the role of RI (catechism) teacher.
44. Valašsko, a region of the far east of Moravia, not Romania.
45. Hasso-Eccard Freiherr von Manteuffel (1897–1978) began his military career during the Great War. During World War II he was a German general, and in 1953–57 a member of the Bundestag.
46. Erwin Freiherr Roszner von Roseneck (1852–1928), Austro-Hungarian politician.
47. Viktor Julius Ignaz Ferdinand Graf Dankl von Krásnik (1854–1941), Austro-Hungarian general.
48. Moritz von Auffenberg (1852–1928), Austro-Hungarian general and politician, in 1911–12 Austro-Hungarian Minister of War.
49. Franz Conrad von Hötzendorf (1852–1925), Austrian field marshal, head of the general staff of the Austro-Hungarian army.
50. Horodenka (Gorodenka), a town in western Ukraine, previously, thanks to nineteenth- and twentieth-century frontier changes, in Austrian Galicia (until 1918), then Poland (until 1939, when it was annexed by the Soviets, subsequently occupied in turn by the Hungarians, then Germans). It is known for one of the most egregious atrocities during World War II, when the town's Jewish population, comprising about half of the total, was murdered piecemeal by the local Ukrainian militia or shot en masse by the Germans and buried in a mass grave (December 1941). About a dozen Jews survived to form a partisan unit, which hid in the local forests from where they fought back. A synagogue in Salford, England, is named in honour of this community.
51. The speaker is alluding to the person known in Czech as Ludvík Jagellonský, in English as Louis II of Hungary (1506–26), of the Polish-Lithuanian Jagellonian dynasty, king of Hungary and

Bohemia. He died at the Battle of Mohács, falling backwards off his horse in retreat and drowning in marshland, after his army had been thrashed by the more powerful Turks.

52. Among a nation like the Czechs, who know their wild edible fungi extremely well and forage for them in a big way, the species *Tylopilus felleus*, known in English as the bitter bolete, is instantly recognisable and specimens are left well alone, thereby becoming very conspicuous in a stretch of woodland otherwise cleared of all its edible companions. Hence the image of conspicuous solitariness.

53. Count Arnošt Emanuel Sylva-Tar[r]ouca (1860–1936), Austro-Hungarian, later Czech aristocrat, lawyer, dendrologist and politician, scion of an originally Portuguese line with property in Bohemia since the 18th century. He had, and his descendants have had, an abiding interest in the famous Průhonice estate on the edge of Prague.

54. The island referred to in note 41.

55. Martin Lecián (1900–27), an army deserter, safebreaker and murderer. He committed his first murder on 19 January 1927 and on April 23rd he and his under-age accomplice Dědek were arrested in Nový Bohumín by constables Halíř and Kaluža. On 3 September 1927 he was convicted of ten murders and condemned to death by hanging, which took place at 6 pm on 6 October 1927 in the yard of Olomouc military prison. Many Czech readers will be aware at least vaguely of this famous case.

56. Leopold Wohlschleger (1855–1929), the Austro-Hungarian and subsequently Czechoslovak state hangman. The last person he hanged was Lecián.

57. Wichterle and Kovařík, the names behind the acronym WIKOV, a company that came into being in 1918 following the merger of two engineering firms. Mostly it produced farm machines, with cars as a sideline. After the Communist putsch in 1948 it was nationalised and renamed Agrostroj Prostějov. (A Wikov car is one

'character' in Antonín Bajaja's *Na krásné modré Dřevnici*, trans. as *Burying the Season*, London: Jantar Publishing, 2016.)

58. A misquotation of Karel Havlíček Borovský's (1821–56) poem *Má hvězda* (My star, 1854): 'Ever since I've known your heart / Juliánka of mine, / I've been seeing a star again, / but this one is yours! // My erstwhile star / has now forever set, / with my childish trust / the star also went out.'

59. A herb-based liqueur (includes *inter al.* aniseed, fennel, coriander and caraway). Widely drunk during the first half of the twentieth century, it earned itself a mention in Hašek's *The Adventures of the Good Soldier Schweik*. It originated in Poland as *kontuszowka*.

60. Charles/Karl I of Austria (Charles III as King of Bohemia, Charles IV as King of Hungary; 1887–1922), great nephew and heir presumptive of Emperor Franz Joseph I. He reigned 1916–1918 as the last Emperor of Austria. He sought in vain to bring the nations of the Empire together and the war to an end; after the break-up of Austria-Hungary he went into exile and died in Madeira.

61. Wilhelm II of Prussia (1859–1941), the last German Emperor and Prussian king. He came from the Brandenburg branch of his family and was its head until his death. After Bismarck's dismissal in 1890 Wilhelm took German politics in a nationalist and militarist direction, thus contributing to the outbreak of the Great War. On Germany's defeat he went into exile in Holland.

62. Meaning Field Marshal Hans Georg Hermann von Plessen (1841–1929), adjutant general of the Prussian high command.

63. Wolf Albach-Retty (1906–67), Austrian actor, husband of Magda Schneider and father of Romy Schneider. He appeared in almost a hundred films.

p. 237 **PROTOCOL or: A contribution on the Renaissance as compiled jointly with my Uncle Josef**
From the original typescript. Note the direct reference in the title to Hrabal's Uncle Josef (more widely known as Pepin) as co-author.

'Protokol' saw publication first in *Schizofrenické evangelium* (A schizo-phrenic gospel, Prague: Melantrich, 1990), and subsequently in Vol. 3 of the Collected Works (pp.129–131).

1. Cf. Luke 10: 40–42: "But Martha was cumbered about much serving and came to him, and said, Lord, dost thou not care that my sister hath left me to serve alone? Bid her therefore that she help me. And Jesus answered and said unto her, Martha, Martha, thou art careful and troubled about many things: But one thing is needful: and Mary hath chosen that good part, which shall not be taken away from her."

2. The 'tinkling cymbal' of Corinthians 13:1.

3. Cf. Matthew 16: 26: "For what is a man profited, if he shall gain the whole world and lose his own soul."

4. See 'The Sufferings of Old Werther' above, note 12.

5. An allusion to *The Dollar Princess*, a musical in three acts by A. M. Willner and Fritz Grünbaum, with music by Leo Fall (Ger-man sources refer to it and other works by the Olomouc-born Fall as operettas). It played in Vienna in 1907 and in London at Daly's Theatre in 1909. In late Victorian and Edwardian Britain, a 'dollar princess' was an American heiress (the phrase doubtless giving rise to the German calque *Dollarprinzessin* and thence to the Czech *dolarová princezna*; the expression is still recorded in modern Czech dictionaries as meaning a rich girl).

p. 243 **A SCHIZOPHRENIC GOSPEL.**
Dedicated to my seventy-year-old muse, my Uncle Pepin
From a typescript dated 1951. It first saw publication in the epony-mous anthology (Prague: Melantrich, 1990), then in *Atomová mašina značky Perkeo* (The Perkeo Atomic Typewriter, Prague: Práce, 1991) and in the Collected Works (Vol. 3, pp. 129–131).

1. This opening paragraph points to the period 1947–49, when Hrabal had a job as a travelling salesman hawking hardware and toys.

02. The charm of this whole text resides in the need to see, behind the biblical names, the author himself and specific members of his family. Hrabal's stepfather, František Hrabal, had a particular fondness for old has-beens where cars were concerned. In his case, the story of Jesus' birth incidentally provides another view on the matter of paternity.

03. Probably an oblique reference to the Trinity Mine in [Silesian] Ostrava.

04. Rokytka, a rivulet that enters the Vltava just below Libeň Manor in Prague.

05. See footote 2 under 'The Sufferings of Old Werther', p. 486.

06. The motifs that follow are developed further in *The Little Town Where Time Stood Still* and *Cutting it Short*, where the hero is Hrabal's stepfather Francin.

07. The source, Romans 12:15, has the two halves in the reverse order.

08. A prelude to the main theme of the novel *Cutting it Short*.

09. This was at 269/1 Betlémské Square in Prague 1.

10. An oblique reference to Blanka Krauseová, a heartthrob of Hrabal's, who lived At the Sign of the Blue Pike, the house on the corner of Karlova and Liliová streets in Prague Old Town. He dedicated to her a letter in verse.

11. This was at Květinářská St., Prague 8 – Libeň; today the site is the Castle Residence restaurant.

12. Cf. Matthew 11: 25–26: "At that time Jesus answered and said, I thank Thee, o Father, Lord of heaven and earth, because thou hast hid these things from the wise and prudent, and hast revealed them unto babes. // Even so, Father: for so it seemed good in thy sight."

13. In Czech Kateřinky, now the psychiatric clinic of the Charles University Faculty of Medicine. Previously it had been a 'Victorian' mental hospital. It owes its name to the monastery originally founded by Charles IV in 1355 in memory of his 1332 victory at San Felice against hostile northern Italian towns, which he attributed to an intercession by St. Catherine.

14. I.e. Vincent van Gogh.

15. Lake Mácha, an artificial lake, originally a fish pond, in the Liberec Region of North Bohemia. Named after the national poet, Karel Hynek Mácha (1810–16), whose name attaches to the surrounding area, known for its beauty and wreathed in legend. The lake is used almost exclusively for recreational purposes.

16. Matthew 16: 6–8: "Then Jesus said unto them, Take heed and beware of the leaven of the Pharisees and of the Sadducees. // And they reasoned among themselves, saying, It is because we have taken no bread. // Which when Jesus perceived, he said unto them, O ye of little faith, why reason ye among yourselves, because ye have brought no bread?"

17. Matthew 20: 1.

18. Cf. Luke 22: 42.

19. Cf. Matthew 7: 6.

20. The John Huss memorial refers to Jan Hus (*c.* 1369–1415), the Bohemian protestant philosopher, preacher, teacher and chancellor of Charles University, and finally unrepentant martyr, burned at the stake in Constance. His memorial is a major landmark on the Old Town Square in Prague.

21. An episode re-used in section 9 of 'Bambini di Praga' (*Pábitelé* [Palaverers]). The reference to an axe in a fairy-tale is a mystery; it has not proved possible to identify any such tale.

22. Also used in 'Bambini di Praga'.

23. In the sense of the political screenings to which many were subjected, usually in connection with their perceived employability, after the Communist takeover of Czechoslovakia in February 1948. Similar procedures were reintroduced under the conditions of 1970s 'normalisation' following the Warsaw Pact invasion and Soviet occupation of the country in 1968.

24. The word here translated as 'obstacle' is *hranice*, which in Czech is neatly ambiguous (a pun) between the meanings (a) frontier, border, (b) the wood pile that is ignited when someone is to be

burnt at the stake. The whole clause also carries shades of the faith that moves mountains.

25. Cf. Mark 12: 33.

26. Here Hrabal has merged three different popes into one: Pius XII, born Eugenio Maria Giuseppe Giovanni Pacelli (1876–1958) was elected Pope on 2 March 1939. It was Pope Pius X (Giuseppe Melchiorre Sarto, 1835–1914) who had been friends with the Emperor Franz Joseph, and Pius XI (Achille Ambrogio Damiano Ratti, 1857–1939, Pope from 6 February 1922) who was the keen mountaineer.

27. According to legend, the sixth labour of Hercules was to clean the Augean stables in a day, which he indeed achieved by diverting the flow of two nearby rivers.

28. The Catalan surrealist was one of Hrabal's favourite points of reference.

29. This sentence is either pure mystification, typically Hrabalesque, or possible evidence of an unfulfilled intention.

p. 265 A JANUARY STORY

From a school exercise book dated 1952. It was published in *Poupata* (Buds, Prague: Mladá fronta, 1970), then in *Schizofrenické evangelium* (A schizophrenic gospel, Prague: Melantrich, 1990) and in Vol. 3 of the Collected Works, pp. 58–61.

1. Grandma is confused by the similarity between the names of Karl Hermann *Frank* (1898–1946), secretary of state at the Office of the *Reichsprotektor*, i.e. the Nazi head of the Protectorate of Bohemia and Moravia, of which he was appointed Minister of State in 1943, later, in 1946, being tried for war crimes and executed, and Spain's General Francisco *Franco*. The grammar-dependent way in which the latter is treated in Czech orthography is the source of her problem.

2. See 'The Sufferings of Old Werther', note 3.

3. Klement Gottwald (1896–1953) was a Communist politician,

general secretary of the Communist Party of Czechoslovakia from 1929 to 1945 and party chairman until his death in 1953. He was the country's Prime Minister from July 1946 to June 1948, after which he became President of the post-war Republic, four months after the 1948 Communist coup. He attended Stalin's funeral in 1953.

4. See 'The Sufferings of Old Werther', note 12.

p. 272 **A FEBRUARY STORY**

From a school exercise book dated 1952. It was published in *Poupata* (Buds, Prague: Mladá fronta, 1970), then in *Schizofrenické evangelium* (A schizophrenic gospel, Prague: Melantrich, 1990) and in Vol. 3 of the Collected Works, pp.62–69.

1. The tincture with the brand name Anker Pain Expeller used to be recommended for a whole range of indications. It was invented by Friedrich Adolf Richter (1846–1910), the owner of a pharmaceuticals factory in Rudolstadt, Thuringia. All the company's products bore the trademark of an anchor (*Anker*).

2. Remanence: a part of Nymburk.

3. *Rudé právo*, the Communist Party daily.

4. Conceivably Hrabal hopes Pepin is referring to Freiherr Otto James Wucherer von Huldenfeld (1888–1964), who is pictured on the geni website in military uniform and would have been active in the First World War, to which many of Uncle Pepin's memories usually attach. In terms of "today's Russians", the reference may be to the former's son, Georg Otto Freiherr Wucherer von Huldenfeld (1924–1944), who may indeed have been involved in trying to "chase the Russians out beyond the Urals": he died as a consequence of injuries sustained at "Janow, Russia", which I take to be Ivanava (Pol. Janów Poleski, Rus. Ivanovo) in Belarus, reoccupied by the Soviets only weeks after Wucherer died; it may be inferred that he was moved to Spantekow, Mecklenburg-Vorpommern, to die. See https://www.geni.com/people/Freiherr-

Otto-James-Wucherer-von-Huldenfeld/6000000025219666605 and https://www.geni.com/people/Georg-Otto-Freiherr-Wucherer-von-Huldenfeld/6000000040888126404.

5. This passage gets re-used in *The Little Town Where Time Stood Still*, though there Pepin is speaking to a German officer.

6. This is taken to be a reference to the period film comedy *Uličnice* (The Minx, 1936), in which the hugely popular Jára Kohout sings a song about nine canaries.

7. Places of interest in Vienna, to which Pepin's mind so often wanders.

8. *Paní Marjánka, matka pluku aneb Ženské srdce* (Mme M., the mother of the regiment, or: The heart of a woman), a play by Josef Kajetán Tyl (1808–56) based loosely on August von Kotzebue's *Das Kind der Liebe* (The Love-child) and first performed in 1845. In Tyl's play a spirited sutler, camp follower, returns to her home town and meets up with her former lover, the father of her son.

9. Vlasta Burian, real name Josef Vlastimil Burian (1891–1962), a comedian of genius, manager of the Rokoko Theatre from 1923, and from 1925 proprietor of the Vlasta Burian Theatre Company, which played in several of Prague's theatres, ultimately (1930–44) at the new Mines and Steelworks House in Lazarská Street, which closed in 1944 (later the site became the Comedy Theatre). After the war Burian was charged with collaboration with the Germans and his property was confiscated. Uncle Pepin could never have seen him at any theatre.

10. I.e. anti-rheumatic.

11. Possibly meaning enterohaematic.

12. Feromantochiol – apparently a Czech liquid version of Feroman-TX, a treatment for anaemia; it is typical of Uncle Pepin that he should treat the name as applying to a wine.

p. 285 **ONE GREAT GUY**

Typescript, part of the now lost collection *Umělé osudy* (Artificial destinies). It was first printed in *HANŤA PRESS*, 18, 1995, pp. 8–24, and subsequently in Vol. 19 of the Collected Works, pp. 22–36. The translation preserves only some of the elements of Hrabal's idiosyncratic punctuation, odder here than many other of his practices, though at least he uses the full stop.

1. The Atom Prince character reappears in the short story 'Anděl' (Angel) in *Inzerát na dům, ve kterém už nechci bydlet* (For Sale ad for a house in which I no longer wish to live, 1965).

2. The labourer Vindy also appears in the short story 'Divní lidé' (Strange people), ibid.

3. Vítězslav Nezval (1900–1958), Czech poet, co-founder of Poetism and a leading Czech Surrealist.

4. Isaak Mautner's (1824–1901) Náchod textile factory (I. Mautner Baumwoll- und Leinweberei in Náchod, founded 1882) blossomed under his son Isidor Mautner (1900–58). The company supplied the army with woollen fabrics and had branches in Prague, Budapest and Trieste. The firm was nationalised in 1946 as Tepna Náchod and finally collapsed in the face of cheap imports in 2006. – Hrabal took this narrative over into 'Divní lidé'.

5. In reality, Charlie Chaplin had only four wives, all very young, three of them under 18.

6. This same episode was worked up by Jiří Kolář in *Prométheova játra* (The liver of Prometheus – written in 1950, first published in 1990). He had derived it from a short story by Zofia Nałkowska, 'Przy torze kolejowym' (Beside the railway line, 1946). Hrabal retold it in his own short story 'Emánek' (Little Eman) in the collection *Perlička na dně* (A little pearl at the bottom, 1963 – also known under other translated titles).

7. In *Něžný barbar* (A tender barbarian) this episode is attributed to Vladimír Boudník.

18. 'O, sweet Naples, o blessed soil, where all of creation smiles...' This Neapolitan song in praise of the port of Borgo Santa Lucia was written in the local dialect by Michele Zezza in 1776, an Italian rendition being produced in the mid-19th century by the composer and music publisher Teodoro Cottrau (1827–79). Hrabal is quoting the latter.

19. In 1946, Václav Kučera (1925–83) founded an ensemble, known as the Kučerovci, which specialised in songs from Latin America and the Pacific. It is still active.

10. He means *Lágrimas negras*, a bolero composed in 1929 by Cuban musician and singer Miguel Matamoros (1894–1971).

11. 'I'm off to Vigo, my black-haired beauty, it's time to say goodbye', a popular song by Cuban Ernesto Lecuona (1895–1963).

12. Beřkovice – an outpost, north of Prague, of the Provincial Institution for the Mentally Sick, set up in Horní Beřkovice in 1891. It is now the Horní Beřkovice Psychiatric Hospital.

13. I.e. in contrast to beer, the beverage of choice among Czechs.

14. I.e. Douglas Fairbanks, Sr (1883–1939), American star of silent films (e.g. *Zorro, D'Artagnan, Robin Hood*).

15. A traditional patriotic song (*Čechy krásné, Čechy mé*), widely sung at funerals, music by composer and musicologist Josef Leopold Zvonař (1824–65), words by Václav Jaromír Picek (1812–69), a civil servant, judge and poet – in the latter role known almost exclusively for this song.

16. I.e. the type of cap worn by Field Marshal Erwin Johannes Rommel (1891–1944), the 'Desert Fox', commander of the German Afrikakorps.

17. The names are all of genuine players in the Kladno and Teplice teams of the day.

18. This tale, retold by Uncle Pepin about "a certain Johnny Sachr", also features in *The Little Town Where Time Stood Still*.

Typescript, part of the now lost collection *Umělé osudy* (Artificial destinies). The text first appeared in HANŤA PRESS, 18, 1995, pp. 8–24, and subsequently in the Addenda in Vol. 19 of the Collected Works, pp. 22–36.

11. Some of the motifs here were to be developed in *Jarmila*, others being taken over into the short story *Miláček* (Sweetheart).

12. Border defence force.

13. Heinz Guderian (1888–1954), German military theorist and tank corps general.

14. Hasso-Eccard Freiherr von Manteuffel (1897–1978), a German general during World War II, in 1953–57 a member of the Bundestag.

15. The 15th Olympic Games, held in Helsinki in 1952, was the high point of Emil Zátopek's (1922–2000) career: he won both the 5,000 metres and the 10,000 metres, earning a third gold in the marathon, which he had never entered previously.

16. Herbert Schade (1922–94), German runner, whose best result was bronze in the 5000 m race at the Helsinki Olympic Games in 1952.

17. [Douglas Alastair] Gordon Pirie (1931–91), British runner, won a silver medal at the Melbourne Olympic Games in 1956.

18. [Sir] Chris[topher John] Chataway (1931–2014), British runner, later television commentator, conservative politician and author. In 1954 he had a world record-breaking win in the 5000 m at a London-Moscow competition at White City.

19. Gaston [Étienne Ghislaine] Reiff (1921–92), Belgian runner who beat Zátopek in the 5000 m at the London Olympics in 1948. He then lost to Zátopek at the 1950 European Championships, coming third.

10. Alain Mimoun (1921–2013), Algerian-French runner, winner of the marathon at the Melbourne Olympics in 1956.

11. I.e. it urgently needs tapping.

p. 321 **THE GABRIEL EXPLOSION. A short story**

This story and the two that follow, probably dating from 1952, have survived as typescripts on lined paper. The three texts jointly constitute the basis of 'Legenda o Egonu Bondym a Vladimírkovi' (The legend of Egon Bondy and Little Vladimír), published in *Morytáty a legendy* (Gory stories and legends). The version of the text translated here came out in *Atomová mašina značky Perkeo* (The Perkeo Atomic Typewriter, Prague: Práce, 1991) and in Vol. 3 of the Collected Works (pp. 70–77).

1. A close friend of Hrabal's, Vladimír Boudník (1924–68), whose dynamic structuralist graphic artworks of the second half of the 1950s anticipated the abstract current in the Czech arts. Hrabal mentions him in numerous texts, most particularly in *Něžný barbar* (A tender barbarian) and *Dandy v montérkách* (A dandy in dungarees).

2. The *Sir Malvaz* tavern at 10 Karlova St. in Prague Old Town was opened during the First Republic by the Pragovar brewery to promote its product. It lives on in the memories of lovers of porter.

3. Jan Reegen (1922–52), Zděněl Bouše (1928–97) and Josef Krauer (1927–90), artists and schoolmates of Vladimír Boudník. Bouše figures in 'Vladimírovi přátelé' (Vladimír's friends, 1982), included in the *samizdat* collection *Pražská ironie* (Prague irony).

4. See 'A Schizophrenic Gospel' above, note 10.

5. A building in Bethlehem Square, Prague Old Town, once a brewery and alehouse of ill repute, now the Náprstek Museum of Ethnography.

6. I.e. the three dolphins fountain outside St Nicholas' church on Prague's Old Town Square. At the time, Hrabal lived nearby and used the fountain for his morning ablutions.

7. Jaroslav Rotbauer (1929–2015), an artist and schoolmate of Boudník's; Hrabal remembers him in 'Vladimírovi přátelé' (Vladimír's friends, 1982), included in the *samizdat* collection *Pražská ironie* (Prague irony).

8. I.e. the primeval animal pictures discovered in the Altamira caves in northern Spain in 1879.

9. See 'A Schizophrenic Gospel' above, note 20.

p. 335 **MADE IN CZECHOSLOVAKIA. A short story**

Later rewritten in *Legenda o Egonu Bondym a Vladimírkovi* (The legend of Egon Bondy and Little Vladimír; Collected Works, Vol. 5, pp. 246–56). Despite the sub-title, this is the storyboard for a film. The version of the text translated here appeared in *Atomová mašina značky Perkeo* (The Perkeo Atomic Typewriter; Prague: Práce, 1991), and in the Collected Works. Vol. 3, pp. 78–85. The title is in English in the original.

1. Egon Bondy (real name Zbyněk Fišer, 1930–2007), a bearded philosopher, writer and poet and a close friend of Hrabal's.

2. A flawed rendering of an aria sung by Anna Lisa in Franz Lehár's opera *Paganini*.

3. See 'Scribes and Pharisees' above, note 5.

4. Egon Bondy described his bohemian existence in the memoir *Prvních deset let* (The first ten years, MS, 1981, in book form, Prague: Maťa, 2002). In it he also describes how he crossed into Austria in the spring of 1950 and his periods spent in Austrian jails: 'At the police HQ [in Vienna] I asked for political asylum, but because I didn't have the money to pay the fine for crossing the frontier illegally (100 schilling), they put me there and then in the local lock-up. It was there that I had the first major shock to my morale: from a shred of paper in the toilet I learned that Záviš Kalandra had been executed in Prague' (pp. 46–55 [52]). Kalandra (1902–50), a Czech journalist, historian and critic, was tried, convicted and executed during the show trial of Milada Horáková. Bondy had been in contact with him, and with Karel Teige, after the war.

5. A misquotation from an aria in Lehár's operetta *Der Graf von Luxemburg* (1909, rev. 1937).

16. See 'A Schizophrenic Gospel' above, note 13.

17. I.e. the youngest members of the Communist Party's youth movement, recognised by their uniform of dark skirt or trousers, white shirt and red neck scarf.

18. The 'he' alludes to Vladimír Boudník. See 'The Gabriel Explosion' above, note 1.

19. Explosionalism: a direction in art forged by Boudník, who largely remained its sole exponent. It is based on association and the free rein given to perceptions mediated to the artists by everyday reality – hence the pictorialisation of scenes latent in stains, patches, blotches and cracks on walls, as recounted in 'The Gabriel Explosion' above.

10. Mikuláš Medek (1926–74), Czech painter whose work was derived from Surrealism.

11. Bondy wrote the long poem *Jeskyně divů aneb Prager Leben* (The Cave of Wonders, or Prager Leben, later called *Pražský život* [Prague Life]) in 1950–51, which, in 1951, constituted one volume of the typewritten series *Půlnoc* (Midnight). It later appeared in Vol. 1 of his collected works (*Básnické dílo Egona Bondyho*, Prague: Pražská imaginace, 1990–93, pp. 5–38), and more recently in Egon Bondy: *Básnické spisy* (ed. Martin Machovec), Vol. 1, Prague: Argo, 2016, pp. 115–155. It carries a dedication to 'Comrade Záviš Kalandra'.

12. On nationalisation, all retail hardware stores became links in the KOVOMAT chain. It is worthy of note that the new company's logo – a letter K stylised into a male figure with a hammer over his shoulder – was designed by Vladimír Boudník. The Kovomat name has survived re-privatisation, though not the logo.

13. I.e. Louis Armstrong, whose later 10-day visit to Prague in 1965 remains unforgettable.

p. 349 **BLITZKRIEG. A news flash**

Later rewritten, along with the two previous texts, in *Legenda o Egonu Bondym a Vladimírkovi* (The Legend of Egon Bondy and Little Vladimír, Collected Works, Vol. 5, pp. 246–56). The version of the text translated here appeared in *Atomová mašina značky Perkeo* (The Perkeo Atomic Typewriter, Prague: Práce, 1991), and in the Collected Works (Vol. 3, pp. 86–87).

11. Cz. *bleskovka* – the term used to describe a single-sided duplicated sheet, or flyer, a typical phenomenon of 1950s underground publishing.

12. See 'The Gabriel Explosion' above, note 1.

13. See 'Made in Czechoslovakia' above, note 1.

14. See 'The Gabriel Explosion' above, note 3.

15. Jaroslav Dočekal (1926–74), artist and schoolmate of Vladimír Boudník.

16. The *samizdat* series *Edice Půlnoc* (Midnight; the name probably echoes the illegally published, French wartime series *Les Editions de Minuit*) was founded at the turn of 1950/51 by Egon Bondy and Ivo Vodseďálek (1931–2017). It formed the basis for the unofficial publication of texts by the circle of their friends, who included Pavel Svoboda, Jana Krejcarová, Adolf Born, Oldřich Jelínek, Bohumil Hrabal and Vladimír Boudník. The series rose to *c.* 50 volumes, large and small, though in many cases only later copies have survived, and in some only the titles, with no certain evidence as to whether they actually saw the light of day or not.

17. There are people still living who recall that in Anenská Street there used to be a semi-legal basement taphouse run by two female pensioners, hence its street-names The Old Ladies, The Two Old Ladies. It was patronised by artists and the criminal classes.

18. See 'The Gabriel Explosion' above, note 2.

19. It used to be very common for people to go to their local pub with a jug for a takeaway pint (or more).

10. This was Hrabal's address at the time.

505

11. The phrase attributed to Galileo following his forced recantation. The Czechs' familiarity with the phrase far exceeds its incidence in English, where it tends to be replaced by 'I told you so'.

p. 355 **MEETINGS BY CHANCE AND BY DESIGN**

The next sequence of texts, up to 'Everyday Talk' (plus 'January Story' and 'February Story'), was published in *Poupata* (Buds, Prague: Mladá fronta, 1970) under the omnibus title of *Setkání a návštěvy* (Meetings and visitors, herein as Meetings by chance and by design). It is highly likely that the stories were separate, each with its own title. Regrettably, the original texts of the first four have not survived, hence their inclusion here in the form given them by Hrabal in *Buds*; the remainder are based on surviving typescripts. The versions here are all taken over from the Collected Works, Vol. 3, pp. 132–151.

1. A well-known pub at 415/10 Uhelný trh in Prague Old Town.
2. The image of skylarks on strings was to be part of the title of Hrabal's first published book (in 1959), except that it didn't see the light of day. Skylarks on strings used to be used as bait for birds of prey being hunted.
3. The pub-restaurant U Pinkasů at 15/16 Jungmann Square (Jungmannovo náměstí) in Prague New Town.
4. On 10 July 1952, Hrabal suffered a nasty head injury at the Kladno steelworks. He was off work until April 1953. He returned to Kladno for only a brief spell before taking a job at the recycling depot in Spálená Street in Prague.
5. The reference is to the murder of St Wenceslas, traditionally dated 28 September 935, by his brother Boleslav at the entrance to the church in Stará Boleslav. Boleslav struck just as Wenceslas took hold of the ring of the door handle in order to enter the building.
6. The statue of Josef Jungmann (1773–1847), philologist, poet and translator, one of the prime movers of the nineteenth-century Czech National Revival, is the focal point of Jungmann Square in Prague 1, where Jungmann Street (Jungmannova ulice) meets

October 28 Street (ulice 28. října). Jungmann is seated in an armchair, here represented only jocularly as a wheelchair.

17. The passage about Prague prostitutes was to be taken over into 'Ingot a ingoti' (Ingot and ingots) in *Inzerát na dům, ve kterém už nechci bydlet* (For Sale ad for a house in which I no longer wish to live).

18. See 'Cain' above, note 3.

19. I.e. Bílá labuť, which passed and passes for a better class of department store.

10. The Cabaret Carioca on Wenceslas Square survives and is now one of the city's best-known strip clubs.

11. Fanda (František) Mrázek (1903–70), Czech folk comedian, songwriter, author and singer, a well-loved film actor and artiste of operettas and cabarets.

12. Nataša Gollová (real name Nataša Hodáčová, 1912–88), actress and film star of the First Republic and the Protectorate. Her career plummeted after 1945.

13. Ruda (Rudolf) Princ (1902–64), comedian, engaged at various Prague theatres before and after the war.

14. In the most popular Czech card game, *mariáš*, Balls, or Bells, equate to Diamonds in a regular pack. For the full rules of the game in English see https://www.pagat.com/marriage/marias.html.

15. *Far from Moscow* (1950, dir. Alexander Stolper [1907–79]), based on the eponymous, Stalin Prize-winning 1948 novel by Vasilii Azhayev (1915–68) about the construction of an oil pipeline in eastern Siberia during World War II.

16. *The Village Doctor* (1951, dir. Sergei Gerasimov [1906–85]), a film about the demanding work of GPs in the Soviet countryside. In it, Tamara Makarova (1907–97), Gerasimov's wife, plays a young doctor whose first job was in the hospital attached to a collective farm.

17. Hrabal reworked the motif of a blind girl travelling alone in the short story 'Diamantové oko' (Diamond eye) in *Pábitelé*. There,

however, it is an entirely new text, quite free of any political undertones.

p. 387   LINE No. 23A

Typescript dated June 1952. Published in the Collected Works, vol. 3, pp. 152–156. The title denotes the railway line from Prague to Lysá nad Labem and Kolín (today numbered 231). The associated line 23B (today's 232) goes from Lysá n. L. to Milovice, a place also mentioned in the story.

1. The run-down estate and château at Lysá nad Labem was granted to General Jan Špork (1597–1697) by Emperor Ferdinand II for sterling service during the Thirty Years' War. Špork restored the estate, purchased others and rebuilt the château. His son, Count František Antonín Špork (1662–1738) carried out further modifications. The various gardens are well maintained. The house itself has been an old people's home since 1961 and is not open to the public, though it is a listed building.

p. 395   ONE PRETTY NONDESCRIPT STATION

Typescript first published in *Poupata* (Buds), translated here from the Collected Works edition, Vol. 3, pp. 157–162. Hrabal later described this text as one of the forerunners to *Carefully Watched Trains*.

1. Hrabal attended a course for train dispatchers from 1 December 1942 in Hradec Králové, taking the exams at Hradec Kr. (theory) and Kostomlaty (practical) in October 1944.

p. 406   A CHRISTENING

Typescript, first published in *Poupata* (Buds), as the seventh item in 'Setkání a návštěvy' (Meetings by chance and by design). It forms the core of the short story, 'Křtiny 1947' (A 1947 Christening) in *Perlička na dně* (A pearl on the bottom). Translated from the version in the Collected Works, Vol. 3, pp. 163–169.

1. Alluding to 1 Corinthians 13:1: "Though I speak with the tongues of men and of angels, and have not charity, I am become as sounding brass, or a tinkling cymbal."
2. The story is told in Genesis 28–32: Jacob had fallen for Rachel and had agreed with her father Laban that after seven years of service he would marry her. However, after the seven years had passed, and mindful of local customs, Laban gave him, instead of Rachel, his first-born Leah. Jacob served another seven years and married both. Rachel remained childless for a long time, while Leah bore Jacob four sons. But Rachel also gave him children through the slave girl Bilhah, and the jealous Leah, now also rendered infertile, gave him the maidservant Zilpah for the same purpose.

p. 419 BE EXPECTING ME

Typescript, first published in *Poupata* (Buds), as the eighth item in 'Setkání a návštěvy' (Meetings by chance and by design). Translated from the version in the Collected Works, Vol. 3, pp. 170–172.
1. I.e. before World War I.

p. 425 TOY SHOP

Typescript, first published in *Poupata* (Buds) as the ninth item in 'Setkání a návštěvy' (Meetings by chance and by design). Translated from the version in the Collected Works, Vol. 3, pp. 173–174.
1. The toyshop milieu suggests that the female shop assistant is Blanka Klauseová (see 'A Schizophrenic Gospel' above, note 10). She had been interned in Theresienstadt during the war and Hrabal met her after the war in the Zinner Bros haberdashery store at the corner of Maisel St. and Jáchym St. (where Hrabal himself lived at the time) in the Old Town of Prague. Blanka later worked at the Dětský dům ('children's house') in Smíchov. That was shortly before she terminated their relationship.

Typescript, first published in *Poupata* (Buds) as the tenth item in 'Setkání a návštěvy' (Meetings by chance and by design). Translated from the version in the Collected Works, Vol. 3, pp. 175–178.

1. The Old Double Base at site no. 452 in Libeň, Prague 8. A single-storey corner building housing the U Libušáka tavern, later The Old Double Base, built in 1895 by local developer A. Wertmüller. It stood at the corner of Kandert St. and Zenkl St. and was demolished in the 1970s to make way for the realignment of the railway line into Holešovice.

2. Hausman's, 18 Ludmila St. on the corner with Na hrázi St., in Libeň, Prague 8, said to have been known previously as Vaništas'. It was demolished in the 1970s, along with many other buildings nearby, in connection with the construction of the Palmovka station of the Prague metro system.

3. A reference to two chains of this name. After 1948, part of the consumer sector was nationalised and part was reorganised under Statute 53/1954 as people's cooperatives and cooperative organisations. Towns and cities had the state chain Pramen. The Včela chain (as Včela-Bratrství in Prague, Vzájemnost-Včela in Brno), which had emerged in 1905 as a workers' consumer cooperative, survived the 1948 regime change. Other cooperatives merged as Jednota.

4. The central area of Libeň, dominated by the manor house.

5. That is, *Roman einer jungen Ehe*, a 1952 film from the German Democratic Republic, directed by Kurt Maetzig from his own screenplay. It describes the ups and downs in the marriage of a two young actors against the background of escalating ideological warfare.

6. The female voice here is again clearly inspired by Blanka Krauseová. See the note under 'Toy Shop' above.

7. The 'revolution' means the 1945 Prague Uprising against the German occupation.

8. See 'One Great Guy' above, note 6.

Typescript, first published in *Poupata* (Buds; Prague: Mladá fronta, 1970) and in the Collected Works, Vol. 3, pp. 86–87. The motifs were exploited in condensed form also in 'Bambini di Praga 1947' (in *Pábitelé*).

1. Egon Bondy, see 'Made in Czechoslovakia' above, note 1. He spent several periods in 'the madhouse', as he put it himself.
2. See 'The Sufferings of Old Werther' above, note 55.
3. That is, the high-security prison at Terezín, notorious under its German name of Theresienstadt as a Nazi concentration camp, as elsewhere in this book.
4. From May 1889 Van Gogh had been kept in the mental institution at the former Augustinian monastery of Saint-Paul-de-Mausole, about two miles from Saint-Rémy-en-Provence. Between bouts of insanity he painted a number of pictures inspired by the institution and its environs. He left in May 1890, shortly before his death.
5. Tatraplan – a fabulous, powerful, streamlined saloon, made by the Tatra car company, years ahead of its time and with a fine history, and the forerunner of the lugubrious, bug-eyed, gas-guzzling limousine, the Tatra 603, so beloved of Communist bigwigs, and of the later, far less striking Tatra 623, ditto. Images of all three can easily be found on the World Wide Web.
6. Towards the end of his life, the composer Bedřich Smetana (1824–84) exhibited signs of progressive paralysis as a consequence of syphilis. He suffered from bouts of memory loss, hallucinations, loss of speech and fits of aggression.
7. Ivan Petrovich Pavlov (1824–1936), the Nobel prize-winning Russian physiologist, psychologist and physician, best-known for his teachings on innate and conditioned reflexes.
8. Referring to Jean Gabin, the charismatic French star of stage and screen.

p. 463 **ONE ORDINARY DAY: a short story**
Typescript dated 1952. The typescript has attached to it the following
appendage: "It's like with the demijohn of plum brandy I buried
in the garden twenty years ago and have never looked for, and I've
quite forgotten where I actually buried it, and then my sister-in-law
turned up this month bearing a large, crumbling parcel, tied up
with a woman's black garter, and she said I've found this behind the
joists in the cellar, you might find some of it come in handy. And
I flicked through it and found texts that I barely even remembered,
and several poems and a short story that I'd be inclined to say was
written by someone else, though it was certainly by me, and so I have
no option but to acknowledge a child aged about twenty, admitting
my paternity, and I'm copying it out on a single top sheet and a few
carbon copies in order to round off my portrait by inclusion of
a period that I believe is firmly behind us, the period of fear during
which I wrote these texts, texts of wartime and of the time of trials
that curdled the blood. I believe that one day, when these texts fall
into the hands of a critic who will be composing a portrait of me,
they will surely contribute to the end product, as they will for anyone
seeking to profile the so-called 1950s. October 1971." The text of 'One
Ordinary Day' was published in *Atomová mašina značky Perkeo* (The
Perkeo Atomic Typewriter, Prague: Práce, 1991) and in the Collected
Works, Vol. 3, pp. 200–211. The characters, events and emotions are
entirely authentic.

1. The phone has been answered by Maxi Marysko (1945–2000),
   the then seven-year-old daughter of Karel Marysko (1915–88),
   a poet and musician and lifelong friend of Hrabal, going back to
   their shared time in Nymburk. Maxi had been born to the sound
   of gunfire (during the 1945 Prague Uprising) out in a corridor
   of a tenement block (inside the flat there was the risk of stray
   bullets), and they named her Šárka. The girl (perhaps also as
   a side-effect of her dramatic birth) felt herself to be a boy and
   having reached maturity she officially changed her name. The

Maxim that she sought was rejected by the registrar, so all her life she was Maxima, though she consistently signed herself just Maxi Marysko. She got her sense of humour and tall story-telling entirely from her father.

12. Václav Černý (1905–87), Czech literary historian and critic, translator from the Romance languages. In 1951 he was driven from his comparative literature post at the university, and in September 1952 he was accused of anti-state activity, arrested and tried, but in the spring of 1953 he was released for lack of evidence.

13. That is, *Kritický měsíčník*, a review of literary and art criticism, founded by Černý and published between 1938 and 1942 and again from 1945 to 1948.

14. An ancient form of graduation whereby outstanding doctoral candidates were granted their title under presidential patronage.

15. Karel Marysko's works, edited by Václav Kadlec and Maxi Marysko, were eventually published by Pražská imaginace in 1995–96 in 12 volumes.

16. Černý had been involved in the anti-Nazi resistance and from late 1944 was a prisoner of the Gestapo. In 1945 he was awarded the Czechoslovak military cross.

17. Psychoton itself is a harmless, freely available food supplement and sedative, based on lavender oil.

18. A quotation, slightly defective, of the opening lines of Marysko's poem 'Zpíváno kraji' (Sung to these parts), subsequently published in Vol. 1 of *Dílo Karla Maryska* (KM's collected works), Prague: Pražská imaginace, 1995, p.62.

19. *Tenner* (Cz. *desítkářka*), under Stalinism, a member of a street committee, put in charge of ten people, on whom s/he passed information to the authorities.

10. Marysko had studied the cello under Prof. Ladislav Zelenka; during the war he had played the cello with the orchestra of the National Theatre and after the war with the Smetana Theatre orchestra in Prague.

11. On 9 September 1947 Hrabal joined the Karel Harry Klofanda company as a travelling salesman hawking pharmaceuticals, haberdashery and toys. One year later he assisted at the firm's liquidation.

12. Konstantin Biebl (1898–1951), Czech poet of the interwar avant-garde. The dentist was his father, the poet himself having studied medicine, which he never actually practised. In an atmosphere in which private individuals were constantly spied on and when the Stalinist show trials were being played out, he committed suicide.

13. A typical piece of Marysko-esque word-play in the title of *The Bride of Messina* (i.e. with *-swin[e]-* for *-sin-*), an opera by Zdeněk Fibich based on the eponymous tragedy by Friedrich Schiller.

The present volume contains a body of prose texts dating back to the period 1945–1952. Their basic corpus came out in Vols 1–3 of *Sebrané spisy Bohumila Hrabala* (Collected Works of BH, SSBH), entitled *Básnění* (Versifying), *Židovský svícen* (Menorah) and *Jarmilka*, in a special edition by Miroslav Červenka, Karel Dostál and Václav Kadlec (Prague: Pražská imaginace, 1992), while some texts discovered later figure in Vol. 19 of SSBH, *Bibliografie. Dodatky. Rejstříky* (Bibliography. Additions. Indexes), drawn up by Václav Kadlec and Claudio Poeta (Prague: Pražská imaginace, 1997). Within the second series of Hrabal's Works (*Spisy Bohumila Hrabala*) the late rediscoveries appeared in Vol. 1, entitled *Křehký dluh. Básnění a rané prózy* (A fragile debt. Versifying and the early prose-works, Prague: Mladá fronta, 2017). All the early prose pieces as they appear in the latter edition (pp. 360–535), prepared by Václav Kadlec and Jiří Pelán and reproducing the texts edited in SSBH by Miroslav Červenka, Karel Dostál, Václav Kadlec and Claudio Poeta, are the source of the present translations, while the original annotations have been adapted and supplemented for the Anglo-Saxon reader by the translator.

These early texts are essentially laboratory experiments, while simultaneously bearing the hallmark of a quest for a pathway through life against the dramatic background of how Czechoslovakia was evolving after the war, from the shaky democracy of 1945–1948 through the first – and cruellest – years of the totalitarian, Communist regime that followed. In this critical time, Hrabal, who graduated in law in 1946, opted for the position of an outsider: having spent the last years of the war as a train despatcher at Kostomlaty, not far from Nymburk (east of Prague), where he grew up, he worked as an insurance agent (1945–47), travelling salesman (1947–48) and casual labourer at the Kladno steelworks (1949–53).

Each of these milieus afforded him a vast wealth of material, observed and recorded by his "eidetic memory", whether stemming from self-dissection or mediated through "the things people say". The key problem of his work at the time was that of trying to balance the lyrical core of his vision (his enchantment with, amazement at, and indestructible longing for that platonic "begetting in the beautiful") with the brutality of the prosaic side of life afforded him by each new environment – finding a way to grasp his material and organise it and then hit on the right literary syntax to go with the grossness of the subject matter. Different attempts to resolve this come time and again, each solution constituting a new variant stylistically and, usually, each one re-surfacing at some or other later stage in Hrabal's output.

All the questing, both in terms of subject matter and form, has given these early texts an extraordinary intensity, which is also precious in terms of comparisons with the later re-writings of the 1960s. This applies *par excellence*, to the "existentialist short-story" *Kain*, reworked later in the novella *Ostře sledované vlaky* (Carefully watched trains): while in *Trains* Hrabal was telling the story, rooted in history, of an antihero condemned to involuntary heroism, in the early version he had tried to bring out the fundamental determinants of human existence by couching the construction of the *syuzhet* symbolically, as the story of an "everyman". In *Utrpení starého Werthera* (The sufferings of old Werther) he applied, for the first time (if in a radical transcription), the non-stop narrative stream of his uncle Pepin (Josef Hrabal, 23. 8. 1882 – 21. 3. 1967), which would be re-used (in a more disciplined literary form) in *Taneční hodiny pro starší a pokročilé* (Dancing lessons for the advanced in age). Hrabal may have also largely reconstituted the motifs of *Pásek* (here as One great guy) and *Atomový princ* (Atom Prince) and of *Exploze Gabriel* (The Gabriel explosion), *Made in Czechoslovakia* (a title not requiring translation) and *Blitzkrieg* (ditto) in the short stories he later included in the collections *Perlička na dně* (A pearl on the bottom), *Inzerát na dům, ve kterém už nechci bydlet* (A for-sale ad for a house in which I nolonger wish to live) and *Morytáty a legendy* (Gory-stories and legends), but these, too, are not so much early versions of texts that were gradually reworked, but the first, largely autonomous – and hugely effective – image of the Kladno steelworks, and the first – quite vivid – image of the intellectual community of Libeň.

Hrabal added a sort of postscript to the 1952 story *Jeden všední den* (One ordinary day) – a brilliant portrayal of everyday life under "real socialism", only rediscovered in 1971 – which has a direct bearing on all his writings from that period. In it, he says, *inter alia*, that the delayed printing of them may "round off my portrait by inclusion of a period that I believe is firmly behind us, the period of fear during which I wrote these, texts of wartime and of the time of trials that curdled the blood." Already back then, Hrabal the 'recorder' was thus acting as a witness giving testimony to things that ought to remain in the collective memory. The autobiographical dimension of these early writings was, then, already functioning as guarantee of the underlying truth.

J. P.

ABOUT THE AUTHOR

BOHUMIL HRABAL (1914–97) was born in Brno, Czechoslovakia and studied law – although, as Josef Škvorecký wrote, "he never had anything to do with any bar other than those where Pilsner beer is served." He spent decades working manual labor before turning to writing and earning admirers such as Milan Kundera and Philip Roth.

Hrabal's work is conspicuous for its range. He began as a poet in the 1930s, before switching to experimental styles of prose. He made a name for himself with his short story collections *A Pearl at the Bottom* (1963) and *Palaverers* (1964), but became truly renowned with the novella *Closely Watched Trains* (1967), which was turned into an Academy Award-winning film. In the early 1970s Hrabal found himself on the list of banned authors, so his writing appeared only in samizdat without information identifying him as the author; books he wrote in this period include *I Served the King of England* (1971), *Cutting It Short* (1974), and *The Little Town Where Time Stood Still* (1974). After 1975 he was allowed to publish, with a measure of (self-)censorship, some of his works 'officially' – such as the masterpiece *Too Loud a Solitude* (1977). From the late 1980s onwards, Hrabal focused chiefly on shorter genres – feuilletons, commentaries, and essays.

When he fell to his death in 1997, he was ranked among the greatest Czech writers of the twentieth-century.

English translations of his novels have been published by Northwestern University Press, Abacus, Doubleday, Vintage, Simon and Schuster, Harcourt Brace, New York Review of Books, Archipelago, and New Directions. *Why I Write?* is the third book by Hrabal that Karolinum Press has published.

ABOUT THE TRANSLATOR

DAVID SHORT is the author of a popular Czech textbook, the coauthor of a number of publications in the field of linguistics, and a prolific translator from Czech. He spent 1966–72 in Prague, studying Czech and linguistics, working, translating, having fun, and eventually marrying a Czech classmate. He then taught Czech and Slovak at the School of Slavonic and East European Studies in London from 1973 to 2011. He was awarded the Jiří Theiner Prize for his significant contribution to the dissemination and promotion of Czech literature abroad, the Czech Minister of Culture's *Artis Bohemicae Amicis* medal, and the Medal of Comenius University in Bratislava.

His translations include:
Vítězslav Nezval: *Valerie and her Week of Wonders*
Bohumil Hrabal: *Pirouettes on a Postage Stamp*
Karel Michal: *Everyday Spooks*
Jáchym Topol: *Gargling with Tar*
Karel Čapek: *Rossum's Universal Robots*
Daniela Hodrová: *Prague, I See a City...*
Jaroslav Durych: *God's Rainbow*
Bohumil Hrabal: *Rambling on: An Apprentice's Guide to the Gift of the Gab*

MODERN CZECH CLASSICS

The modern history of Central Europe is notable for its political and cultural discontinuities and often violent changes, as well as its attempts to preserve and (re)invent traditional cultural identities. This series cultivates contemporary translations of influential literary works that have been unavailable to a global readership due to censorship, the effects of the Cold War and the frequent political disruptions in Czech publishing and its international ties. Readers of English, in today's cosmopolitan Prague and anywhere in the physical and electronic world, can now become acquainted with works that capture the Central European historical experience – works that have helped express and form Czech and Central European identity, humour and imagination. Believing that any literary canon can be defined only in dialogue with other cultures, the series publishes classics, often used in Western university courses, as well as (re)discoveries aiming to provide new perspectives in the study of literature, history and culture. All titles are accompanied by an afterword. Translations are reviewed and circulated in the global scholarly community before publication – this is reflected by our nominations for literary awards.

Published Titles

Zdeněk Jirotka: *Saturnin* (2003, 2005, 2009, 2013; pb 2016)
Vladislav Vančura: *Summer of Caprice* (2006; pb 2016)
Karel Poláček: *We Were a Handful* (2007; pb 2016)
Bohumil Hrabal: *Pirouettes on a Postage Stamp* (2008)
Karel Michal: *Everyday Spooks* (2008)
Eduard Bass: *The Chattertooth Eleven* (2009)
Jaroslav Hašek: *Behind the Lines: Bugulma and Other Stories* (2012; pb 2016)
Bohumil Hrabal: *Rambling On* (2014; pb 2016)
Ladislav Fuks: *Of Mice and Mooshaber* (2014)
Josef Jedlička: *Midway upon the Journey of Our Life* (2016)
Jaroslav Durych: *God's Rainbow* (2016)
Ladislav Fuks: *The Cremator* (2016)
Bohuslav Reynek: *The Well at Morning* (2017)
Viktor Dyk: *The Pied Piper* (2017)
Jiří R. Pick: *Society for the Prevention of Cruelty to Animals* (2018)
Views from the Inside: Czech Underground Literature and Culture (1948–1989), ed. M. Machovec (2018)
Ladislav Grosman: *The Shop on Main Street* (2019)
Bohumil Hrabal: *Why I Write? The Early Prose from 1945 to 1952* (2019)
Jiří Pelán: *Bohumil Hrabal: A Full-length Portrait* (2019)

Forthcoming

Jaroslav Kvapil: *Rusalka*
Jan Procházka: *The Ear*
Ivan Jirous: *Collected Works*
Jan Čep: *Common Rue*
Jiří Weil: *Lamentation for 77,297 Victims*

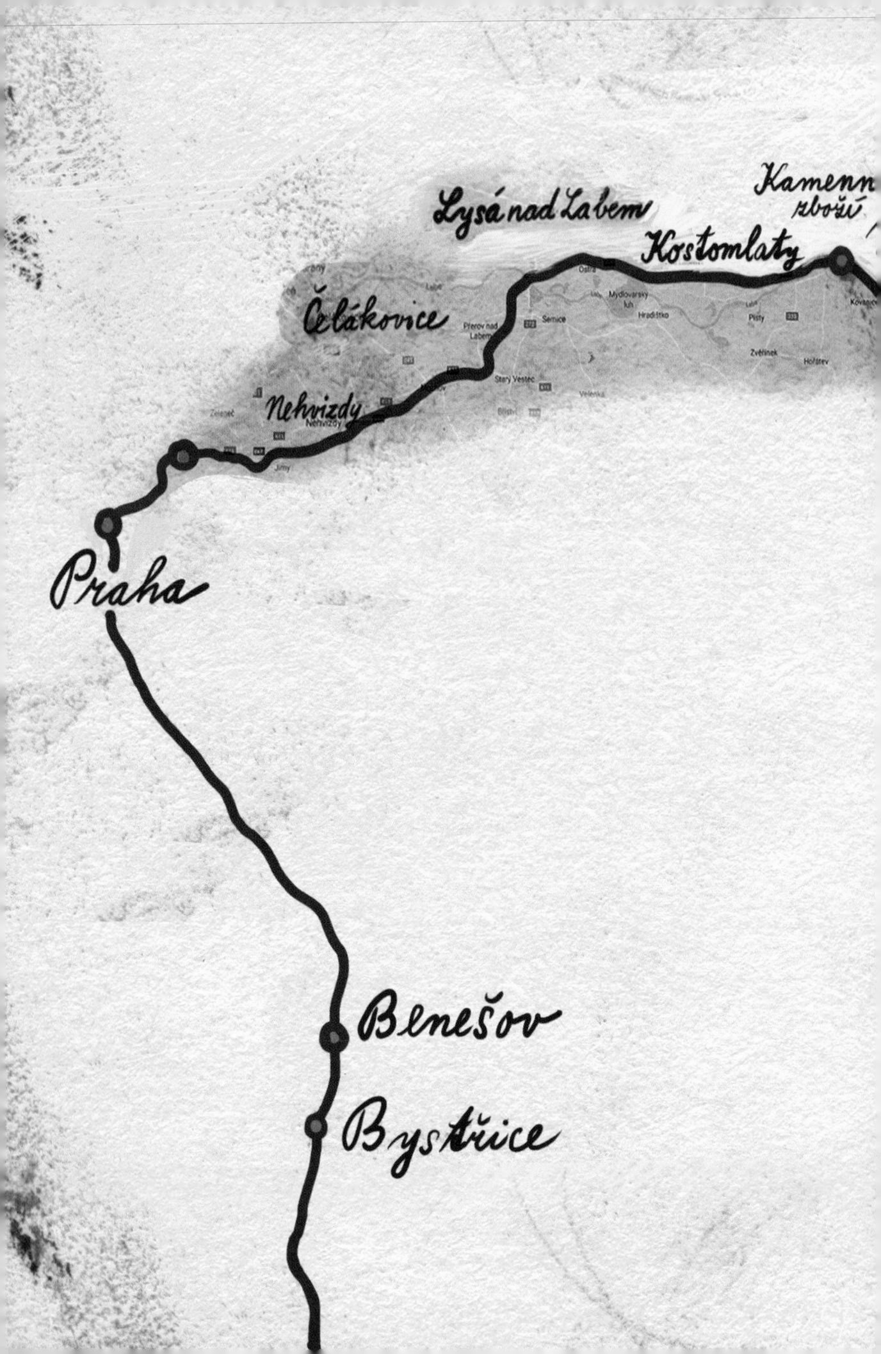
Kamenn
zboží
Lysá nad Labem
Kostomlaty
Čelákovice
Nehvizdy
Praha
Benešov
Bystřice